W9-BCA-634

# No One You Know

∞

ALSO BY MICHELLE RICHMOND

*The Year of Fog*

# No One You Know

*a novel*

## Michelle Richmond

DOUBLEDAY LARGE PRINT HOME LIBRARY EDITION

*Delacorte Press*

This Large Print Edition, prepared especially for Doubleday Large Print Home Library, contains the complete, unabridged text of the original Publisher's Edition.

NO ONE YOU KNOW
A Delacorte Press Book / July 2008

Published by Bantam Dell
A Division of Random House, Inc.
New York, New York

Delacorte Press is a registered trademark of Random House, Inc., and the colophon is a trademark of Random House, Inc.

ISBN 978-0-7394-9765-4

Printed in the United States of America
Published simultaneously in Canada

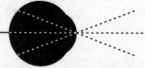

This Large Print Book carries the
Seal of Approval of N.A.V.H.

*For my sisters,*
*Monica and Misty*

*There are three main aims that one can have in studying the truth.*
*The first is to look for it and discover it.*
*The second is to prove it when one has discovered it.*
*The third is to distinguish it from falsehood when one examines it.*

—Blaise Pascal, "On the Spirit of Geometry and the Art of Persuasion"

# No One You Know

# *One*

────────── ∞ ──────────

When I found him at last, I had long ago given up the search. It was late at night, and I was dining alone in a small café in Diriomo, Nicaragua. It was a place I had come to cherish during my annual visits to the village, the kind of establishment where one could order a plate of beans and a cup of coffee any time of the day or night.

I had spent the evening wandering the dark, empty streets. July days in Diriomo were scorching; come nightfall, the buildings seemed to radiate heat, so that the air possessed a baked, dusty scent. Eventually I came to the familiar intersection. Going left would lead to my hotel, with its hard bed and uncooperative ceiling fan. Straight ahead was a baseball diamond where I had once seen a local kid beat a rat to death with an old wooden bat. To the right was a wide road giving way to a crooked alleyway, at the end of which the café beckoned.

Some time past midnight, I stood on the doorstep, ringing the little copper bell. Maria appeared, dressed in a long blue skirt, white blouse, and no shoes, looking as though she'd been expecting me.

"Did I wake you?"

"No," she said. "Welcome."

It was a ritual greeting between us. I had no way of knowing whether Maria was actually asleep on those nights, or whether she was sitting patiently in her kitchen, waiting for customers.

"What are you serving tonight?" I asked. This was also ritual, for we both knew that the menu never changed, no matter the time or season.

"*Nacatamal,*" she said. "*Está usted sola?*"

"*Sí, señora,* I am alone." My answer, like the menu, had remained unaltered for years. And yet she asked it, each time, with a kind of naked hope, as if she believed that one day my luck might change.

The café was empty and dark, somehow cool despite the heat outside. She pointed to a small table where a candle burned in a jar. I thanked her and sat down. I could hear her preparing coffee in the kitchen, which was separated from the dining area by a narrow doorway in which hung a curtain of red fabric. I watched the patterns made by the candlelight on the far wall. The images seemed too lovely and symmetrical to be random—a bird, a sailboat, a star, followed by a series of rectangular bars of light. It was a feeling I often had in that town, and one of the reasons I kept returning when my work as a coffee buyer brought me to Nicaragua—a feeling that even the simplest natural acts were somehow ordered, as if some unnamed discipline reigned over both the animate and inanimate. I rarely felt this way at home in San Francisco. It was no wonder the locals referred to Diriomo as *pueblo brujo*—bewitched village.

Maria had just set my plate on the

table when the bell clanged outside. Together we looked toward the door, as if something miraculous might materialize. In all the times I had taken a midnight meal among the porcelain dolls and carnivorous plants in Maria's café, I'd rarely met another customer.

Maria went to the door and opened it a crack. For a moment my table was flooded with moonlight.

*"Buenas noches, Maria,"* a man's voice said.

*"Buenas noches."*

The door closed, plunging the room once again into near darkness.

The man passed by my table. His face was turned away, but in the pale light from the kitchen I observed that he carried himself in the way very tall men often do, shoulders slumped in a sort of apology for taking up so much space. He wore a baseball cap pulled low on the forehead. A hardback book was tucked under one arm. He went to a table in the corner, the one farthest from my own. When he sat down, his back to me, the wooden chair creaked so violently I thought it might break.

Maria took a match out of her apron pocket, struck it against the wall, and dipped the flame into a crimson jar on the man's table. Only after she had retreated into the kitchen to fetch his coffee did he turn around and glance at me from beneath the brim of his hat. In the flickering red candlelight only his slightly jutting chin was visible, the rest of his face receding into shadows.

"Hello," I said.

"Good evening."

"You're American," I said, surprised. Foreigners were scarce in Diriomo. Encountering a fellow American at this particular café in the middle of the night was utterly strange.

"I am," he said.

He gave a polite wave of the hand before leaning over the table and peering into his book. He held the candle above the page, and I considered warning him it was bad for his eyes to read in the darkness. He seemed like the kind of man who needed to be told these things, the kind of man who ought to have someone taking care of him. Soon Maria brought him coffee.

Something about the way he lifted his cup, the way he turned the pages of his book, even the way he tilted his head toward Maria in silent thanks when she brought him a napkin and a bowl of sugar cubes, struck me as familiar. I watched him closely, wondering if the feeling that I knew him was simply an illusion brought about by my having been traveling alone for too long. The longer I sat there, however, the more I became convinced that it was not the vague familiarity of one countryman to another, but something more personal.

While he drank his coffee and read his book, seemingly oblivious to me, I tried to recall the context in which I might have known him. I sensed, more than knew, that it had been a long time ago, and that there had been some degree of intimacy between us; this sensation of intimacy coupled with my inability to remember was completely unsettling. The thought crossed my mind that I might have slept with him. There had been a period following my sister's death when I slept with many men. This was a long time ago, though, so long that now it almost seemed like a different life.

Maria brought my food. I waited for the steaming plantain leaves to cool before peeling them away, picking up the *nacatamal,* and biting in. Back home, I had tried several times to replicate Maria's combination of pork, rice, potatoes, mint leaves, raisins, and spices, but it never came out right. When I tried to tease the recipe out of her, she just laughed and pretended not to understand my request.

"You should try these," I said to the man between bites.

"Oh, I know Maria's *nacatamal,*" he said, glancing my way once again. "Delicious, but I already ate."

What could he be doing here so late at night, I wondered, if he had already had his supper? In Diriomo, men did not sit alone in cafés reading books, even American men. A few minutes later, when I took my wallet out to pay, he closed his book and stared at the cover for a few seconds, as if to gather courage, before standing and walking over to my table. Maria watched us shamelessly from the doorway of the kitchen. The red curtain was pulled aside, filling the room with soft light. For a moment it occurred to me that perhaps Maria had set this whole thing up for my benefit, perhaps she was trying to pull off a bit of matchmaking.

The man removed his baseball cap and held it in both hands. His shaggy hair grazed the low ceiling, gathering static. "Pardon me," he said. Now I could see his face completely—the large dark eyes and wide mouth, the high cheekbones and prominent chin, covered with stubble—and I knew at once who he was.

I had not seen him in eighteen years. There had been a period of several months in college when I thought of him constantly. I had watched for his name in the paper, had performed drive-bys of his ground-floor flat in Russian Hill, had taken lunch at a certain small Italian restaurant in North Beach that he frequented, despite the fact that the menu stretched my student budget beyond its limits. At that time I suspected that if I shadowed him without ceasing I could begin to understand something—maybe not the thing he had done, but the mechanism by which he had been able to do it. That mechanism, I was certain, was a psychological abnormality; some moral tuning fork that was present in others was absent in him.

Then, one afternoon in August of 1991, he vanished. That day I walked into the restaurant in North Beach at half past noon, as I had been doing every week for three months. Immediately my eyes went to a table in the corner, above which hung a miniature oil painting of the Cathedral Duomo of Milan. It was where he always sat, a table that seemed to be reserved specifically for him. He always arrived on Monday at a quarter past noon, and after sitting down would place a notebook on the table to the right of his bread plate. He rarely bothered to glance up at his surroundings as he scribbled furiously in the notebook with a mechanical pencil. He would pause only to order spaghetti with prawns in marinara sauce, which he ate quickly, followed by an espresso, which he drank slowly. The whole time, he worked, scribbling with his right hand and eating with his left. But that day in August, he wasn't there. Immediately I sensed something had changed. I dipped my bread in olive oil and waited. By the time the waiter brought my salad, I knew he wasn't coming. At one-fifteen I called in sick to the University of San Francisco library, where I held a work-study position, and took the bus to Russian Hill. There was a *For Rent* sign in front of his flat, and the shutters were open. Through the large windows I could see the place was stripped clean, all of the furniture gone. It occurred to me that I might never see him again.

# *Two*

∞

"A story has no beginning or end," my sophomore English professor used to say. "Arbitrarily one chooses that moment of experience from which to look back or from which to look ahead." It was a motto that Andrew Thorpe managed to work into every session of class, no matter what book we were discussing. One could almost anticipate the moment he was going to say it, as the statement was always preceded by a lengthy pause, a lifting of his eyebrows, a quick intake of breath.

I would choose a Wednesday in December 1989. Again and again, poring over the details, I would choose that day, and it would become the touchstone from which all other events unfurled, the moment by which I judged the two parts of my life: the years with Lila, and those without her.

On that morning I was in the kitchen, listening to Jimmy Cliff on the radio and waiting for the coffee to brew. Our parents had already left for work. Lila came downstairs, dressed in a ruffled black blouse, green corduroy skirt, and Converse high-tops. Her eyes were red, and I was startled to realize she'd been crying. I couldn't remember the last time I'd seen Lila cry.

"What's wrong?"

"Nothing. It's just been a stressful week." She gave a little wave of her hand as if to dismiss the whole thing outright. She was wearing a ring I'd never seen before, a delicate gold band with a small black stone.

"Dance with me," I said, attempting to cheer her up. I grabbed her hand and tried to twirl her around, but she pulled away.

The coffeemaker beeped. I turned down the radio and poured her a cup. "Is this about him?" I asked.

"About who?"

"It is, isn't it? Come on. Talk to me."

She was looking out the kitchen window, at a small limb that had fallen onto our deck the previous week during a rainstorm. Only later, as I replayed the events of those days, would it seem strange that none of us had bothered to remove the fallen limb from the deck.

"How long has that been there?" Lila asked.

"A while."

"We should take care of it."

"We should."

But neither of us made a move toward the kitchen door.

"Tell me his name," I said finally. "I know guys on the basketball team. I'll have his face rearranged." I was only half joking.

Lila didn't respond; it was as if she hadn't heard me at all. I had learned long before not to be offended by her silences. Once, when I accused her of ignoring me, she had explained, "It's like I'm wandering through a house, and I happen to step into another room, and the door shuts behind me. I get involved in what's going on in that room, and everything else sort of vanishes."

I reached across the counter and touched her hand to summon her back. "Nice ring. Is it opal?"

She slid her hand into her pocket. "It's just a trinket."

"Where did you get it?"

She shrugged. "I don't remember."

Lila never bought jewelry for herself. The ring must have been a gift from *him,* whoever he was. The very thought of a romantic entanglement was new to Lila. She hadn't had more than half a dozen dates in high school and college combined. Throughout those years, my mother was fond of saying that boys didn't know how to appreciate a girl of such exceptional intelligence, but I suspected my mother had it all wrong. Boys were interested in Lila; she simply had no use for them. During my freshman year of high school, when Lila was a senior, I'd seen the way guys looked at her. I was the one they talked to, the one they invited to parties and asked on dates, the fun and freewheeling sister who could be counted on to organize group outings and play elaborate pranks on the teachers, but Lila was far from invisible. With her long dark hair, her general aloofness, her weird sense of humor, her passion for math, she was, I imagined, intimidating to boys in a way I would never be. When she walked down the hallway, alone and deep in thought, clad in the eccentric clothes she made on my mom's old Singer sewing machine, she must have seemed completely inapproachable. Although boys didn't talk to her, it was clear to me that they *saw* her. I was well-liked, but Lila had mystery.

Even after she had graduated from UC Berkeley and started the Ph.D. program in pure mathematics at Stanford, Lila was perfectly content living in her old bedroom, eating dinner with the family most nights, watching rented movies with Mom and Dad on weekends while I was out with my friends. Lately, though, she had begun going out several evenings each week, coming home after midnight with a smile on her face. When I tried to get her to tell me who she was with, she would say, "Just a friend."

Our mother, like me, was thrilled at

the prospect of Lila dating. "I don't want her to go through life lonely," she had said more than once, although I suspected that Lila wasn't entirely capable of feeling loneliness in the way most people did. There was so much going on inside her head, she never craved the company of friends. Although we could pass hours talking quietly in the dark, I knew that she was just as content to be alone, pencil in hand, working through some complicated math problem. I thought that, for other girls, having a sister was like standing in front of a milky pane of glass in which your own past and personality were reflected back to you with interesting variations. But aside from our physical resemblance, Lila and I were so different that, had we not been born into the same family, I doubted we would have been friends.

Lila finished her coffee, took an apple from a bowl on the counter, grabbed her backpack, and said, "Tell Mom I'll be home late tonight."

"How late?"

"Late."

"Whoever he is," I said, "don't go too easy on him. You can't let him think he's running the show."

I saw the beginning of a smile on her face. "Is that a rule?"

"A cardinal rule."

I followed her to the foyer and took her black peacoat down from the peg beside the stairwell. As I was helping her into it, she said, an afterthought, "Any chance I could have the car today?" We'd been sharing a blue Toyota ever since I got my license three years earlier. It was Lila who wrote out our schedule every month, and on that month, she'd given me Wednesdays.

"I would, but I get off work at the library at four and I have a dentist's appointment across town at four-thirty. I'd never make it on the bus."

"It's not important," she said.

Before she walked out the door, I gave her our traditional half salute. For two seconds, maybe three, I heard the familiar sounds of the outside world infiltrating our quiet house—a car passing, a kid riding a skateboard down the steep sidewalk, a snatch of music from an open window across the street. Then the front door clicked softly behind her, and she was gone. In the months to follow, when I recalled that moment, I would suspect that the clicking sound I'd heard wasn't the door, but something in my own mind, some barely audible psychic signal. I would tell myself that if only I had listened, if only I had paid attention, I could have somehow changed the story.

That night, I passed Lila's message on to our parents, and we all went to bed as usual. The next morning, when I came downstairs, my mother stood at the kitchen counter eating cereal and perusing a legal brief, while my father sat at the table with his newspaper and buttered toast. "Go wake your sister, Ellie," my mother said. "I can't believe she's not up. She has a nine-o'clock class."

I went upstairs and knocked on her door, but she didn't answer. I opened the door and saw that her bed was undisturbed, the white pillow shams and coverlet pristine. The small bathroom we shared was attached to my room, and Lila always listened to KLIV while getting ready in the morning. There was no way she could have showered and dressed without my hearing her.

I went downstairs. My mother was rinsing her cereal bowl in the sink. "She's not here," I said. "It looks like she didn't come home last night."

My mother turned to face me, her hands still wet. "What?"

My father looked up from his paper, startled. "She didn't call?"

"Did she tell you where she was going last night?" my mother asked.

"No. She was upset yesterday morning, but she wouldn't say why."

"This person she's been seeing," my mother said to me. "Do you know who he is?"

"She won't tell me anything."

I went up to her room and retrieved her schedule from the bulletin board above her desk. We called the office of the *Stanford Journal of Mathematics*, where she worked part-time. She hadn't been at her five-o'clock meeting the night before. "Weird," the editor said. "It's the first meeting she's missed in two years." Next, we called a guy named Steve who led a seven p.m. study group Lila was in; she had also missed the study group.

At that point, my father called the police and filed a missing person report. An officer came to our house and asked for a photograph of Lila, which he slid into a plastic sleeve. After he left, we went into the living room and waited for the phone to ring. That was Thursday. For two days there was no trace of her. It was as if my sister had walked to the Greyhound station, bought a ticket to Somewhere Else, and vanished.

On Saturday of that week Lila's backpack was found in a Dumpster in Healdsburg. It still contained her wallet, her house keys, and her books. The only thing missing was a perfect-bound notebook, about an inch thick, with a blue plaid cover. I knew the notebook would have been in her backpack when she left home because she never went anywhere without it. It wasn't a journal in the traditional sense. Instead of words, it contained numbers, page after page of formulae. For me, trying to read one of her calculations was akin to saying an ordinary word as fast as possible a dozen times in a row; the numbers and letters, taken separately, each looked familiar, but grouped together so densely they seemed mysterious, like some alien code that only a savant could crack. While I immersed myself in indie music and Eastern European novels, Lila filled her time with equations and algorithms, long sequences of letters and numerals stretching across and down the graph-paper pages.

"What's all this?" I had asked her once, sitting on her bed and flipping through the notebook. I read aloud from a dog-eared page. "Every even integer greater than two can be expressed as the sum of two primes."

She was trying on a new dress. My mother was always buying Lila fashionable clothes, trying to spiff up her quirky, homemade wardrobe. Out of kindness Lila would try them on, model them for our parents, and make some positive comment before hanging the clothes up in her closet, where they would remain untouched until I co-opted them for myself.

"Only one of the most famous math problems of all time, Goldbach's conjecture," Lila said. "Mathematicians have been trying to prove it since 1742."

"Let me guess. My brilliant sister is going to be the one to solve it."

"You don't solve a conjecture, you prove it."

"What's the difference?"

"Math 101," she said, cramming her feet into the pumps our mother had purchased to go with the dress. "A conjecture is a mathematical statement that appears *likely* to be true, but hasn't been formally *proven* to be true. Once there's proof, it becomes a theorem. While it's a conjecture, you can use it to try to construct other mathematical proofs, but anything you come up with using a conjecture is only a conjecture. Get it?" Lila turned her back to me so I could zip her up.

"Thanks for being the family genius," I said. "Takes the pressure off me."

Lila kicked off the shoes and plopped

down on the bed. "When I do prove it,
I can only take credit for being half a
genius. I have a partner. It's a pact—
we're going to solve it together, even if
it takes us the next thirty years."

"A partner, huh? Who is it?"

"Just this guy I know."

"If it's going to take thirty years, you
might as well marry him."

"His wife might object."

"Does she know that her husband is
mathematically betrothed to you?"

Lila adjusted a bra strap and tugged
at the neck of the dress. "She's an
artist. I doubt she's ever even heard of
Goldbach's conjecture."

When the news of the backpack
reached us, we went to Mass. Even my
father, whose only concession to reli-
gion my entire life had been to step
through the wide church doors once a
year on Easter Sunday, agreed to go.
Together, we lit a candle for Lila. While
my mother prayed aloud, I prayed, too,
something I hadn't done since I was a
child. I didn't exactly believe, but if
there was a chance God was listening,
I wanted to do everything right.

On Monday, two days after Lila's backpack was found, a hiker in Armstrong Woods, near the Russian River town of Guerneville, left the trail and stumbled over a body partially covered by leaves. There was no hiking gear, no identification. It was four o'clock in the afternoon when my parents left for Guerneville, about seventy-five miles north of the city. I stood before the large front windows of our house and watched their dark gray Volvo pull out of the garage below. Thursday had been trash day, and in the chaos following Lila's disappearance none of us had thought to retrieve the cans. The car stopped in the driveway, and my father got out and rolled the empty bins into the garage. Then he climbed in the car again, and I heard the hum of the garage door closing. Through the windshield I could see my parents, but only from the shoulders down. My mother's navy skirt rose just above her knees. Her purse rested in her lap. In the space between the two front seats, she and my father held hands. As the car slowly backed into the street, I felt a sense of panic.

I sat at the kitchen table and waited, staring at the clock. At 5:43, the phone rang. It was my father. He was using the phone at the morgue, and the connection was poor. Muzak played in the background, the Beach Boys' "Little Surfer Girl." I strained to make out my father's words, and made him repeat himself twice. "It was a positive ID." Even when I was certain of the words themselves, it was a struggle to comprehend their meaning. "Her necklace is missing," he added, more as a question than a statement, and I thought of the thin gold chain she always wore, with a tiny topaz stone suspended in a delicate gold pendant. The necklace had been a gift from me for her eighteenth birthday, purchased with three months' worth of babysitting money. My father went on. "The coroner listed the cause of death as blunt trauma to the head."

At that moment I didn't stop to question the strange evenness of his voice, or the fact that he would deliver such

horrifying news by phone while I was
home alone. In hindsight I would realize
he had been out of his mind with shock
and grief; he could not be expected at
that moment to make rational decisions. As I hung up the phone I was
thinking about the car. If I had given it
to Lila on Wednesday, as she requested, how might the chain of events
have been altered? If I hadn't been
thinking of my dentist appointment,
might Lila still be alive?

Once, in trying to explain to me the
strange concept of imaginary numbers,
Lila had quoted Leibniz, who called the
imaginary number "an amphibian between being and non-being." After my
sister's death, I sometimes felt as if I
were trapped in such a state. All my life
I had been Lila's little sister. Then, without warning, I was an only child. My
parents, to their credit, did their best to
maintain our sense of family, to replicate the harmony we had shared before Lila's death. In a world where
"dysfunctional" was the common language of domesticity, we had considered ourselves lucky to be a happy

family. But no matter how well-adjusted a family may be, no matter how hard its individual members try to move on, grief is not a thing that can simply be managed. The shape of our family had changed.

Almost immediately, I would come to see the world in terms of before and after. In my memories of before, there was a certain lightness of feeling, an intensity of color, the comfortable chaos of family life. After was a different story. After consisted of weight: the weight of guilt and that of grief. The shutters were closed, the house was quiet. At night, my mother kept to her garden, clawing at the dirt by the light of electric torches, tearing up weeds and planting bulbs. Past midnight I would hear her come in through the back door, drop her trowel and gardening shears in the big metal bucket in the garage. There would be a few moments of silence, followed by the rush of water through pipes, the sound of the washing machine shuddering to life. Then her footsteps up the interior stairs from the garage to the main level of the house, and the rat-a-tat-tat of the shower in the porcelain tub. Meanwhile, my father sat in the Stickley chair in their bedroom, reading, a glass of water on the table beside him. It was not a comfortable chair; before, he had always read in the recliner in the living room, his hand curled around a wineglass, Bob Dylan or Johnny Cash playing softly on the stereo. After, there was no wine, no music.

Some years after Lila's death, at a garage sale on Collingwood, I reached into a cardboard box and pulled out an old hardback copy of Graham Greene's *The End of the Affair.* The jacket had been torn and taped back together, and the pages were warped and swollen. A sticker on the cover declared *25 cents.* It was a warm Saturday morning in September, the whole weekend stretching before me. I had nowhere to go, and the sun felt good on my bare arms, so I turned to the first page. "A story has no beginning or end," it began, "arbitrarily one chooses that moment of experience from which to look back or from which to look ahead." It was Andrew Thorpe's old motto, there in black and white.

I scanned the line with my eyes twice, three times, to make sure I had read it right. Then I placed a quarter on the table, tucked the book under my arm, and began walking. It had happened before, I imagined it would happen again: just when I thought I had managed to outdistance the past, to put Lila's story behind me, some unexpected thing would surface, bringing it all back. It could happen anywhere, anytime: a glimpse of someone who looked like her, a mention in the news of some significant mathematical discovery, a snippet of a certain song on the radio, a review of one of Andrew Thorpe's books.

It should not have surprised me that the man who had made a career out of Lila's story would have appropriated the novelist's words as his own. What disappointed me was my own gullibility, my willingness to believe a thing I had been told without examining it for flaws, never stopping to question the source.

Every story is an invention, subject to the whims of the author. For the audience on the other side of the page, the words march forward with a certain inevitability—as if the story could exist one way only, the way in which it is written. But there is never just one way to tell a story. Someone has chosen the beginning and end. Someone has chosen who will emerge as the hero or heroine, and who will play the villain. Each choice is made at the expense of an infinite number of variations. Who is to say which version of the story is true?

# *Three*

∞

In the year following Lila's death, Andrew Thorpe interviewed dozens of people, including the editor of the *Stanford Journal of Mathematics,* three of Lila's professors, and several classmates. If there had been friends, Thorpe would have interviewed them, too, but Lila had always been more interested in numbers than in people. Even my parents confided in Thorpe on a couple of occasions—but that was before any of us knew that he was planning to write a book.

Before he talked to anyone else, Thorpe talked to me. During the first semester of my sophomore year at the University of San Francisco, he was my professor for Contemporary American Literature. Lila died in early December, as the semester was coming to an end. Three weeks after her funeral, having failed to turn in my final paper, I arranged to meet Thorpe in a café across the street from campus. I'd met him a few times in the fall to talk about a semester-long project I was doing on Richard Yates and *Revolutionary Road.* Each of our previous conversations had veered off course, lasting well beyond its allotted hour. I had found him to be easygoing and funny, well versed on a variety of subjects, and perfectly willing to admit that he was a fan of action movies, Tears for Fears, and canned ravioli. He was originally from Tuscaloosa, Alabama, and I could still hear a trace of an accent, which I found charming. Even though he was only thirty years old, technically an adjunct instead of a professor, he was one of the best teachers I'd ever had.

"No problem," he said, when I asked for an incomplete. "Take as long as you need." We were sitting on an old loveseat tucked into an alcove. He had insisted on buying me coffee and a sandwich, which I had barely touched.

"Not hungry?"

I picked up the sandwich, put it down again. "For the past three weeks people have been showing up at our house with all this amazing food, but it's impossible to eat anything. The very idea of food seems absurd. We finally started pawning it off on the neighbors."

"When my dad died a few years ago," Thorpe said, "his friends in Tuscaloosa did the same thing. We had enough fried chicken and banana pudding to feed the Crimson Tide."

He looked me in the eyes for a few moments before saying, "How are you holding up, Ellie?"

I fought off tears. What could I say? It was too soon after the event to process it in any coherent way. There was still an element of shock about the whole thing. I found myself telling Thorpe about something that had happened that morning: upon waking, I had pushed back the covers and hurried into the bathroom with the thought of getting in the shower before Lila, who never failed to use up most of the hot water. As I was turning on the faucet I remembered that Lila was not there, that she would not be taking a shower that day or any day. Her death was a realization I had faced dozens of times since it happened, but each time it was a fresh wound. I would wake in the middle of the night, and for a moment everything would be fine, until I remembered that she was gone, at which point I would lie there in my bed, unable to fathom how our family would go on without her.

"One of the strangest things about all of this is living alone in the house with my parents," I said. We were sitting beside the heating vent, but I was shivering. "Before, there was balance: two of them, two of us. Now, I feel like a third wheel in my own home, more like a houseguest than a daughter. When my parents and I weren't getting along, whenever I was in trouble, Lila was always a buffer between us. Now, we just sit there trying hopelessly to make conversation." I wiped my eyes. "I don't know why I'm telling you this."

Thorpe's expression conveyed concern, but not pity. "Tell me whatever you like," he said. "Maybe it will help."

The conversations Andrew Thorpe and I had in the weeks and months following my sister's death were not, to my knowledge, interviews. I turned to him because he was there, and he was sympathetic, and I never felt that he was judging me or my family. It was difficult to talk about Lila's death with my peers, who were careful to be somber in my presence, as if laughter might make light of my grief. It was impossible to talk to my parents, who had in a way shut down. It wasn't as though they stopped functioning: they both got up and went to work in the morning, and in the evenings, as it had always been, we took turns making dinner. My father played golf every other Friday, and my mother continued to work in her garden, weeding and planting and watering at night after her long days at the law firm. The difference was not one of action, but rather of emotion. My parents had always been joyful people, but after Lila died, they rarely laughed. On the rare occasion when one of them smiled, it seemed forced. The silliness that had been a common feature of our house subsided. And the lingering romance of their marriage, which I had come to take for granted, faded entirely.

When they talked about Lila, it was almost always the result of the occasional and momentary mental relapse of believing her to still be alive. For example, one morning a few weeks after she died, when I was taking the car out for the day, my father said, "Be sure to fill up the tank for Lila." Another time, when I was taking plates down from the cupboard to set the table, my mother said, "You need one more," and reached into the cupboard for a fourth plate before realizing that my count had been right.

It was as though my parents had made a conscious decision to forget. In hindsight I would find it strange that we did not sit around talking about my sister, calling up our fondest memories of her. But at the time it seemed natural that we danced around the subject, as if removing Lila from our conversation might somehow excise the grief.

But with Thorpe, I held nothing back. I talked to him about things Lila and I had done together as children. I out-lined her odd habits and neuroses: she always put her left shoe on first and took a few steps around the room, as if to test the floor, before putting on the other one. She formed relationships with certain numbers in the same way avid readers develop relationships with characters in books—one of her fa-vorite numbers was 28.

"Why 28?" Thorpe asked.

"Because it's one of those rare phe-nomena that falls under the category of 'perfect numbers,' " I said. "Its divisors, 1, 2, 4, 7, and 14, add up to 28. It's the sum of the first five primes. There are exactly 28 convex uniform honey-combs. Our universe is 28 billion light years from edge to edge. Twenty-eight is also a harmonic divisor number, a Keith number, and the ninth and last number in the Kubera-Kolam magic square."

"Interesting," Thorpe said.

Encouraged, I told him more. Despite being pretty, Lila couldn't stand mirrors and would go out of her way to avoid them. There were no mirrors in her bedroom, and when my mother finally got her to start wearing lipstick her senior year of college, it would often be a bit off-kilter because she put it on blindly.

One thing that came up often in our conversations was the question of who had killed Lila. The fact was, I didn't have a clue. To my knowledge, no one had disliked her. I couldn't imagine her getting on anyone's bad side. I told Thorpe what I did not tell my parents: that whoever did it, I hoped he had been a stranger. I couldn't bear the thought of it having been someone she knew and trusted.

"What about the man she was seeing?" Thorpe asked once. "Could he have murdered her?"

I flinched. "Please don't use that word." *Murder* was the term favored by reporters, but I couldn't bring myself to say it. It was too graphic. I was grateful for the official terminology, *homicide,* which was somehow softer around the edges. "Of course the police are very interested in him," I said. "But no one knows who he is. The two of them were extremely discreet."

He jotted something on a notepad, and I kept talking. With Thorpe, I felt free to say anything. He listened, nodded, asked questions. In hindsight, I should have been alarmed by the pen that was always at the ready, the way he would sometimes start scribbling into his notebook in the middle of a conversation, but every time I met with him, he was reading student essays or writing lecture notes, so I thought nothing of it.

The semester after Lila died, I enrolled in Thorpe's survey of Eastern European literature. It was the only class I attended faithfully. Our private conversations always began with whatever we were reading in class that week—Milan Kundera's *The Book of Laughter and Forgetting,* Václav Havel's *Temptation,* Bohumil Hrabal's *Too Loud a Solitude*— and ended with Lila. I began to suspect that my friends found me morose and difficult to tolerate; though I understood that grief makes for unpleasant company, I couldn't get my mind off what had happened to my sister. Thorpe was the one person who never seemed to tire of the subject. It occurred to me more than once that he might have a romantic interest in me. Why else, I wondered, would he continue to indulge me?

Most often we met at the café, but sometimes I stayed after class. The classroom had large, rounded windows, through which I could see the mouth of the bay and the Golden Gate Bridge. The sight of the bridge rising up through the fog, so aloof and yet so familiar, was comforting. Lila and I had walked across the bridge together many times, it was something we had done twice a year for as long as I could remember—on her birthday, and on the first day of fall. Talking about her in that setting, with this man whom I'd come to consider a friend, felt natural.

After the spring semester ended, we continued to get together. We'd meet in Dolores Park, which was close to his apartment, or at Creighton's Bakery in Glen Park. A couple of times we saw a movie at the Roxie.

It wasn't until June, six months after our talks began, that Thorpe told me he was writing a book. We were having lunch at Pancho Villa. We sat by the window, and while we dug into our burritos, Thorpe kept up a running commentary on the passersby. He had a story for each of them: the ratty-looking woman pushing the five-hundred-dollar stroller had stolen it from an unsuspecting yuppie mom; the attractive couple, hand in hand, was in town on a bogus business trip, both cheating on their spouses. It was a habit of Thorpe's, creating backgrounds and motivations for complete strangers. I always suspected their actual lives were far less interesting than the stories he built for them.

At one point Thorpe sipped his orange soda and said, "Actually, I have some interesting news."

"Really? What?"

"I'm writing a book."

"That's wonderful," I said, and meant it.

Thorpe had confessed to me early on that his secret desire was to be a writer.

While in graduate school he had attempted to publish a number of short stories, but after a string of rejections he gave up. I knew there was a partially written novel in a drawer somewhere— "Half the English department has one of those," he'd said to me once, dismissing years of his own work with a wave of his hand.

"A novel?" I asked.

"No, this is nonfiction."

"About what?"

He bit his lip, fiddled with his silverware, and after a long pause finally said, "It's about Lila."

At first, I was certain I'd heard him wrong. "What?"

"A celebration of her life and an investigation of her death."

It sounded rehearsed, as if he had said it before. But the very notion that he would write a book about Lila was so outlandish, I thought for a moment he was joking.

"That's not funny," I said. "Why would you say something like that?"

"It's a fascinating story. I think people would want to read about it."

I pushed my plate away. "You can't be serious." I kept waiting for him to tell me he was kidding, but he didn't. A man passed by with several dogs on leashes and Thorpe tried, stupidly, to lighten the mood with a joke. "This one gave up a lucrative career in medicine to pursue his dream of being a dog walker."

"Lila isn't a story," I said, so loudly the couple at the next table turned to stare. "She's my sister."

Thorpe glanced apologetically at the couple and spoke quietly. "I'm sorry. I shouldn't have said it that way. It's just that, listening to you talk about Lila these last few months, I've realized there's so much about this case that hasn't been brought to light. The police are strapped for resources. To them, solving the crime is just a job, an un- welcome distraction. Maybe I can bring a fresh pair of eyes to the case."

"What stone could you possibly over- turn that they haven't already looked under?"

"Look, somebody knows something.

At the very least, maybe I can figure out who Lila was seeing."

"If you want to play private eye, go ahead, but please don't put it in a book. Lila would hate that."

I could tell that, as I spoke, Thorpe was already planning his response. "She was an exceptional person, enormously gifted," he said. "The book is a tribute to her."

I felt my face getting hot. "But you didn't even know her."

"I feel as though I did. If it weren't for you, she would have been nothing more to me than an item in the news. But you made her real to me. You made her matter."

"I'm begging you," I said, "seriously, as a friend."

I had told Thorpe in the past about Lila's almost obsessive desire for privacy. It was the reason she lived at home rather than in an apartment; having an apartment would have required her to have roommates. It was why she rarely answered the phone, and she had so few friends. It probably had something to do with why she liked

numbers, too: numbers kept their distance. They communicated without the
messiness of emotion. Numbers possessed an inherent order that was impossible to find in human relationships.
She would have been sick about having her face splashed across the papers, her name mentioned on the TV
news. A book would be even worse.
Books get passed from hand to hand,
preserved in libraries. In a book, she
would always be the victim.

Thorpe leaned back. "I'm too far into
it to back out now, but I'll feel better if I
have your approval. The first draft is almost halfway done. I'd love for you to
take a look at it. I've already found an
agent."

"Didn't it occur to you to ask me before you started?"

He said nothing.

"I trusted you," I said, feeling stupid.
I thought about his endless questions,
his incessant note-taking, and how I'd
answered every question he asked,
never really stopping to consider his
motives.

He reached across the table and put his hand on mine. I pulled away.

"I thought you might be reluctant, and I completely understand. That's why I wanted to get the ball rolling before I told you." He reached into his bag and pulled out a file folder, which he slid across the table to me. I opened it. The stack of papers inside was two inches thick. I read the title page, feeling sick to my stomach.

## MURDER BY THE BAY
A True Tale of San Francisco Noir
*by Andrew Thorpe, Ph.D.*

During the next few weeks, I saw Thorpe on several occasions. Each time, I begged him not to go ahead with the book, and each time, he refused. "Have you read it?" he would ask eagerly. "If you read it, I think you'll change your mind." But I didn't want to read it. I didn't need to relive, through someone else's lens, the horror of Lila's death.

The last time Thorpe and I talked was a foggy day on Ocean Beach, after I'd told my parents about the book. They had been devastated, and my normally calm father had been unable to hide his anger.

"You brought Andrew Thorpe into this house," he said. "He had dinner with us. We trusted him because he was your friend."

Thorpe and I walked along the shoreline, faces cold and wet from the fog. "I'm asking you one last time," I pleaded. "For me, for my parents, for Lila. Just let this go."

"Ellie," he said. "I can't."

"That's it?" I asked.

He looked out at the ocean, where an enormous ship was making its way slowly toward the bay. "I'm sorry," he said.

I turned and walked away. When I was halfway to the boardwalk, he shouted something, but his words were drowned out by the waves.

# *Four*

∞

For several years after Lila died, I wandered. It took me longer than it should have to complete my B.A. in literature, after which I worked as a waitress and an office temp in order to finance my travels around the U.S.—endless road trips in beat-up cars with on-again, off-again boyfriends. Eventually, I went alone to Europe. The summer after I finished high school and Lila graduated from Berkeley, our parents had paid for the two of us to spend six weeks backpacking by Eurail. We had so much fun on our trip, we vowed to do it again in five years. With Lila gone, the five-year mark came and went without fanfare. I lived in a kind of suspension, having never found a clear path forward. Four years later than planned, I bought a one-way ticket across the Atlantic. I spent the summer of my twenty-seventh year retracing the steps that Lila and I had made together. I traveled the same route we had traveled, from Amsterdam to Paris, Paris to Barcelona, across to Venice, up through Germany, and finally back to the Netherlands. I visited the same museums, even tried to sleep in the same hostels, though more often than not I couldn't find them, as I'd never bothered to keep a journal.

I bought a book of mini-biographies of famous mathematicians and visited several of their graves—Blaise Pascal at Saint Etienne-du-Mont in Paris, Carl Gauss at the Albanifriedhof in Göttingen, Germany, Leibniz in Hanover, Christian Doppler at the Cimitero di San Michele in Venice. Visiting the gravesites of the mathematicians Lila had admired was a posthumous gift to my sister, one which served no practical purpose, but in some way I couldn't quite explain, it made me feel closer to her.

Upon my return home, I continued

working temp jobs, moving from one office to the next with no sense of joy or purpose. I often wondered what Lila would be doing, had she lived. Surely, it would be a great deal more than this; her life, I knew, would have amounted to something. A decade after her death I could not quite banish the thought that I was still living life as an imaginary number.

Then, when I was beginning to doubt that I would ever find anything to be passionate about, I found my calling in coffee. The discovery was accidental, what some might call luck. Lila, for her part, had never believed in such a thing. Once, when I exclaimed over her good luck at having won a Walkman in a high school raffle, Lila had said, "What we call luck is really just the result of natural laws playing themselves out, a matter of probability."

A cupper, like a sommelier or a perfumer, must have an excellent nose. I inherited mine from my mother, an avid gardener who arranged her plants not by color, but by smell. Walking through my mother's garden as a child, I was enthralled by the way the heady sweetness of jasmine gave way to the tartness of lemon trees, or the way musky wisteria was buttressed by the piney smell of sage. I loved the crispness of peppermint against a carpet of cedar bark mulch, the earthiness of roses paired with delicate lavender. Once, when I was in elementary school, my mother told me I had a natural nose. I relished the compliment, and clung to it for years. My mother was always supportive, and nothing would have pleased her more than to have many fronts on which to praise me. But while Lila's intellectual gifts made her a magnet for spontaneous and genuine praise, I knew our mother had to work a little harder with me.

Decades after the fact, I still remembered my first cup of coffee, enjoyed on the sly with my father one Sunday morning when Lila and my mother were at church. I was eight years old, homebound with poison oak following a family camping trip.

I'd always loved the smell of coffee, the way it filled the house in the mornings when my parents were getting ready for work. But that day, I noticed something new in the kitchen: a small wooden box on the countertop, with a metal cup affixed to its top and a crank on the side. A few dark beans rested in the bottom of the cup. My father was sitting at the kitchen table, reading the paper.

"What's this?" I asked.

"A coffee grinder."

"Where did it come from?"

"Your mother and I bought it in Venice."

"What's Venice?"

"A city in Italy. We went there on our honeymoon."

"Why haven't I ever seen it before?"

"I found it when I was cleaning out the garage. Why don't you give it a whirl?"

I turned the crank round and round, watching the teeth in the bottom of the cup break the beans into smaller and smaller bits, releasing a rich, nutty fragrance. I continued cranking until the beans disappeared. Then I pulled out the little drawer where the coffee grounds had fallen, brought it to my nose, and sniffed. It was wonderful.

"I want some," I said.

Dad smiled. "Aren't you a bit young?"

Many years later, I would take a temp job doing administrative work at Golden Gate Coffee in South City. When the owner, Mike Stekopolous, offered me a permanent position as his assistant, I accepted without hesitation; it was the first office where I felt I truly fit in. I'd been at Golden Gate Coffee for a year when I first accompanied Mike on one of his trips. I was thirty-one years old, searching for something I couldn't quite pinpoint—a sense of peace and well-being that had eluded me since Lila's death. On a small plot of land in the Quezaltenango region of Guatemala, I stood side by side with three generations of a *campesino* family and picked ripe coffee cherries from glossy trees. By the end of the day my back was aching, my fingers sore, and my burlap bag only half full; I was stunned to learn that it required two thousand hand-picked cherries to produce a single pound of coffee. The next day, I took a tour of the processing shed, where the floaters were separated from the good cherries, which were then fed into the pulping machine before the beans, still wrapped in a thick skin of parchment, were separated by size. I saw the fermentation vats, dipped my hands into the soggy beans, and rinsed away the gooey mucilage, revealing the smooth, greenish beans with their delicate seams. Finally, I helped spread the beans on gigantic tarps to dry, raking them back and forth in the sun.

It was only after I had experienced the process from start to finish that Mike allowed me into the cupping room—a small shed in a clearing, with whitewashed walls and a floor of packed dirt. There, as I broke the dark crust with a heavy spoon, I remembered the morning I sat sipping coffee with my father. It was the first time in my adult life I could envision some version of my own story in which the disparate parts somehow came together, in which the various plots began to merge.

# *Five*

∞

---

*Murder by the Bay* appeared in stores on a Tuesday in June, eighteen months after Lila's death. The following Sunday, a reviewer named Semi Chellas gave it a glowing front-page review in the *San Francisco Chronicle,* promising that it was destined to become "a true crime classic." Days later, I came across a piece Thorpe had written for *San Francisco* magazine, titled, "Lila's Story," in which he detailed his friendship with me and claimed that while Lila had been the main character of his story, I had been his muse. It made me sick to my stomach. I hoped my parents hadn't heard about the article; if they did, they said nothing.

I watched the book section, alarmed to see it debut at number seven on the

*Chronicle* nonfiction best-seller list. Week by week, it rose, from seven to five to two, and eventually to number one, where it remained for twenty-three weeks. I couldn't walk past a bookstore without seeing it prominently displayed in the window, often with a large poster, on which the cover art—a photograph of Lila's face ghosted over the Golden Gate Bridge—was paired with Thorpe's headshot: victim and author, side by side. I hated the thought of all those people reading about Lila, hated the fact that her private tragedy had become public entertainment.

During its third week on the stands, I was in the waiting room of a service station on Geary Boulevard, having the oil changed in my car, when I noticed that the woman across the aisle was reading *Murder by the Bay.* She saw me looking at the cover and asked, "Have you read it?"

"No."

"You should. It's fascinating. Slow in parts when the author gets into the math stuff, but overall I'd recommend it. It's chilling to think this happened right here, in San Francisco. I know the streets he mentions, I've eaten in the restaurants, my son even went to the same high school as Lila—Lowell. He remembers her, she was apparently very quiet, pretty, a little strange. I'm three-quarters of the way through. The author just named the murderer."

"He did?"

"Yes. I won't spoil it for you."

She looked at the cover, then back at me. "Actually, you kind of look like her."

After paying for the oil change, I drove to Green Apple Books on Clement. Until then, I had been determined not to read Thorpe's book. But the woman at the service station had caught me off guard. Was it possible that Thorpe had actually done what he said he would do—that he had ultimately found something that the police had not? The book was on the shelf of new releases, front and center. A gold sticker on the cover, just above Lila's left eye, said *Autographed*. It was a staff pick. A card handwritten by someone named Pate said the book was "reminiscent of *In Cold Blood,* a chilling account of a grisly murder that will have you on the edge of your seat." If the sales clerk hadn't been looking straight at me, I would have ripped the card off and moved the stack to the calendar section at the back of the store. Instead, I just picked up a copy, placed it on the counter, and paid cash for the story of my sister's life and death. That night in my bedroom, I began reading.

The book opened with a detailed description of the manner in which Lila's body was found. Thorpe quoted the hiker who found her in the woods: "There I was unzipping my pants, getting ready to take a leak, when my foot caught on something and I tripped. When I caught my balance and saw that it was a body, I freaked out. I leaned against the nearest tree and puked my guts up."

For weeks afterward, I couldn't shake the image of this stranger in his unzipped pants, vomiting beside my sister's body. I would have given anything to be the one who found her, to comb her hair with my fingers and wipe the mud off her face. I would have given anything to make her look more like herself, less exposed, before the detectives arrived with their notebooks and Polaroid cameras.

Thorpe found no detail too intimate or too gruesome to report. He described the crime scene photos as if he were describing a series of paintings: the pale bluish color of my sister's skin, the high arch of her dark eyebrows, the way her bloodied hair fanned out around her face. Even, agonizingly, the way the police covered their noses when they approached her body, as it had been several days since she died. She was lying on her back in a straight, prim line, arms resting at her sides, a pile of leaves beneath her head like a pillow—a position which led the detectives to surmise that her murderer must have known her.

*The killer appeared to feel some compassion for his victim,* Thorpe wrote. *Almost as if he was putting her to bed, tucking her in for the long night.*

She had been clothed when the hiker found her, but her shirt was gaping open beneath her peacoat, the top four buttons missing. Thorpe took several sentences to describe her pale yellow bra, a full paragraph to describe a small tattoo above her left breast. She'd gotten the tattoo a few weeks before she died, and had shown it to me proudly one night before bed.

"What is it?" I'd asked, tracing my fingers over the dark purple ink.

"A double torus, or as good an approximation of one as I could get on Haight Street."

"What's a double torus?"

"It's a sphere with two handles and two holes, formed by connecting two torii. Picture two doughnuts glued together, side by side."

"What possessed you to get a tattoo of two doughnuts?" I asked.

"The double torus is a very elegant topological construct. It can be plotted like so—" She went to her desk, jotted something down on a scrap of paper, and handed it to me: $z^2 = 0.04 - x^4 + 2x^6 - x^8 + 2x^2y^2 - 2x^4y^2 - y^4$. A few days after her body was discovered, I came across the paper tacked to her bulletin board. I realized it was the last thing she had written down specifically for me. I never threw it away. For years it would travel with me in my wallet, like some secret code.

Lila buttoned her pajama top to cover the tattoo. "Someone dared me."

"Who?"

She smiled, a private smile, as if I wasn't even in the room. "No one you know."

Standing beside Lila's body in the morgue in Guerneville, holding hands, my parents saw the tattoo for the first time. This scene, too, was described by Thorpe, who, of course, had not been there, but who claimed in his book's preface that a "dramatization of this and other events, though fictional, was necessary to telling the story in a truthful way." But there were things he got right: my parents' surprise at the tattoo, the smell of Chinese takeout coming from the mortuary office, my father's monotone phone call to me—things Thorpe only knew because I had told him.

For him, it was a story, pure and simple. Prior to the book, he'd been teach-

ing part-time at various Bay Area uni-
versities for several years. He confessed to me that the only reason he
ended up at USF was that it had the
best views and the shortest semesters.
"I used to think teaching was the perfect career," he told me early in our
friendship. "I had this idea that everyone was in it for the love of literature.
But that was before I discovered how
much jealousy and petty politics is involved. I love the students, but I hate
the system. I have to come up with a
way out."

The book was Thorpe's solution. He
was thirty-two years old when *Murder
by the Bay* made him a minor celebrity.
Every time I glanced at the literary
events section of the *Chronicle,* he was
there. One morning, while eating breakfast in front of the television, I saw him
on the *Today* show, being interviewed
by Bryant Gumbel. He looked completely different from the Andrew Thorpe
I knew, slick and polished and decked
out in beautifully tailored clothes, expensive shoes. The next week, *Murder
by the Bay* appeared on the *New York*

*Times* best-seller list. His byline began cropping up in slick magazines like *Harper's* and *GQ,* and eventually he landed his own column for *Esquire.* He went on to pen three more books in the true crime genre, growing richer murder by murder. Occasionally I would see him on CNN, talking about some new unsolved case as if he were an expert in forensics. And maybe, by then, he was.

While I despised the exploitative nature of *Murder by the Bay,* there was one thing I could not deny: Thorpe had done his research.

Ultimately, evidence about the crime was scant and the police investigation was unenthusiastic. Lila's case was never much of a priority for the San Francisco Police Department, which was caught up in a scandal involving the police chief's son. The Guerneville police, for their part, were underfunded and short on staff. Although Lila's death was labeled a homicide, no one was ever charged. Thorpe, however, had a theory, which he pieced together using a complex series of clues and seemingly well-reasoned conjecture. He laid out his case meticulously, convincingly, over a span of 296 pages. Added to the details about the case itself were long passages about Lila, my parents, me.

*This isn't only the story of the murdered girl,* Thorpe wrote in the preface. *It is also the story of her sister, the one who was left behind. I knew her personally. It would be fair to say I knew her very well. Portions of this book are directly transcribed from conversations I had with Ellie Enderlin, who would strive, in the weeks and months following her sister's death, to be exactly what her parents needed, to transform herself, as if by magic, into the good daughter.*

The irony was that, if there had ever been a chance of my becoming "the good daughter," it ended with the publication of Thorpe's book. While my mother tried valiantly to treat me exactly as she always had, my father could not hide his disappointment. I heard it in his voice when he spoke to me, saw it in his face when he looked at me. Mine was an ambitious family—my father's successful financial consulting business, my mother's well-regarded law practice, Lila's burgeoning genius. Only one of us was average—a break in the genetic code, perhaps, a dilution of the Enderlin family determination to succeed. My mediocrity was a fault which my father had largely chosen to overlook when Lila was alive. With a prodigy like Lila, he could afford for me to be average. Even after her death, there was a grace period during which I suspected he was trying to give me the benefit of the doubt; for the first time in my life, he took an interest in my studies, frequently asking about my classes, my goals. I tried to come up with worthy answers to his questions, never letting on that I skipped most of my classes or that my promises to follow in my mother's footsteps as an attorney were meaningless. For a short time, he seemed to harbor a genuine faith in me. But after the book came out, everything changed. Our conversations became shorter and shorter, the silences between us more strained.

I suspected it was an effort for him not to say what he was thinking: that the book was my fault, that, through my indiscretion, I had turned our family's private tragedy into a public spectacle.

# *Six*

∞

The sixth chapter of *Murder by the Bay*, more than any other, shined a spotlight on our home life. Entitled "A Tale of Two Sisters," it focused in particular on the relationship between me and Lila. As I read the book that night, three weeks after its publication, I cringed at the picture Thorpe painted of the two of us, the idea that we could be so easily summed up.

*One was tall and dark,* the chapter began, *the other petite and fair. One was a math prodigy, while the other was always lost in books.*

Both of these sentences were basically true, although the language implied a kind of fairy-tale dichotomy that had not existed in real life. Lila did indeed have almost three inches on me, and she shared my father's olive complexion and brown hair, while I had inherited the pale skin, red hair, and small stature of my mother's Scotch-Irish family. Aside from those differences, though, we looked very much like sisters—a fact that people often commented on when they saw us together. We both had dark brown eyes, dimples, and rounded faces. We shared my mother's mild cheekbones and my father's straight, serious nose. And both of us had lucked out when it came to our mouths, a happy accident of genetics that combined my mother's bow-shaped lips and my father's full pout.

On the page facing the opening paragraph of chapter six, there was a photograph of me and Lila standing together on the day of her graduation from Berkeley. She looked academic and respectable in a cap and gown, her long hair fastened in a low ponytail. I fit the image of the carefree younger sister, with my low-cut sundress and sandals, hair falling loose around my shoulders. To further the contrast, Lila never wore more than a dab of mascara and a hint of pale lipstick, while I wore lipstick in rich shades of red. The photograph had originally been in color, so that when it was rendered in black-and-white on the cheap, porous paper, my lipstick appeared even darker. Readers might study the photograph and be utterly convinced that we were just as Thorpe had described us.

Thorpe went on to portray Lila as painfully shy, me as wildly sociable. But to anyone who actually knew us, it would have been clear that Thorpe had grossly exaggerated our differences for dramatic effect. Anything that might disrupt the narrative as he saw it was omitted: he never said that until Lila's death, I had always been quite studious when it came to the classes I enjoyed. He never mentioned that Lila, while basically a loner, could be quite friendly with strangers.

I understood why. "It's all about character," he had said, in one of several lectures he gave on storytelling during my first class with him. Even though the class was called Contemporary American Literature, Thorpe took liberties with the syllabus, frequently requiring us to write short stories of our own. "Plot, setting, style—none of it means anything if you don't have interesting characters, preferably in conflict with one another." From his standpoint, I could see how the contrast of the shy, intellectual sister with the wild, artistic one might have made the book more entertaining. And that, I believed, was what he was after. It wasn't accuracy that mattered in Thorpe's mind, so much as the overall effect.

From page one, there was a "lean closer and I'll tell you a creepy story" feel to *Murder by the Bay.* I had read and enjoyed many such books myself over the years. While I liked my Chekhov and Flaubert, my O. Henry and Pavese, I could always get into a well-written detective novel or a riveting true crime tale. *In Cold Blood* was one of my favorite books of nonfiction. The fact that Truman Capote had allegedly taken liberties with the truth had never really bothered me. Years after I first read the book in high school, I still had a clear picture in my mind of sixteen-year-old Nancy Clutter, "the town darling," pleading for her life in the upstairs bedroom. I could still see the farmhouse as Capote had drawn it, with each member of the Clutter family isolated from the others at the moment of his or her death. But the unthinkable depravity of the crime didn't keep me from feeling a voyeuristic thrill as I turned the pages of Capote's book.

There are two characters in *In Cold Blood* who are mentioned only in passing, so that one easily forgets all about them.

*The eldest daughter, Eveanna, married and the mother of a boy ten months old, lived in northern Illinois but visited Holcomb frequently . . . Nor did Beverly, the child next in age to Eveanna, any longer reside at River Valley Farm; she was in Kansas City, Kansas, studying to be a nurse.*

In the aftermath of the murders, Eveanna and Beverly must have felt the blow more deeply than anyone else. I wondered if they had ever read the book, and if so, what they thought of it. When Capote was writing the story that would make him famous, did it ever occur to him to consider how painful it would be for the surviving sisters?

At some point that night, as I sat alone in my room, reading, I heard my mother shuffling down the hall. She tapped on my door, and I stuffed the book under the covers. "Come in."

She walked in and sat on the edge of my bed. "Your light was on," she said, smiling. I'd noticed lately that she was always smiling, or trying to, but the expression never looked quite natural. I reached over and held her hand. It was soft and moist with night cream. She was a woman who believed in minor luxuries. As long as I could remember, she'd used the same expensive lotion on her hands that she used on her face, claiming that you could always tell how well a woman took care of herself by looking at her hands. It worked; despite the endless hours of gardening, hers were beautiful.

"You don't have to do that, Mom," I said.

"Do what?"

"Smile. You don't have to smile for me."

She looked down at the comforter, and with her free hand she rubbed at a dot of dried red nail polish that had been there for months. "Windex will take care of that."

"Mom?"

Finally she looked up and said, "I'm not doing it for you, sweetie. I read somewhere that if you force yourself to smile, it will actually improve your mood."

"Does it work?"

"Not yet."

I had an idea. "You and Dad should take a vacation."

She looked at me as though I'd suggested she quit her job and join a commune. "Whatever for?"

"Maybe it would help."

I wondered if she entirely understood what I was saying. Over the past year and a half, my parents had become so distant with one another that I worried their marriage might end. It was a thought that had never occurred to me before Lila died—I'd never known a married couple who seemed more solid in their commitment, more certain of their love. But lately they had begun moving around the house like room-mates who feared invading one an-other's space. I couldn't remember the last time I had seen them touch.

She reached up and smoothed my hair. "We could go to Timbuktu, it wouldn't matter, I'd still miss her so much I could hardly breathe."

I wished, at that moment, that I could have traded places with Lila. I imagined a scenario in which my mother's grief was smaller, more manageable, a sce-nario in which she had not lost her bril-liant eldest daughter. Surely, if she'd only lost me, the recovery would have been quicker, the devastation less complete. Perhaps the family would have inched closer together rather than farther apart.

She hugged me good night, got up, and closed the door behind her.

It was four in the morning when I finished the book. I hid it under my bed and switched off the lamp.

What I felt for Andrew Thorpe could only be described as disgust. When I read the long passages about Lila—passages in which my sister was painted as a math prodigy, a loner, something of an oddball, a late-blooming beauty—it was clear that Thorpe had used me. Stupidly, blindly, I had delivered Lila right into his hands.

Nonetheless, in the matter of the murder itself, he was very convincing. By the time I got to the end of the book, I was compelled to believe his version of the story. The case he made wasn't foolproof. There was no forensic evidence, for one thing, and some questions remained unanswered. In no way would Thorpe's theory stand up to Lila's own rigorous test—the standard of absolute proof. She would probably scoff at it, calling it what it truly was: mere conjecture. Nevertheless, Thorpe's prime suspect—Peter McConnell—made perfect sense.

# Seven

∞

"We live our lives by way of story," Thorpe said one afternoon, a couple of months after Lila died. "Over time, we construct thousands upon thousands of small narratives by which to process and remember our days, and these mini-narratives add up to the bigger story, the way we see ourselves in the world." He was talking to the class, in a lecture loosely based on *The Book of Laughter and Forgetting,* but I knew his words were really meant for me.

Looking back, it was easy to see that the major story of my own life had been my sister's death. Andrew Thorpe's book had deeply influenced the way I constructed this story. I was twenty years old when I read *Murder by the Bay,* young enough to believe that the things he said about Lila's murder, and the things he said about me, were true.

*In the world of mathematics,* he wrote, *Lila had found her place. When Lila was murdered, Ellie had yet to find hers. The sense of belonging and clarity of direction that simplified Lila's short life would continue to elude Ellie.*

There were times when I wondered if, in describing my flaws in relentless detail, in using me to create a character to fit the story he wanted to tell, Thorpe had somehow altered the course of my life. The Ellie he put on the page was uncertain, unanchored, incapable of finding her way. Did I take his words too much to heart?

But there was one part of the story even the author couldn't have foreseen.

Nearly two decades after the fact, in a South American café, the villain of Thorpe's book stood before me, tall and soft-spoken, nervous as a schoolboy, saying, "Do you know who I am?"

Gazing into Peter McConnell's dark eyes, I had the same impression I'd had the first time I saw him outside his office at Stanford—the sensation that his face was comprised of perfectly ordinary features which, put together, added up to something memorable.

"Yes," I managed to say.

"May I sit down?"

This was not part of my story, not part of the plot of my life as I saw it. My sister's murderer would not simply walk up in a café and ask to join me. I must have nodded again, or perhaps answered in the affirmative, because Peter McConnell proceeded to sit down in the chair opposite me, lay his book on the table, lay his hat on top of the book, and place his large hands palms down, on either side of the book and hat, as if he did not know what to do with them.

"How did you find me?"

I was disappointed in my voice, which came out weak and uncertain. All the anger I had silently directed toward this man in the past, all the disgust, remained locked somewhere inside me, in a place I couldn't, at this crucial moment, quite reach. All that came was my astonishment, which must have been as obvious to him as the sound of Maria's footsteps in the kitchen.

"I didn't. You found me."

"I'm just here for work," I protested. I was still trying to wrap my mind around the fact of his presence, trying to make sense of how he could have shown up here, of all places, from out of the blue. "I've been coming to this village for years," I added.

I had given up looking for Peter Mc-Connell a long time ago. My travels to the coffee regions of the world—Hua-tusco, Yirgacheffe, Poas, Sumatra— were, if anything, an attempt to leave that part of my past behind, to erase it, as much as possible, from the geography of my life. Although I still consid-ered San Francisco home, I spent a good deal of my time elsewhere, among people who did not speak my language, landscapes that looked nothing like my hometown, places where I would not be reminded of Lila. I felt at ease wander-ing among the coffee trees, feeling the mist of a foreign climate and smelling unfamiliar earth. At home, I was always nervous, always looking over my shoulder. Abroad, I found a kind of peace.

"I know," he said. "I've seen you in the past."

"Pardon?"

"It's a small town. You stand out. The first time was almost five years ago. You were at the outdoor market. I was going to say something, but then it started to rain, and you hurried away."

I didn't know how to respond. It occurred to me that perhaps he had followed me here, that he planned to do to me what he had done to my sister. It felt surreal, as if I had dreamt him out of thin air. I looked to Maria—for confirmation of his existence or, absurdly, for some kind of protection, I'm not sure. But she just smiled.

"You said 'the first time.' There were others?"

"Yes."

"How many?"

He paused for a moment. "Three."

"Do you live here?"

"For the past seventeen years."

I found myself staring at Peter McConnell's hands, at his long arms.

These were the hands, according to Thorpe, that had killed my sister, the arms that had carried her into the woods and left her there.

"I came to Nicaragua because of the book," he said. "My wife, Margaret, didn't believe what Thorpe wrote, of course. But it was too much for her. It didn't matter that she knew I wasn't a murderer, everyone else thought I was."

I wanted to add, "You were, you *are,*" but McConnell kept talking, in a steady, unrelenting rhythm, as though he had something to say and did not plan on stopping until he was finished.

"Margaret and I held it together for a little while," he continued. "Not for us, it had been over between us for a long time. We only made an effort to stay together because of our son, Thomas. He was three years old when the book came out. We picked up at the end of the summer semester and moved to the Midwest, where Margaret's parents lived. We had hoped to leave the media circus, the suspicions, back in the Bay Area. By then the police had already questioned me twice, and they had no evidence on which to charge me, but that didn't matter. As far as most people were concerned, I was guilty. Even in Ohio, we couldn't escape that book. It seemed like everyone in my wife's hometown had read it. In a way, I don't blame Margaret for cutting me out of her life. She had Thomas to think of— she was afraid of what it would do to him to grow up under that kind of microscope, with that kind of stigma. And then there was Lila, of course. Margaret knew that I would never get over Lila."

McConnell talked with the urgency of a man who had not spoken to anyone in a long time. It struck me as strange that he would be defending his wife to me. I kept wondering how this was relevant. His wife, their son—it was just a minor side note, I thought, to the larger story: what he had done to my sister.

"I used to follow you," I said. "After I read the book, I went to Stanford and found your office. You had hours posted on the door. I was afraid to be alone with you, but I wanted to see you, to put a face with the name."

"My picture was in the paper."

"More than a face, I guess. I wanted to see you up close, in person. So I waited in the hallway outside your office one Monday. I wore a big hat and sunglasses. I felt ridiculous. You had the door shut. There was a line of students waiting. I kept hearing Lila's name. It was obvious they weren't all there to talk to you about class. It was more like they wanted to be a part of the action. One boy actually wanted you to sign Thorpe's book. I was furious. Lila was dead, and here they were treating you like a celebrity."

As I spoke, I tried to keep my voice steady, so as not to betray my fear. "After a couple of hours you finally came out. The first thing that crossed my mind was that you weren't what I expected. The way you looked, the basic physical description—yes, Thorpe had gotten that right. But everything else—the way you moved, the way you spoke—he'd gotten it wrong."

"Of course he did. He never met me."

"What?"

"I know," McConnell said. "In the

book, he gave the impression that he spent a lot of time interviewing me, but we actually spoke only once, on the phone, for five minutes." He rubbed his thumb back and forth over the bill of his cap; the cloth in that spot had faded to a pale purple. "What did you expect?"

"I expected you to seem more, I don't know, dangerous. I thought there would be something about you—" Here, I stopped, surprised to hear myself saying these things to him. I remembered distinctly thinking that there should be something obviously *off,* something in his eyes, maybe, or his bearing, that marked him as a murderer, but there wasn't.

"You took the train back to the city," I continued. "I left my car behind and followed you. You ended up at Enrico's in North Beach. I got a table and watched you eat. After that I didn't go to Stanford again, but every Monday I went to Enrico's. And every time, you were there—spaghetti with prawns in marinara sauce, ice water, followed by espresso. You were always alone, always working, scribbling away in your notebook, as if the world was invisible to you. I always wore a hat and sunglasses, but I expected that, one day, you would recognize me."

McConnell shifted in his seat. His face in the candlelight was striking. I could see now what Lila would have seen in that face—the interesting angles, the depth of the eyes, the enormous pupils, the flat, honest width of the mouth. "I did," he said.

"You did?"

"Of course. Lila had shown me pictures—some of you together in Europe, another of the two of you on the beach, pictures from childhood. And there were the photographs in Thorpe's book. But even if I hadn't seen pictures, I would have known." His voice grew quieter, and his gaze moved from my eyes to my mouth, my neck. I looked toward the kitchen for Maria, but I could neither see nor hear her.

"Why didn't you say anything?" I asked.

"I assumed you would approach me one day. I would have liked to talk to you. For several months before Lila died, I saw her constantly. Aside from the time I spent with my son, she was the best part of each day. I loved talking to her. More than that, I loved listening to her. Then she was gone. You looked so much like her, I wondered if you sounded like her, too. I wanted to hear your voice. But you just sat in a corner, watching."

"I kept planning to confront you," I said, "but I never could work up the nerve. Even in that setting, with all those people around, I couldn't be sure how you would act. And then one day, you were gone."

There had been a time, a period of years, when I looked for Peter McConnell everywhere, and because I was looking so intently, on a number of occasions I thought I saw him. On the street, I would catch a glimpse of a profile and hurry toward the man, only to realize it wasn't him. Or I would see a movement in a museum, a tilt of the neck or a certain gesture of the hands, and sidle up beside the person, who would invariably end the illusion by turning his face toward me.

After a strange, unsettling year of sex and alcohol following Lila's death, I had spent my twenties in a series of brief relationships, never willing to truly commit. At the time I told myself I was too busy, but I later realized that the problem was Peter McConnell. I had created a sort of personal mythology around him. He had done such enormous damage to my family, had taken on such absurd proportions in my mind, that no one could make me feel the depth of emotion he elicited. It was hatred I felt for him, and when hatred goes deep enough, no affection can compare. For love to take hold there must be available space in the mind and heart; I was so eaten up with anger toward him, I could not make room.

"Why did you do it?" I said quietly. This was the question I had been asking myself for almost half of my life. I had long since given up hope that I might find the answer. It didn't occur to me, at that moment, to believe his claim of innocence. I had believed far too long in his guilt to simply let that conviction slip away.

I waited. He sat there staring alternately at his hands, and at me. Maria emerged from the kitchen, carrying a jar filled with insects. She went over to the windowsill, where her Venus fly-traps sat, opened the jar, and shook it gently over the plants. Finally, McConnell said, "That's what I'm trying to tell you. It wasn't me."

# *Eight*

∞

Strange things were rumored to happen all the time in Diriomo—ghosts dancing in the churchyard, candles spontaneously igniting, music from unknown quarters drifting through deserted streets—but until that night, they had never happened to me.

"I don't deny that I was the most likely suspect," McConnell said, looking directly into my eyes. "But that doesn't make me guilty." He didn't flinch, didn't glance away.

"You were having an affair with my sister."

"Yes, I admitted that to the police."

"Only after they already knew. Only after the book was published. In the beginning, you told them nothing."

"It was on Margaret's bidding that I

decided not to say anything. As angry as she was about the affair, she was terrified of what would happen if the suspicion was cast on me. In hindsight, of course, I knew how stupid my decision was. But under the circumstances, I didn't think I had the right to deny Margaret anything."

"You had dinner with Lila the night she disappeared," I said. "After the book was published, a hostess came forward who placed you at Sam's Grill together."

"I don't deny that."

"And you left the restaurant together."

"We did."

"You walked her to the Muni station at ten p.m."

He nodded.

"That makes you the last person to see her. And the hostess said that she looked upset when you left the restaurant. That morning, before she left home, she'd been crying."

McConnell nodded again.

"Well?" I felt the old anger simmering up again. "Everything was going well in her life. She'd just gotten all that attention for the paper she presented at Columbia. She was a shoo-in for the Hilbert Prize at Stanford. Everyone knew she was on her way. You were obviously the source of her distress—it couldn't have been anything else."

"Do you remember what Thorpe proposed as my motive?" McConnell asked.

"He said you were breaking up with Lila that night at the restaurant, and she threatened to tell your wife about the two of you."

He looked at me in silence.

"What?" I said.

"Tell me, does that sound like something Lila would do?"

He was right. Although I wasn't about to confess this to McConnell, that part of Thorpe's argument had always nagged at me. It simply wasn't in Lila's character. She would never have told McConnell's wife, nor would she have threatened to do so. Over the years, I'd tried to sweep my discomfort with this detail away by telling myself that I didn't really know Lila as well as I thought I did.

"Were you breaking up with her?"

"Quite the contrary. A few days before, I had come clean with my wife."

Maria emerged from the kitchen and pointed at a clock on the wall. It was two a.m. *"Cerrado,"* she said.

"Just a few more minutes," I pleaded. I wasn't ready for this conversation to end. There was so much more I wanted to ask.

*"Cerrado,"* she said again, indicating with her hands that it was time for bed.

*"Por favor,"* I said, but it was no use. As McConnell and I stood to go, Maria smiled and winked at me. She must have believed she was doing me a favor, sending me off into the night with the handsome American.

Moments later, McConnell and I were standing on the dirt road in front of the café. He was wearing the baseball cap again, pulled low on his forehead. The effect was to make him look younger than he was. He had been seven years Lila's senior; that put him at about fifty. The book that he had been reading in the café was tucked under his arm. I had glimpsed the title as we got up to leave: Faraday's *The Chemical History of a Candle.*

The village was silent, deserted. The white buildings shone in the moonlight.

"You shouldn't be wandering around alone at this hour," he said. "I'll walk you back to your hotel."

If I hadn't been so frightened, I might have laughed at the absurdity. "You can't be serious," I said, looking back at the closed door of the café. "Anyway, I do it all the time."

"You shouldn't."

I reached into my bag, feeling for my tryer. It's a basic tool of the coffee trade, a long, scooped metal object with a sharp point on one end and a small cylinder on the other, which tapers into a handle. To take a random sample, you jab the sharp end into the burlap coffee sack, and beans slide along the stem into the cylinder. With one hand, I slid the tryer out of its leather case.

My hand shook, my pulse sped up. I'd spent so many years believing McConnell to be a monster, capable of the most terrible crime. But I'd also spent that time wishing I could confront him, wishing I could discover the truth, however painful, about Lila's death. I didn't want to be left wondering, for the rest of my life, about the end of hers. At that moment, what I wanted was to keep talking, to make McConnell tell me everything. My desire to know what had happened to my sister was even greater than my fear.

The dust rose around our feet as we walked down the narrow path to the main road. Each time he moved closer, I inched away. "If it's true that you weren't breaking up with her, why was she so upset?"

"You know what kind of person Lila was. The entire time we were together, she felt horribly guilty. She hadn't wanted me to tell Margaret about us, didn't want to be responsible for all that. I tried to make her realize it wasn't her fault, it was mine, and that my marriage had been over long before I met her."

We arrived at an intersection, where a small white church sat sentry. A life-size Virgin Mary with a broken glass eye gazed out at us from a roadside altar. The gravestones in the churchyard looked like giant slabs of white soap in the moonlight.

Suddenly, McConnell reached out and grabbed my elbow, pulling me toward him. I jerked out of his grasp and took two steps back. I pulled the tryer out of the bag and held it in front of me. I was trying to find my voice, wondering if anyone would even hear me, when he pointed to a long snake lying in the path a few inches from his foot. The snake was still, its body covered with dark green diamonds.

"It's a fer-de-lance," he said quietly, stretching his arm toward me. "Give me that."

I had no choice but to trust him. I handed him the tryer. He grasped the handle with his right hand, and with one swift, powerful motion, brought the sharp end down a few inches from the snake's head, severing it from the body. The long green body slithered and shook for a moment, then lay still. The yellow mouth gaped open.

McConnell stood, visibly shaken, and

wiped the tryer on his pants before handing it back to me.

"If it bites you, you bleed to death internally."

"I'm sorry, I—"

"It's okay," he said. He stepped over the dead snake and looked back at me. "If you want, I'll turn around right now. You should be all right from here."

I hesitated for several seconds before joining McConnell on the path. I looked back at the snake, then at him. We continued down the road, my heart beating wildly.

"Why Lila?" I asked. "You must have known how inexperienced she was. If you wanted to cheat on your wife, why couldn't you have found someone else?"

"It wasn't like that. Margaret and I had made a decent life together, and our son was everything to me. But Margaret didn't understand my work. None of it mattered to her. As long as I continued to advance in my career, she was content. When we met, I liked that about her. She was into art and dancing, things I'd never understood. It was a nice balance, and I believed she was the kind of woman who could take care of things at home, give our children a happy life while I concentrated on work. But then I met your sister, and realized I wanted something more."

"How did you meet her?" I asked.

So long ago, I had tried to get this very information out of Lila. Over the years I had told her everything about the guys I dated. She seemed to take pleasure in my escapades, and had said more than once that she was living vicariously through me. So I was hurt that, when there was finally someone in her life, she wouldn't tell me anything.

"I was in my fourth year in the Ph.D. program," McConnell continued. "I loved fatherhood, but it took its toll; my dissertation was going much more slowly than I had expected, and for some time I had been attempting to collaborate on a paper that was going nowhere."

McConnell's voice in the quiet night was deep, a smooth and calming voice. I imagined Lila sitting with him in one of those private booths at Sam's on the final night of her life. Was his the last voice she ever heard, or was there someone else, someone I had never allowed myself to imagine—a taxi driver, a stranger on the street?

One number in Thorpe's book had been burned into my memory: 23,370. It was the number of people who were murdered in the U.S. in 1989, the year Lila died. *Only 13.5 percent of murder victims do not know their assailants,* Thorpe wrote. *Murder is rarely random.* I remembered thinking that his word choice was inaccurate. There was nothing rare about 13.5 percent. 13.5 percent of 23,370 was actually a very large number. I couldn't recall exactly how the paragraph was written, but one thing I did remember was that Thorpe had accused Lila of being a *tragically poor judge of character.* And I had been angered by the way he manipulated the words, as if Lila bore some responsibility for her own death, as if only the victims of "random" acts of violence were truly innocent.

"Then Lila came along," McConnell was saying. "I remember the day she walked into the office of the *Stanford Journal of Mathematics.* She was wearing this orange dress and purple sneakers, and her hair looked like she'd just rolled out of bed."

"I remember that dress," I said, surprised to be complicit in this story, to add my memory to his own. "She made it herself. She made all her clothes herself. She didn't use premade patterns. She'd just take her measurements and sketch the dress on a legal pad, then make calculations as she went."

"The outfit was completely outlandish." I was looking straight ahead, but I could hear the slight change in McConnell's voice, and knew that he was smiling. It was strange to think that the man standing beside me had been intimate with my sister, had even been loved by her. I could not deny that there was a magnetic quality about him—something in the tone of his voice, his direct and unapologetic gaze. There was something unmistakably sensual about him that I hadn't noticed during my spying missions at Enrico's.

"She looked beautiful," he continued. "The editor, a stodgy old guy named Bruce, looked at her and asked how he could help her. He seemed to think she had wandered in there on accident. Lila thrust a folder into his hand. It was a paper on numerical evaluation of special functions. She wanted to submit it.

"Bruce looked at her like she was out of her mind. You have to understand, the journal published the work of highly respected mathematicians. And here was this disheveled, great-looking girl, very young, waltzing into the office as if she had a right to be there and asking us to publish her paper. It was unheard of. I fell for her instantly. I took the paper home with me, and I was blown away. I called Lila that night and asked her to meet me the next day for lunch."

We had reached another intersection. With no cue from me, McConnell took the lane to the right, in the direction of my *pensión*. I asked myself what I would do if he led me straight to my hotel. Would that be the thing that brought me to my senses?

A minute later we were standing in front of the small yellow building, which was flanked by large trees with knotted, twisting trunks. Blinking white Christmas lights hung from the branches, connected to the hotel by a thick orange extension cord. "Here we are," he said.

Again, I took a step back. "How did you—"

"It's a small town."

I still wasn't ready for the conversation to end. There was so much more I wanted to know. I remembered something that I had confided to Thorpe and which he had quoted in his book. "I hope it wasn't someone she knew and trusted," I said to him more than once. What McConnell seemed to be offering me, all these years later, was an alternative version of the story, one in which Lila's murderer wasn't also her lover. Whatever the truth was, I needed to know.

I felt a warm drop of water on my hand, and another. McConnell looked up at the sky.

"Can we talk again tomorrow?" I asked.

He toed the dirt with his shoe. "You won't see me again. I just wanted to meet you and have my say. It's been a long time. I'm not sure what you think happened, I'm not sure what you think about me, or that awful book. I'm not even sure if you think about it at all. But it's important to me to tell you this, Ellie—I didn't do it, I never could have done it. I loved your sister. I loved her more than you, or she, will ever know. It all happened so long ago, it hardly matters to me now what people think. But your opinion does matter, because Lila talked about you all the time, you're the person she was closest to in the world."

He was wrong about that. I loved her, but we weren't as close as I would like to have been. She hadn't told me about him. She hadn't been willing to tell me, that morning, why she was crying. I suspected that Peter McConnell, not me, was the one person with whom she hadn't held back.

The rain began in earnest now, slapping the leaves of the trees, pitting the dirt road. Impulsively, I said, "Don't go yet." I stepped under the awning of the hotel and McConnell followed.

"Are you inviting me inside?"

"Yes."

José, the owner of the *pensión,* always locked the door at midnight. Accustomed to my late-night walks, he had given me a key. I made some unnecessary racket as I opened the door, just to let him know I was there. We passed through the empty lobby. In an alcove behind the desk was a shrine to the Virgin Mary. The candles had burned out. McConnell walked behind me, his long shadow preceding me up the single flight of stairs. As we passed José's room I talked loudly. If anything happened to me, I wanted someone to know I wasn't alone that night. I heard bedsprings creaking in José's apartment, feet shuffling toward the door, the cover of the peephole sliding open.

At the end of the hall I slid my key into the lock, opened the door of my room, and waited for McConnell to follow me inside. There was no overhead light, just a single lamp with an ancient shade that gave off a dingy yellow glow.

# *Nine*

∞

My room was simply furnished: a bed, a hardback chair, a cupboard, and a small table. A narrow doorway opened onto the tiny bathroom. The room was hot. I turned on the overhead fan, and it began to click and hum.

"I have rum," I said. "Drink?"

"Just a little, please."

I took out the bottle and two glasses and poured some for both of us. I still had my satchel over my shoulder, the tryer easily accessible.

"Have a seat," I said, gesturing toward the chair. The furniture was small by any standards, and when McConnell sat, his knees jutted absurdly in the air. He laid the hat and book beside him on the floor. I sat on the edge of the bed directly across from him, the bag on the mattress beside me.

He took a sip of his rum, closing his eyes when he swallowed. "This is very good."

My mother was always giving me bits of advice gleaned from her experience as an attorney. One point she frequently came back to was that, if you wanted someone to tell you anything of significance, you had to build trust by offering them some personal information about yourself first. "It was a gift," I said. "From a local coffee farmer. That's why I'm here. There will be a cupping tomorrow, and I fly back to San Francisco day after that. I always stay here when I visit the farm, and there's always a bottle of rum waiting for me when I get here." I took a sip, felt the warmth slide down my throat.

"A mathematician is a machine for turning coffee into theorems," McConnell said. Then, noticing my look of confusion, "Paul Erdos. There's some truth in it. I go through nine or ten cups a day."

"The book," I said, glancing at the

small volume on the floor beside him. *"The Chemical History of a Candle.* What is it?"

"It's from a series of lectures delivered during Christmas at London's Royal Institution in 1860. Faraday writes that 'there is no more open door by which you can enter into the study of natural philosophy than by considering the physical phenomena of a candle.' Faraday delivered the lectures to schoolchildren, but there's quite a lot to them. A great essay is like a mathematical proof in that its argument is elegant, its truth universal." He took another sip of his rum.

"You read a lot?" I asked.

"It passes the time. As you've probably noticed, this is a rather quiet little corner of the universe."

"You were telling me why you're in Diriomo."

"After my wife kicked me out, I didn't know where to go. I couldn't go back to San Francisco, because I'd been vilified there, a walking pariah. I couldn't go back to Stanford. For several months, I drifted around Ohio, working as a house painter. I figured that if I stayed in the area, then maybe, every now and then, I'd get to see Thomas. But Margaret convinced a judge to give her sole custody, I didn't even get visitation rights—it all came back to the book. I was devastated. First I lost Lila, and then I lost my son. My work had ground to a halt, and my career was over. At that point it was difficult for me to imagine any reason that I ought to continue living."

"Why did you?"

"Have you heard of Alan Turing?" he asked.

"Rings a bell."

"In 1950 he devised the Turing Test, to determine a machine's capability to demonstrate intelligence. A human judge engages simultaneously in natural language conversation with a machine and another human being."

He must have read the confusion on my face, because he smiled and said, "I apologize. This is exactly why I would make a terrible teacher. When I speak, I follow whatever path my thought processes may be traveling at the moment, but I forget to make the necessary connections for the person I'm speaking to. With Lila, when I went off on a tangent, I always had the feeling that she was following along with me. I never had to write down the steps to a proof; she could connect the dots on her own, as if she were reading my mind. There you go, I'm doing it again."

I poured him another shot. He didn't hesitate in drinking it down.

"Turing killed himself by biting into an apple laced with cyanide," he said, "just a few days shy of his forty-second birthday. The suicide came after he was persecuted by the British government for homosexuality. Which leads me to the point I was attempting to make: I've never believed that suicide is a viable action, except in the most extreme cases—by extreme I mean that one is about to be captured by the enemy, or is suffering horrific physical pain from a terminal illness. Although I could see no immediate reason to live, ceasing to live was not a scientifically sound option. While Lila was gone for good, there was always the possibility that I would be reunited with Thomas, or that I would, despite my detachment from the math community, make a significant mathematical discovery."

There was a noise in the hallway, just outside the door. McConnell heard it, too. He stopped speaking for a moment, we both glanced at the door.

"It's José," I said. "Probably checking to make sure I'm okay."

As José's footsteps retreated, I realized that I had relaxed somewhat. But I wondered if this was part of the man's talent, part of his charm; perhaps Lila had felt exactly the same way in the hours before she died.

"I'd been separated from my son for almost seven months when my advisor at Stanford told me about his cabin in Nicaragua," McConnell continued. "He'd purchased the cabin a few years before, but he'd only used it a handful of times. I had nothing else to do, and nothing to lose, so I came. I instantly felt comfortable here. It was the kind of place a person could start over. I've been here ever since."

"What about work?"

"I contract for an engineering firm in San Marcos—calculations, figuring out load-bearing weights for bridges, that sort of thing. I do it by hand, with paper and pencil. It's a very satisfying way to work. You can't imagine how much time can flow into a single lengthy calculation. Days and nights pass when I hardly leave my house—although perhaps it's a stretch to call it a house. So much was subtracted from my life when Lila died, I thought there would never be an addition that could make up for what I had lost, and that's certainly true. But I've tried in the last few years to think of my move to Nicaragua as a kind of gift. Prior to coming here, I relied extensively on computers. Without them, I feel a kinship with Ramanujan, Gauss, even Archimedes. Of course I don't mean to compare myself to them, only to say that there's something pure about approaching mathematics with only the most basic tools—one's own intellect, a blank page, a pencil."

He eyed the bottle of rum, and I filled his glass again. This time, he stared at it for several moments, moving his hand in a circle so that the brown liquid swirled in the glass. The motion of his hand was measured and delicate, the movement of the rum in the lamp's dim yellow light hypnotic. McConnell had been the obvious choice all along, the most likely suspect, but I was beginning to doubt that he could have brought a stone down upon Lila's head, as Thorpe had theorized. The wound was too large, the manner of death and its aftermath too messy for a man of such obvious precision: the blood on her hair, the way her body was only partially covered by leaves. I imagined that, even in the most extreme circumstances, McConnell was a man who would tie up all the loose ends. The buttons of her blouse, for one thing— surely, if it had been him, he would not have left the blouse gaping open. Another thing: her cheap topaz necklace, the gift from me, had been taken. But the opal ring, which must have been a gift from McConnell, was still on her finger when she was found. If it was Mc-Connell, why would he have left the ring but taken the necklace? This detail, like Thorpe's theory that Lila had threatened to tell McConnell's wife about their affair, had always bothered me. But Thorpe's narrative had been so forceful, and so widely accepted as truth, that I had not trusted my own misgivings.

"Here's the funny thing," McConnell said. "If you tell me about a bridge you want to build—where you're going to build it, what materials you're going to use, the depth of the river—I can tell you exactly, to the most minute fraction, how much weight it can handle. But I've never been able to apply the same rigor to my own life. I failed to recognize how much Margaret would endure before she took my son from me. I simply counted on her—not her love, but her desire to have a certain kind of life. I believed that there was nothing she wouldn't overlook."

I listened for a false note in his voice, watched his face and hands for some twitch or subconscious gesture that might indicate that he was lying. There was a part of me, I realized, that wanted to believe everything he said. If Lila had really loved him—and I saw now how she could have, I understood his charm—I did not want him to be the person who had taken her life. Was the very nature of the village itself to blame? I'd never been superstitious, but I was beginning to feel as if I were under the influence of some strange spell.

"Thorpe's book," I said. "I read it twice, cover to cover."

"Really?" McConnell said, looking at me with an unnerving intensity. "Then you know that Thorpe proved nothing. His accusations against me were purely conjecture. He could not find a single piece of physical evidence linking me to the crime. Not a single eyewitness. When I read it, I was furious. All I could think about was how offensive Lila would have found it—the lack of precision, the leaps in logic dismissed in a single sentence."

"You were the most probable choice."

"Probability is a strange thing," McConnell said. "In terms of evolution, an instinct for probability should be built into our brains as a way of avoiding danger, but the reality is that most people are terribly inept when it comes to calculating probability. Our running into one another, for example, might at first glance seem totally improbable. But you're a traveler, I'm an exile, and Diriomo isn't all that far off the beaten path. In general, people want to believe that the world is safe. Random acts of violence make them feel unsafe. Therefore, when someone is murdered, the initial instinct is to blame someone close to the victim, despite the fact that probability dictates that all of us come in close contact with dangerous individuals on a regular basis."

"What about the math problem?" I asked. "Goldbach. What about Thorpe's suggestion that the two of you were getting close to solving the problem, and you didn't want to share the credit."

"Close to *proving* it," he corrected me. "But that's ridiculous. We were nowhere near. Thorpe didn't know what he was talking about. I didn't give up on it, though. After I moved here, I spent most of my free time working on it. It was soothing, something to pass the time. More than that, I'll admit, the Goldbach Conjecture reminded me of Lila. It was a pact we'd made with one another, that we would once and for all prove it. I felt so guilty after she died. Whatever happened to her, I hadn't been there for her. I should have driven her home that night after dinner. But I didn't, because we had stayed out too late, and I needed to get home to my son. He wouldn't fall asleep until I tucked him into bed. So I walked her to the Muni station. Every day, I live with the fact that I failed her."

The rain was coming down hard, thrashing the trees outside and making everything smell earthy and green. Because the room had no air-conditioning, I had left the window open. A screen kept out most of the rain, but a few drops splashed onto the floor beneath the window.

McConnell leaned forward. His chair scraped against the floor, and his knee touched mine. Instinctively, I reached into my bag for the tryer. His eyes followed my hand. His expression was pained. "Don't be afraid of me," he said. "You have no reason to be afraid. I loved your sister, Ellie. I would never, ever, have done anything to hurt her."

I wanted to believe him. For Lila's sake, I wanted it to be true.

He stood to leave. In his face, I saw defeat. He must have felt that he would never convince me. "Wait," I said. "I have one more question."

"Hmmm?"

"Your son, Thomas."

"He turns twenty-three this year. A few months after I came to Nicaragua, I called my in-laws. Margaret's father told me that Margaret had remarried and moved out of state. He wouldn't tell me her new last name, or where they'd gone. I sent birthday and Christmas cards care of my in-laws' address up until three years ago, when they began to come back marked 'wrong address.'"

"Do you ever think about looking for him?" I asked.

"Every single day. But at this point, I

think that if he wanted to find me, he would have."

He picked up his book, his hat. "It's late. You've been kind to listen to me."

"Wait," I said again, but I had nothing with which to stall him. I realized I wanted to hear more about my sister, to reminisce with this man who had known an entirely different side of her. How quickly, in the course of one's day, the unthinkable can become reality.

He moved toward the door, placed his hand on the knob, and then seemed to remember something. He dropped his hand and turned to face me. "Did Lila ever tell you about Maria Agnesi?" he asked.

"Yes, along with the others—Sophie Germain, Olive Hazlett, Charlotte Angas Scott, Hypatia."

"Then maybe you recall how Agnesi used to solve problems?"

I shook my head.

"According to biographers, Agnesi was a sleepwalker. After laboring over some impossible problem, she would go to bed in defeat. The legend is that when she woke up in the morning she would find the solution on her desk. But I've always believed that's only a pretty myth. I think it was simply that when she woke up the next morning it was a new day, and she was able to see things in a different way."

He opened the door and disappeared into the dark hallway. I stood there for several minutes. Part of me believed I must have conjured the whole night from my imagination. Finally I went to the window and parted the curtain. In the distance, I could see his dark silhouette moving slowly down the street in the rain.

# *Ten*

$\infty$

That night, after McConnell had left, I thought back to the conversation Lila and I had just weeks before she died, the day she tried on the slinky blue dress and told me about her plans to solve the Goldbach Conjecture.

*Every even integer greater than two can be expressed as the sum of two primes.*

Lila had explained the conjecture to me quite plainly. It was part of her on-going effort to educate me in a subject in which I was hopeless. I think she believed that if she worked on me long enough, she might be able to convince me of the inherent beauty of numbers. I humored her in large part because, by some miracle, she managed to make the stuff seem interesting, something

not one of my teachers had ever managed to do. She loved to tell me about
the people behind the numbers—Poincaré and Agnesi, Fermat and Ramanujan, Euler and Leibniz and Pascal.
While the subject itself was dense and,
for the most part, impenetrable, I found
the human side of math and all of the
stories surrounding it to be fascinating.

One of the things that makes the
Goldbach Conjecture so unique is that,
despite the notorious difficulty of finding a proof, its basic terms are actually
quite simple. A prime number is a
counting number whose only divisors
are itself and one. Dividing it by any
other number will result in a fraction.
While the Goldbach Conjecture is generally assumed to be true, in the two
and a half centuries since it was first
proposed, no one had managed to
prove it. One can say that 4 is the sum
of the primes 2 and 2, that 6 is the sum
of the primes 3 and 3, or that 8 is the
sum of the primes 5 and 3. You can
continue making these calculations for
months, years, even decades, finding
that every positive even integer you en-

counter fits the conjecture, but no one has come up with a way to prove that no positive even integer exists that is not the sum of two primes. Because the even numbers are infinite, a case-by-case proof is impossible. What is needed is a general proof, an argument that covers every possible even number to infinity. Therefore this simple, elegant, and seemingly true statement— *every even integer greater than two can be expressed as the sum of two primes*—remained only a conjecture, rather than a solid theorem on which others could be built.

This, Lila explained to me, is the particular onus of mathematics. Whereas scientific proofs are based upon a body of observations which, taken together, add up to what appears to be overwhelming evidence in favor of a particular hypothesis, scientific theories are not absolute. They are always subject to change. When new evidence comes along that disproves an accepted theory, the theory goes out the window. With science, there is always some degree of doubt.

Not so with mathematics. In order for something to become a mathematical theory, it must have absolute proof. Once a theory is proved, it is true forever, and the advance of mathematical knowledge is powerless to change it. This means that mathematicians are held to a higher standard of proof than anyone else. Take for example the Pythagorean theorem, that bit of triangle logic that forms the basis of every sixth-grade geometry class. The concept had been used by the Chinese and Egyptians for millennia when it was finally proved by Pythagoras around 500 B.C. More than two thousand years later, it's still true, and it always will be. For eternity, humans can count on the fact that, in any right triangle, the square of the length of the hypotenuse will be equal to the sum of the squares of the lengths of the other two sides.

For the past eighteen years, one thing had been firm in my mind: the identity of Lila's killer. My meeting with McConnell had changed that. What McConnell left me with was a problem. I could believe what he had told me, and allow the story of my life as I knew it to completely unravel. "What is a life but a compendium of stories?" Thorpe had said. Thorpe's story of Lila's death had become my own; it was the windowpane through which I had viewed the world for my entire adult life. If I chose to believe McConnell, I must face the possibility that the identity of Lila's killer would never be known, that the person who truly committed the crime had duped everyone, and had paid no price at all. Or I could go on believing Thorpe's version of events, in which case there was still no justice for my sister, but at least there was an answer—an answer that made some kind of sense—a story with a beginning, middle, and end.

# *Eleven*

∞

The next day, I replayed the evening's events in my mind—the meeting at the café, the walk to the *pensión,* the long conversation in my room. In the bright light of morning, the previous night took on the fuzzy contours of a dream. I opened the cupboard beside the bed where I kept the rum. Part of me believed the bottle of rum would be full, the glasses unused; but the bottle was half empty, and the bottoms of the glasses were coated with an amber film. On the white tile floor, the ghostly imprint of McConnell's big shoes.

I had breakfast downstairs with José and his wife—strong coffee, fried beans, and bland, warm tortillas. José did not ask about the stranger in my room, but he and his wife looked at me differently.

Their usual friendly chatter was replaced by silence. I had the uncomfortable feeling that I had disappointed them by bringing a man to my room—thereby acting out of character—and that I had surprised them in an unsatisfactory way.

At half past nine a car arrived to take me to Jesus's farm. It was sixteen miles along a bumpy, unpaved road, the morning sun beating through the windows. The driver chain-smoked and sang softly to himself, occasionally glancing at me in the rearview mirror. On the seat beside me was my bag, containing only a wallet, a couple of small gifts, and my cupping journal. The latter was a thick, tattered, 8×10 moleskin notebook in which I recorded my impressions of various beans. During my career as a cupper the journal had traveled around the world with me—to Ethiopia, Yemen, Uganda, Brazil, Colombia, Costa Rica, Jamaica, Java, New Guinea. This was my diary of sorts, but instead of people and faces it was filled with detailed notes on aroma and body, acidity and balance. The words associated with cupping were as varied as the coffees, and I found comfort in their simple, precise poetry: a taste described as sweet could be further broken down into piquant, nippy, mild, or delicate, while a sour-tasting coffee was acrid, hard, tart, or tangy. Aromas were dry, sugary, or enzymatic, the latter of which could be further described as flowery, fruity, or herby. A flowery aroma was either floral or fragrant, a fruity aroma was either citrusy or berrylike, and an herby aroma was alliaceous or leguminous. Most people sipping their morning java wouldn't identify the aromas of onion, garlic, cucumber, or garden peas that characterized the herby coffees, or the cedar and pepper aromas in a spicy coffee of the warming variety—but to me a major part of the joy in drinking a cup of coffee came from noticing these subtle variations.

In addition to my cupping notes, the margins of the notebook were crammed with descriptions of cupping houses, notes on local customs, names and birth dates of farmers' children, anecdotes about the time I spent with them.

If I were to be struck by a bus, my cupping journal would be the most significant thing I left behind, the record by which a stranger might deduce my personal history.

When the car stalled three-quarters of the way up the steep mountain road, I thanked the driver, paid him, and set out on foot. Walking always calmed me, the feel of earth beneath my feet and the rhythmic motion of my legs and arms. I happened to agree with Henry David Thoreau on the nature of a good walk: "You must walk like a camel, which is said to be the only beast which ruminates when walking."

Behind me I could hear the driver working on his car—metallic clangs that made it sound as though he was tearing it apart, punctuated alternately by cursing and impassioned prayers to the Virgin Mary. Soon I was beyond reach of his voice, and could hear animals rustling about on the forest floor, warblers in the branches, the rat-a-tat-tat of woodpeckers. At this altitude the air was thin; my breaths were short and my lungs felt tight. It helped, at least, that I was in shade, protected from the sun by a canopy of trees. I was on farmland now, less than a quarter-mile from Jesus's home. The rich aroma of the coffee berries was mixed with the tart, sweet smell of lemon trees and the mild scent of plantains. I heard a familiar, raspy note, a series of bright, slurred whistles, and followed the sound to find the bright yellow underbelly of a Baltimore oriole in the branches above.

A young girl appeared in the clearing. "Ellie!" she called, running out to me, arms outstretched. It was Rosa, just shy of six years old. I'd known her since she was a baby, and was amazed each time I returned by how much she had changed, her hair styled shorter and shorter, her features becoming more defined year by year. I imagined that by the time she was sixteen she would be all elegant angles, with a stylish bob and starlet bangs. I dropped my bag on the ground and lifted her in my arms.

"I have something for you," I said.

She beamed. "What is it?" she said,

eyeing the bag. "A present? Can I open it?"

"Listen to you! When did you learn English so well?"

"A lady comes to teach us on the weekends," she said. "Angel is learning, too."

I reached into my bag and pulled out a gift wrapped in bright red paper. It was a leather-bound diary and red pencil, each inscribed in gold with her name. Rosa started to untie the ribbon. "It's for your birthday," I said. "Promise you'll wait until next week to open it."

"I promise." She grabbed my hand. "Come on. Papa's waiting."

When we got to the little house, Jesus was standing on the porch. He came down the stairs and greeted me with a hug. I'd first met Jesus five years before, when Mike and I had traveled to Nicaragua to investigate some of the new co-ops that were beginning to take shape in the country following years of civil war. At the time, Jesus had teamed up with three other small coffee growers to form the Rosa Cooperative. Mike and I had been impressed from the beginning by their commitment to shade crops, and their eagerness to learn about the preferences of specialty coffee buyers in the U.S. Since then, they had invited five other small operations into the fold, and their coffee was gaining a solid reputation.

Jesus invited me inside, where we talked business over a plate of fried plantains. Occasionally my Spanish faltered, and Rosa stepped in to act as translator. There was a burst of conversation outside. Jesus's wife, Esperanza, came through the door, Rosa's little brother Angel at her heels. I caught up with Esperanza and played with the children for a little while.

When Esperanza left to put Angel down for a nap, I followed Jesus out the back door, across a dirt path to the wooden shed that served as a cupping house. I could hear Rosa behind me, her bare feet padding softly in the dirt. Not once had I seen her in shoes. I remembered her feet when she was a baby, the thin, straight toes. Once, I had seen Esperanza lift her, naked save for a cloth diaper, up into the air and pop the baby's tiny foot into her mouth. Rosa had laughed and squirmed in her mother's arms. It was the first time I had felt that maternal pang other women talked about so often—the first time I had actually been inspired to envision myself with a child of my own. Several days later, back home in San Francisco, I had told my boyfriend Henry about Rosa's little foot, how it fit so perfectly into her mother's mouth, and how Jesus had beamed with pride when he showed me the wooden cradle he had made for their first child.

"Soon, that will be us," Henry had said. I was surprised to realize that the idea wasn't the least bit frightening. I could imagine the two of us together, standing over a crib, gazing down at a sleeping baby that looked like the best parts of each of us—Henry's nose and chin, my mouth and dimples.

In the cupping house, Jesus had set out three samples of fresh-roasted beans. While he ground the beans, I boiled water on a Bunsen burner. Meanwhile, Rosa arranged nine small glasses on the table—three cups for each sample. Jesus scooped a bit of coffee into each one, and I poured in the boiling water. The grounds rose to the surface, and steam lifted off the dark liquid.

Jesus and I sat on stools on either side of the table. Rosa stood beside her father, both of them watching intently as I began to break the crust with a heavy silver spoon. I loved this part of the cupping process, the way the aroma of the coffee wafted up when the spoon broke through the wet grounds. I closed my eyes and breathed deeply. Then I cleared the grounds off the surface and rinsed the spoon in clean water before I began tasting. For the next few minutes, I was able to put everything else aside, to forget the events of the previous day as the coffee slid over my tongue, down my throat. I rarely spit the coffee out when I was cupping. It wasn't just the taste and aroma that brought me calm and clarity, but also the way it warmed me going down, and the way I felt for hours after, that sweet rush of energy, followed by the slow descent.

That evening, I returned to my hotel room in Diriomo to find that someone had been there in my absence. At first, upon entering the room, it wasn't obvious, just a feeling that something was off. Immediately I went to the safe on the floor of the closet and found it locked. I punched my code into the keypad and opened the door to find my passport and spare cash just as I had left them. But when I went to the sink to wash my face, I saw that the basin was wet, and the tiny bar of soap had been unwrapped. By habit, I always wipe down the sink after each use, and I always carry my own soap with me when I travel. I told myself that I must, for some reason, have broken routine that morning, even though I couldn't remember doing so.

I turned on the ceiling fan, took off my T-shirt and skirt, and lay on top of the clean white sheets. The breeze felt good against my skin, and the sensation of lying half-clothed on the firm bed in the simple room, with the fan clacking overhead, brought to mind a similar afternoon three years before, in Guatemala. On the afternoon in memory, I had not been alone, but with Henry. Early in the evening we had eaten at a little restaurant in the hills, and upon returning to our room had partially undressed and lain down together on the bed, intending to make love. For some reason, before we got around to doing so, we had begun to argue.

Lying alone on the bed in Diriomo, I couldn't remember what Henry and I had argued about, or what had instigated it. I only remembered that, at some point, several minutes into the argument, Henry attempted to make a joke, and I accused him of not taking anything seriously. Before long the argument grew all out of proportion—we were both yelling, saying the sort of things that hours later you can't believe you've said to someone you love—until finally, in tears, I asked him to turn around so I could get dressed. We had been naked together hundreds of times and the request struck him as melodramatic. Eventually he complied, and I dressed and went out. I took a walk through an adjacent park and had coffee at the same restaurant where we had eaten dinner not long before. By the time I finished my coffee I had replayed the argument in my mind, and had realized how ridiculous it was, that a point of minor contention had brought us to such a passionate standoff.

On my way back to the room to apologize, I stopped at a roadside stall to buy a present for Henry, a handmade silver lighter that he had admired the day before. Henry was the only man I had ever dated who smoked—"only cigars," he rationalized, "and only on weekends"—and I knew that the gift of the lighter would be especially meaningful to him, because it was a full concession on my part, a display of genuine affection in that it asked him to change nothing. I paid extra to have the girl who sold me the lighter wrap it in printed yellow paper and add an elaborately tied ribbon, which she did slowly and with a show of great care.

I had left the hotel in such haste that I'd forgotten to take my key, so when I returned to the room I had to knock. I waited for the sound of Henry walking to the door, but my knock was met with silence. I knocked again, called his name, and stood there for a good five minutes, knocking and calling to him with a rising sense of unease, before finally going downstairs and getting a key from the concierge. When I opened the door I saw that the bed had not been touched. Henry wasn't there. His suitcase and passport were gone. I postponed my appointments and spent the next two days in the hotel, waiting for him, only going out for coffee and meals.

On the third day, when I returned to the hotel after work, the concierge had a message for me. Henry had called from San Francisco. We could talk, he said, when I got back home. Over the next few days I attempted to reach him several times, to no avail. I had farms to visit, and another three days passed before I was able to return to California. When I did, it was too late. Henry had already begun packing his things. He said he had "reevaluated." He was moving to the East Coast, starting over. No amount of reasoning, and ultimately pleading, on my part could dissuade him. I tried to give him the lighter—I didn't know what else to do with it—but he wouldn't accept it. I ended up putting it in a wooden box on my dresser, where I kept my meager collection of earrings and necklaces, and every time I opened the box to retrieve a piece of jewelry, there was the silver lighter, a reminder of our terrible, stupid fight, and of his subsequent departure. For some reason I couldn't bring myself to throw out the lighter or give it away, nor could I find a different, better place for it in my apartment, the apartment which Henry and I had shared for almost two years. Eventually I moved my jewelry to a smaller porcelain box, but the wooden one was still there on my dresser, a repository for an object that was neither usable nor disposable.

I was lying on my bed in Diriomo, remembering that strange and painful time, remembering how the most significant relationship of my adult life had simply dissolved without warning in a room very similar to this one, when I glanced over at the bedside table and noticed that the small stack of books appeared to have grown in height. I picked them up one by one: a newly published history of the indigenous peoples of Nicaragua; a novel by a friend of a friend whom I'd met back home in San Francisco; the latest copy of *Fresh Cup* magazine. But underneath these familiar items was something else, book-sized, wrapped in plain brown paper. This, I knew for a fact, I had not brought with me.

I got up and checked to make sure the door was locked, pulled the curtains closed, and stood there holding the package, as if it might contain something dangerous. Then I placed it on the desk and stared at it for a minute or two. Finally, I picked it up again, turned it over, and broke the two seams of tape with my fingernail. When I unfolded the paper and glimpsed the faded blue-plaid pattern on the cover, I could not, at first, believe what I saw. But when I opened it to the first page there was no mistaking what lay before me on the battered hotel desk: it was Lila's notebook, the one that had gone missing with her almost twenty years before.

# *Twelve*

∞

How to describe that notebook?

To me, for whom mathematical formulae were opaque, impenetrable as hieroglyphs, it was like a book of mysteries. It had remained in my memory all these years, my sister's notebook, the lost thing that I imagined held her deepest secrets. With a sense of awe I opened it, and there they were, just as I remembered them, the stately numerals, letters, and symbols marching across and down the page. Lila's handwriting was beautiful in its precision. I admired the darker impression of the ink at the endpoint of each number, as if she had lingered there before moving on to the next, as if every single number was not merely part of a larger whole to her, not just a figure in a calculation, but individual, a world unto itself.

On the first page of the notebook, in her tiny, neat cursive, was this:

*"A mathematical proof should resemble a simple and clear-cut constellation, not a scattered cluster in the Milky Way."*
                                    *G. H. Hardy*

Below the quote, she had used a black felt-tip pen to delineate the six stars of the constellation Lyra. In pencil, she had traced the jagged line among the stars and noted the names—Vega, Sheliak, Sulafat, Epsilon, Aladfar, Alathfar.

"Who's ever heard of Lyra?" I asked her once, when she told me it was her favorite constellation. We were lying in the cool, damp grass in our backyard, looking up at the sky. It was the summer before Lila started high school, there was a rare electrical blackout in our part of the city, and we had snuck outside in the middle of the night after our parents went to bed to eat cupcakes and plan our futures. I tasted the waxy sweetness of chocolate frosting on my lips, crunched the candy sprinkles between my teeth. All around us, insects ticked and chirped. These were sounds I'd only heard at our Russian River cabin, never in the city, and the effect of the night sounds, combined with the smell of grass and my mother's newly planted star jasmine, made me feel as if we had entered a different world.

"The lyre was given to Orpheus by Apollo," Lila said. "When Orpheus played it, the sound was so beautiful that even the animals were entranced. One day, his wife, Eurydice, was killed by a snake. Orpheus was devastated. He couldn't eat, he couldn't sleep, all he could do was think about his beautiful dead wife. Finally, he went to the Underworld and played his lyre for Pluto and Persephone. Like everyone else, the king and queen of the Underworld found his music irresistible, and so they gave Orpheus permission to take Eurydice back to the land of the living with him, on one condition."

I held my breath. To be under the stars with Lila, in the backyard on a night without electricity, when everything about our little plot of land in the city seemed entirely different and new, was wonderful. She must have felt it, too, because she reached across the grass and took my hand in hers. "What condition?" I whispered.

"He couldn't look back until he had left the Underworld, or Eurydice would be taken from him."

"What happened?"

"For the longest time he kept his promise," Lila said. "He held his wife by the hand, leading her up, step by step, to the surface of the earth. They had almost reached the surface when he couldn't stand it another second, he had to see her beauty, and he looked back."

"And then?" I asked. Surely, I thought, the gods would understand. After all, he'd made it most of the way. And he loved her so much.

"When Orpheus reached out to put his arms around her," Lila said, "she slipped away into the darkness. He had to return to earth alone. Back in Thrace, his hometown, Orpheus was so devastated at losing his wife a second time that he completely ignored the company of women. The women of Thrace were so angry they stoned him and tore him to pieces, and threw his head and his lyre into the river."

I heard a noise over the fence and gripped Lila's hand harder.

"It was Zeus who retrieved the lyre from the river and tossed it into the sky," Lila said. "Come here."

I scooted closer, and she raised her hand, still clutching mine, up to the sky and pointed. "At the tip of my finger is Vega, see?"

I strained to make out the star. There were so many, and they were so far away, how could I tell which one she meant for me to see?

"It's the upper right point of the summer triangle, the brightest star visible from the Northern Hemisphere. If you can find Vega, you can find Lyra."

We lay out there for a long time. At some point, I fell asleep. When I woke up Lila was standing over me, her long hair wet from the grass. "Get up," she whispered, reaching down to take my hand.

A few nights after Lila went missing, I stepped into our backyard and tried to find Vega. I lay on the grass, just as we had as children, but the city lights were bright, so that only a few stars were visible. I looked for the second brightest star in the Northern Hemisphere. Just when I thought I had spotted it, and was attempting to trace a line in the sky with my eyes to the upper left point of Orpheus's harp, I realized my star was moving. It wasn't Vega, just a satellite.

It had been a long time since Lila had mentioned Lyra, a long time, in fact, since we'd had a conversation of any significance. At that point I was aware that something was terribly wrong, but I couldn't have imagined that she was actually gone. The next day, we would receive the phone call from Guerneville.

To me, the cruelest part of Orpheus's story was not that he had lost Eurydice twice, but that, as she was slipping away from him the second time, he was unable to touch her. When we were children, Lila and I had been in constant physical contact—braiding one another's hair, tumbling on the floor, dancing together to my mother's old records. But the older we got, the less we touched, so that by the time she was in graduate school, the only time our skin made contact was when we accidentally brushed against one another in passing—or when I crossed her invisible boundary, putting a hand on her arm to bring her back from some deep concentration. Unlike me, Lila was not a physically affectionate person, and on those rare occasions—a birthday, a good-bye at the airport when I was dropping her off for one of her trips to a math conference—when I tried to hug her, I could sense her reluctance the moment my arms circled her neck.

The night that I lay alone in the backyard, searching for Lyra, it occurred to me that it had been a very long time since I had hugged my sister. And I decided that when I saw her again, I'd pull her close and hug her for a long time, whether she liked it or not. It did not occur to me, even for a moment, that she might never be coming home.

# *Thirteen*

∞

"Every story entails a contract with the reader," Thorpe used to say. "The contract is laid out in the first page, possibly the very first line: the setting, the main characters, the rhythm of the language, and most important, the point of view—who is telling the story, from what distance. At any point in the story, if the point of view wavers, the contract with the reader is broken. The foundation falls apart, and the reader is reminded that it's all just a fiction."

I'd gone through life believing a certain story about my own history, a story which happened to be told from Thorpe's point of view. The person I was as an adult was deeply influenced by this story. If Lila could be murdered by the man she cared most about, the one man she had invited into her life, then how was it possible to trust anyone? Since Lila's murder, I had allowed myself the luxury of complete trust only once—with Henry; only with him had I truly let down my guard. When that relationship fell apart, I threw myself into my work. I convinced myself that the way to happiness was to excel at the thing I did best. When I felt lonely, I could travel to a coffee farm or retreat into my cupping notes. This was the shape my life had taken, and I had made peace with it. It wasn't the life I'd imagined for myself, and it wasn't the life my parents would have chosen for me—they wanted a son-in-law, grandchildren. Somehow, though, it was a good enough life.

As much as I hated what Thorpe had done, I realized that his book, his answers, had provided a kind of relief. But now, like a mathematical structure that had been built upon a faulty theorem, all the certainties of my life had come crashing down.

Back home in San Francisco the morning after my return, I unpacked my suitcase. Everything smelled like travel, the chemical air of the airplane mixing with the green, wet smell of my hotel. I had stashed three pounds of coffee beans in a side pocket of the suitcase, so the shirts and skirts and everything else bore the aroma of coffee as well. After tossing my clothes into the washing machine, I showered and chose a clean pair of jeans, T-shirt, and sweater. The neighborhood outside my window was sunny, but I could see the fog bank to the west, a wall of brilliant white, and knew that, out in the avenues, it would probably be damp and fifteen degrees cooler.

I walked to Twenty-fourth Street and bought a small coffee at Tully's. It was my tide-me-over coffee. With the first sip, I felt the mental cobwebs clearing. I found a vacant table in the corner and opened Lila's notebook. On the third page, she had made a list entitled *Unsolved. Unsolvable?* The first, the Goldbach Conjecture, took up more than half of the notebook, and the rest of the pages were devoted to the remaining problems. The second item on the list

was the Poincaré Conjecture: *Every simply connected compact three-manifold
(without boundary) is homeomorphic to
a three-sphere.*

I stared at the problem for a long
time, unable to make heads or tails of
it. It amazed me that Lila—with whom I
shared the same genes, the same loving parents, the same good schools,
the same summer weekends at the
Russian River—could get her mind
around this sentence.

Although the meaning of Poincaré's
conjecture eluded me, I remembered
the man himself for one reason: during
our backpacking trip through Europe,
Lila and I had gone to the Montpar-
nasse Cemetery in Paris, where Poincaré was buried. Beside his gravesite,
she had told me his story. Poincaré was
known as The Last Universalist; he ex-
celled in every field of mathematics,
both pure and applied, that existed
during his lifetime. But what had
caught my interest was the story of his
testimony on behalf of Alfred Dreyfus,
the Jewish army officer who was
charged with treason by anti-Semitic

colleagues and sentenced to life im-
prisonment on Devil's Island in 1895.
Poincaré's attack on the invalid scientific claims made by Dreyfus's accusers
was in large part responsible for Dreyfus's exoneration.

Lila placed a piece of paper on Poincaré's gravestone and rubbed over it
with a pencil. Then she helped me lo-
cate someone else on the cemetery
map: Simone de Beauvoir. De Beauvoir
had been buried just a year before in
the same grave as Sartre. The ivory-
colored gravestone with its simple
double inscription—names and dates—
was laden with fresh flowers and gifts.
I'd read *The Second Sex* and *Memoirs
of a Dutiful Daughter,* I'd read *The
Words,* but the only line I could conjure
at that moment was by Lloyd Cole and
the Commotions—*She looks like Eva
Marie Saint in* On the Waterfront/*As she
reads Simone de Beauvoir in her American circumstance.*

"Can you imagine being so deeply in
love that you want to have your body
tossed on top of your lover's bones?" I
asked.

Lila didn't even take a moment to consider the question. "No." She didn't have to elaborate. I knew her perspective on romance, marriage: it would only get in the way of her work.

One might argue that true universalism is no longer possible. Surely even Poincaré would be unable to keep up with all the esoteric fields of his subject, as they existed a century after his death. But there was a part of me that liked to think Lila might have had it in her to at least approach universalism. I believed that she might have been, if not *the* great mathematician of her time, certainly one of them. And this was where the cosmic numbers seemed to be all out of whack, this is what my parents must have considered a thousand times over the years, though they would never, ever say it: they had two daughters. To subtract me from the equation would have been to rob the world of some decent cupping notes, a well-trained palate, a few articles for trade journals about the more elusive qualities of the world's finest coffees. But it didn't happen that way. The subtraction that was made turned out to be a far crueler one. Who knows what Lila might have discovered, what problems she might have solved, what elegant proofs she might have constructed, had she been given time? Unlike me, she was poised to do important work, work with significant repercussions.

In hindsight, it was easy for me to see what I was doing in the year immediately following Lila's death, when, over and over again, I found myself drunk and in bed with some guy from school, or someone I'd met at a party. I wasn't just trying to forget what had happened to Lila. I was trying to forget that I was the product of a warped mathematics that had managed to end the life of a genius while allowing her sister, who was ordinary in every way, to live.

"It's like I'm wandering through a house," Lila used to say, as a way of explaining her frequent silences. "I happen to step into another room, and the door shuts behind me. Everything else sort of vanishes."

Sometimes I felt as though I'd wan-

dered into the wrong room twenty
years ago, and the door had shut behind me. On one side of the door was
my parallel life, the one I was supposed
to have. On the other side, the room
where I was trapped, was the life I had
stumbled into in the aftermath of Lila's
death. I wanted to go back to where I
had started before I crossed the thresh-
old, but the door was shut so tight,
there was no way out.

Like all condemned men, Dreyfus had
been convicted because the judges believed a certain story about him. Poincaré came forward with a different
version of the story, and it changed the
course of Dreyfus's life. Was there a different story for Lila as well, one that
might change the course of Mc-
Connell's life, and perhaps my own?

I had never, in thirty-eight years, done
a single extraordinary thing. I often told
myself that it was a matter of circumstance—that I had neither the talent nor
the opportunity to make much difference for anyone. Maybe this was my
opportunity. McConnell was the one
person outside our immediate family

whom Lila had let into her life, the one person she had trusted. Like Dreyfus, McConnell had been hanged in the court of public opinion on the basis of a story—quite possibly a fraudulent one. Maybe, after all, I could do one thing right; maybe I could restore to McConnell something of what he had lost.

And in the process I might do something for my parents as well. A decade before, they had divorced. I think they had finally given up any hope of trying to be happy together. The crack that opened between them in the aftermath of Lila's death had grown wider year by year. At some point they had begun taking separate vacations, my mother spending as much time as she could alone at the Russian River. Eventually they came to a mutual agreement that their marriage could not be salvaged. On the night the divorce was finalized, my mother came over to my apartment for dinner. "I think if there had been something official," she said, "an arrest and a conviction, then we might have been able to get through it. When it comes down to it, this whole business with Peter McConnell is nothing more than a story in a book. Maybe it's a true story, but it's not justice. No one has ever paid a price for what happened to our baby."

When she was having trouble making sense of a problem, Lila used to turn the piece of paper she was working on upside down. "It helps to see it from a new perspective," she would say. "This way, I have to concentrate on each number, each symbol. It's like having a second set of eyes with which to view the same picture. Sometimes a completely different angle is all I need to break through."

Over the years, I had become so accustomed to Thorpe's picture of Lila's death that it seemed like the true picture. Now, I had to admit that I'd been lazy to accept Thorpe's story. Grief had blinded me to logic. If Thorpe was at fault for writing a deeply flawed book, I was equally at fault for believing it without putting it through any sort of rigorous test. After my strange encounter with McConnell in Diriomo, everything looked different, as if the page had been turned upside down.

# *Fourteen*

∞

Outside Green Apple Books, the wooden gnome stood sentry. Inside, I took the creaking steps to the second level. Between Frank Thistlethwaite— *The Great Experiment: An Introduction to the History of the American People*— and Grant Uden—*Hero Tales from the Age of Chivalry*—I found Andrew Thorpe. That cover: my sister's face, ghosted over the Golden Gate Bridge. On the back jacket of *Murder by the Bay,* above several complimentary endorsements from other writers, was a photograph of my old teacher, looking serious but good-natured in a dark sweater and glasses. The photo had been taken outdoors, so that his wavy hair blew back from his face. Hands on his hips, staring confidently into the camera, he looked like the kind of man you would trust to tell you a story, the kind of man who would get all his facts straight. The odd thing about the photograph was that, by the time I knew Thorpe, his hairline had already begun to recede. This photograph had obviously been taken years before the book was published, probably when he was in his early twenties. The man who stared out at me from the jacket was, indeed, the same man, but in a very different manifestation. The man in the picture was an optimist, while the man I knew, the one who wrote the book, gave off a very slight but unmistakable air of disappointment bristling with nervous ambition.

Next to *Murder by the Bay* was a paperback copy of Thorpe's second book, *In Step with a Sadist,* about the kidnapping and torture of the wife of a prominent Sacramento businessman. The jacket bore the same photograph of Thorpe as a much younger man. There were two copies of his third book, *Runner Up, Runner Down*—the story of a journalist who had been assassinated in broad daylight during a marathon in Dubai—same photograph yet again, as if he had never aged. There was a fourth book stamped with his name, although this one had a title I'd never seen, *Second Time's a Charm.* It was a remaindered first edition, priced at $4.95. According to the jacket copy, it was a memoir of marriage, a love story, a message of hope for lonely men. *Think you'll never find love? So did Andrew Thorpe. Then he found Jane, the woman who would give him a second chance at happiness.*

This photo must have been more recent; Thorpe had gone a bit pudgy in the face, and no attempt had been made to hide the fact that he was balding. The picture had been taken in what looked like a home office. He sat behind a desk, hands poised on an old electric typewriter. I figured the typewriter must be a prop, probably calculated to make him look like a romantic figure. When I knew him, he wrote everything on his computer. On the desk, to the left of the typewriter, were

two wooden bookends carved to repre-
sent the bow and stern of a boat.

"It's an allusion," I had said, when I
gave him the bookends at the end of
spring semester, just five months after
Lila's death. "To *The Odyssey.*" It was
one of his all-time favorites.

"You didn't have to get me anything."

"I know. I just wanted to thank you."

He looked surprised. "What for?"

"You've been kind. You've been a
good listener."

"It wasn't kindness," Thorpe said. "I
happen to enjoy talking to you."

Standing in the aisle at Green Apple,
looking at an older, happier Andrew
Thorpe, I was surprised to discover
that he had kept the gift.

Down the street at Blue Danube café,
I began reading. I couldn't bring myself
to start at the beginning, with Thorpe's
detailed description of how Lila's body
had been found. Instead, I skipped
ahead to chapter four, "First Love."

*When Lila was eleven years old,*
Thorpe wrote, *she discovered horses.*

This much was true. I remembered it
well, and it was my account, only

slightly altered, that appeared in the book. It happened when she was ten years old, spending her first week-end—indeed, her first night—away from home at the innocuously named Girls' Adventure Camp in Sonoma County. Lila was crying when we drove through the gate. When we pulled up in front of the clubhouse, she clung to her seat belt and vowed not to get out of the car until she was safely home in the city.

It was tall and lanky Sara Beth, the counselor for the Chipmunks Cabin, who finally coaxed Lila out of the station wagon by bringing an old mare named Spice up beside Lila's window. Sara Beth gave Lila an apple, and Spice ate it right out of her hand. That was all it took. When we went to pick her up Monday morning, all she could talk about was Spice.

After that, Lila took riding lessons in Golden Gate Park once a week. For her thirteenth birthday, when they knew the horse thing wasn't just a fad she'd grow out of, our parents finally acquiesced and bought her a quarter horse named Dorothy. Dorothy was chestnut brown, with white patches above her hooves that looked like socks and a white stripe running down her face. My parents rented space for her in a stable in Montara, about thirty-five minutes down the coast. Montara was a small town comprised of newish wooden houses marching up the hills from a long stretch of golden-sand beach. Behind the houses were hundreds of undeveloped acres shaded by redwoods, and a couple of small farms. The stable where Lila kept Dorothy was in a clearing about a mile back from Highway 1; on clear days, I could stand on top of the riding ring gate and see cars passing on the winding, rickety highway, and beyond them, the famous waves of Montara State Beach.

"I've been thinking about it," Lila said to me once, not long after she got Dorothy. We were sitting on the fence of the riding ring, waiting for her riding teacher. Dorothy was huffing and stomping, kicking up great clouds of dust that made me sneeze. "I've decided that we can share her," Lila said, swinging her legs back and forth so that her boots tapped out a rhythm on the fence. "Not forever. Just until Mom and Dad buy you your own horse."

"I don't want my own horse," I said. I didn't tell her that I disliked the feel of dust under my fingernails, and although I could appreciate Dorothy from a distance, the coarse feel of her fur made my skin crawl. Lila looked at me as if she'd just discovered that I was adopted.

She kept riding through high school. When the stable in Montara closed down during Lila's senior year, she began boarding Dorothy just north of Petaluma, about an hour and a half drive from the city. The new place was a pasture attached to an apple orchard. The owners also kept half a dozen milking cows, a few ostriches, and a pig. There was no riding ring, and that suited Lila just fine. When she wanted to ride, she loaded the saddle onto a golf cart and took off through the fields. When she spotted Dorothy in the distance, she would whistle and call her by name, then saddle up on the spot. It would be way past dinnertime when she got home, tanned and exhausted and smelling of horse.

The summer before her final year at Berkeley, my parents and I were shocked when Lila announced one evening over dinner that she was giving up riding altogether. "I have to get serious about math," she said.

"Why not do both?" my mother said. "You love riding. You should always keep something in your life that you do purely for pleasure." My mother knew what she was talking about. Although, by that time, her law practice took up most of her energy, she always found a few hours a week for gardening.

"I've made up my mind," Lila said. "I have to focus. All the great mathematicians in history have made sacrifices."

A few days later, she placed an ad in the *Chronicle* and in the *Sonoma Index-Tribune.* She drove out to Petaluma several times during the next couple of weeks to meet with prospective buyers. One afternoon, I went with her. We drove over the Golden Gate Bridge, past the Marin Headlands. Eventually the highway became less crowded, and the buildings gave way to gently rolling hills dotted with cattle and baobab trees. Lila turned off onto a dirt road, and we made our way slowly over the bumps and potholes until we came to a long gravel driveway. At the end was a big white farmhouse, the kind of house I would have loved to live in, with a wide porch and dormer windows, and a couple of rooms off to the side that looked as though they had been haphazardly nailed on. To the left of the house was a potato patch—long rows of dry brown dirt, with an occasional swatch of green sprouting up from the mounds.

I followed Lila to the fenced-in pasture. We could see Dorothy out in the distance, grazing beneath a Joshua tree. When Lila whistled, Dorothy perked up her ears and came running. Lila rubbed Dorothy's muzzle and talked quietly into her ear, while Dorothy just stood there, blinking calmly. I wondered if Lila talked to Dorothy in the way she'd never really talked to me, if she shared her deepest secrets with this silent creature. A few minutes later a car came up the driveway. It was a father and his ten-year-old daughter, who lived in the city. Lila helped the little girl up onto Dorothy's bare back.

"She's spirited," Lila told the girl. "If you're firm with her, she'll respect you. She doesn't like carrots, but she goes nuts for apples and blackberries. She's also a fan of Cheerios. She likes when you sing in her ear. If she's testy, you can usually calm her down with a Simon and Garfunkel song."

I recognized that look in the little girl's eyes, the look Lila had gotten when she saw Spice all those years ago. The man said he'd come by our house the next day with a check.

After they left, a guy came walking toward us from the farmhouse. He was big and handsome and full of swagger, probably in his late twenties or early thirties. He looked somewhat tired and unwashed, like he'd been out partying all night.

"Hey, William," Lila said.

"Hey there, Lila."

"This is my sister, Ellie."

William reached out to shake my hand, and his grip was so tight it hurt.

"We met once before," I reminded him. He seemed confused. "When the car broke down a while back. You gave us a hand with the jumper cables."

"Oh, that's right," Lila said. "I'd forgotten."

"Good to see you," he said, but I could tell he didn't remember me. He was chewing on a sprig of mint. He turned to Lila. "Sold her yet?"

"I think so. The kid who was just here fell in love."

When William was out of earshot, I said, "He's cute."

"You think?" Lila said, looking at his back as if it was something she'd never considered. "I don't know about that, but he's good with Dorothy. I wish he'd buy her. At least I would know she was in good hands."

That afternoon, Lila rode Dorothy one last time. Then she bathed her, moving her soapy hands in circles over Dorothy's thick fur. She put her mouth close to Dorothy's ear and said softly,

"Good girl." Finally, she gave her an apple and hugged her around the neck. I wondered if Dorothy realized that Lila was saying good-bye.

As far as I know, Lila never saw Dorothy again. She rarely talked about her. I wondered if she would be the same way with me. If I died in a car accident, or broke my neck diving into a swimming pool and was in a coma for the rest of my life, would she adjust as easily to my absence as she had to Dorothy's?

*From then on,* Thorpe wrote at the end of the chapter, *there were no distractions. Lila had only one true passion, one devotion: math.*

At home that night, I went back to the beginning. It was strange to read the book again after so many years, strange to see Lila before me on the pages, alive and real, riding her horse, or sewing, or sitting at the kitchen table, pencil in hand, working through a mathematical formula. It was Lila as I had known her, as I had described her. For all the liberties Thorpe had taken with my sister's life, there was no denying that he had captured her essential spirit, her personality: the way she walked, the way she held her head when she spoke, her turns of phrase.

With McConnell, on the other hand, he had gotten it all wrong. *Looking into McConnell's eyes,* Thorpe wrote, *one had the impression of having met a man without an ordinary conscience, a man who might be capable of anything. There was a kind of cruelty in his eyes, a hardness in his speech.*

I knew this to be false. I had been struck by the softness of McConnell's eyes, the gentleness of his voice. I couldn't reconcile the man I'd met in Diriomo with the character in the book, could not believe the picture that Thorpe had painted of McConnell as a heartless, calculated killer.

Still, I came away from the book with no answers, no clue as to who else might have been involved. It was as though Thorpe had put every bit of his energy into making a case against McConnell, quickly and categorically eliminating everyone else. Why had he done that? What did he have to gain?

# *Fifteen*

∞

Andrew Thorpe's website was a multi-media affair, complete with flash graphics, background music by a local band called Sugar dePalma, podcasts, and video clips. He was running a couple of contests, including a "name the villain" contest, whereby one lucky winner would name a character in Thorpe's first novel, which was currently in progress, and a "first draft" contest, the reward for which was the original, handwritten draft of one of Thorpe's books. As the Thorpe I knew had never handwritten so much as a memo, I imagined he'd probably hired some poor sap to copy an MS Word file out by hand. The most popular contest appeared to be the one in which the winner would get to visit Pelican Bay State

Prison with Thorpe. "Enjoy a one-on-one conversation with Johnny Grimes, the subject of *Blood in the Valley*—the riveting tale of the gruesome murder of two Yahoo employees," the website promised. The book had just been released two months before, and, judging by the slew of reviews and reader comments on his website, it was getting a lot of attention.

I clicked on the events page and saw that the San Francisco Ladies' Bureau would be hosting a luncheon with Thorpe that Thursday. The ticket price of $85 included a light lunch, a glass of chardonnay, and an autographed copy of *Blood in the Valley*. I called and made a reservation. The woman who took my call was very enthusiastic. "Good timing," she said. "We only have a couple of spots left. Have you read the book?"

I confessed that I hadn't.

"It's brilliant. You're going to love it."

As I marked the date of the luncheon in my calendar in red ink, I thought back to a strange night I'd spent with Thorpe, just months before he told me he was writing the book. By then, I had moved on to higher level English courses, but we still met frequently for coffee or lunch. One afternoon over the phone, he asked me offhandedly if I'd like to have dinner at his place. From the way he phrased the invitation, I assumed he was having a small dinner party.

The apartment was on the third floor of a twelve-unit building at the top of Dolores Park. When Thorpe opened the door, I saw that he had forgone the usual blue jeans and sneakers and was dressed instead in a black oxford with pinstripe slacks and loafers. It was an odd look for him, and he seemed uncomfortable in the clothes.

"Smells good," I said.

"It's lasagna, my mom's recipe. It needs another half hour in the oven. Want some wine to start?"

I followed him into the small, spotless apartment. There was no one else there. I was surprised to realize that it would just be the two of us.

By the time the lasagna was ready, we were into our second bottle of wine.

I was drinking faster than usual out of nervousness, and he was drinking considerably more than I was. He didn't have a dining room, so we sat on the sofa with our plates on the coffee table, a black-framed, glass-topped affair that screamed bachelor pad. Over the course of the night, the wine took the edge off our nervousness, and he kept touching my arm, patting my leg, and brushing up against me. By the time we finished our dessert of strawberry cheesecake, which came from the freezer and hadn't entirely thawed, I understood there would be no good way to extricate myself from the evening. He put his arm around me, pulled me closer on the couch, and said, "Promise me you'll never take one of my classes again."

"Why?"

"Because if you're my student, I can't do this." Then he kissed me.

I was still grateful for his friendship, for the way he had helped me through the long months since Lila's death. If I had allowed myself to dwell on the fact that he was eleven years my senior, I might have been more reluctant—but I was drunk enough to brush the age difference aside. I went to bed with him because I could think of no terribly good reason not to, but even as we were undressing in the dim light of his bedroom, I realized I would not do it again. Over the course of the evening, he had undergone a subtle transformation. The outfit, the coffee table, the incense that he lit on the bedside table, all served to cast him in a different, somewhat pathetic, light. Prior to that night, I had known him only in a certain context. When the curtain parted and I glimpsed his private life, I couldn't help but feel a bit sorry for him. After that, he asked me over to his apartment a couple more times, but I declined. I was grateful to him for not pressing the issue, for following my lead in acting as if it never happened.

It had been such a glitch in our relationship, such a minor part of our months-long friendship, that it had, for the most part, slipped my mind. After all, during that year I'd been with a number of guys whom I didn't know very well at all. In comparison, Thorpe was a dear friend, a trusted confidant, and it wasn't very surprising that we would end up in bed together, if only for a night. But when I thought about it now, with the added perspective of age, I couldn't help feeling somewhat ill. I'd been only nineteen years old at the time. Apparently, it hadn't been enough for Thorpe to have my story. For one night, at least, he had to have me, too.

# *Sixteen*

∞

As I drove out of town toward South City, San Francisco's picturesque skyline gave way to the flat, industrial landscape of the Peninsula. I'd taken a couple of days off work after the Nicaragua trip, and I was glad to be returning to Golden Gate Coffee. From a quarter mile away, I could smell the rich caramel scent of roasting coffee. I pulled around to the back of the building. It was a warm day, the sun glinting off the flat, shining bay.

Inside, Dora was on the phone with the broker, buying coffee on the futures market. Soon, giant sacks of the stuff would be loaded onto a ship in Ethiopia, the birthplace of coffee, and begin their journey west. It would be several weeks before they arrived at the port of Oakland. Before the coffee was unloaded, samples would be brought back to the office, where Mike and I would roast and cup them.

"Wait until the Yirgacheffe hits $114," Dora said into the phone. She covered the mouthpiece with her hand and greeted me. "Hi, stranger."

I'd visited the coffee trading floor only once, in the summer of 2001, when the New York coffee exchange, the largest coffee auction in the Western Hemisphere, was still housed in the World Trade Center. A few months later, the obliterated trading pits were at the bottom of tons of rubble, and the coffee traders had relocated to dismal, low-ceilinged rooms across the East River. Just days after 9/11, the new, makeshift trading floor was doing a robust business; no matter what happened in the world, people still wanted their coffee.

In the cupping room just beyond the office, several trays were laid out with samples waiting to be roasted and cupped. I plunged my hand into the mound of Tanzanian peaberry beans and breathed in the musty smell. Next to the peaberry was an Ethiopian Harrar. I'd also brought some beans from Nicaragua, which I poured into trays and labeled for later. I already knew we'd be ordering a large shipment of Jesus's coffee, but Mike liked to taste every sample himself. He was a perfectionist. His great-grandfather Milos had started the business during the Gold Rush, and it was Milos's likeness that still graced the packages of coffee bearing the Stekopolous family name.

I fed the peaberry into one of three small metal drums on the sample roaster, a Jabez Burns that had been passed down through generations. In the second drum, I placed the Ethiopian Harrar. I lit the gas burner and waited. After a few minutes, the beans began to sizzle and pop. The room filled with a rich floral scent. I took the peaberry beans out first, scooping them into the perforated metal cooling tray. For the Harrar, I wanted a slightly darker roast, so I waited for the second round of popping to begin and end. When the beans were roasted to my satisfaction, the papery chaff removed, I checked the beans for color and ground them coarsely before scooping a bit of coffee into each of the clear glass cups.

"Good to have you back," Mike said, emerging from his office.

"Good to be back."

We began tasting. Between slurps, Mike caught me up on office gossip. During my absence, Jennifer Wilson, one of the sales reps, had announced that she was pregnant, and Gabrielle, the daughter of the owner of a rival company, had started dating one of our warehouse guys. Debbie Dybsky from accounting was retiring and moving to Muir Beach. Hearing news of my co-workers made me feel at home. Aside from my mother, they were the people I was closest to in the world.

There was a large brass spittoon beside each stool, but neither of us used them. Instead we swallowed the coffee, sipping water between tastes. I had inherited Mike's down-to-earth tasting style, which got the job done without all the Sturm und Drang.

"Some guys make it all about the performance," Mike had told me in the beginning. "For me, it's about the coffee. That's why I like you. You can smell an exceptional bean from a mile away."

Early on, I'd learned to appreciate Mike's mentorship, and I would always be grateful to him for giving me a chance. When I started in the business in the late nineties, there were still men who wouldn't deign to sit at a cupping table with a woman. Like the kitchens of fancy restaurants, the bowels of mining shafts, and the most prestigious math departments, the coffee industry was a man's world. Odd, considering that, from the beginning of coffee's popularity in the U.S., it had been primarily women who purchased the stuff and brought it to the table.

For my thirty-fourth birthday, Henry had given me a rare copy of William Harrison Ukers's 1922 book *All About Coffee,* the Bible of the coffee industry. Weighing in at eight hundred pages, it was filled with fine print and elaborate illustrations. One of my favorites was an 1872 Arbuckle Brothers advertisement, picturing a perplexed-looking woman in an apron standing over a smoking stove, complaining, "Oh, I have burnt my coffee again." Another ad, titled "A Mistake Many Women Make," urges housewives to buy Arbuckle Brothers pre-roasted coffee instead of roasting their own, claiming falsely that "every time you roast four pounds of coffee you lose a whole pound." The ad wasn't just offensive; it was inaccurate. Like any narrative, the story of coffee was peppered with half-truths. It took a discerning eye to separate fact from fiction.

Even after the relationship with Henry ended, *All About Coffee* retained a prime position on the buffet table in my dining room. Like the silver lighter I bought for him in Guatemala on the day he left, the book served as a reminder of our history together. So did Golden Gate Coffee. Everyone there knew him. His blue eyes still gazed out from the huge staff photograph that hung in the lobby. In the picture we stood side by side, his arm around my shoulders, mine around his waist. Every now and then, when I stayed late at the office after everyone else had left, I'd find myself standing in front of the photograph, staring, trying to figure out what exactly had gone wrong.

# Seventeen

∞

The San Francisco Ladies' Bureau luncheon was in the restaurant of a downtown hotel. The round tables were set with white plates and pink napkins. A stack of *Blood in the Valley* formed the centerpiece of each table. I took a seat near the back.

On my right was an attractive woman in her late forties who turned to me and said, "And who might you be?"

"Ellie."

"Welcome," she said, offering me her hand. "I'm Maggie. This is Dwight, Barbara, Stella, and my daughter Claire."

"I'm going to interview him for the paper," Claire said. She was petite, blonde, and blue-eyed, with the kind of skin that's featured in Cover Girl commercials.

"Which paper?"

"Mercy High."

I suddenly felt very old. After Lila died, my father had retreated into himself, to such an extent that my mother turned to me for companionship. The result was that, for quite some time, I had been her frequent companion at luncheons, law firm parties, and wine tastings. We spent so much time together that I felt I had more social interaction with people my mom's age than my own. Her friends seemed to welcome my presence, and always took a sincere interest in what I was studying, whom I was seeing. I remembered so clearly how it felt to be Claire's age—grateful for the attention of my mother's friends but also smugly proud of my youth. It was impossible, at that age, not to be aware of the power that came with being young. Claire, it was clear, possessed that same pride and confidence. When the waiter came to fill our water glasses, he couldn't stop looking at her, and she accepted the attention as if it was her due.

Lila, on the other hand, never possessed the arrogance of youth. Maybe that had something to do with the fact that, in math years, she was already getting on. "If I'm going to make my mark, I don't have much time," she told me during her final year at Berkeley. "Niels Henrik Abel was only nineteen when he proved that there is no finite formula for the solution of the general fifth-degree equation. Gauss published *Disquisitiones Arithmeticae* at twenty-four. Galois discovered the connection between group theory and polynomial equations before dying in a gunfight at the age of twenty. It's like Hardy said, 'Mathematics is a young man's game.' Or, in my case, young woman's."

Stella pulled two cell phones and a beeper out of her purse and lined them up above her plate, as if some urgent matter might whisk her away at any moment. She was dressed in an ugly but expensive-looking green suit. "I've read every one of Andrew Thorpe's books, even *Second Time's a Charm,*" she said.

"This was my first," said Claire. "I loved it. After I finished this I borrowed *Runner Up, Runner Down* from Mom, and now I'm working my way back."

"Just wait until you read *Murder by the Bay*," said Barbara. "That was his best by far."

"I met the mother once," Dwight said. There was a visible shift of attention at the table; all heads turned toward him. "At a fund-raiser for the San Francisco Ballet. She was the nicest lady you could hope to meet. We swapped tips on growing geraniums."

I doubted very much that my mother had ever been at a San Francisco Ballet fund-raiser. I knew for a fact that she'd never taken an interest in geraniums. He must have remembered her green thumb from Thorpe's book. Thorpe had taken two pages to describe the intricate layout of my mother's garden, which she showed him once when I invited him to dinner at our house. Now, I wondered—did Dwight really think he had met her, or was he just pretending he had in order to make himself appear more interesting? One thing I'd discovered over the years is that tragedy is like a major earthquake or an act of terrorism: no one wants to experience it firsthand, but everyone wants to be able to place themselves close to the scene of the disaster.

Maggie tapped me on the forearm. "Have you read it?"

"Yes, but it was a long time ago."

"Well? What did you think?"

I took a sip of my water. A bit of lemon pulp stuck in my teeth. "It was well-written." I couldn't bring myself, at that moment, among those people, to say that the whole book was a betrayal of my family on a monumental scale.

"Personally," Maggie said, "I don't think Thorpe has yet to write another book to even compare to his first." She turned to Claire. "It's a classic, you know. Write *that* in your school paper."

"But there are plenty of true crime books out there," I said. "What was it about *Murder by the Bay* that left such an impression?"

It was a question I'd never asked anyone before. After I read the book the first time, I wanted to forget it existed. Even several years after the fact, a perfectly good day could be ruined by spotting someone with it on the bus, or coming across a used copy in a bookstore. Every time I caught a glimpse of it, my memories of the day when my parents pulled out of the driveway in their gray Volvo, headed to the morgue in Guerneville, came flooding back.

"When I read it," Stella said, "I felt like I was there in the woods with that poor girl where her body was dumped. My own daughter was ten years old at the time, and it chilled me to the bone. For the longest time I couldn't let her out of the house without worrying that something terrible was going to happen."

"It wasn't just that," Maggie said. "That's part of it, of course—the fear that it could happen to someone you love. But for me, more than that it was the fact that I felt like I knew Lila. What a sweet, smart girl she was, with such amazing promise. The kind of daughter any parent would be proud to have. You invest everything in your child—

time and money, of course, but also your emotions, and your hope. So much goes into a life, so much goes into nurturing a child. As a mother, it's just absolutely horrifying to think that one person can put an end to all of that."

"At least it wasn't a random act of violence," Stella said. "Nothing's more terrifying than the idea of being attacked by someone you don't even know."

Nods all around. I believed that Stella had hit on a key aspect of the book's success. The ultimate effect of naming Peter McConnell as the killer was to reassure readers that it couldn't happen to *them*. Thorpe's version of the story gave the impression that violence wasn't random, it wasn't something that happened to good, ordinary people going about their good, ordinary lives. *In the vast majority of cases,* he wrote in the prologue, *murder victims know their killers.*

There was a slight commotion in the room, and I turned to see Andrew Thorpe walking through the door.

Thorpe had lost weight. Back when I knew him, he wasn't overweight, but he'd always had a slightly dumpy look, a result of his distaste for the outdoors and his affinity for pasta and beer. Now he was trim and tan, his head entirely shaved. He wore black pinstripe pants, a snug black Oxford, and side-zip boots. The overall effect was a kind of Bruce Willis flair, but he wore the style self-consciously, as if someone else had chosen his clothes. At fifty, he appeared to be in better health than he was when I knew him at thirty.

A woman in a yellow pantsuit led him to a pedestal and introduced him.

"It's a real pleasure to be here with you," Thorpe began, smiling broadly. "You work on a book in solitude for such a long time, when you finally get out into the world to talk about it, it feels like you've been released from prison." The Southern accent which had been just a faint holdover when I knew Thorpe was much stronger now, and I couldn't help but wonder if he was playing it up for the crowd.

"Speaking of prison," he continued,

"I've just returned from Pelican Bay State penitentiary, where I went to see Johnny Grimes, who, you might recall, is serving twenty to life in a second-degree murder charge for the deaths of Stacy Everett and Greg Simmons."

There were nods and murmurs. The waitstaff came around with the salads, iceberg wedges with blue cheese dressing. I couldn't remember the last time I'd had iceberg lettuce in a restaurant. In a hipper establishment, I would have thought the iceberg wedge was a new fad, but in this case I knew it had probably been on the menu for decades. Our waiter glanced down Claire's shirt when he set her salad in front of her; she leaned forward to give him a better look.

Thorpe spent a few minutes talking about how he'd become interested in the Silicon Valley murders. He mentioned his friendship with families of the victims, and I wondered what their take on the relationship would be. Had they let Thorpe into their lives? Had he eaten dinner in their homes as he did in ours? Had they shown him the family photo albums, played him home movies of their kids in happier times? I imagined that, if they'd had a say in the matter, they would have chosen not to have a book written at all.

The waiters cleared away the salad plates and brought out the main course, grilled chicken with rice, a side of broccoli florets. Thorpe had finished his preamble now and began reading. I wondered if anyone else found it strange to be gnawing on chicken and broccoli while Thorpe eagerly read a particularly bloody scene from his book. It was the first chapter, and like the book about Lila, it opened with a description of the bodies as they had been found in the aftermath of the crime. It was his thing, what he was known for—what one reviewer had called his "unflinching portrayal of the crime scene."

While he was reading, Thorpe looked up from the book, made eye contact with the audience. I waited for him to see me. Would I throw him off balance? Would he fumble his sentence, lose his place on the page? But then I realized he wasn't actually making eye contact with anyone. Instead, as he glanced around the room, he kept his gaze just slightly above eye level, so as to create the appearance of interacting with the crowd without actually doing so. And I remembered that he used to do the same thing during class. He confessed this to me one afternoon over ice cream at Mitchell's. "If I look in the students' eyes, I get nervous," he said, "so instead I just pretend."

Dessert came. Just as the lunching ladies tucked into their flourless chocolate cake, Thorpe said, "Any questions?"

A frail-looking woman at the table next to mine raised her hand, and Thorpe acknowledged her with a nod. "What was the most difficult thing about writing this book?" she asked.

"Just untangling the web," Thorpe said. "When you write a novel, you have complete power over the events and the characters, complete control of the story. You start with a blank canvas. But with nonfiction, obviously, you're at the mercy of the facts. I interviewed dozens of people for this book. Everyone had his or her own version of the story, and every version was different."

Someone asked how his wife felt about *Second Time's a Charm.* "She hated it," he said. "Then she saw the first royalty check."

People laughed. Forks clinked. The waiters came around with coffee.

"How do you find stories to write about?"

"I don't really find stories," Thorpe said. "The stories find me. In this case, for example, I had a friend who was working at Yahoo at the time of the murders. We were golfing together one day, and he began to tell me about how the organization had been turned upside down by the events. He talked about how fearful people had become, about the culture of mistrust that arose on the Yahoo campus after it happened. To me, that was a story begging to be told. I wasn't interested in the murders so much as I was interested in their aftermath, and I was less intrigued by the victims than I was by the people

who were left behind, the way those relationships shifted."

Watching Thorpe work the room, I
tried to recall what it was about him
that made me willing to tell him such
personal details, things I had revealed
to no one else. Now, even more so than
before, his persuasiveness was in full
form, as if he'd spent the last twenty
years perfecting it. He'd passed the
Sundays of his childhood in a Southern
Baptist church in Tuscaloosa, and I
couldn't deny that he had something of
the evangelist's flair about him—a stagy,
folksy presence that made everyone
lean slightly forward in their seats.

There were still hands in the air when
Thorpe smiled and said, "Well, if there
are no more questions . . ." and stepped
away from the pedestal.

The woman in the yellow pantsuit in-
structed everyone to form a line in front
of the signing table.

Thorpe signed quickly, head down,
exchanging a couple of words with
each person before sliding the book
back across the table with a smile. As
the line inched forward, I felt my stom-

ach knotting up. So many times over the years, I had wanted to confront him, but something had always stopped me; for one thing, I didn't know that I could face him. More important, a confrontation seemed futile. The book was written, the damage done. What possible good could it do—for me or my parents, or for Lila—to open up the wound? But now, everything had changed. If the book was made of lies, as McConnell alleged, then Thorpe's betrayal was even greater. I needed to hear from Thorpe himself how much truth was in those pages.

When it was my turn, he took the book without looking at me. "And whom should I sign this to?"

I didn't answer.

"Would you like me to inscribe it to you or just sign my name?" he asked, growing impatient. Then he looked up, pen poised over the page. His mouth opened, but he said nothing. He laid the pen down and moved as if to stand, but then appeared to think better of it, and sat down again. "Ellie, I—"

It was the first time in my life I'd seen him speechless.

"Hi."

"Hi," he managed, his voice soft. His eyes looked wet, but the Thorpe I knew would never have become so emotional as to find himself on the verge of tears.

Finally he pushed his chair back and stood, leaning forward across the table, arms outstretched. Realizing he meant to hug me, I stepped back. He dropped his arms to his sides, glanced at the fans still waiting eagerly behind me in line, and sat down again. "I can't believe you're here. You don't know how good it is to see you." He was quiet again for a moment. And then, "God, Ellie, you really haven't changed at all." His Southern accent was all but gone. For a moment, he was the old Thorpe— the friend I knew before the whole terrible business with the book began.

The woman in the yellow pantsuit tugged at his sleeve. "Mr. Thorpe, we only have the room until one."

"Of course," he said, regaining his composure.

He leaned toward me, as if to talk in private, although it was clear that the woman in the yellow pantsuit and the people in line behind me were eavesdropping. "Look, I'm taking a taxi straight to the airport after this. I'm flying out to New York, but I'll be back in a couple of days. Call me." He wrote his phone number in the book. "No, better yet, come by, please. We have so much to catch up on."

He was already jotting down his address. "I mean it, come by anytime."

I tried to formulate a response, but the woman in the yellow pantsuit had me by the elbow and was ushering me on.

"Wait," Thorpe said, coming out from behind the table. "Ride to the airport with me. I'll pay for your cab ride back."

Seeing him in this room full of people was unsettling enough. I pictured us together in the cab, side by side in the closed space. "I have to get back to work," I said.

"You'll come by my house?"

"I don't know."

"You will," he said, his voice firm now, full of certainty. "I'm back on Tuesday."

A couple of minutes later, I stood outside the restaurant in the din of Market Street traffic, clutching Thorpe's latest best seller, feeling the same way I'd felt all those years ago, when he'd called out to me in the fog on Ocean Beach, having just told me he was going through with the book, no matter what. Then, as now, he'd had the final word. It was Thorpe's talent, the thing he did best: every story he told, every conversation he engaged in, ended on his own terms.

# *Eighteen*

∞

"For every human event," Thorpe used to say, "there is a story. For every emotion, every mystery, every historical point of reference, there is narrative that seeks to explain."

It stands to reason that there is a story for coffee. It was Henry who told me this story, on our second date. We had met just a few days before in the offices of Golden Gate Coffee, where he'd recently taken a job in sales. Henry had begun his career as a warehouse boy at Welsh's Coffee Roaster in San Mateo when he was still in high school. By the time I met him, he was spending much of his free time working as an advocate for the farmers. At that time there was such obscene wealth among young San Franciscans, it was a turn-on to meet a guy who genuinely didn't care much about financial profit—at least not his own.

He told me the story not over coffee but over beer, at the 500 Club in the Mission. While he could certainly appreciate the finer things, and would splurge once a year on a meal at Chez Panisse, he had a soft spot for dive bars. Early in our relationship, he would confess that the meeting at the 500 Club had been a kind of test. "If you were snobby about the red vinyl booths and pool table," he said, "it would mean you weren't for me."

But I'd been too intrigued by Henry to pay much attention to the décor. At five foot ten, he seemed to own the space he walked through more authoritatively than much taller men often did. He had light brown hair, blue eyes so pale they made me think of that Velvet Underground song, and milky skin that tended to go pink in the sun. His slightly lopsided smile exuded kindness and made him appear more shy than he actually was. He rarely wore anything other than jeans and a dark sweater, but his taste in shoes tended toward the adventurous. On the day we met, he was wearing boots made of a shiny black material that looked like hair, which he jokingly referred to as his horsehair boots before reassuring me that no horses had died in their manufacture. In public he had a pleasantly resonant voice that tended to draw attention his way, but in private he spoke so quietly that I often had to make him repeat himself.

"The story begins in Abyssinia in the ninth century," he said. Two glasses of beer stood on the small table between us. I leaned forward to hear him. "It begins with a young goatherd named Kaldi, and with his goats, who refuse, one evening, to follow him home. They are absorbed in a new discovery, a tree Kaldi has never seen before, with dark glossy leaves and red berries. They eat and eat, and it takes Kaldi a long time to coax them down from the mountain."

Henry used his hands when he spoke. Even though he had an office job, he possessed the rough, calloused hands of a manual laborer. I would later learn that he moonlighted as a furniture mover to save money to start his own business.

"That night," he continued, "the goats don't sleep. The next morning, when Kaldi takes them again to their grazing place on the mountain, they return immediately to the same tree. Like Eve, Kaldi is curious; he must have some for himself. The berries of the strange plant give him a feeling of alertness and well-being. He feels more energetic, more clever. He goes back home and tells his family and friends what he has experienced. Within a fortnight, the dervishes at a nearby monastery have discovered that chewing the leaves of the mystical plant allows them to spend less time sleeping, more time enacting their passionate devotions to God."

I wondered how it was that I'd spent years at Golden Gate Coffee without ever bothering to look this stuff up. Over time I would realize that Henry had something I'd lost a long time ago—a passion for the details, a keen memory not just for dates and place names, but for the oddities that made a story unique. He picked up the details because he paid attention, and he asked questions, and he burned things into his memory by sharing them with others, repeating stories until they became his own. For me, life was a house that I passed through quietly, trying not to unsettle the dust or bump up against the furniture. Henry was just the opposite; he moved through life with his hands outstretched, picking everything up and measuring its weight in his hands, knocking on walls to test their strength.

"I wish I could be more like you," I told him once, about six months into our relationship. "I wish I could just rush into life without analyzing everything so much."

"What's holding you back?" he asked. We were lying face-to-face in bed, fully clothed because of the cold, and he was looking at me with those intense blue eyes, waiting.

"I don't know."

It felt as though he was always waiting for me to tell him something, but I never could quite get the words out, never could let go enough to say exactly what I was thinking. With Henry I did make a sincere effort to open up, but most of the time I stopped short of the complete truth.

For a few minutes neither of us said anything, we just lay there, close together but not touching. I had closed my eyes and was beginning to drift off to sleep when his voice pulled me back. "You're nothing like her, you know," he said.

"What?"

"The girl in the book. She may have your name, your history, your face, but she's a fabrication. Andrew Thorpe made her up. You're not her."

I wanted to believe him, but I wasn't convinced. Really, how could Henry think that he knew me any better than Thorpe did? I had told Thorpe everything.

"Then who am I?" I asked, not expecting an answer.

"You're you," he said, without missing a beat. "You're Ellie Enderlin, and I love you."

"You do?"

It was something he'd never said before. I felt it, too, but I hadn't planned on saying it yet. I figured we were still a bit early in our relationship to be making such an enormous statement, the kind of thing you couldn't take back.

"I do," he said. And then he was waiting again. I tried to work up the nerve, but the words wouldn't come. One thing I would always appreciate about Henry was the fact that he didn't turn away. That night, despite the fact that I failed to say I loved him, he pulled me close. My body relaxed, and I realized that, for the first time in my adult life, I was beginning to feel truly safe.

# Nineteen

∞

*"It was the view which finally made us take the place."*
Aldous Huxley, *Young Archimedes*

I turned off Market and took the winding road up to Diamond Heights, past rows of sixties- and seventies-era condos. I had always liked this neighborhood, which had the feel of a suburb plopped on a mountain in the middle of the city. It was just after midnight, and the steep streets were dark and quiet. I knew Thorpe would be surprised to see me show up on his doorstep so late, and I hoped this would work to my advantage. Nighttime was when my mind was most alert, and also when I felt most comfortable in my skin. If Diamond Heights was Thorpe's territory, then nighttime was mine.

Thorpe's house was at the top of Red Rock Hill. It was a two-story Eichler, with a white beam roof overhanging the gray front wall. A small garden was laid out in a triangle pattern in the front yard, a Japanese maple and several lavender bushes providing a bit of privacy from the street. I parked at the curb, sat in the car for a couple of minutes gathering courage, and walked up to the front door and rang the bell. Soon, I heard footsteps. The door opened, and Thorpe stood before me, clad in a striped cotton bathrobe, his head covered in gray stubble, save for a large bald patch on top. There were dark bags under his eyes, and he gave off a faint medicinal scent.

"Ellie?" he said, rubbing his eyes. "What are you doing here?"

"You told me to stop by anytime."

He smiled and said groggily, "So I did. Come on in. I'll make coffee."

I followed him through the open courtyard, where a stone fountain gurgled. The courtyard led into a large living room, the back wall of which was floor-to-ceiling glass. The high ceiling featured exposed white beams. Having grown up in a pretty but cramped Victorian in Noe Valley, an Eichler on the hill was my idea of a dream house. But Thorpe had made a mess of the place. The hardwood floors were covered with tatty Turkish rugs in deep reds and drab browns, the floor-to-ceiling shelves on either side of the fireplace were filled with magazines and knickknacks. The flat-panel TV was shoved inside a huge mahogany armoire, the doors of which were open to reveal a jumble of audiovisual equipment. There were two sofas, a leather recliner, a coffee table, and a couple of mismatched side chairs. Even the glass wall was obstructed by an enormous bamboo console. Stacks of newspapers and magazines were everywhere. I imagined Joseph Eichler turning in his grave.

The house reeked of stale smoke, and I noticed several empty ashtrays strewn about. "You took up smoking?" I said.

"Not anymore. I've been clean for almost two months, knock on wood. The ashtrays are a visualization technique my life coach suggested to help me kick the habit."

"Life coach? I always wondered who their clients were."

"I hired her because I was suffering from a severe case of writer's block."

"Did she fix it?"

"Ask me next month. We're currently in week nine—uncluttering my living space." He gestured helplessly at the room. "We've hit a bit of a snag there. Week ten and eleven are spiritual awakening. Next stop, writer's block. She said we had to work our way up. Laurie Giordano—she's tough, but good—remind me to give you her card."

I waited in the living room while he went into the kitchen to make coffee. The kitchen was separated from the living room only by a low countertop. The sink was full of dishes, the refrigerator door covered with newspaper clippings, calendars, receipts, postcards, and photographs. He rummaged around in a drawer, then another, and finally said, "I can't find the coffee filters. We'll have to settle for tea."

He filled a red kettle with water and set it on the stove.

"I hope your wife doesn't mind my showing up so late," I said, "but I was in the neighborhood."

"Wife?"

"I saw *Second Time's a Charm* in the bookstore."

"Ah, *that.* Well, the second time didn't really turn out to be such a charm after all. Jane filed for divorce a month after that one came out."

"I'm sorry to hear."

"Apparently, so was Oprah." He laughed. "I was *this* close. Who knows, maybe I could have been the next Deepak Chopra or Dr. Phil. Oh well, there's always another book, eh?" He gestured toward the general chaos of the living room. "Have a seat. You're making me nervous."

I cleared a spot on the sofa. The cushions caved in when I sat down, so that my knees were up in the air. Something smelled weird. I realized the cloying vanilla odor was coming from an enormous, flesh-colored candle on the coffee table.

"Sorry, I couldn't find saucers," Thorpe said, handing me a steaming mug that bore the insignia of a hotel in Cleveland.

He sat down in the recliner across from me, adjusting the hem of the bathrobe to cover his knees. The top slid open to reveal a pale, broad nipple ringed with curly black hair. A fake palm tree rose up behind his head. On the wall beside the tree were several wooden masks bearing macabre and pained expressions. I thought of Colonel Kurtz in the jungle. I thought of the drunken night almost twenty years before when I'd ended up in bed with this man. He had been an earnest and awkward lover; the night had ended badly. Then, as now, nothing seemed quite real. I'd long ago learned that the world was filled with grotesque and unsettling encounters that could be funny or just depressing, depending upon one's perspective; the jury was still out on this one.

"I wish you'd told me you were coming," he said, running his hand over the gray stubble on his head. "I would have cleaned up. As you can see, I don't get many visitors." The Southern accent was entirely gone; as I suspected, it was just part of the performance.

Because of the relative height of the recliner and the depth of the sofa cushions, my eyes were level with the soles of his feet. It had been a mistake to come here. Nighttime, after all, didn't neutralize the territory as much as I'd hoped. I cleared my throat to speak, but I didn't know where to begin.

"How long has it been?" he said.

"A long time."

"I've wanted to see you, Ellie. Very much. Things didn't turn out the way I hoped between us. Losing your friendship, that was harder on me than you can possibly know."

"It was your choice," I said.

"Hardly."

"I begged you not to write that book."

Thorpe gave the footrest a shove, set his feet on the floor, and leaned forward. "This is true, but I swear, I never wanted to hurt you or your family. I was at the end of my rope, and the book was my way out. Did I ever tell you about the day I decided to write it?"

I shook my head. "No."

"It was a Sunday night, and I'd just spent three hours in a departmental meeting listening to my colleagues argue over which short story should be used for a diagnostic essay—Alice Walker's 'Everyday Use' or Hemingway's 'Hills Like White Elephants.' I kid you not, three hours. About halfway through the meeting I started thinking about what had happened to Lila, and to your family. I couldn't believe they hadn't arrested anybody. I'm sitting there, and some uptight white guy in a turtleneck is going on and on about how we can't ignore the literary canon, while the new women's studies hire is harping about marginalized feminist writers, and I knew that if I was still having the same conversation in five years I'd have to kill myself. So I just tuned out and started writing. By the time the meeting adjourned, I'd filled six pages. I reread it as soon as I got home, and I knew right then it could be really good.

If I hadn't taken that chance, I'd still be holed up in some little apartment grading freshman essays, fucking around with a Hemingway story I never liked in the first place."

"Would you do it again?"

He didn't say anything. The silence was answer enough. He finished his tea and set the cup on the table. "I've thought about you over the years, Ellie."

"I'm not that hard to find."

"Actually, you are."

"I'm sure you have resources. Not to mention, until a year ago, my mother lived a quarter mile from here."

"What? I'm going to show up on your mother's doorstep? I was hoping you'd come to me. I knew if I was the one to make the first move, you'd shoot me down. You made it clear that you didn't want anything to do with me."

I couldn't argue with that.

"Listen," he said, "do you mind if I go change?"

"What?"

"I feel weird, sitting here and talking to you in my bathrobe. To be perfectly honest, it's been a rough couple of days. I've got this new book I'm working on, and I've hardly left my desk. In fact, I was up in my office writing—or trying to—when the doorbell rang."

He stood. "Make yourself at home," he said. "Wander around. Who knows, you might find something interesting."

"You mean that?"

He smiled. "Eat my food, drink my liquor, read my mail, rifle through my drawers. Just don't leave."

I knew that he meant it. There had, after all, been a reason we got along so well all those years ago. He was easy to talk to. He was generous with his time. He liked me. I never bothered with how I looked when I went to see him, never worried that I'd say the wrong thing. When we talked, I could always tell he was really listening. The camaraderie we shared, the genuine ease I felt in his presence, had made his betrayal all the more devastating.

When I heard a door close upstairs, I went into the kitchen to examine the collection of photographs on Thorpe's fridge. There were snapshots of him with various local personalities—Barry Bonds, Bill Gates, Jim Mitchell, Armistead Maupin—as well as national media types like Barbara Walters, Ted Turner, and that narrow, white-haired guy from *60 Minutes.* There was a calendar featuring *The Simpsons,* the page turned to the month of June, which had already come and gone. I flipped to July—almost every square was filled. There were radio shows, readings, book clubs, an elementary school fund-raising luncheon. I wondered what kind of grade school would enlist the services of a true crime author to raise money for crayons and monkey bars.

On the wall above the counter was a corkboard, on which was tacked a schizophrenic mishmash of ticket stubs from a couple dozen movies—*The Lives of Others, Ocean's Thirteen, The Squid and the Whale, Shrek*—and music shows—Sugar dePalma at the Rockit Room, Walty at Hotel Utah, Steve Forbert at the Great American

Music Hall, the Polyphonic Spree and Pilar Dana at Slims. There was also a two-day pass to the New Orleans Jazz Festival from 2003. I was impressed with his musical tastes, surprised to see that we still had so much in common on that front, until I saw the $115 stub for a Journey revival tour.

There was more: a year-old receipt for an $800 coat purchased from Neiman Marcus—maybe he'd planned to return it but never got around to it—and a postcard from Hawaii, post-marked five years ago in November, addressed to "Mr. & Mrs. Thorpe," bearing the handwritten message: *Memo to self: remember the honey-moon,* and the signatures *Jane & Andy.* Apparently they hadn't followed their own advice.

I took the stairs to the second floor. I passed a closed door, behind which I could hear him moving around. I liked the freedom of being able to wander around his house unimpeded. I had come prepared to ask Thorpe for an-swers, but a few minutes with him had led me to understand what I should have known all along—that it wouldn't be as easy as asking a simple question and getting a direct and honest response. Socially, beneath the dishevelment and disorganization, Thorpe had always been a crafty, clever man.

I turned right and came to a square room equipped with a large metal desk, which was flanked by industrial filing cabinets. The desk was shoved against a large window. Books and papers were everywhere, and the chair was covered with file folders. On top of the desk, anchoring a stack of papers, was a pair of binoculars. The hardwood floor had ring-shaped stains where potted plants once stood. I flipped the light switch, but nothing happened.

Thorpe was walking around, opening and closing drawers. I heard him curse to himself. The fountain gurgled in the courtyard.

I was amazed by how quiet his house was. Having lived in apartments for years, I'd grown accustomed to the constant noise of neighbors—garage doors opening, toilets flushing, televisions blaring. It didn't matter how nice

an apartment building was, how exor-
bitant the rent, you could never escape
the sounds of your neighbors. I imagined that if I were ever to move into a
proper house, one without any shared
walls, I would find the silence somewhat creepy. I liked the proximity of
neighbors, even those I didn't know. I
figured, if need be, I could always call
for help. I could never entirely banish
from my mind the image of Lila, alone
with her killer in the woods. If she called
out, no one heard her. Urban places
provided at least the illusion of safety. It
was hard to believe that houses like
this existed in the middle of San
Francisco—solitary houses, where you
could scream and no one would hear
you. Of course, that was probably why
Thorpe's neighborhood was the last
piece of land in the city to be devel-
oped. Despite its amazing views and
central location, Diamond Heights had
an eerie, windswept quality.

I leaned over the desk and peered
out the window. Whereas the living
room windows faced north, the office
had an eastern view. There was a

steep, wooded hill beside the house. Beyond the hill the streets of Noe Valley glowed vaguely under the automatic lamps. I felt unnerved, but I couldn't pinpoint the source of my discomfort— it was just a vague sensation of something not being quite right. I moved the file folders off the chair, sat down at the desk, and peered down the hill. Midway down, someone had set up a makeshift encampment. The end of a cigarette glowed. That was unremarkable, it was part of the accepted absurdity of San Francisco—homeless people living within yards of multimillion-dollar homes. At the bottom of the hill was a fence, and beyond the fence a small playground, and beyond that a narrow street lined with rows of Victorians. There were many such streets in Noe Valley, of course, but I realized with a shiver that this wasn't just any street. From the house on the corner, I counted down the block until I came to the sixth house on the right. A light burned in an upstairs room. A person appeared in front of the window and stood there, still as a photograph. I

lifted the binoculars to my eyes and experienced several seconds of confusion as the binoculars picked up the
objects in front of me on the desk, absurdly magnified. I moved them back
and forth, finally finding the house, the
window. Affixed to the outside frame of
the window was a wooden bird feeder,
a Victorian house in miniature. I recognized the bird feeder immediately—the
small scalloped roof, the little red
door—I'd built it from a kit and painted
it myself during my freshman year of
college. There had been a hummingbird with an iridescent blue throat that
came at ten every morning. It was Lila
who cleaned the feeder and kept it
supplied with nectar. After she died I
forgot to fill it, and the hummingbird
stopped coming.

I was looking at my old bedroom.
Thorpe had a perfect view. The person
standing before the window was a
woman, not much older than I was,
dressed in a pale green bathrobe, arms
crossed. She shifted, lifted her arm in a
wave. For a moment, I thought she was

waving at me. Then I saw the person on the street below her window—a man, waving up at her. I couldn't be sure, but he looked like an old neighbor of mine.

# *Twenty*

∞

I sensed him before I heard him. Several seconds passed. I kept waiting for him to announce himself, but he didn't. Finally I turned and saw Thorpe standing in the doorway, watching me. He was wearing a white cable-knit sweater, linen slacks, and leather sandals. His head had been shaved clean, and he smelled of aftershave—a combination of orange blossom, musk, and leather, with a hint of patchouli and tonka bean. The fragrance was familiar, but I couldn't trace it to a particular person or time.

I had witnessed the third transformation of Thorpe in as many days. He looked nothing like the man who had answered the door a half hour before. His demeanor had changed as well. He had a bit of swagger now. The total effect of the clothes, the aftershave, the smooth and gleaming head, was of a man who'd come to take me out to Sunday brunch in Marin.

He walked into the room and looked out the window, down the hill toward my house. For a moment we stood side by side in the darkness. His arm brushed mine, and I moved away from him.

"Bulb's burnt," he said. "Wait here."

In a couple of minutes Thorpe returned. He stood on a chair to remove the light fixture, and handed me the old bulb. I shoved it into the overflowing wastepaper basket and wiped the greasy dust on my jeans.

"How many Marxists does it take to screw in a lightbulb?" he asked, as the new bulb flickered to life.

"I give up."

"None. The lightbulb already contains the seeds of its own revolution."

"Not bad."

He stood in front of me, hands on his hips, breathing a bit faster from the exertion.

"How long have you lived here?" I asked.

"Almost ten years." He was standing so close I could smell his toothpaste. It smelled minty, organic—I recognized it as Tom's of Maine, the old wintergreen flavor. "Turned out to be a great investment. I got it for $400,000. Last month the fixer-upper across the street sold for 1.7 million."

"You could cash out, move to the tropics, and take up a life of leisure." I thought of Peter McConnell in Nicaragua, living off the grid. I wondered what he was doing tonight, what he would make of my trek into Diamond Heights to confront the man who had ruined his life.

"Ah, yes," Thorpe said, "but what about my fans?"

"You can write anywhere."

"True, but then it's not really just about the writing, is it? You can write the best book ever, but if you're not around to do interviews, have your picture taken for magazines, show up at the book festivals, then your book is sunk, your readers evaporate, and you're alone with the blank pages."

"Is that why you do it—so you won't be alone?"

"Isn't that ultimately why anyone does anything?" He glanced out the window, then back at me. "Are you seeing anyone?"

"No one in particular."

I didn't like where the conversation was headed, but I wasn't sure how to get it moving in the right direction. I had come here to talk about Peter Mc-Connell, and now I was distracted by the window. I imagined Thorpe sitting at his desk, watching the comings and goings of my childhood home. Until a year before, it would have been my mother he observed pulling out of the garage each weekday morning, my mother he saw traipsing down the street, yoga mat slung over her shoulder, on the way to her Saturday afternoon class.

And, of course, every Thursday night, he would have seen me, because every Thursday I came over for dinner. I would arrive at six, and my mother and

I would have a glass of wine—either in the living room or on the back deck, depending on the weather. At six-thirty we would walk to Alice's at Twenty-ninth and Sanchez, where we would order pot stickers, orange chicken, garlic prawns, and bok choy. Around seven-thirty, we would climb the steep hill to my mother's house and stand on the sidewalk for a couple of minutes, saying our good-byes. This had been our routine ever since my father moved out after the divorce, and unless I was out of town or had something pressing to attend to, I honored the commitment. It was something we counted on, my mother and I. When she sold the house and moved to Santa Cruz, I had found myself on those Thursday nights feeling completely adrift. It had been such a regular part of my life for so long, I didn't know what to do with myself. Eventually I began filling the newly freed time with classes—Bikram yoga, conversational Russian, Italian cooking, even hip-hop dance—but I always felt out of sync; the only place I wanted to be was in my old neighborhood, with my mother, talking casually about our week. During those Thursday-night dinners with her, I felt I could truly be myself, relaxed, with no need to put up my guard. Knowing that Thorpe had been there, probably watching us from above, cast the whole thing in a different light.

Although the clear view of my house was the most obvious topic, Thorpe simply passed over it as if it did not exist. It was his way, again, of controlling the conversation, so that any dialogue advanced according to his own terms.

"There was a woman I was seeing for a while, a long time ago, before I met my ex-wife, Jane," Thorpe said. He was sitting on the edge of the desk now, legs crossed at the knees, hands resting at his sides, in a posture I remembered from class. I sat down in the desk chair. "Her name was Florence, I called her Flo. We'd been together for a couple of months when I took her to a dinner party at the home of one of my former colleagues, Pio Schunker. Do you remember him?"

I thought for a moment. "Yes, he was

the good-looking fellow with the unidentifiable accent and a taste for action movies. I had him for twentieth-century British lit. Whatever happened to him?"

"He ended up abandoning academia and becoming a major advertising executive, but that's beside the point. So we went to his house, and after dinner we were sitting in the living room having coffee when he said to Flo, 'Funny, the moment you walked in I thought you looked very familiar, and all night I've been trying to figure it out, and it just hit me.' At that point he turned to me and asked if I knew who he was talking about.

"Of course I knew," Thorpe continued, "but I'd never mentioned it to Flo, so I pretended to have no idea. 'You remind me of a student Andy and I used to have,' Pio said, 'Ellie Enderlin.' "

All this time, I'd been looking out the window. The light went off in the upstairs room of my childhood home. Thorpe stood and began pacing. Because the room was so small and overcrowded with furniture, he could only go three or four steps before turning around and pacing in the opposite direction. "What I'm trying to say is that I needed you."

The intimacy was too much, too fast. I felt myself instinctively leaning away from him, scooting the wheeled chair back a couple of inches.

He moved closer. "No, not in *that* way," he said, as if he were reading my mind. "Not that I would've objected— the night we spent together was terrific, I still think about it."

I backed away again. Again, he stepped closer. My chair was pressed against the bookshelves and I was looking up at him, his face tired and pale in the unflattering light of the new bulb.

"You were amazing, so open to me."

I remembered that night at his Dolores Park apartment differently. I remembered the bad lasagna he made, the strawberry cheesecake he served before it had completely thawed. I remembered sitting on the couch with him, well into our second bottle of

wine, wondering how to extricate myself from the evening.

"But I'd have been fine with never
touching you again if I could have had
you in my life," Thorpe said. "Not as a
romantic partner, as something more
than that—a friend, an inspiration. Because I couldn't have you, I found
someone who looked like you." He
stopped pacing. "Funny, huh? Kind of
pathetic. In fact, I have pictures. Come
with me."

He was out of the room before I could
protest. I followed him down the hall
into a bedroom, and was surprised to
see that the room was clean. The bed
had recently been slept in, but only one
side of the covers was turned down;
the other half was in order, the pillows
stacked neatly. The bedside table was
clear except for a tidy stack of books,
and the marks on the rug showed that
it had been recently vacuumed. In the
corner by the window stood a black
leather Aeron chair, with a wool blanket
folded over the back. The room was
softly lit by a tall, modern lamp. This,
too, was in keeping with the man I had

known so many years before. Just when I thought I was beginning to understand him, I would be confronted with some aspect of his character that made me reevaluate.

"Don't look so surprised," he said. "I am at least capable of keeping one room of the house clean. I sleep better when I have no distractions."

He took a leather box off the chest of drawers, placed it on the bed, and removed the lid. The box was full of photographs. He began to go through them one by one. "I'm certain I have one in here," he said. "The two of you could be sisters."

As he searched, I caught glimpses of him as a young boy and as a teenager, mostly with his family—vacation snapshots from Disney World and Six Flags, Christmas morning pictures taken in front of a tree, a Polaroid of him and a young woman in a cap and gown at what appeared to be a high school graduation. He went too fast for me to get a good look at any of them, the effect being that I felt as though I was seeing a fast-forwarded version of his personal life. During all those hours I had spent spilling my heart to him, telling him the most intimate details of my life, he had revealed almost nothing about his own. There was a series of photographs of him in a gondola, and in each one—there must have been twenty or more—he was with a different girl.

"Where's this?" I said, taking one from his hand. The girl in this photograph was blonde, plump, and pretty, wearing a red gingham jumper and white Keds. She looked like the punch line to a farmer's daughter joke.

"Oh, the gondola ride in the harbor at Marina del Rey," he said. "For a couple of years during grad school at UCLA it was where I took girls on first dates. The girls seemed to like it, and I enjoyed the consistency. I figured if I put all of them on a level playing field— same date, down to the restaurant and the gondola ride—I'd have a better basis for comparison."

"Did it work?"

"I don't know that I ever went on a second date. None of them inspired me."

He flipped through a few more photos, and finally found what he was looking for. "Here," he said, thrusting a
snapshot into my hand. "This is Flo."

The picture had been taken at Candlestick Park. Flo was sitting in the
stands, holding a hot dog in one hand,
a plastic cup of beer in the other. She
was smiling, looking directly into the
camera. Judging from the coat and
scarf that she wore, it was a typical day
at Candlestick, cold wind blowing off
the bay. Lila and I had been to a few
games there with our parents when we
were kids, but I'd never been a big
enough Giants fan to weather the frigid
temperatures. When the Giants moved
to the more comfortable China Basin in
2000, I began going to the games on a
regular basis.

But this picture wasn't from China
Basin, it was Candlestick. It could have
even been a 49ers game. The woman
in the photograph was petite, with
strawberry blond hair and dimples, but
the similarities ended there. I didn't
think she looked much like me at all.
Thorpe was living in his own little world.

He sat down on the bed and pulled me down beside him. "You were a turning point, Ellie. I was a frustrated writer, bored with my job, headed nowhere. Then you walked into my life, and everything changed. If I hadn't met you, Lila's story would have been no more to me than an item in the news, something I quickly forgot. Because of you, I stopped *talking* about writing a book and actually sat down and wrote one. You were my muse. Without you, I floundered."

"You wrote four more books."

"Yes, but they weren't the same. There's a reason everyone thinks my first book was my best. The others were forced—competent, maybe, because by then I knew what I was doing—but forced. Every sentence was an effort. With *Murder by the Bay,* the writing just flowed. During the day, I would see you, or at least talk to you by phone. At night, I wrote, energized by our conversations."

"You're leaving one thing out," I said.

"Hmm?"

"All that time, when I was talking to

you about Lila, and about my family, you were using me. I considered you a friend, you considered me a source."

"It wasn't like that," he said, turning his whole body to face me. "People know Lila's name. Twenty years later, they're still talking about her. They love her. If it weren't for the book, she'd just be another dead girl."

"They don't love her," I said. "They're fascinated by her. To them, she's just a corpse somebody found in the woods, a catharsis. Anyone who reads that book feels relieved that it wasn't their daughter or girlfriend or sister. It's someone else's tragedy. Your readers can enjoy the spectacle, but they don't have to pay a price."

"You're wrong," he said, shaking his head. "That's not how it is at all."

I could tell that he believed what he was saying. He really believed he had turned Lila into some sort of cult hero-ine. In his version of the story, he'd done little wrong.

# Twenty-one

∞

At two in the morning Thorpe and I were sitting at the large glass-top table, facing each other over a half-eaten pizza and a near-empty bottle of wine. He'd insisted on feeding me, and the only thing he could find to cook was a frozen spinach and artichoke pizza from Trader Joe's. I was surprised how good it tasted, and how hungry I was. The wine was delicious, a 2003 pinot. I tasted raspberries and smoke, and poured myself a second glass. Thorpe was on his third.

I was all talked out, and yet I hadn't gotten any answers. Every time I tried to steer the conversation in the direction of Peter McConnell, he steered it back to something else. We talked about a recent trip he'd taken to Lisbon, an angry letter he'd received from the now ex-wife who was immortalized in *Second Time's a Charm,* and an early photograph by the Hungarian photographer Martin Munkácsi which he had recently acquired at considerable cost. I'd seen Munkácsi's spare, beautiful black-and-white photographs at the San Francisco Museum of Modern Art a couple of years before. The exhibit had featured famous portraits of American celebrities, aerial photos of female pilots, and the well-known "Three Boys at Lake Tanganyika." But the photograph Thorpe had purchased was from the early 1920s, when Munkácsi was at the very beginning of his career.

"Do you know Munkácsi's story?" Thorpe asked, lifting his glass.

"Didn't he take some iconic photo of Fred Astaire?"

"Yes, but what's really interesting is what came before all that, before he fled Hitler and moved to New York, back when he was completely unknown. One day Munkácsi was walking along with his camera when he came upon a street fight. He started taking pictures. By the end of the brawl, someone was dead. Munkácsi's photographs were used in court to clear the accused—this was what launched his career. I've managed to get my hands on one of these photographs of the brawl. It's being shipped from a gallery in Budapest next month. It will go right there, above the fireplace."

I imagined the image of a bloody street fight hanging above Thorpe's mantel, hovering over the room. What kind of man would want to gaze, every day, at a portrait of a murder-in-action?

"Lucky man," I said.

"I know. You should have seen me at the gallery, trying to talk the owner into parting with it. He was determined to only sell to a Hungarian. I was speaking through an interpreter, to whom I'd promised a handsome commission, and it turns out he did more than translate. He apparently made up some elaborate story about my ancestral connection to the Hapsburgs."

"I wasn't talking about you," I said.

"Pardon?"

"When I said 'lucky man,' I was referring to the man who was cleared of committing the crime."

"Oh," Thorpe said, "of course."

It was late, and I was afraid of leaving without getting what I'd come for. As a night owl, I was always aware of the coming daylight, could sense the minutes ticking away. All of my best conversations with Henry had occurred in the middle of the night. Sunrise had a way of putting an end to intimacy; the vulnerabilities men displayed in the middle of the night seemed to disappear with the moon and stars.

Thorpe picked up his knife and began cutting his pizza into small bites. I'd forgotten his annoying habit of treating his food like he was dissecting it.

"There's something I wanted to ask you about."

"How does anyone live without Trader Joe's?" Thorpe said. "I'd go hungry if it weren't for their frozen food aisle. Did I ever tell you I met Joe Coulombe once? At a fund-raising soiree for the LA Opera. He's a big opera fan."

"Peter McConnell," I said.

Thorpe peeled an artichoke off the

pizza and ate it slowly, gazing intently at his plate. If I didn't know him so well, I would have thought he hadn't heard me. "Trader Joe's didn't get really huge until it was bought out in 1979 by one of the German brothers who own Aldi. People still think there's a California guy named Joe in a floral shirt and Panama hat running the whole show."

I was determined not to give up. "Did Peter McConnell do it?"

Thorpe blotted his lips with a napkin. "You read the book. You know my theory."

"I'm not asking about your theory. I'm asking whether he did it."

"Off the record?"

"Sure," I said. "Who am I going to tell, anyway?"

"He had opportunity. He had motive. Most of the circumstantial evidence certainly pointed in his direction."

"Most?"

"In any case like this, there are shades of doubt."

I poured the last of the wine into his glass. "When you wrote the book," I

continued carefully, "were you doubt-
ful?"

"Any rational person, given the facts,
would experience an element of doubt.
That's unavoidable."

"But in the book, you made it sound
as though it *had* to be him."

Thorpe picked up his glass. "It did."

"Why?"

"Because if anyone else did it, it
would have just been another sordid
murder for the police ticker, suitable for
nothing more than an item in the newspaper. But if McConnell did it, it was a
great story—a young, beautiful math
prodigy, murdered by her married lover,
who knew that he would never be as
brilliant a mathematician as she was."
His voice had become slightly un-
steady from the wine, and a shadow of
stubble had reappeared on his head.
"At the end of the day, everyone wants
to be taken away by a great story.
Everyone wants to read about people
they're unlikely to meet in real life. From
the moment I stumbled upon Mc-
Connell, I knew he was the character
I'd been looking for, the one who had

eluded me in all my previous attempts to write a novel."

"But your book wasn't a novel."

"Nonetheless, I had to think like a novelist. If I'd approached it as a straightforward piece of journalism, I never would have found the heart of the story."

"What if the character in your book is nothing like the actual man? What if McConnell didn't do it?"

"One can't rule out the possibility."

"You don't care that you might have ruined an innocent man's life?"

"It's a stretch to call him innocent," Thorpe said. "Let's suppose for a moment that he didn't kill Lila; he would still be guilty of having an extramarital affair, and of using your sister to further his ambition of proving the Goldbach Conjecture."

"When a book is labeled nonfiction, people expect to read the truth."

"Remember what Oscar Wilde said in the preface to *The Picture of Dorian Gray*: 'There is no such thing as a moral or an immoral book. Books are well-written or badly written.' Hopefully, mine was well-written and provided some pleasure. I was only trying to tell a good story. And the deeper I got into the book, the more clear it became to me that there could be only one ending. Once I understood what it was, writing the story was like following a map."

Thorpe leaned back. "Listen, I was thinking maybe we could get together soon. I'm doing a signing at Books Inc. in Opera Plaza on Saturday. We could have lunch in the neighborhood afterward."

The sky was beginning to lighten. Soon, it would be five a.m., and the world would yawn to life. I realized the only way to get what I wanted from Thorpe was to use his own tactics against him. My mother had once told me that her success as a trial attorney had to do with her approach to the witness stand. Many attorneys, she said, made the mistake of beginning a cross-examination from the standpoint of the aggressor. In their eagerness to make their own case, they bullied the witness. She said she saw herself, at the outset of any cross-examination, as a negotiator. Prior to a trial, she'd find out everything she could about the witnesses, and tailor her questions to each personality. In this way she could lead the conversation in the direction she wanted it to go.

By asking me to see him again, Thorpe had opened a door.

"Let's assume for the sake of argument that it wasn't McConnell," I said. "Who else could have done it?"

Thorpe stood and began clearing the dishes. "We could walk down to Mangosteen afterward. Great little Vietnamese place. Best garlic beef in the city."

I ignored his invitation and pressed on. "You interviewed dozens of people for the book. There must have been others who stood out as possibilities."

"Have you ever had mangosteen berry juice? It's delicious."

He took the plates into the kitchen, and I followed him with the glasses and leftover pizza.

"I'm not asking you to remember offhand. You must have notes tucked away somewhere."

He put the dishes in the already-full sink, squirted some dishwashing liquid into the pile, and turned on the hot water. "We'll let them soak."

"I like Vietnamese food," I said after a pause. "I haven't had it in a while."

Thorpe turned and leaned against the counter. A few seconds passed. "John Wheeler," he said finally. "He was a janitor at Stanford. A student claimed to see him talking to Lila in the math building the night before she died."

"I don't remember him from the book."

Thorpe shrugged. "I talked to him once. He was in the first draft, but he ended up on the cutting-room floor— he wasn't very interesting."

"Do you have any idea where I might find him?"

Thorpe shook his head. "That was forever ago. But I can probably find his old address. Come with me."

If the bedroom was the one place in Thorpe's house where neatness reigned, the garage was where he had completely abandoned any pretense of order. It was designed to hold two cars, but was so overrun with boxes, gardening tools, sports equipment, and old furniture that it would have been difficult to even fit a motorcycle in there. The garage was lit by fluorescent tubes, and in the exaggerated brightness Thorpe looked increasingly haggard in his wrinkled slacks and wine-stained sweater, his morning beard. Beneath the scent of aftershave, I detected a faint but unmistakable tinge of body odor. There was a spot in the book where he described Peter McConnell as a modern-day Jekyll and Hyde, but I thought the comparison could be more aptly applied to Thorpe himself. I had the feeling that the garage, more than any other room in the house, represented the real Thorpe— not the stylish, put-together author persona he presented to the world, but the man he was in his most private moments, ripe-smelling and uncertain amidst the detritus of his lonely life.

"Welcome to the wine cellar," he quipped.

I tripped over an old rug that was rolled up on the floor, and Thorpe took my arm to steady me. We picked our way through tottering shelves, a weight bench, and several full recycling bins to a metal file cabinet crammed into a corner. "It may look like a disaster," Thorpe said, "but believe it or not, I actually have a system. All the notes for my old books are in this cabinet, arranged top to bottom, first book first."

He opened the top drawer and began thumbing through the green hanging files, which emitted a musty, old-paper smell that made me think of a chiropractor's office where I'd temped one summer after college. The temp job lasted an interminable three weeks. Just days after I left, a disgruntled former patient had walked in and shot up the office, killing the chiropractor and critically injuring the receptionist, for whom I had been the replacement while she was on her honeymoon. The event only confirmed what I knew to be true: the world was unsafe, and danger lurked in the most innocuous places. It was a lesson I had learned with Lila's death, and over the years I saw it repeated over and over, an unrelenting pattern.

I looked over Thorpe's shoulder, trying to read the labels on the files, but they appeared to contain only dates instead of names. Finally he pulled out a folder and flipped through it until he came to a 4×6 green notebook with the word *Memorandum* embossed in gold across the cover.

"Great notebook, isn't it?" Thorpe said. "FBI issue. A friend of mine in the Bureau, Lucy Ranahan, gave it to me ages ago. I think it's positively Hooveresque. Unfortunately, they don't make them anymore." He licked his index finger and flipped through it. "Oh," he said, "it's James."

"Pardon?"

"James Wheeler, not John Wheeler. I remembered it wrong. Here's his old contact info. He was in his fifties then, not in the best of health. It's quite possible he's dead now. A much younger wife, though, if I remember correctly." Thorpe ripped the page out of the notebook and handed it to me. It had a name, address, and phone number.

"What's this?" I said, pointing to a sketch of a face beneath the number.

"Oh, just a habit. When I interview people, I draw them. I draw the victims, too, from photographs. Helps me get into the characters. I tried to get my editor to include the drawings in the book, but she said it sent the wrong message."

I wondered if he had drawings of Lila, of me. I reached for the book, but he held it out of my reach. "I promised you *one* name."

"Are there others?"

He didn't answer. We walked back through the house. In the entryway I paused in front of the fountain, stalling. I still wanted to ask him about the view. Close up, I could see that the water in the fountain was green and scummy. Dead bugs floated on the surface.

"You want it?"

"Pardon?"

"The fountain. It was Flo's idea. I've been meaning to get rid of it. You can have it if you like."

"Thanks," I said, "I'll think about it," but we both knew I wouldn't. Then we were standing in the open doorway, and I knew the opportunity to ask him about the window had passed. His garden looked shabbier in the morning than it had when I arrived. The lavender was dull and brown, and the small patch of earth needed weeding.

"See you next Saturday?" he said.

I nodded. He stood at the door, watching me, while I fished through my purse for the keys and got in the car. Just as I was about to pull away, he ran out to the curb and knocked on my window.

"Comfortable shoes," he said.

"Comfortable shoes?" I thought for a moment he was providing me with a clue, offering some enigmatic puzzle that might lead me to Lila's true killer.

"On Saturday," he said. "It's a walk to Mangosteen."

"Of course."

Driving the winding road down from Diamond Heights, I remembered a story I'd once told Thorpe, over a picnic at Lone Mountain. The story was about Boris, the German shepherd that had been in our family since Lila and I were children. In 1986, he had become very ill. It was terrible to see him that way, and we did everything we could to make him comfortable. All his life, he had decided each night when he went to bed which of us he would grace with his presence—our parents, or me, or Lila. He would enter the chosen bedroom with a great show, plopping down on his haunches and sniffing the air, before sauntering over to the bed and climbing on. As much as we loved him, over the years, each one of us had come up with countless schemes to lure Boris into one of the other bedrooms; he was a terrible snorer and he took up so much room in the bed, it was hard to get any sleep with him curled up at your feet. But after he became ill, we stopped playing those games. We realized that, one day before too long, we were going to miss that loud, wet snoring and his unwieldy bulk at the foot of the bed.

A couple of weeks before Boris died, when it was clear that he might pass away at any time, we made a schedule so that someone would always be at home. None of us could bear the thought of Boris dying alone. If one of my parents couldn't arrange to work from home, either Lila or I was allowed to stay home from school. One Tuesday it was my turn. Our habit on those days was to stay next to Boris's side in the living room, from which he rarely budged. I'd done just that all day long, stroking his fur and reading aloud to him, when the doorbell rang.

It was Roxanne, a neighbor girl from two houses down. I'd babysat for her family for a few years, but since she'd turned ten a few months before her parents had started leaving Roxanne and her little brother, Robbie, home alone. The moment I opened the door, I knew something was terribly wrong. She had a look of sheer panic in her eyes, and all she said was, "Robbie's choking! Nobody's home!" I took a quick look back at Boris, who was staring up at me from his pallet on the living room floor. "I'll be right back," I promised. Boris let out a faint sound, lifted his head, and attempted to move. I could tell he was about to try to follow me, even though he'd not moved more than a few inches at a time in days. "Stay," I said, then bolted out the door and ran to Roxanne's house, where I found six-year-old Robbie, whom I'd never liked very much, writhing and blue-faced on the kitchen floor. I lifted him to his knees and did the Heimlich maneuver, and a big chunk of something flew out of his mouth. Roxanne, who was shaking and crying at this point, declared, "It was a frozen banana. I told him not to eat it!" I made sure Robbie was all right, told Roxanne to call her mother, and then raced home.

When I got there, Boris was lying on the floor of the entryway, perfectly still, eyes open but vacant. He wasn't breathing. He had no pulse. While I was performing the Heimlich on the bratty kid down the street, Boris had died trying to get to me. Even though my parents commended me for coming to Robbie's rescue, I never forgave myself for not being there for Boris, for letting him die alone.

Years ago, when I told the story to Thorpe during the picnic, he had listened intently. When I was finished, he remained silent for several seconds. I expected him to say something about what a sad story it was. I was shocked, then, when he finally spoke. "Wow," he said. "What a perfect ending."

*There is an office on the third floor of Sloan Hall at Stanford,* Thorpe had written in the final chapter of *Murder by the Bay. In the office sits a man—tall, imposing, the kind of man whose very presence changes the chemistry in a room. His concentration is as fierce as his ambition. At this moment, perhaps, he is working on the Goldbach Conjecture, certain that he will one day find the proof. When he does, there will be no one to share the glory.*

Looking back, I realized I should have put two and two together long ago. Thorpe hadn't discovered the ending in the process of writing the book. He had written the book toward his perfect ending.

# *Twenty-two*

∞

When I got home at half past six, I threw my clothes into the washing machine, then showered to get the smell of Thorpe's house off my skin. Even though he hadn't smoked for two months, I came home reeking of stale cigarettes.

It was still too early to call the phone number he had given me. Despite my exhaustion, I knew I wouldn't be able to sleep, so I took Lila's notebook from its hiding place beneath my bed and drove to Hayes Valley. I parked on Octavia and walked down the narrow alley, past the graffiti-spattered mechanic shops, past the black leather corsets on display in the windows of Dark Garden. A line stretched into the alley outside the Bluebottle coffee kiosk. On more than one occasion I'd seen unsuspecting customers step up to the counter and order a "half-caf double latte" or "short soy hazelnut cap," only to be subtly rebuked by the barista, whose attitude made it clear that if they wanted some hyped-up, tricked-out excuse for a good, solid cup of coffee, they could take their business to Starbucks. I'd never been much for the bells and whistles myself, and couldn't imagine watering my *Coffea arabica* down with soy milk or injecting it with flavored syrups. Bluebottle had no seating, just a small counter perched over the sidewalk, but in a way this added to the place's charm.

I breathed deeply, enjoying the huge aroma of the Yemen Sana'ani, before taking my first sip. I tasted hints of apricot, tobacco, wine, and spice. The first sip of the morning was always the best, when I could feel the cobwebs of my mind clearing, the blood rushing to my head. I tuned the world out and opened Lila's notebook, determined, once again, to try to make sense of it.

On the page where I'd left off, Lila

had written down the Continuum Hypothesis: *There is no infinite set with a cardinal number between that of the small infinite set of integers and the large infinite set of real numbers.*

The next couple of pages contained notes on the problem's history. I was reminded of a conversation we had late one night in her bedroom, after our parents had gone to bed. I couldn't quite place when the conversation had occurred—maybe weeks before she died, maybe months?—but I remembered the gist of it.

The Continuum Hypothesis was special in that it was the first problem on David Hilbert's famous list of twenty-three unsolved problems, which he proposed in 1900. In the early sixties, someone had proved that the Continuum Hypothesis could never be determined to be either true or false. But the famous mathematician Paul Erdos had another take on it. His thought was that, if there were such a thing as an infinite intelligence, it might have the knowledge, which is lacking in humans, to decide whether the hypothesis was true or false.

"So unless the human race somehow manages to get infinitely smarter," Lila said, "the planet will die out without us solving this basic problem about infinity."

"What if your Goldbach Conjecture is the same sort of problem?" I asked. "What if you spend the next thirty years pursuing a proof that doesn't exist?"

"Then at least I'll know I tried," Lila said. "At least I'll know I did everything I could, and I didn't give up."

Every day since my meeting with Mc-Connell, I had come up against the limits of my own knowledge, the frailty of my imagination. If the situation had been reversed—if it were my body that was found in the woods—I knew that Lila would not have taken some story in a book at face value. With determination, she would have examined the facts and methodically pieced the puzzle together. I was convinced that she wouldn't have stopped until she knew the truth. And I was certain it wouldn't have taken her twenty years to begin the search.

At eight a.m., I took the slip of paper from my wallet and dialed the phone number. A woman answered on the second ring. "Good morning," I said. "Is this the number for Mr. James Wheeler?"

"This is Delia Wheeler. Are you calling about a bill?"

"No."

A dog barked in the background. "Are you sure? Because the only person who ever called him James was his mother, God rest her."

"I promise I'm not a bill collector."

"This is Jimmy's number, then. Who am I speaking to?"

"You don't know me, but our paths crossed a long time ago. Lila Enderlin was my sister."

"Who?"

"Lila Enderlin."

She paused. I could hear the dog, closer now, panting near the phone.

"We don't know anything about that," Delia said.

"I'd just like to come by and talk to Mr. Wheeler for a few minutes, please."

"The police talked to him thirty years ago," she said. "He told them everything."

"Twenty," I said.

"What?"

"It was twenty years ago that Lila died."

Another pause. "I could've sworn it was 1979. Lord, if my mind goes, too, we're sure up the creek."

"Are you still living on Moultrie?" I asked.

"We are."

"I can come by anytime."

I fully expected her to shoot me down, at which point I'd have to start pleading, so I was surprised when she said, "Well, I guess we'll be here all day. Jimmy can't go out anymore and I don't like to leave him alone."

"I'll be there in an hour. Thank you so much for seeing me."

The house on Moultrie was a brown-shingled cottage with dark yellow trim, the front door situated just a few feet from the sidewalk. The street was packed with cars, so I had to drive around for a couple of minutes before finding a spot.

I was just about to ring the bell when the door opened. A tiny, pale woman, about four foot eleven and no more than ninety-five pounds, stood before me in a Google T-shirt and black pants. Her long brown hair was in a ponytail, and she wore pink blush and matching pink lipstick. She was even younger than I expected—probably in her early sixties.

"Ellie Enderlin," she said, studying my face. "My goodness." She seemed about to say something else, but instead she just stepped aside to let me in.

"Thank you for letting me come over on such short notice."

"Well, I doubt I can help you, but it's nice to have a visitor."

To the right of the entryway was a blue curtain, partially opened to reveal a nook just big enough for a bed. On a narrow table at the foot of the bed was a small television, the lights of which played over a yellow quilt. No sound came from the TV. There was someone in the bed—James Wheeler, I assumed—but because of the curtain I could only see his feet, white and bony. Next to the feet, a small black dog slept. We passed through the entryway into a small, immaculate living room. It was a shotgun house, with the kitchen in the back, and a bathroom off the kitchen. A tea kettle rattled on the stove.

"Sorry for the mess," she said. "I didn't have time to clean."

"It looks perfect." I sniffed the air— ginger and cinnamon. "What smells so good?"

"Oh, that's just coffee cake. I'd have made you lunch if you came later."

"You didn't have to do that."

"I grew up in Mississippi," she said, opening the oven to examine the cake. "My mother would roll over in her grave if I had a guest over and didn't offer them something to eat. Just last week Matthew—that's our oldest—took me to a lady's house out in Pinole to buy a wheelchair that he found on the computer. For Jimmy, you know. The lady didn't so much as offer us a glass of water."

Only after we were sitting at the table with the cake arranged on a pretty china platter between us did Delia Wheeler bring up the purpose of my visit.

"It's that Peter McConnell fellow that did it," she said, looking into my eyes with conviction. "I read that book, it's clear as day he was the one. It was a terrible thing. I feel so for your parents, hon. For you, too, but especially your parents. I can't imagine if somebody did something like that to one of my boys. It still breaks my heart to think of it."

I nodded. "It's been a long time, but not a day goes by that I don't think about my sister."

"If I remember correctly, that Mc-Connell fellow just up and disappeared. Did they ever end up arresting him?"

"No."

"That's a shame. Nothing can bring her back, I know, but if it was my own, I'd want somebody to be held account-able."

She sipped her tea and chewed thoughtfully. "Honestly, hon, I'm not sure why you're here. I don't see what we can do for you."

"I understand your husband talked to my sister the night before she died. I thought he might be able to fill in some blanks for me."

"I wish he could," Mrs. Wheeler said, "but Jimmy had a stroke three years ago. He hasn't spoken since. He used to communicate by writing, but he can't even do that anymore." She stretched her fingers and fiddled with her wedding ring. "Jimmy wasn't in the book. I remember. I went out and got it from the library as soon as it came out, and I read the whole thing cover to cover. I was scared out of my mind that he might be mentioned by name. I worried he couldn't handle it, after everything that had happened. I'm just wondering, hon, how did you know about him?"

"I talked to a detective who worked on the case," I said. The truth was far too complicated.

She frowned. "Then you must know what happened to Jimmy after."

I shook my head.

"The police took him in for questioning. It was horrible. They showed up one night when we were getting the kids ready for bed and hauled him off like some kind of criminal. I stayed up all night, praying and crying. The kids were scared to death. When he came back the next morning, he looked awful. They hadn't let him sleep, hadn't given him anything to eat. They tried to make him confess. They just kept saying, 'You're the janitor. What's the janitor doing talking to a pretty young college student?'

"But he was just like that, you see. He talked to anybody who would listen. And I'll be the first to admit, he talked way too much. Once he had your ear, he wouldn't let go. Drove me crazy, but now that he can't talk, I miss it. Your sister was such a sweet girl, she always said hello to him in the hallway. He really liked her, but not in the way the police wanted to believe. We had two boys, and Jimmy had always wanted a girl. He told me once, before all this happened, that if we had a daughter, he wanted her to be like Lila. She was a good girl, he said, always acted modestly, never talked loud or tried to attract attention to herself."

I sat quietly, listening. It was easy to believe that Lila would have been friendly with the janitor. She was most comfortable around people who didn't fit into her peer group, people who wouldn't demand more than a few minutes of her time, who wouldn't ask for her phone number or invite her to a movie.

"Did the police ever talk to him again?"

She shook her head. "Oh, there was no need to. The reason they kept Jimmy so long that night was that he wouldn't give them an alibi. He kept refusing to tell them where he had been on the night she died. But after a while they started getting rough with him, saying real terrible things, and he realized they honestly believed he could have done it. That's when he told them about his second job—he worked at a steel mill in South City. We were having a real hard time back then, poor as church mice and a third baby on the way. He was working two full-time jobs to keep us afloat. But there was a strict policy at Stanford back then against moonlighting. That job was our bread and butter, and Jimmy couldn't afford to lose it. He knew if he told the cops about the steel mill, it would make it back to his boss at Stanford, and he'd get fired."

"So what happened?"

"He finally gave in and told the police, and they went out and talked to his boss on the night job, and sure enough, he'd gone straight from one job to the next. He clocked out at Stanford at seven p.m., then clocked in at the steel mill in South City at eight-thirty and worked all night. After that they left him alone."

She reached across the table and took my hand. "I know why you're here, hon, and I don't blame you for trying to figure some things out. But I want you to know, it wasn't Jimmy. You believe me, don't you?"

I did.

"It tore him up what happened to her, and that they thought he could have done it," she said. "Things fell apart after that. Within weeks he lost his day job at Stanford, I miscarried, and we almost lost the house. It changed him. He'd been so strong before, so eager. He grew up real poor, got a late start in life, and he had this idea that if he just worked hard we'd be able to move up in the world.

"The crazy thing is, now this little place is worth a fortune, but we'll never sell. Jimmy hardly gets out of bed, he's got all sorts of problems with his lungs and everything else. He worked his whole life for something he'll never get to enjoy."

There was a thumping noise from the front room. "Oh, that's Jimmy," Mrs. Wheeler said. "Two thumps. That means he's thirsty." She got up and poured water into a glass.

"Thank you so much," I said, standing. I felt there was something else I had to say, even though I knew I was far too late. "I'm sorry your family got caught up in all this."

She smiled. "Well, what can you do? You just try to get by as best you can. Fortunately Jimmy and I were always pretty much head over heels for each other, that helps."

I followed her through the living room into the entryway. She pulled the curtain back, and there was James Wheeler, a skeleton of a man with a wild swirl of gray hair. The dog had climbed up onto the pillow beside his head. "I'm here, hon," Mrs. Wheeler said.

He looked up at me and for a moment, something flashed across his eyes. He raised an arm, as if to wave, but it dropped back to the sheet.

"I know," Mrs. Wheeler said, holding the glass of water to his lips. "She looks just like her sister, doesn't she?"

# Twenty-three

∞

On Saturday, as promised, I met Thorpe at Opera Plaza. When I arrived he was still signing books, a line of customers stretching through the store. He looked up, saw me, and mouthed "Ten minutes."

A good-looking guy walked into the store, carrying an ugly baby in a Maclaren backpack. He wore an expensive leather jacket, brown Skechers, and rocker jeans cut so low and tight it was a wonder he could walk. The baby wore a pink hat that said *Nader 2008.*

The guy's shaggy haircut and sideburns were too perfect to be real. He was of the class of young, disaffected San Francisco hipsters who had long baffled me with their seemingly unlimited supply of free time and money, none of which they appeared to spend on food. He turned and gave me a lopsided grin. "Who's the author?" he said.

"Andrew Thorpe."

"Any good?"

"I haven't read the book."

I excused myself and walked to the coffee shop attached to the store, where I bought a tin of chocolate-covered espresso beans. Back at the store, I popped one in my mouth and let the chocolate melt on my tongue. By the time Thorpe was finished, I'd had a dozen and was beginning to feel the buzz.

"Ready to walk?" he asked.

Half an hour later we were sitting at a little table at Mangosteen, crowded in on both sides by noisy lunchgoers. The place smelled of lemongrass.

"I recommend number ten," Thorpe said. "Cubed steak with potatoes over rice, or number twenty-two, same thing but with noodles."

I went with the noodles. The service was slow, but the food was good. Thorpe talked about a meeting he'd just had with his life coach before launching into a series of questions about my personal life. Without exactly knowing how it happened, I ended up telling him about Henry, our breakup in Guatemala three years before.

"Was he the one?" Thorpe asked.

I just shrugged, but he asked again. Reluctantly, I said, "I thought he was, at the time."

"Do you still think about him?"

"On occasion." The truth was I'd been thinking about him a lot lately, but that was none of Thorpe's business.

"Then he wasn't the one," Thorpe said. "If he was, you'd think of him every morning when you wake up. You'd think of him when you go to bed at night, when you drop off your dry-cleaning, when you're sitting in a movie."

"I saw James Wheeler."

"You went through with it." He sounded surprised.

"Why didn't you tell me he'd been cleared by his alibi?"

"Was he? I don't remember that. Like I said, he just wasn't that interesting."

He swirled the last bite of steak around in the sauce and popped it in his mouth. The server came over with the check, and Thorpe handed her his credit card before I could protest. "I'm stuffed," he said, patting his stomach. "What say we take a walk, work off the lunch?"

The sun was out, scorching the sidewalk, glinting off the parked cars that lined the street. I took off my sweater and twisted my hair up in a bun to get it off my neck. The Tenderloin smelled atrocious in the heat, like dog shit, petrol, and baked piss. Guys urinating on the sidewalk were one of the commonest features of the neighborhood, second only to drug-addled prostitutes working their trade at all hours. This was a part of the city I'd never learned to love.

We walked South on Larkin, block after block in silence.

By the time we got to Market, my shoes were beginning to pinch and I wondered where Thorpe was taking me. Every minute with him made me feel uneasy, but I was determined to ask him for more names.

"Do you like horse races?" Thorpe asked. "I sometimes go to Bay Meadows. It's more fun than you think. I was planning to go next Saturday. You should come."

Fortunately, I didn't have to answer, because just then we were overtaken by a posse of a dozen men linked together by a complex matrix of chains, clad in leather vests, kilts, and combat boots.

"Oh, I forgot, it's the weekend of the Folsom Street Fair," Thorpe said.

I had the feeling he hadn't forgotten, that this had been our destination all along.

We continued walking south. Within a few blocks, we were caught up in the crowd: men in leather chaps with nothing underneath, women in painful corsets, towering trannies in six-inch heels. I felt out of place in my knee-length summer skirt and T-shirt, like Exhibit A in the Suburban Soccer Mom display at the Museum of Mainstream Morality.

"If I'd known this was our destination, I'd have worn something a bit more dramatic," I said.

"You look great. Maybe people will think you're being ironic."

Eventually we came to a barricade in the middle of the street.

"Three bucks to enter," said an extremely tall man in a bit and harness. He whinnied, stomped his big foot, and shook his hair extensions. He was so convincingly horselike, I wondered if he dressed like this every day.

"Well, since we're here already," Thorpe said, fishing a five and a single out of his wallet.

One thing I loved about San Francisco was that, when it came to public exhibition of all varieties, the vibe was decidedly laissez-faire. At any moment, you might wander into what seemed like a scene from a movie. Years ago, I'd been folding my towels at a Laundromat on Diamond when the theme song from *Grease* came on the radio, and all five patrons literally burst into spontaneous song. If you had the time and inclination, you could live your life as a picaresque without ever leaving the city.

Thorpe turned his attention to a whipping demonstration going on at a booth a few feet away. The sun was oppressive, the smell of leather and mysterious lubricants overpowering. Someone swatted me on the backside with a wooden paddle, but when I turned to identify the spanker, I met a sea of guileless faces. I felt like Alice in a freaky San Francisco version of Wonderland, where the Mad Hatter and all his loopy friends were into S&M.

And then I saw a familiar face.

"Jack?"

He wrapped me in a hug. "Ellie. God, it's been ages."

His thick black hair hung down to his shoulders. He wore a Mickey Mouse T-shirt and brown leather pants. "You look great," I said, and he did. Thorpe beamed his most confident smile. "This is Andrew Thorpe," I said. "And this is my friend Jack, from college."

"Jackson," he corrected me. That's when I remembered how he'd insisted on being called Jackson, even though his actual given name was just Jack.

We'd met at the beginning of my senior year and had been together morning and night for several weeks before he went to Senegal with the Peace Corps. It was good to see him. The city was full of men whom I'd had brief relationships with in the year following Lila's death. Every now and then, I'd run into one of them. It was always interesting, if somewhat unsettling, to see who they'd become, how they turned out.

A tall blonde in a red leather dress came up and put her arm around Jack's waist. "This is my wife, Stacy," he said. To my surprise, he introduced me as "an old girlfriend."

There was an awkward pause. "The kids are at home with the sitter in Atherton," Stacy said.

"Kids?"

"We've got two. First grade and preschool. They think we're at a company picnic."

Stacy was friendly and quick, and I got the feeling that when she wasn't dressed like a hooker, she wore serious business suits and pulled in a serious income—maybe as an attorney or a realtor. But I remembered Jack/Jackson as a skinny guy with a joint in one hand and a book in the other, lounging naked on his ratty mattress in the aftermath of sex. It was strange to think of him married with kids.

He handed me his business card. "Give me a call. We'll have you over for dinner. You can meet the little monsters."

"That would be great," I said, but I knew I'd never call.

Thorpe and I pushed past booths selling giant dildos and gold-plated cock rings, vendors peddling anatomically vivid funnel cakes, posters advertising special events for various fetishes. A woman in a rubber nursing uniform thrust a flier into my hand. It read, *Meet Your Submissive. First consultation free.*

Finally we came to the end of the street and exited the fair. I was trying to figure out how to phrase my request when Thorpe said, "I've got another one for you."

"Pardon?"

"Another name. Something else I didn't put in the book. There was a car out at Armstrong Woods around the time Lila went missing, a white Chevy. Somebody thought it looked weird and took down a license plate, reported it to the cops."

He pulled a slip of paper out of his pocket and handed it to me. On it was printed a name: William Boudreaux.

"He was some sort of musician, went by Billy. I originally planned to follow up on it, but then I just got busy. And anyway, by the time I discovered it, I already liked where the book was going."

I folded the paper carefully and slid it into my wallet. "Thank you." We walked for a couple of minutes in silence before I said what was on my mind. "I have to ask—why are you doing this?"

Thorpe smiled. "I guess I've got this crazy thought in my head that if I do you a good turn, maybe I can win you over."

We kept walking. The crowds thinned out, the fog moved in. When we got back to Opera Plaza, where my car was parked, I said, "Hey, before I go, could you clear one thing up for me?"

"Yeah?"

"Your house. The view from your desk."

"Ah, that."

"Well?"

"Would you believe it's a coincidence?"

"No."

He looked away. For a moment, he actually seemed to be blushing. "When it came up for sale, I'd gone almost two years without writing a word. I'd sit down to type, and I'd just stare at the blank page for hours. This had gone on for so long, I'd finally decided to abandon writing altogether and go back to teaching. I was visiting a friend in the neighborhood one Sunday, when we drove by and saw the open house sign. He wanted to have a look, so I joined him. I wasn't looking to buy, and it's not really even my style—too modern, somewhat cold—but when I realized I could see your house from the upstairs window, I knew I had to have it, and I knew that the room with the view would be my office."

"That's a little creepy."

"Maybe, but it worked. Within two months of moving in, I had three chapters of a new book. I did my writing at night, but only on those nights when the light was on in your room."

"By then, it wasn't even my room," I said. "My mother had turned it into an office."

He rested his hand on the roof of my car. "Oh, I knew you weren't there anymore. But when the light was on, I could pretend you were. I imagined you sitting at your old desk, reading books, listening to music. I at least had the illusion of your being nearby. And sometimes you were. Until your mother moved away last year, I rarely went out on Thursday nights. That was the one night of the week when I could be almost certain of seeing you. Even though I couldn't speak to you, I still could conceive of an imaginary line running from my desk to you. I would watch you down there, standing on the sidewalk in front of the house with your mother. I wondered what you were talking about. I'm somewhat ashamed to admit that there were times when I wondered if my name came up."

"You must understand that's weird," I said. "Very weird."

What I didn't tell him was that even the one man in my life who had truly loved me, Henry, had never been so devoted to me. In comparison with Thorpe, Henry had given up on me relatively easily. Did obsession breed a deeper loyalty than love?

He rubbed at an imaginary spot on my car. "What can I say? You were my Zelda, my George Sand, my Stella. My books, the house, the mild celebrity I've enjoyed—it's all because of you."

It was easy to see he'd put me on a pedestal. If the circumstances had been different—if his book had been about anything other than Lila—I might have been flattered. I could see how, under the right conditions, it might be really nice to be someone's muse.

Finally, I unlocked the driver's-side door, but before I could open it, Thorpe did it for me. "Really," he said, once I was settled behind the wheel, "it might not be a bad idea to look up Billy Boudreaux."

# *Twenty-four*

$\infty$

"What about Thorpe?" Henry asked me once.

It was December 8, 2004, the fifteenth anniversary of Lila's death, and we had just visited her grave with my parents.

It was a cool day in Palo Alto, the sun shining after a night of heavy rain. As there were no civilian cemeteries in San Francisco, we had been at a loss as to where to bury Lila. We ended up choosing Alta Mesa Memorial Park because it was the closest cemetery to Stanford. Even though it was a longer drive from the city than the large cemeteries in Colma and Daly City, it seemed like a more fitting place. We liked that trees had grown up around some of the older headstones, and that the grounds were well-kept without appearing overly manicured.

Much of that day is a blur. I remember that we rode to the cemetery in Henry's Jeep Cherokee, because my car was in the shop. I remember that he had made a mixed CD for the drive, which began with Lila's favorite song, Elvis Costello's "Peace, Love & Understanding," and ended with Gram Parsons's "She Once Lived Here." I remember that he held my hand while we drove, and that we had to stop at a 76 station in Burlingame because the gas light came on. I remember that, when we arrived, we had a difficult time finding Lila's grave, despite the fact that I'd been there many times, and I felt embarrassed that I got lost. Surely, if the situation were reversed, Lila would have had a clear picture in her mind of the layout of the cemetery, would have been able to remember not only the plot number, but exactly which path we needed to take to get there.

After wandering for a few minutes, we finally saw my parents standing in the distance, and made our way to them. My mother was wearing a navy dress and matching knee-high boots. She'd gotten a new haircut, with bangs, that made her look younger than she had in years. My father was dressed in a suit, and it took me a moment to realize he was going to the office later that day. It angered me that he would treat it like a regular day, that he would abandon my mother on such an important anniversary. Even though they had seen each other rarely in the five years since their divorce, this was one day I believed they should be together. When I pulled him aside and whispered, "I think Mom would really like it if you hung around today," he replied, "Actually, sweetheart, that's the last thing your mother would want." He gave me a quick squeeze on the shoulder and walked away. And I couldn't be angry anymore, because he had used that simple term of endearment left over from my childhood, a word he hadn't used for me since Lila died.

It was early that afternoon, while Henry and I were eating lunch with my mother at Maven Lane Café, Lila's favorite restaurant, that he posed the question: "What about Thorpe?"

I sat across the table from the two of them. I shot him a look, but he didn't seem to understand.

"What about him?" my mother said warily.

"I just wonder about his motives," Henry said. "I wonder why he went to great lengths to make a case against Peter McConnell."

"It wasn't that hard to do, Henry," my mother said. I recognized the tone of voice—I'd heard it when I watched her trying cases in court. It meant he was on thin ice. I tried to telepathically will him to back off, but he continued.

"I'm just saying, did anyone ever look at him?"

"Look at him?" my mother asked.

"You deal with crime all the time," Henry said. "Surely the person who appears at first glance to be guilty isn't always the one."

"Henry," I said. "This isn't the time."

"Actually," my mother said, "nine times out of ten, the person who appears to be guilty is."

Henry's face flushed.

"Please pass the salt," I said.

But it was too late. My mother had laid down her fork and had turned to face Henry. "Go ahead."

Henry took a sip of water and looked at me, as if I might rescue him. But I knew my mother. Now that he'd baited her into this, he wasn't getting out until he'd made his case, whatever it was.

"I just can't help but think that Thorpe's interest in the whole thing was bizarre. In the book, he tried to make it sound as if McConnell had something to gain from Lila's death, but in truth McConnell could only lose. His career was at stake, his marriage. Everything about him pointed to his being a rational man, the kind of person who would weigh the consequences of his actions. To me, something about it just doesn't add up. Technically, the only person who came out at an advantage in the end was Thorpe."

"Where is this coming from, anyway?" I asked. "Why on earth are you bringing this up now?"

"I saw something in *Esquire* last

week," he said. "An article about the three murders last year in Golden Gate Park."

"The homeless men who were killed in their sleep?" my mother asked. I remembered it, too. It had been a big local news item for a couple of months. People in the Outer Sunset, near where the murders occurred, had begun to get nervous.

"Yes," Henry said. "The article was by Thorpe."

"Big deal," I said. "That's how he makes a living. Other people's tragedies."

"But there was something strange about the tone of the article," Henry said, "something almost gleeful. I got the feeling Thorpe actually took pleasure in the details. The police have never linked the three murders—one was a stabbing, one was a shooting, and the other was a strangulation—but Thorpe kept referring to the Golden Gate Park serial killer, as if it was a given that they were all related. As if he knew something no one else did."

It was unlike Henry to have such bad

timing, such lack of subtlety. I regretted bringing him along. My mother had enough to contend with on the anniversary of Lila's death. She didn't need this. "You're coming out of left field," I said. "Leave it alone."

My mother picked up her fork again and began moving her salad around on her plate. "It's okay, Ellie," she said. "It's not like it's something I've never thought of."

"It's not?"

She looked at me, her eyes soft. "Oh, I don't think there's any credibility to it. But I've thought of pretty much everything. Every possibility, no matter how far-fetched. In my mind, I've, diagrammed a hundred different scenarios. For what it's worth, I do believe, in my heart, that it was probably Peter McConnell. But if I were to look at it objectively, as a prosecutor, I'd have to say the case against him is flimsy. There's only one thing I know for certain." She reached across the table and squeezed my hand. "Not a day goes by that I don't think about your sister. Fifteen years, not one day."

# Twenty-five

∞

There were over a hundred hits for "Billy Boudreaux" on Google, but when I added the search term "San Francisco," it narrowed the results to half a dozen. One of the links was to a sparse Wikipedia page dedicated to a band called Potrero Sound Station. Two brief paragraphs identified it as a San Francisco band that formed in 1975 and was defunct by 1979. The person I was looking for received a single mention— *Billy Boudreaux on bass*.

A search for "Potrero Sound Station" turned up a fan site, which had last been updated five years before. The site was devoted mostly to the lead singer, who went by the name Sound. Following the breakup of the band, Sound had embarked upon a lackluster solo career before opening a mechanic shop in Aurora, Colorado. His real name was Kevin Walsh. His first solo album in sixteen years, *Engine Days,* had been released in 2003 and had received a favorable review from an alternative Denver weekly, as well as *Time Out* Scotland. The writer lamented the fact that the album had been passed over by all of the major publications, save for a one-line mention in a trivia question in *Paste* magazine. According to the site, the other original band member, Drew Letheid, was living with his banker wife and two children in Greenwich, and he never gave interviews. As for Billy Boudreaux, the site said only "whereabouts unknown."

It didn't take long to find a Walsh Mechanics in Aurora, Colorado. It was four-thirty p.m. mountain time when I dialed the number.

"Walsh here," a voice said. "What can I do for you?"

"Kevin Walsh?"

"That's me."

"I'm calling about the band," I blurted.

"What band?"

"Potrero Sound Station."

He laughed. "Now there's a blast from the past. Are you with VH1? No offense, but I'm not interested in going on *Bands Reunited.* That was a long time ago, a totally different life."

"I'm just an old acquaintance of Billy Boudreaux," I said.

"Acquaintance? Sounds like he owes you money. You might want to take a number."

"It's nothing like that. I've just been wondering what became of him." Walsh hadn't hung up yet. I figured that was a good sign and plunged on. "Do you by any chance know where he is?"

"Sorry, doll. You're asking the wrong person. I haven't heard from him in decades. He got messed up in some bad stuff, you know."

"What kind of bad stuff?"

"Coke, meth, whatever."

"Do you know if he stayed in San Francisco after the band broke up?"

"He was there for a few years, but I don't know how long. He alienated all of us pretty well. Just became a major asshole, impossible to be around. Sad, too, because before he got messed up with the drugs, he was the nicest guy you could hope to meet, genius on bass." He paused. "You know, we got a mention in a *Rolling Stone* article in, I don't know, '84 or so. Ben Fong-Torres was the guy who wrote the piece. I was already out here by then, had a bad taste in my mouth from those years with the band, and Drew had gone corporate. Fong-Torres ended up interviewing Billy." He paused for a minute. "I guess that's pretty much all I got for you."

"Thanks," I said. "You've been helpful."

"You bet. If your car ever breaks down in Colorado, you know who to call."

I knew about Ben Fong-Torres. I'd seen the movie *Almost Famous*, and over the years I'd read a number of his profiles of famous musicians. He still lived in San Francisco, where he did a weekly radio show. Four days later, I found myself standing in front of his towering three-story house at the top of a hill in the Castro. I'd contacted him

through KRFC and he'd e-mailed right
back.

I rang the bell. The intercom crackled.
"Is this Miss Enderlin?" Ben's voice
was deep and resonant, just like on the
radio. I imagined, with a voice like that,
he'd never had any trouble meeting
women.

"Hi, yes."

"You're an hour early. You'll have to
come back later."

"I'm sorry," I said, before I realized he
was joking.

"Elevator's straight ahead and on
your left. Take it to the third floor." I
thought that was a joke, too, but after
he buzzed me through the entrance, I
saw that, indeed, there was a small elevator, outfitted with leopard-print carpet and gold-painted walls. I climbed
in, punched 3, and checked my teeth
for lipstick. I hated riding elevators in
my hometown, imagined worst-case
scenarios in which the big one struck.
In the aftermath of the earthquake, as
sirens wailed and aftershocks shook
the building, I'd be trapped alone between floors while the building crum-

bled around me. Lila used to make fun of my overactive imagination. She'd tried to reassure me by calculating the probability that I'd actually be in an elevator at the exact moment of a major earthquake, but logic did nothing to quell my fears.

The elevator shuddered to a stop and the door opened. Ben stood in front of me in black pants and a gray shirt, looking dapper and not a day over forty-five. I quickly did the math. He'd begun writing for the fledgling *Rolling Stone* in 1967, which meant he had to be at least sixty. Maybe rock and roll had kept him young.

"Welcome to the manse," he said, grinning.

I thrust a box into his hand. "I brought you something," I said. "From Chow. It's the half-chicken with mashed potatoes. I saw the interview in *SanFrancisco* magazine where you said it was your favorite."

"Thanks. You shouldn't have."

I suddenly felt stupid for bringing him an entrée, but I hated to arrive empty-handed and couldn't think of an appropriate house gift for a man who surely had everything he desired. Normally, if I wanted to give a casual, heartfelt gift, I'd make someone a mixed CD, but I figured making a mixed CD for Ben Fong-Torres would be like making *boeuf bourguignon* for Anthony Bourdain.

"Make yourself at home," he said. "I'll go plate this up."

The living room, like the elevator, was carpeted in a leopard print. The first thing I noticed was the view, a wall of windows facing north. At the far bottom of the hill the neon marquee of the Castro Theatre blinked on and off; the missing T on the sign gave San Francisco's grandest old movie theater a pleasingly shabby look. Judging from the sign, you'd never guess that the interior of the theater was a throwback to baroque splendor, or that an organ rose from the orchestra pit each night before the seven-o'clock showing. It was a clear night, and the Golden Gate Bridge was visible beyond the twinkling city lights.

I walked over to the windows for a

better perspective. In the patchwork of streets below I could see familiar houses, the roofs of apartment buildings I'd known all my life. It was strange to gaze down on my city from such a tremendous height. I knew these streets intimately, from the ground up. I'd walked the sidewalks thousands of times, looking up into the windows, spying on the lives of families. Our own family, I knew, must have been spied on this way as well by countless passersby. When I was growing up, the windows of our living room were always uncovered. My mother loved the natural light and the bottlebrush tree beside our driveway, loved being able to glance out into the street and see friends and strangers walking by. After Lila died, she put up shutters. For the first several years after that, the shutters were rarely open, so that our once cheerful house became dim and sunless.

I imagined the people in the houses far below, looking up at the house on the hill, making up stories about the lives of the people who lived here. Did

it ever occur to Ben, when he stood before his windows surveying the brilliant
city, that someone might be watching?
Most of us go about our lives with a be-
lief in our own privacy. I had done so
myself for many years. But then I sat in
Thorpe's office, looking through binoculars at my old bedroom window. And
just weeks ago, in a café in Diriomo, I
ran into a man who had been aware of
my presence in the town long before I
was aware of his. Nearly two decades
before, in the restaurant in North
Beach, I had been the voyeur, watching
Peter McConnell during his Monday
lunches. How far did this network of
spying eyes extend? We were all the
watchers and the watched. Privacy
was just a comforting illusion.

As I stood staring out the window,
lost in thought, I glanced up and saw
Ben's reflection in the glass. He stood
completely still, hands in his pockets.
Some moments are almost too perfect,
their symmetry too precise. I recognized this as one of those moments: as
I was looking out at San Francisco, Ben

was looking at me. Our eyes met in the glass.

"Funny," he said. "When someone walks in the house for the first time, it never takes more than five seconds for them to gravitate to that exact spot."

"Great view."

"It is. Now if only the city would invest in a gigantic fog blower so it could look this good all the time."

Ben had insisted on pouring me a glass of 2002 Malbec from a friend's winery in Patagonia. We sat at the breakfast table off the kitchen, eating chicken and mashed potatoes, which he had split onto two plates, and sipping our wine. I hardly knew him and yet I liked him already. I appreciated the casual way he received me into his home, the immediate intimacy he invited by joking with me as if I was an old friend. I could tell he was a person who lived at ease in the world, a talent I'd always envied. I would have preferred to live that way myself, and was often embarrassed by my own formality, a slight but unnerving social stiffness that I could never quite get past.

I sipped my wine. "How is it?" he asked.

"It's good."

"A bit fruity for my taste, but not bad," he said. "The chicken on the other hand is excellent. Do you cook?"

"A bit. What about you?"

"I know a few tricks."

The phone rang and he went into the living room to answer it. The breakfast nook opened onto a small den, which was outfitted with a television, comfortable chairs, and a karaoke machine. A couple of Emmys stood atop the TV, which was on, tuned silently to the TiVo menu. I took the opportunity of Ben's absence to look at what he'd recorded: *Top Chef*, *Project Runway*, *Storytellers* with Elvis Costello, *Waterland*, and *The Last Waltz*, Martin Scorsese's classic documentary about The Band.

I was still craning my neck to see the TiVo screen when Ben returned. "You're busted." He picked up the remote from the couch and turned off the TV. "So, you're here about Billy Boudreaux?"

I told him about Lila, and about Boudreaux's white Chevy parked out at Armstrong Woods. I reached into my purse and pulled out a copy of the article from *Rolling Stone,* which I'd dug up at the library. I handed the article to Ben.

"Ah, yes, I remember this," he said. "Billy was living in the Lower Haight in those days. We met at a bar in his neighborhood. This was '83 or '84, but he was still living like it was the good old days"—Ben ended his sentence with a line from a song—"all strung out on heroin on the outskirts of town." His singing voice was clear and deep. Maybe all that karaoke paid off. "Know that one?" he asked.

It felt like it was a test. I was glad I knew the answer. "Warren Zevon. 'Carmelita.' "

"Not bad." He dropped the article on the table. "I asked Billy, off the record, what the hell he was doing. He was an amazing bass player, and he was throwing it all away. He told me he was going to clean up his act, and I remember exactly what I said to him—'I hope

you do, but the odds are against you.'
By then I'd covered the deaths of Jim
Morrison, Janis Joplin, Elvis for *Rolling
Stone.* I could see where he was
headed."

"At the end of the interview," I said,
"the two of you agree to meet up exactly one year later at the Top of the
Mark. He says he'll be a different man
by then. He even promises to buy you
a drink. Did that ever happen?"

Ben shook his head. "I waited forty-
five minutes and he never showed.
There I was at four o'clock on a Wednesday afternoon, drinking Scotch
alone at the Top of the Mark. It was just
me and a bunch of rowdy guys from a
bachelor party. I figured Billy was either
dead or strung out in some motel in the
Tenderloin."

"And that was it? You never saw him
again?"

Ben thought for a moment. One thing
I'd noticed in talking to him was that
there were no false starts in his speech,
no *um*s or *ah*s or other verbal tics. His
words and sentences came out pre-

cisely, as if they'd been planned. It must have been his radio training.

"I did run into him once, in the rhythm and blues section of Amoeba Records. He was dressed strangely, in overalls and boots. He shook my hand, apologized profusely for standing me up that day at Top of the Mark, and offered to buy me a drink. We walked over to Zam Zam and sipped martinis in the back room.

"That was in the days when the bartender refused to serve anything other than martinis. Billy made the mistake of ordering a bourbon and Coke, he got into a huff with the bartender, and we almost got kicked out of the place. He eventually settled on a martini, and then he proceeded to tell me the story of his past few years. He'd hit rock bottom in the late eighties, and by ninety, having had a brush with mortality, as he put it, he finally decided to get sober and pull his act together. He moved back to Petaluma to work on his brother's dairy farm—apparently he'd lived there off and on over the years. That's what he was doing when I ran into him. He had come into the city to see old friends, but the reunion hadn't gone well, and he was on his way back to the farm that afternoon. As much as he loved the city, he felt that it was a dangerous place for him, too many of his old habits lurking in the doorways, I guess.

"I was happy to see him sober, but I got the feeling he was still fragile, like his mind could crack at any moment and send him spiraling back into the abyss. In the conversation he kept referring to his demons. It was freaking me out a little bit."

"What was he like as a musician?"

Ben thought for a moment. "He never quite got there, but he could have been a great one. When I saw him, he hadn't entirely given up on the music. I was in a hurry, due down at KSAN to interview Sheryl Crow, but he insisted that I follow him out to his car several blocks away so that he could give me a tape. It was something he'd recorded in his brother's basement, four new songs he'd written. I can't tell you how many people have given me tapes over the years—in San Francisco, half the young guys you run into on the street have a band and a tape. But this was one I actually wanted to hear, because I knew what Boudreaux had been capable of."

"How was it?"

"Pretty good. Nothing like the stuff with Potrero Sound Station, but there was definitely something to it. I might still have it lying around somewhere."

I followed him downstairs, where the hallway was covered with black-and-white wedding photos—Ben in a mustache and shaggy seventies hair, his wife, Dianne, looking like an inspired emblem of the times with her pixie haircut and flowy white dress.

"Great pictures," I said.

"Annie Leibovitz took them. There she is." He pointed to a photo of him and Dianne lying across a bed. His face was deadpan, and she was laughing, like he'd just told some fabulous joke. The camera was aimed at the mirror, and Leibovitz herself was in the corner of the frame, her camera covering a portion of her face. "There's Jann

Wenner," he said, pointing to another photo, "and this is Cameron Crowe."

The office was down the hall. It had huge windows, a built-in desk that wrapped around the room, and floor-to-ceiling shelves. On the walls were photos of Ben with Ray Charles, Johnny Cash, Bob Dylan, Jim Morrison, George Harrison, Janis Joplin, Grace Slick, Bill Clinton.

"Wow," I said. "You're like Zelig."

"I just happened to be in the right place at the right time. Used to be you could hardly walk the streets of San Francisco without running into an up-and-coming rock star."

"I just saw Damon Gough buying records last week at Street Light," I said. "And a couple of years ago, I saw Nick Cave on Ocean Beach. It was this weird, foggy day, no one out but the surfers, I'm sitting on a log watching the waves, and this tall, rail-thin figure dressed all in black comes striding down the beach toward me. It scared me until I realized who it was. He said hello, and I managed to mumble something stupid like 'Nice day for a walk.'

When I got home I checked the Pink Sheet—he was doing a show that night at the Fillmore."

"Oh, yeah," Ben said. "I was at that show, backstage. I interviewed him afterward. Nice guy."

"Oh, neat."

"Neat?" He grinned. I wanted to crawl under the desk. Being in Ben's presence made me feel like I'd lived a pretty boring life. It was another hazard of life in San Francisco: people of my generation were destined to feel uncool.

On the shelves of Ben's office were dozens of magazine files labeled by date and publication. While I browsed the shelves, he rifled through a desk drawer, looking for the tape.

"Are you in all of these magazines?" I asked.

"Yep."

"It must be pretty cool to leave a record of yourself behind in the world."

Ben looked up. "It's not a record of me, my dear. I'm just the observer."

I walked over and peered over his shoulder. There were hundreds of tapes in the drawer, which appeared to have no system of organization. After about ten minutes, he gave up.

"Sorry," he said. "I may have loaned it out."

Ben turned off the light and led me back upstairs. At the third-floor landing, he paused. "I'm curious," he said. "Why are you doing this now, after all this time?"

I didn't quite know how to answer. I could see how, from a stranger's perspective, it might look pointless. "Can I show you something?" I asked.

"Sure."

I retrieved my bag from the couch and pulled out Lila's notebook. I told Ben the story of the notebook, how it came to be in my possession. "It may sound weird," I said, "but having her notebook with me for the past few weeks, I've felt closer to Lila than I have since she died. It's almost like hearing her voice."

"I hear you."

"Ever heard of the Kepler Conjecture?"

"Nope."

I laid the notebook on the table and flipped through the pages. "It was first stated in 1611 by Johannes Kepler," I said. "Kepler became interested in the problem while he was corresponding with an Englishman named Thomas Harriot, who was trying to help his friend Sir Walter Raleigh figure out the best way to stack cannonballs on ship decks. The goal was to find the densest possible spherical arrangement, in order to get as many cannonballs as possible onto a ship."

"Okay," Ben said. He must have wondered where I was going with all this, but he listened patiently, as if it was perfectly normal for him to have a strange woman standing in his living room, lecturing him on math.

"Kepler's conjecture holds that the greatest density of stacked spheres that can be achieved is this." I held out the notebook for him to see Lila's notation:

$$\frac{\pi}{\sqrt{18}} \simeq 0.74048$$

"To achieve this density, the bottom level of the stack should be arranged in a hexagonal lattice, and the next layer should be placed on the lowest points atop the first layer. Each layer should follow this principle until the top layer of the pyramid—a single sphere—is reached—basically, the way grocers stack oranges."

"Okay," he said, nodding.

"Kepler's conjecture *seems* perfectly sound," I said.

"That it does," Ben said.

"But here's the thing. The conjecture has never been proved, to this day. I looked it up and discovered that, in 1998, a proof had finally been put forward by an American mathematician named Thomas Hales. In 2003, a committee that had been assigned to verify Hales's work confirmed that they were ninety-nine percent certain of the proof's correctness. But that one percent was key. The mathematical world is still waiting for the publication of the data that will prove the Kepler Conjecture definitively."

"Sucks for Thomas Hales," Ben said.

"I agree. But it makes sense that they have to be certain, doesn't it? The thing is, I'm ninety-nine percent sure that Peter McConnell didn't kill Lila, but until I find the final piece of evidence, until I can stack it all up in a neat configuration and make sense of it, everything is just conjecture. I just need to know for sure. Does that make sense?"

"It makes perfect sense," Ben said, placing a hand on my shoulder. "I wish you luck, my friend."

# Twenty-six

∞

One Friday six months after Lila's death, I walked into her bedroom, following my mother's request to "see what you can do." Already, I realized I would not be able to throw away a single thing. The fact that Lila had never been a pack rat should have made it easier, but what her possessions lacked in quantity was made up for by the intensity of her attachment to them. Each item in the room had been cherished by her. There was little organizing to be done, as Lila had been obsessively neat. Most of her possessions fit into a series of red file boxes that she kept in the floor-to-ceiling shelves beside her desk, each box labeled with a white card on which she had typed the contents: *keepsakes, financial papers, correspondence.* Her math notebooks were arranged by date, left to right, on a bookshelf above her desk. Her sewing machine sat on a wooden table that fit snugly into the bay window; beneath the table was a basket containing bobbins, thread, scissors, a pincushion, and a slim metal sewing ruler. In the days before her disappearance, she had been working on a a patchwork skirt, and on the table to the left of the sewing machine was a neat stack of silk squares in various prints and colors. I picked up the stack and arranged the squares across her bed. None of them seemed to go together, but I knew that if Lila had finished the skirt it would have somehow worked. Lila had been sewing since third grade, when she'd taken a kids' class at City College. After the class was over, she'd gone on to teach herself new techniques, becoming more competent with every garment. She'd tried more than once to teach me, but I'd never had the patience. My hems came out messy, my zippers and buttons off-kilter, the proportions all wrong.

"Why do you do it?" I'd asked her once, during one of those hopeless sewing lessons. "You know how Mom is about clothes. She'll buy you whatever you like."

Lila had a needle between her teeth and a seam-ripper in her hand, and was in the process of tearing out a dart I'd botched on a simple A-line skirt. "It makes me feel calm," she said, her words slightly slurred by the needle. "Sewing has a lot in common with math. You're looking for the most elegant outcome, putting things together in a way that's precise, unexpected, and ultimately beautiful." She held the fabric up to the light. "There!" she said, having extracted the dart. "Now, let's start from scratch."

That Friday, alone in Lila's room, I could still hear her voice as clearly as if she were there with me, but I wondered how long that would last. My parents hadn't bought a camcorder until a couple of years before. We had very few recordings of Lila's voice. I knew there must be some point at which the basic imprints of a personality begin to fade in the mind. I dreaded the day when my memories of Lila would become foggy.

I wrapped the fabric in tissue paper and placed it in the top drawer of my dresser. I wasn't sure what I'd do with it. Not a skirt, as Lila had planned—I'd only make a mess of it. But I thought perhaps I could pay someone to sew the squares into a quilt. I liked the idea of having them close—something tangible that I could touch, that would somehow convey her spirit. Dozens of times in the months to follow, I would remove them from my drawer, unwrap the tissue, and lay them out across my bed, arranging and rearranging them for hours, searching for some sign of her in the elaborate patterns. When I moved out of my parents' house my junior year of college, I took them with me. When I traveled alone to Europe several years after she died, I sewed a couple of silk squares to the interior lining of my backpack. In later years, wherever I traveled, one or two of them made the trip with me.

I went back to Lila's room and opened the closet door. All of the hangers were white and faced the same direction. Shirts came first, then skirts, pants, and dresses. "Keep the clothes you can wear and give the rest away to Lila's friends," my mother had said that morning before heading to Napa with my father for a friend's wedding. In hindsight, as an adult, I would consider it so strange that they had left me alone to deal with the ghosts in Lila's room, but at the time, I simply chalked it up to the absentmindedness and weird behavior that had hounded both of them since Lila's death.

Standing alone in Lila's small walk-in closet, sliding the hangers across the rack, I thought back to what my mother had said that morning. What world was she living in, that she believed in some bevy of phantom friends waiting in the wings to accept Lila's old clothing? For all their attempts to be loving, involved parents, my parents had never really understood how solitary an individual Lila was. And I began to wonder if I, too, had been wrong about her all along. I had assumed that she spent all those weekend nights of high school and college at home with the family out of choice, because that was where she wanted to be. But maybe she *had* wanted friends and boyfriends, but hadn't known how to go about it.

Ultimately, I ended up going to the hardware store a couple of blocks away and buying several large rubber containers, into which I placed the red file boxes, the sewing basket, the books and notebooks and bed linens. The only thing I kept for myself was Lila's well-worn copy of G. H. Hardy's *A Mathematician's Apology*, a slim volume that I would read several times in the years to come, impressed by the simplicity with which Hardy described the beauty of pure mathematics.

One by one I carried the rubber containers into my parents' closet, then pushed them through the small door that led into the crawl space. Once all the boxes were all inside, I took a flashlight and ventured into the stale, hot space, climbing through cobwebs and balls of dust. I shoved the boxes to the farthest corner. No one ever went in there. It was with no small degree of guilt that I contemplated the fact that Lila's belongings would be completely alone. I knew my mother would not ask what I had done with them. Embedded in my parents' departure that morning for Napa was an unspoken command: they wanted Lila's things to disappear, and the responsibility was mine.

Later I would regret the fact that on that afternoon, I had called the one person in whom I could confide, Andrew Thorpe. Still reeling from the events of the day, I let him into our home and told him everything.

"Can I see?" he had asked.

So I led him up to my parents' room and opened the door to the crawl space, and watched as he stooped and went inside, shining a flashlight on the boxes. I could not fathom why he would want to see that dusty attic space, could not make sense of his interest in Lila's old things. Only later would I realize that he'd gone in there for the sake of authenticity—so he could describe the cramped dimensions of the crawl space, its musty smell, the blue sheen of the cheap rubber boxes.

Many years later, when my mother was preparing to sell the house and move to Santa Cruz, I received a phone call from her. "I went into the crawl space," she said, her voice breaking. "I thought you'd given those things away."

I realized that, for all those years, she had been unaware that Lila's things were stored just a few yards from the bed where she slept. I left work early and drove to the house where I grew up. Together my mother and I went through the boxes. Among the things we found was an album by Cat Stevens called *Numbers,* which was released in 1975. Although it was part of a three-album box set, along with *Izitso* and *Back to Earth,* Lila had only *Numbers.* There was a period of several months when she played it every day after school, so often that the songs became stuck in my mind. At some point she stopped playing it, and I had forgotten all about it. I dusted it off and read the song titles on the back of the jacket, at which point some synapse fired in my brain, setting off a tangled stream of melodies and their accompanying lyrics. My first thought was to play the album, but then I realized I had nothing to play it on. My parents had long since done away with the turntable, and I couldn't think of a single person who owned one.

"If you really want to hear it, I'm sure you can find a record player on eBay," she said.

"Maybe I will," I said, but I never did.

# Twenty-seven

∞

"First name Steve," Thorpe said, "last name S-t-r-a-c-h-m-a-n."

We were sitting at Simple Pleasures out in the avenues on a Monday night. I'd had an appointment earlier in the evening with the owner, Ahmed, who had been buying his beans from Golden Gate Coffee since the eighties. Although we still provided the beans, he had recently begun roasting them himself in a storefront two doors down from the popular café. The beautiful bronze machine was situated right in front of the window, and around four in the afternoon, neighborhood kids would gather on the sidewalk to watch it rumble to life. It was live music night, and a folksinger named Patrick Wolf

was setting up in the little alcove beyond the kitchen.

I jotted the name Steve Strachman
into my notebook, and read it back to
Thorpe to make sure I'd spelled it correctly. "It rings a bell," I said.

"He was a grad student in the math
department at Stanford," Thorpe said.
"He was a contender for the Hilbert
Prize."

"The one Lila was supposed to get."

Thorpe nodded.

The Hilbert Prize was awarded in the
February of even-numbered years to a
promising graduate student for work
related to any one of David Hilbert's famous unsolved problems. Nineteen-
ninety was rumored to be Lila's year.
The prize had been a sort of beacon on
the horizon in the months leading up to
her death. She was giddy about the
prospect of winning it.

"At the same time Lila was working on Goldbach," Thorpe explained,
"Strachman was working on the Hodge
Conjecture. Not one of the Hilbert
problems, mind you, but Strachman
believed that progress on Hodge might

ultimately shed light on the Riemann Hypothesis. Like Lila, he was somewhat of a prodigy. He'd made a name for himself as a high school student during the International Mathematics Olympiad in 1982. From what I gathered during my interviews, he wasn't well-liked at Stanford. He was arrogant, competitive, used to irk the other students by trying to hone in on what they were doing, listen in on conversations without ever adding anything to the soup. Mathematicians as a group are extremely interconnected, constantly sharing information. But Strachman was notoriously cagey. Anytime he came up with an idea that he considered particularly interesting or valuable, he mailed it to himself in a sealed envelope so he'd have evidence of exactly when he'd first made note of it. He was so paranoid that someone would try to steal his ideas that he kept his math notebooks, and all those sealed envelopes, in a locked drawer at home. And here's an odd little detail—the cops once came out to the house on a domestic disturbance call. Seems he caught his mother trying to break the lock while she was cleaning his room, and he went ballistic."

"He lived with his mother?"

"Indeed he did."

"Strike one," I said. "Then again, Lila lived at home, and I never thought twice about it."

"Right, but he was a guy—it's different. *And* he was older."

Wolf began to sing. He sounded good.

"Let's move outside," Thorpe said. "It's getting noisy in here."

On my way out I said hello to Wolf's girlfriend—a preschool teacher named Mary—and to Peggy and Matt, who owned the Pilates studio across the street. I loved that about San Francisco cafés: spend enough time in any one of them, and you started to recognize the faces, learn the personal stories.

The temperature had dropped a good fifteen degrees in the last hour. The fog, which had been gathering over the ocean when I arrived in the early evening, was advancing up the avenues. When the fog was low to the ground like this, it reminded me of the cloud forests of Costa Rica and Peru. I pulled on my jacket and sat down opposite Thorpe at a small wooden table. He leaned over to pet a shaggy white dog that was tied to a parking meter.

"Are you cold, little guy?" His tenderness caught me off guard. Then he glanced up, as if to make sure I saw him, and it occurred to me that his affection with the dog, like so many other things about him, might actually be a calculated move to manage his image. After all, if he loved dogs so much, wouldn't he own one?

"This Strachman," I said. "So he was weird and competitive. That description fits a lot of people I know."

"Granted. But listen to this. A few days after Lila died, Strachman asked one of his professors about the prize."

"No crime there."

Thorpe leaned forward. "His exact question, according to my source, was, 'Who's next in line for the Hilbert Prize now that Enderlin is out of the picture?' "

"And you didn't find this important enough to put in your book?"

"I did put it in," Thorpe said. "My editor cut it. She thought it confused matters to throw yet another Stanford mathematician into the mix. She had a point; a reader can only keep up with so many characters before they all start to run together."

"Who was your source?"

"The professor to whom Strachman posed the question."

According to Thorpe, everyone had known for months that the prize would go to either Lila or to Strachman. They had been neck and neck. But following the success of a paper Lila presented at Columbia in November, the odds had shifted; Lila's victory was almost certain. Although she never would have admitted it, I knew that Lila wanted that prize so much she could almost taste it.

"Did Strachman win the prize?"

"Yes."

"Where is he now?"

I braced myself for the news: that he was a world-renowned mathematician, that the Hilbert Prize had paved the way for grander successes, that he had

proved the Hodge Conjecture and become something of a star. He'd be well
into his forties now, living off the
largesse of his earlier accomplish-
ments. But I had it all wrong.

"He gave up math a long time ago.
Tried his hand at engineering, and
when that didn't pan out he became a
contractor. He was in the news a couple of years ago for repairing the Treasure Island on-ramp to the Bay Bridge
after that fuel tanker disaster."

"You're kidding. It's *that* Strachman?"

"Yep."

The story had been big at the time. A
truck carrying three hundred gallons of
fuel had crashed through a barrier in
the middle of the night, sending a fire-
ball shooting high into the sky. The
driver had been killed, but what really
caught the public's attention was that
the much-used on-ramp had been de-
stroyed. With one crash, a tanker truck
had turned a twenty-minute commute
into three hours, minimum. Strachman's company had won the bid to re-
build the ramp. It was supposed to take
six months, but Strachman did it in

thirty days. The entire Bay Bridge had been closed down on Labor Day weekend to complete the project early, and there was a lot of speculation in the news that the bridge couldn't possibly reopen by Tuesday. But folks heading home late Monday night found that the bridge had actually reopened eleven hours ahead of the new schedule. It was this last bit of engineering finesse that had made Strachman somewhat of a local celebrity. His picture had appeared on the front page of the *Chronicle,* under the headline, "Most Efficient Man in SF."

What was it about the Bay Area, that people always stuck around? The place was a vortex, an inverted pleasure dome on the banks of the frigid Pacific. Despite the outrageous cost of living, the gloomy fog, the certainty of an impending major earthquake, and the blight of homelessness, the Bay Area behaved like a giant swatch of flypaper. I couldn't remember how many people had told me over the years that they'd arrived in San Francisco with a plan of staying for a couple of years, but had ended up digging their heels in for decades. Would-be rock stars, genius mathematicians, struggling writers, aging hippies—it seemed no one could find it in their hearts to leave. Maybe it had something to do with the water that flowed down from Hetch Hetchy. Maybe it was the climate. Or the food. Maybe it was the music. No matter—I understood completely.

That night, after leaving Thorpe, I went home and found Strachman's problem in Lila's notebook. At the top of one page she had written *Hodge Conjecture,* and below it:

*Let* X *be a projective complex manifold. Then every Hodge class on* X *is a linear combination with rational coefficients of the cohomology classes of complex subvarieties of* X.

It was impossible to understand a problem when I couldn't even comprehend its most basic terms. It felt like reading an excruciatingly complicated passage in a foreign language.

That night, I read every page of Lila's

notes on the Hodge Conjecture. I copied them out and read them again. I looked up the problem online, parsing each of its parts, bit by bit. I discovered that the conjecture remained open, and was considered so difficult and so important that a million-dollar prize awaited anyone who could prove it. I found several different math sites which approached the problem with varying degrees of complexity, and studied each one until my vision blurred. I stayed up all night. In the morning, I was still no closer to understanding. It was the same way I felt about the problem of Lila's murder. I could come at it from every angle. I could look at every possibility, compose any number of different stories. I could even turn the page upside down for a completely new perspective, as Lila used to do when she was stuck.

"Imagination is more important than knowledge," Einstein said. I had found this quote, along with several others, written in tiny cursive in the hidden margins of Lila's notebook. It was as if Lila had gathered these bits of wisdom and stashed them away—encouragement, perhaps, for those days when a problem seemed insurmountable. I suspected that Lila's genius had lain in her fierce imagination, her ability to envision things that she had not yet been taught, to put seemingly disparate concepts together in order to come up with something meaningful. Ultimately, I feared, my own imagination was not up to the task of figuring out what had happened to Lila. The problem might simply be beyond my means. Nonetheless, I had to try. I had to keep looking until I found the answer, or came to a complete dead end.

I ran my fingers over the page, brought the notebook to my face, and breathed in the musty smell of the paper, the very faint scent of lead. The meeting with McConnell had turned my life upside down. But in a way it had brought Lila back to me. This object from her life, this record of her days, was a window through which I could glimpse my sister as she had been at her best, her happiest. For so long, the missing notebook had nagged at me. I couldn't stand the idea that the book into which she had poured all her greatest ideas might have ended up in a landfill, or worse, in the hands of the person who had killed her. Having it back provided an enormous sense of relief. More than that, it made me feel closer to her than I had in years.

# Twenty-eight

∞

The following morning at Golden Gate Coffee, Dora wasn't sitting in her usual place at the front desk. The cupping room was also empty. I pulled on the required paper cap and opened the door to the warehouse, where Reggie was feeding a batch of beans into the roaster. I had to shout to be heard over the noise of the machine. "Where is everybody?"

Reggie pointed over his shoulder.

"What's going on?"

He grinned and shrugged.

In the holding room, Jennifer Wilson and the warehouse foreman, Bobby Love, were standing in a circle with Mike and Dora. The group was talking animatedly with someone else whose back was to me. "Ellie, look who's here!" Dora said.

He turned around and smiled. He looked good, as always. Jeans, black sweater, unusual boots, messy hair.

"Hey, girl," Henry said. "Long time no see."

"Hi," I said, and then, because it had barely been audible the first time, I repeated too loudly and cheerfully, "Hi!"

I moved into the group. Henry pulled me into a bear hug. I squeezed back.

Since the night Henry disappeared in Guatemala three years before, there had been many times when I'd imagined our reunion. But I'd never envisioned it like this, with a small audience of our friends. I never imagined I'd be dressed in jeans and a formless sweater, wearing a stupid paper hat.

Dora caught my eye and pointed at her tooth, the universal indicator that I had lipstick on mine. I rubbed my teeth with a finger.

"A little déjà vu?" Mike said. Everyone knew the story of how Henry and I met, right here in this warehouse seven years before. That day, he'd been interviewing for a job, and Mike had taken him around to meet everyone. Then, as now, I'd been wearing the paper hat. It wasn't the kind of first impression I wanted to make. Moments after introducing us, Mike had been called to the office. As soon as Henry and I were alone together, he said, "The hat's a good look for you. Emphasizes your dimples."

"If you're saying that so I'll put in a good word with the boss," I said, "I should warn you I have absolutely no pull around here."

"I don't care. Want to see Graham Parker with me this weekend at the Great American Music Hall?"

I already had plans, but I knew at that moment I was going to cancel them. When I finished showing Henry around the warehouse, Mike still hadn't come back, so we walked outside into the sunlight.

I pulled off my hat. "I like that look even better," Henry had said.

That afternoon, I told Mike he'd be a fool not to hire Henry.

At the Great American Music Hall,

during a break between sets, Henry told me the story of Francisco de Melho Palheta, the Portuguese Brazilian official who was called upon to mediate a border dispute between French and Dutch Guiana in 1727. Although Palheta was thought to be a neutral party, in truth he wanted desperately to get his hands on Guiana's coveted coffee seeds, which could not be legally exported.

"So how did he do it?" I asked. My hand lay on the table between us.

"He seduced the French governor's wife," Henry said, touching the tips of my fingers lightly with his own. "When he left, she gave him a bouquet of flowers in which she had hidden a few coffee cherries. They ended up in Brazil." He moved his hand so that it covered mine completely. "Have you ever heard Rumi's poem about coffee?"

"Don't tell me you're going to start reciting poetry."

" 'When the black spirits pour inside us,' " Henry said, speaking so softly I had to lean forward to hear him, " 'Then the spirit of God and air/ And all that is wondrous within/ Moves us through the night, never-ending.' "

If it had been anyone else, I might have laughed in his face. But that was Henry. He had a gift for delivery.

Now he was back, and I didn't know how to act around him anymore. This was the man with whom I had hoped to make a life, with whom I'd thought I would have a child. Standing beside him in the warehouse, hearing his voice and breathing in the sand-and-pine-cones scent of his skin, I was reminded once again that my feelings for him were not merely nostalgic.

In my addled state, I picked up enough of the ensuing conversation to understand that he'd just moved back to San Francisco from the East Coast, and that he was starting his own café. He wanted to buy his beans from us.

Mike excused himself for a meeting, clasping Henry firmly on the shoulders. "We're glad to have you back," he said. "I never did think you'd last long in New York. Blizzards, deli-style sandwiches, who needs that stuff?"

"We'll see."

"I'm going to leave Ellie in charge of you," Mike said. "There's some great coffee coming out of Nicaragua. She'll tell you all about it." The others excused themselves, too, leaving me and Henry alone together.

"You haven't changed," Henry said.

"Neither have you." My mouth was dry. I had that old feeling I'd always had with him, like I wanted to get closer. Even during those last few months together, when we were fighting so much, the need to touch his skin and feel his hands on me never diminished.

"I'm actually heading out," he said. "I have to go sign the lease on the new place. Want to have dinner on Friday?"

I couldn't believe he would ask so casually, as if he'd never left. As if the last three years hadn't happened.

"I'd love to, but I already have plans," I said. And it was true. Ben Fong-Torres had called. He'd found the tape Billy Boudreaux gave him in 1999. He thought I might like to hear it.

We walked outside. The fog hung low over the buildings, and the world felt cool and quiet. There was a car parked just outside the door, a silver Prius.

"This is me," Henry said, putting a hand on top of the car.

"You've gone green."

"It's a good city car," he said, "pretty zippy. I still couldn't bring myself to give up the Jeep, though. It's sitting on the street outside my place as we speak. I have to move it every couple of days so I won't get a ticket."

"I loved that Jeep."

"We were in an accident about a year ago in upstate New York," he said. "The Jeep behaved like a dream. I was actually in the hospital for a couple of weeks. I'd probably be dead if I'd been driving this little thing."

My first thought was, *What would I have done if I'd received news that Henry was dead?* And my second thought was, *Why is he using the plural pronoun?*

For three years I'd wondered what had happened to him, what exactly had gone wrong. Dozens of times, I'd replayed that final fight in my mind, and had admonished myself for going out instead of staying in the hotel room with him to work it out. I wanted to ask him what had happened, why he had left, whether he had simply stopped loving me. And if so, when? But I couldn't ask. Instead, we were talking about cars.

I looked at his left hand. He wasn't wearing a ring. And then I said it, because I couldn't stop myself. "Who's we?"

"Come again?"

"You said *we* were in an accident." Now I wished I hadn't asked, but it was too late to back out.

"The Jeep," he said, grinning. "I meant me and the Jeep."

# *Twenty-nine*

∞

At home that night, I turned my attentions to Strachman. I began with the article from the *Chronicle,* "The Most Efficient Man in SF." Then I read an interview in *Marin* magazine, in which he talked about his two kids, his love of deep-sea fishing, his affection for Frank Sinatra, and a café near his office, Crossroads, where he bought his coffee every morning. In the interview, he seemed like a normal, nice guy. But twenty years had passed since he took home the Hilbert Prize. Was it possible for people to change? Given enough time and favorable circumstances, could a violent criminal transform himself into a productive, even likable, member of society?

The next morning, I went to Crossroads in South Beach. I was there at six forty-five but a sign in the window said the café opened at seven, so I went for a walk to kill time. There had been a Giants game the previous night, and the sidewalks were littered with pennants and commemorative plastic cups. I passed a man in a bathrobe and sneakers, hosing vomit off the sidewalk in front of his multimillion-dollar loft. I passed a schoolgirl in a plaid skirt and saddle shoes waiting for the bus, alternately puffing on a cigarette and glaring at it as if it had done something to piss her off.

When I got back to Crossroads, it was open. I ordered a Sumatra and browsed the bookshelves. The place had an interesting, eclectic selection of fiction and biographies. A handwritten note on one of the shelves said that the month's theme was fog. The books on display included *Footsteps in the Fog: Alfred Hitchcock's San Francisco*; *Moon Palace,* by Paul Auster; and *A Dream in Polar Fog,* by Yuri Rytkheu, among others. On the bottom shelf I spotted a novel that I'd read recently, a

sort of literary mystery about a kidnapping set in San Francisco. The book
had been interesting, if somewhat
drawn out. Halfway through I started
skipping long passages on memory
and guilt just to get to the meat of the
story. As I was reading it I found myself
thinking that, sometimes, a story just
needs a beginning, middle, and end.
Maybe that was what made Thorpe's
books so popular. He never dillydallied
with esoteric matters. He drew the
characters early in the book and
quickly, almost methodically, got on
with the plot. If I could look at his work
objectively—which was almost impossible to do under the circumstances—
then I could see that he knew how to
get into a story, pull you along, and
bring the whole thing to a satisfying
conclusion just a few pages before you
were ready for the book to end; he left
you wanting more.

"A lot of writers think popularity is the
literary kiss of death," he told me once,
months before I knew anything about
his plans to write about Lila. "If too
many people enjoy their books, they

think they've sold out. But if and when I ever publish a book, knock on wood, I want people to read it. Lots and lots of people."

I'd been struck, at the time, by the nakedness of Thorpe's ambition. I'd wondered if I'd ever feel such a surge of ambition myself. I was the kind of literature major who wanted to read books, not write them. I had no idea what I'd do with my degree when I finished college. Unlike Lila, whose path was set for her the moment she opened her first math textbook in grade school, I was clueless about my future. Ultimately, it had been chance, not ambition, that led me to a career in coffee. Chance was exactly the kind of thing that Lila had no use for.

By now, people had begun filtering into Crossroads. I studied their faces, looking for Steve Strachman. According to the article, he came in for a double latte and newspaper every weekday morning. His routine was to read the newspaper at the café before walking to his office a few blocks away. I was certain I would recognize him from the photo in *Marin* magazine.

By a quarter to eight, Strachman still hadn't shown. I'd finished my second cup of coffee, had perused all of the bookshelves and skimmed the *New York Times,* and I was beginning to feel anxious.

Eight o'clock. Still no Strachman. I considered just walking over to his office, but somehow that seemed more likely to scare him off than if I bumped into him at the coffee shop. I wondered what a private investigator would do. Or Thorpe. How had Thorpe gotten all those people to talk to him?

At ten past eight, he walked in. At first I didn't recognize him, because he'd lost a lot of weight, and his face was much thinner than in the photograph. He wore khaki pants, steel-toed boots, and a denim shirt. Despite the casualness of his attire, he exuded money. You could tell that his clothes came from some outrageously pricey store, the kind of place where customers might drop hundreds of dollars on a shirt designed to project a kind of rugged appeal. His stylishly floppy hair was beginning to gray, and his dimples had turned into permanent creases. He was Northern California handsome, which is to say his good looks had more to do with pricey organic food and weekends in Tahoe than with any obvious genetic gifts.

He picked up a newspaper. Over the din of the espresso machine, I heard him talking to the girl behind the counter.

"Morning, Isabelle. I'll take a plain bagel, no trimmings, please. Double latte."

He turned from the counter, juggling his bagel, newspaper, and coffee, and looked around the crowded room for a spot. When he glanced over in my direction, I smiled and said, "This seat's free."

"Lucky me. I know it's going to be a good day when a nice young woman invites me to share her table." He opened his paper and said, "Did I just say that? Forgive me, I was thinking aloud."

The funny thing was, he seemed genuine. As if the words really had just slipped. I was waiting for that moment when he would look at my face and see Lila's features staring back at him.

"You're Steve Strachman," I said.

He raised an eyebrow. "How'd you know that?"

"I use the Yerba Buena on-ramp. Pretty impressive what you did."

He shrugged. "It's my job. The only reason people got excited about it is that things like that usually move so slowly around here." He dusted bagel crumbs off his paper. He didn't appear to recognize me at all. "What's your name?" he asked.

"Ellie," I said. "Ellie Enderlin."

He reached his hand across the table to shake. As our skin made contact, I saw something cross his face. He withdrew his hand quickly and took a gulp of coffee.

"Is something wrong?"

"I once knew someone named Enderlin. It was a long time ago." He paused and looked down at his paper, but he wasn't reading. After a few seconds he looked up again. He seemed to be studying my face. "Her name was Lila," he said. "She had a sister." He continued to stare. I could tell he was trying to put the pieces together.

"I know," I said finally.

"That's a coincidence," he said. "It is a coincidence, right?"

On the one hand were his nice clothes, his dimpled smile, his kind eyes. You could tell he was the kind of guy who carried pictures of his kids in his wallet, the kind of guy who surprised his wife with flowers for no reason. He knew the girl behind the counter by name, had asked how she was doing. He was nothing like the portrait Thorpe had painted of an arrogant, secretive person. On the other hand, he'd clearly been taken aback. My presence made him very uncomfortable.

"Are you still working on the famous problem?" I asked.

"Pardon?"

"The Hodge Conjecture."

He waved his hand in the air as if shooing away a fly. "That was a different life. I gave up math a long time ago."

"Why?"

He made a move as if to go, but again, he stayed. I hoped he wouldn't leave. I had no Plan B.

"I just wasn't that good."

"You must have been," I said. "You won the Hilbert Prize."

He frowned. "Only by default. It was Lila's. Everyone knew that."

"Still." I didn't know what to say. I was simply stalling. This was nothing like talking to Delia Wheeler. In that situation, there had been a kind of logic, a way of approaching the subject. But with Strachman, I had nothing.

"Truth be told, she's probably why I quit," Strachman said. "I knew I would never be as good as your sister. Not just her. There were others who by their very presence made me feel like a fraud. Lila's friend, McConnell, for one. It wasn't enough that this beautiful, incredibly smart girl was in love with him—he also happened to be brilliant."

My throat felt dry. "Did you know about them? Back then, before everything happened?"

"Yes."

"But how? I thought they'd kept it a secret from everyone."

"Almost everyone. I saw them together once, in the office of the *Stanford Journal of Mathematics.* I walked in and they were—" He scratched his neck, looked away.

"They were what?"

"Involved." He took a sip of his coffee.

"How involved?"

"Very."

"That's not possible," I said. "Not there."

"It was shocking to me, too," he said. "She'd always been so shy. I figured it must have something to do with McConnell's charisma. He had a lot of it, you know. Good-looking, charming. For some reason, girls fall for that sort of thing."

Was it just my imagination, or was there an edge of jealousy in Strachman's voice?

"I walked away. Never mentioned it to anyone." He paused, looking at me as though something was just dawning on him. "You're still trying to figure it out, aren't you? After all these years." He hesitated for a second, as if he was making a quick calculation, extrapolation, trying to figure out whether he would've been doing the same thing if the roles had been reversed. "All right," he said, "I can respect that.

"Anyway, what I was getting at was that there was an awful lot of talent in that math department. Your sister's was the most obvious, but there were others. At twenty-six, I was already losing my edge. I suspected the Hilbert was as far as I would go, and I only got that far because of Lila's—" He paused, looked away. "Her misfortune," he said finally. "It didn't help that I wasn't much liked in the department. Back then, I had a rather overbearing personality. The prize didn't bring me any joy. I felt ashamed. I was certain everyone hated me for taking what was rightfully hers. If I'd continued, maybe I could have been good, but I knew I'd never be great." He shrugged. "So I quit. I've never regretted it."

"Did you read Andrew Thorpe's book?" I asked.

"I skimmed it." He paused. "I'm embarrassed to admit it, but I was only interested in whether or not I made an appearance. I'm telling you, I was pretty insufferable back then."

"Why would you have?" I asked.

"What?"

"Made an appearance. Say you'd been in the book—"

"Which I wasn't."

"No, but if you had been—"

"No reason," Strachman said. "Except, I guess, I was there. For a few weeks, pretty much everyone in the department was under a cloud of suspicion. The police questioned all of us. Not very well, in my opinion, but they did question us. It was what everyone was talking about in the hallways, the cafeteria, even in the study sessions. I remember thinking at the time that I was caught up in a real-life game of Clue. Was it Mr. Boddy in the ballroom with a rope? Professor Plum in the conservatory with a candlestick?"

I grimaced.

"I'm sorry," he said. "I don't mean to make a joke. But you've got to understand, we were all living mathematics night and day. It was very stressful, highly competitive, a petri dish of obsessive personalities. And then this terrible and, I must admit, fascinating thing happened. We were horrified and riveted at the same time. And the women—there weren't many of them, you know—were afraid. We all knew that Lila didn't have much of a life outside of the department, which seemed to raise the probability that the killer might have been one of us."

"And what do you think?" I asked. I was watching his face for something—a flinch or nervous tic that might incriminate him, an obvious sign like sweating or looking away. But he looked me in the eyes and said, "I have no idea."

"What about McConnell?"

Strachman shook his head. "Honestly, I think he was just an easy target. The obvious choice, perhaps, but I don't believe he did it."

"Why?"

"It just seems out of character. Granted, we weren't best buddies or anything, but we did have a few classes together, and I had worked on a project with him during my first year. I didn't like him much, but then I didn't like anyone very much in those days. I envied his confidence, his ease with women. They loved him, you know. He was tall, good-looking, funny, and when he walked down the hall you could just tell he had an effect on people. Women would stop in mid-sentence to look at him. I was this average-looking guy, clammed up whenever I tried to say so much as hello to a girl, and for him it all just came naturally."

It had never occurred to me before to ask this, but hearing McConnell described in this way, I couldn't help but wonder. "Were there other women?" I asked. "Besides my sister?"

Strachman thought for a moment. "There was one," he said, "a girl in the philosophy department. Petite, willowy, brunette—very pretty. I used to see them eating lunch together all the time, she was obviously smitten. He put an end to it soon after it started—maybe a couple of months—but it was an ugly breakup. Sometimes she'd show up at his office late at night, demanding to see him alone. There would be shouting, and he'd have to practically push her out the door. She threatened to tell his wife, but I don't know if she ever did. The other guy who was working with us on the project used to get very annoyed, but to be honest, I wished McConnell would teach me how he did it. I couldn't imagine any woman would ever feel that strongly about me."

"Do you remember her name?"

"Melissa? Melanie?" He shook his head. "I never knew her last name. I don't know what McConnell did to finally get rid of her, but by the time your sister showed up she wasn't coming around anymore."

"I'm very curious," I said. "Why did you keep McConnell's secret? Why didn't you tell the police what you knew about him and Lila?"

He looked at his watch. "I have a meeting in fifteen minutes." And then, as if to prove to me that he wasn't just making the meeting up to get out of there, he elaborated. "We're bidding on the tunnel to Montara. If you want to make a good investment, buy property on the coast now, before the tunnel goes in. People still think it's too far from the city, they're turned off by Devil's Slide. But once the tunnel opens, property's going to skyrocket, mark my word."

He stood to leave. "I assume you've talked to Carroll."

"Carroll?" I repeated, trying to re-member where I'd heard the name.

"Don Carroll, McConnell's mentor at Stanford. Carroll knew McConnell bet-ter than anyone. I'm sure he's still teaching."

Driving to work after my conversation with Strachman, I tried to banish from my mind the image of Lila and Peter McConnell, naked in the offices of the *Stanford Journal of Mathematics*. When I talked to McConnell in Diriomo, he had somehow managed to make his affair with Lila appear almost inevitable, inspired, driven by a deep intellectual and emotional connection that was more powerful than his will, or hers. From his telling, it looked more like a tragic love story than a sordid affair. But the image of them in the office together late at night—his wife would have probably been waiting for him at home, the child tucked into bed—made me confront something about Lila that I didn't want to think about, something I'd never wanted to think about. She'd knowingly had an affair with a married man, a father. Their relationship had not been based purely upon intellectual attraction, but also upon something earthly and common, something I had succumbed to more times than I cared to admit: lust.

All these years I'd thought of her more as a girl than as a woman. Even though she was three years older, I'd always been the more worldly one. This perception had to do with her naiveté in social matters, her lack of romantic and sexual experience. I'd never once gone to her for advice on men, and had assumed that, when the time came, she would come to me. But the fact was that she had been twenty-two years old when she died, old enough to know what she was doing, old enough to understand what an affair might do to a marriage. I tried to chase the thoughts away. To even contemplate that Lila might have been at fault in any way felt wrong. In my story, she had always been blameless.

# *Thirty*

∞

On Friday evening, I went to see Ben Fong-Torres.

"Red or white?" he asked, when he greeted me at the elevator door.

"Red."

"Perfect. We have a Syrah I've been wanting to try."

We took our glasses outside, where a steep wooden staircase led down to a shady garden of fern trees, luxuriously blooming rose bushes, and banana palms. I could imagine sitting in the garden in the morning, sipping my coffee and reading a book. I asked Ben if he and his wife, Dianne, ever did that.

"Oh, we're not coffee people," he said. "We drink tea."

While I could enjoy a good cup of tea every now and then, I had a hard time relating to people who didn't drink coffee at all. Granted, they were probably calmer, kinder, and less prone to anxiety—but I couldn't imagine going a day, much less a month or year, without coffee.

"Did you know that, in Turkey in the fifteenth century, there was a law allowing women to divorce their husbands if they didn't provide them with adequate amounts of coffee? But a century later in the Ottoman Empire, anyone caught operating a coffeehouse could be officially beaten as punishment. On the second offense, they were sewed into a leather sack and tossed into the Bosphorus River."

Ben nodded politely. It was always my first instinct when there was a hole in a conversation—talk about coffee. I worried that I was like a dentist who regales strangers with stories of molar extractions, or a realtor who can't stop talking about fluctuations in the thirty-year rate.

"Thanks for finding the tape," I said.

"No problem. After we talked about it, I became a little obsessed."

"Where did it turn up?"

"I'd loaned it to a friend years ago. I had to make several phone calls. Turned out my friend let his cousin borrow it, who let her son borrow it, who listed it on eBay last year. But no one bought it. Imagine the kid's surprise when I e-mailed him through his eBay account and told him I wanted my tape back."

In the TV room, we sat side by side on the plush sofa. The recording was low quality, the sound scratchy. You could tell it had been recorded in somebody's basement. The first song was good but not great, a slow, Dylanesque ballad about mornings on Haight Street, before the bars had opened. The second was an acoustic number, the kind of guitar work that made you feel both lonely and inspired. I could almost feel Boudreaux in the room with us, sipping whiskey and weeping over the strings. Before the third song came on, Ben paused the cassette player and said, "Pretty amazing, huh?"

"It is."

"This next one caught me off guard. It's the first time I ever heard Boudreaux on keyboard, but that's not the half of it. I almost didn't call you. Didn't know if I wanted to open up that can of worms. But then I talked to Dianne, and she said you really ought to hear it."

I swallowed. "All right."

He pressed play. I leaned forward and listened. The first couple of minutes were just Boudreaux on keyboard. The notes were less certain than when he was on bass, but there was still something about the music that surpassed the brain and went straight to the heart, like Boudreaux was feeling every note of it. There was something very private about it, too, as if Boudreaux didn't expect another living soul to hear this music. It felt like I was listening in on someone's dreams. And then he began to sing. His voice faltered through the first few lines, then grew stronger, but it never did become entirely confident. Later, listening to the song again, dozens of times, alone in my apartment, I realized that it was this uncertainty in the voice, the emotional rawness, that made it beautiful. His voice reminded me a little of Townes Van Zandt, and I thought of a night more than thirty years before, when my parents had taken me and Lila to see Van Zandt perform at the Fillmore. We waited in line out in front of the building on Geary on a cold night in February. Next door to the Fillmore was the imposing three-story building that served as headquarters for the People's Temple. Mingled in with the people waiting for the Van Zandt concert were Temple members, and indigents waiting to be fed in the church dining hall. At one point a man with dyed black hair stepped out of a limousine, and he was instantly surrounded by people who seemed to want to touch his hair and his clothes. He smiled and hugged everyone, kissing several women, and even a few girls who didn't look much older than Lila, on the mouth.

"Is that Townes Van Zandt?" I asked.

My mother pulled me and Lila close. "No," she said. "That's Jim Jones."

Not long after, the man with the dyed black hair would be dead, along with hundreds of his disciples in Guyana. A few days later, Dan White would assassinate Harvey Milk and Mayor George Moscone, and eventually be found not guilty because he was under the supposedly mind-altering influence of Twinkies. Growing up, I didn't know that San Francisco was any different from any other place. Only when I was older would I realize how strange my city seemed to people from other parts of the country. To me, it was simply home, a place where you might wake up one morning to find that someone you knew had followed a cult to Guyana, or that someone else you knew had died of AIDS, or that your mayor had been murdered. Strange things happened here all the time: some were beautiful, some were horrible, all were part of life in the city by the bay.

# *Thirty-one*

∞

The third song on the tape was entitled "The Forest." When Boudreaux sang the simple refrain, his voice was choked with emotion:

*Deep in the trees I'm on my knees*
*Looking at you and not believing*
*What have I done, my beautiful one*
*What have I done*

The song gave me chills. I tried to be objective about it. One thing my mother had taught me during her years as an attorney is that, if you're looking for something hard enough, you can almost always find it. If we believe a thing to be true, we look for clues that will lead us to our foregone conclusion, filtering out anything that might contradict our beliefs. She'd seen it happen with juries. She'd even seen it happen with my father.

One night, about a year after Lila died, wanting to borrow a belt, I knocked on my parents' bedroom door. "Come in," my mother said, in a falsely cheerful voice.

My father was out that night, and when I entered the room I saw my mother sitting on the edge of the bed, wiping her eyes.

I sat down beside her. "What's wrong?"

She smiled and put an arm around my shoulders. "Just something your father and I need to work out."

"Tell me."

She plucked a Kleenex from the bedside table, blew her nose, and said, "He's got this crazy idea that I'm cheating on him."

"What? You've got to be kidding."

"He says I've been distant lately. Maybe I have. If so, it's got nothing to do with your father. I'm just—" She paused, as if looking for the right word. "Sad," she finished. "I've been sad for

a while now. And your father is accustomed to a certain level of—" Here she
paused again, then looked me square
in the face. "Attention, if you know what
I mean."

"Mom!" I said. "How gross."

"Well, you asked. Anyway, somehow
he got this idea, and now he can't let
go of it. Every time I have to stay late at
work, he gets suspicious. Yesterday, I
told him I couldn't have lunch with him
because I had a meeting at noon that I
expected to run for a few hours. Which
I did, but at the last minute, it got
moved to one-thirty. By then it was too
late to call your dad and have him drive
all the way across town, so I grabbed
lunch across the street with Liam instead."

Liam was one of the younger associ-
ates at her firm. I'd met him a couple of
times at the office. He was great-
looking and had once come this close
to making the U.S. Olympic skiing
team, but when I tried to engage him in
a conversation, I'd discovered that he
was painfully boring.

"And?"

"And your dad, for some crazy reason, had been waiting outside the building, and he watched me go into the restaurant with Liam. We're sitting there eating our pasta, talking about the case, and your dad storms in and says he needs to talk to me."

"Dad did *that*?"

"I excused myself," my mother said, "and we went to Dad's car to talk. He said he knew something was up, and seeing me at lunch with Liam when I was supposed to be with him was proof. So now he thinks I'm having an affair with Liam! Can you believe it?" She was laughing and crying at the same time.

After leaving Ben's house, I went home and listened to the song over and over again, for hours on end. I had to consider that I might be making myself crazy like my father had done all those years before, looking for something where there was nothing. After all, the lyrics were vague enough that they could have been written by anyone, and could have myriad meanings. But the song appeared to be laced with guilt—"what have I done"—and the reference to the trees unnerved me. The lyrics, taken alone, would have been perfectly innocent. And yet I had to consider the context: Boudreaux's car at Armstrong Woods.

During our first meeting, I'd asked Ben if he knew of any reason why Boudreaux might be there. I asked if he was into hiking, or if perhaps he had family at the Russian River. Ben didn't know about the latter, but as for hiking, he told me he got the feeling that Boudreaux wasn't much of a naturalist. "He was more comfortable inside a bar or a recording studio," Ben had said. "The first time I met him, he looked like he hadn't been out in the sun in months. Which is why I was so surprised years later when he told me he was working at the dairy farm. It just didn't seem to fit his personality."

Through my bedroom window I could see the muted lights of the city. A slender moon—the kind that Lila had dubbed a "fingernail moon" as a child—hung high in the sky, and a swath of fog seemed to be hanging from its tip like a giant white overcoat. For perhaps the thirtieth time that night, I pressed the rewind button on my portable stereo, waited for the whir and click of the tape, and listened to "The Forest."

"Deep in the trees, I'm on my knees," Boudreaux sang, his raspy voice nearly cracking on the final word. "Looking at you and not believing." As the keyboard grew quieter and the song came to an end, I sang along: "What have I done, my beautiful one? What have I done?"

The next morning I called the Boudreaux Family Dairy. A man's voice, gruff and sleepy-sounding, answered on the third ring.

"Mr. Boudreaux?" I asked.

"This is he."

My heart did a little jump. But I realized that in my nervousness I'd forgotten to ask by first name. Could this be the same voice I'd heard on the tape, or was this the voice of Billy Boudreaux's brother?

"I was wondering if I could take a tour of your farm," I said.

"This is a pretty busy time of year. You'd probably see more at one of the bigger farms, anyway. Stornetta does tours."

"I was hoping to see how one of the smaller operations works," I said.

"I tell you what. Farm Trails weekend is coming up at the end of the month. August 29. All the farms out here open up on a Saturday so you can see what we do. There's a pumpkin farm, a goat ranch, a bee farm, you name it. We'll be participating in that. You're welcome to stop by."

After we hung up, I wrote FARM TOUR on my wall calendar in red marker.

# *Thirty-two*

∞

"I'm a bit of a night owl," Don Carroll had said when I called to ask if we could meet. "Can you come by late?"

Arriving at the math building at Stanford just after ten p.m., I felt a sense of déjà vu. I remembered tracking McConnell down in this very building when I was twenty, sitting outside his office, listening to the students talk about him as if he were a celebrity. Now the building was empty, my footsteps echoing in the hallway. I shivered in my thin sweater, wishing I'd worn a jacket. The place had a bland institutional smell— floor cleaner and cardboard, a slight chemical odor that might have been dry erase markers. The smell of the world was changing, I noticed it every day. When I was in college, the buildings of USF smelled like chalk, old books, and mimeograph ink.

I turned down a couple of wrong hallways before finding the office number. The door was open, Carroll's back to me. He sat at his computer facing the window, a coffee cup perched precariously on the edge of the desk. He was so still he might have been sleeping. I tapped on the door, but he didn't seem to hear, so I cleared my throat and knocked more loudly. He turned to face me. He had gray hair and glasses, a kind face with light brown eyes.

"Ellie Enderlin?"

"Yes. Thank you for taking the time to talk."

"Sorry about the strange hour. I find the older I get, the less I sleep. Did you know that Thomas Edison claimed to sleep only three hours per night? He invented the lightbulb so that humankind wouldn't waste its time in bed. He believed sleep was the enemy of progress."

Carroll looked down at his hand as though he'd just noticed the large envelope he was holding. "Pardon me, I

have to go slide this under the secretary's door."

While waiting, I glanced around the
office. The walls were covered with
plaques, cheaply framed announce-
ments of various awards, and photographs—there he was with Jimmy
Carter, hammer in hand, standing in
front of a house-in-progress; there with
Stephen Hawking; there with Paul
Allen; there with Baron Davis. On Carroll's desk were more personal photos—an attractive woman in her sixties,
probably his wife; a black cocker
spaniel; a little girl on a blue bicycle.
One in particular caught my eye—a
photograph of Carroll standing in the
rain beside a young Peter McConnell,
in matching white parkas. From the angle of the Golden Gate Bridge in the
background, I could tell the photograph
had been taken at Crissy Field.

On top of a stack of papers was a
hardback book. When I saw the cover,
I did a double take. The book was in
German, so I couldn't read the title. I
was holding the book, staring at the

cover, when Carroll came back in the room.

"Ah, you have an interest in topology?"

"Not exactly. It's just—this symbol on the cover. I recognize it."

"Ah, the double torus." Carroll took the book from me and placed it on top of a stack of file folders. "This is a review copy, just came in the mail today. Apparently I coauthored a paper with this gentleman twenty years ago, but I've been racking my brain all day, trying to remember him. Complete blank. That's what happens when you turn seventy. Did you know that the lower mantle of a volcano flows in a double torus pattern?"

I shook my head.

"Makes perfect sense, but somehow I'd forgotten it. I'm liable to forget my own name pretty soon. My daughter Genna recently put me on a strict ginseng regimen, but so far it hasn't made a difference." He smiled and sat down, crossing his legs and folding his hands in his lap. His hands were smooth and unmarked, as if they belonged to a much younger man. "Please, have a seat. On the phone, you said you wanted to talk about Peter McConnell. Like I said, I doubt I can be of any help. I haven't seen him in over a decade."

"I was more interested in what he was like back then."

"What he was like?"

"This is an awkward question, but I'd heard that McConnell had—" I glanced at the picture on his wall of him and McConnell together. I couldn't think of a delicate way to phrase it.

"Yes?" Carroll leaned forward.

"I heard he had girlfriends."

He settled back in his chair, frowning. "Who told you this?"

"A former student in the math department, Steve Strachman."

"Strachman," he said, with obvious distaste.

I waited.

"Ah, yes. Well, Peter was very handsome. Very charming. Women certainly liked him, no question. But I don't remember girlfriends, per se, other than your sister. To be honest, I was glad when he met Lila. His wife always struck me as a climber, more interested in what he might become than in who he was."

"What he might become?"

"Yes. I don't think it mattered at all to her what his field was—it could have just as easily been science or literature. Peter rarely said an unkind word about Margaret, but he confided to me once that she'd always been insecure about her own lack of education—she'd given college a try briefly but apparently it didn't work out for her—and she felt that she could redeem herself in the eyes of her parents by marrying an academic. It bothered him, I think, the idea that he might not live up to her expectations.

"Naturally, when she found out about Lila, she was furious. She made all sorts of threats, but Peter didn't take her seriously. When I told him he should be concerned he assured me that it was just hot air."

Now I was the one leaning forward. "What kind of threats?"

"That she would make a stink around the department. That she would confront Lila personally. That she would leave him and take their son Thomas. But Peter knew that Margaret was all about appearances. She couldn't stand to go home to her parents in defeat. Despite her very justifiable unhappiness about the affair, there were certain things she wanted out of life—prestige, mainly. She believed that Peter could give her that."

"That confirms what McConnell told me about her."

"You've talked to him?"

"Yes."

He uncrossed his legs. On his right foot he wore a blue sock, on his left foot a yellow one. "When?"

"A month ago. In Nicaragua."

"He didn't mention it," he said, more to himself than to me.

"You talk to him?"

"Not by phone, of course," Carroll said. "Letters."

"But I thought you said—"

"Ah, that. It's true, I haven't *seen* him in a decade. I didn't say we have no contact. You'll understand if I'm protective of him. I feel responsible, in a way, for what happened."

"Responsible? How?"

"It would be fair to say I encouraged the relationship. A perfect match is as rare as a perfect number. I've always considered myself fortunate that I found mine early in life and had the good sense to marry her. Anyone could tell that Margaret and Peter had nothing in common, and there was no tenderness between them. Lila, on the other hand—it was clear when I got to know her that they were right for one another."

"You knew my sister?" I asked, startled.

"Yes, Peter introduced us soon after they met. He wanted her by his side when he broke the news that they were going to tackle Goldbach. I think he knew I would be alarmed. I'm not sure how much you know about the conjecture . . ."

"Only what Lila told me—that it was proposed in 1742, and many great minds had been stumped by it. Every even integer greater than two can be expressed as the sum of two primes?"

"Exactly. A mathematician can easily derail himself by focusing on a single, unattainable goal. Look at Louis de Branges and the Riemann Hypothesis. Along with Goldbach and, until fairly recently, Fermat, the Riemann Hypothesis is one of the most difficult open problems in the world. De Branges spent twenty-five years working on it, and in 2004 he published his proof on the Internet. But no one paid much attention, and it has yet to receive a peer review. What's strange about this is that De Branges is no upstart; in the eighties he proved the Bieberbach Conjecture, by any accounts an important achievement. When he published that proof, there was a lot of skepticism—very similar to what has happened with his Riemann proof—it was as if everyone *wanted* him to be wrong. But in the end, the work won out. At issue in the Riemann case is the fact that he used mathematical tools in which he is one of the few experts—spectral theory, for example—so assembling a team who would be qualified to review the proof would be an enormous undertaking. It doesn't help that he's a bit of a wanker. Added to that is the fact that, in 1964, he claimed to have a proof for the existence of invariant subspaces for continuous transformations in Hilbert spaces. But his claim was false, and he has paid dearly for his mistake in terms of his credibility. Mathematicians, for better or worse, have a long memory. Now De Branges is in his seventies. I have to admit I'm rooting for him, if only because I'd love for him to show the world that an old guy can still have the mettle to make a huge contribution."

Carroll smiled. "You must forgive me. One doesn't easily abdicate the role of math professor. It's in the blood. As Poincaré said, 'Mathematicians are born, not made.'"

"McConnell and my sister," I pressed. "You encouraged them?"

"Yes, early on, Peter came to me for advice. I could find no logical support for continuing in an unhappy and unproductive marriage. When the opportunity for happiness presents itself so clearly, I said, one should take hold of it. I don't believe in this business of the tragic genius. I think a man does his best work when his domestic life is happy. Look at Ramanujan, all his brilliant results and astonishing insights—the infinite series for pi, the Ramanujan Conjecture—but dead at thirty-two of tuberculosis in some slum in India. An arranged marriage at twenty-one to a nine-year-old girl. He'd have contributed far more to the world of mathematics if he had carved out for himself a tranquil home life with a compatible partner.

"So you see, my advice to Peter was not entirely without self-interest. I had the conviction that if he and Lila worked together, they could accomplish something extraordinary. Of course, I didn't expect them to prove Goldbach, but I knew that if they worked toward that nearly impossible goal, they would no doubt come upon other important discoveries in the process. Look at the history of Fermat's Last Theorem. Along the path to its proof, a number of significant advances were made: the proof of the Taniyama-Shimura Conjecture is inextricably linked to the search for the Fermat proof."

Carroll unfolded his hands and placed them on the armrests of his chair. He wore a wide gold wedding ring and had a perfect manicure.

"I digress. Beyond the advice, I facilitated the relationship in a very practical way. Peter once confided that he and Lila felt uncomfortable working in the math building; your sister was afraid that people would begin talking. So I offered them my house to work. My wife was a muralist and was often away doing commissioned work, and by then Genna was off at Columbia."

He paused, watching my face. "Don't look so surprised. Just because I'm a mathematician doesn't mean I have no concept of romance. Do you know what Voltaire said?"

"Hmmm?"

" 'There is far more imagination in the head of Archimedes than in that of Homer.' We mathematicians get a bad rap for being the cold-hearted purveyors of reason and common sense, but the truth is that one can make important mathematical discoveries only by employing the imagination. Lila's imagination was fierce. I used to come home late from my office and find them bent over the kitchen table, hard at work. We'd order out and sit in the kitchen over our take-out containers from the Good Earth, talking number theory. I'd just turned fifty, and I can't tell you what a delight it was for me to be allowed into the intimate circle of their mental gamesmanship. We worked well together, the three of us. I had the knowledge, see, the decades of experience, but they—especially Lila—had the ability to come at something from an entirely new angle, to conjure a surprising connection or intriguing question from thin air. Sometimes, when we'd talked so much our heads were about to explode, we'd retire to the living room and play a video game that Peter had turned Lila on to— some Atari-age game involving rapidly rotating triangles." He smiled at the memory. "I wouldn't be surprised if the

game is tucked away in a box somewhere in the basement."

"That explains where Lila was on
those nights when she stayed out so
late. We never did piece together where
it was that she and McConnell met." I
hesitated. "I'm not sure how to put this,
but did they use your house for—"

Carroll looked alarmed. "Goodness,
no. There was a small hotel in Half
Moon Bay. I would have preferred not
to know, but Peter offered the information one day, out of the blue. I think he
just needed to tell someone. He desperately loved your sister. I know from
experience that's the sort of thing one
doesn't want to keep secret. You want
to tell the world. Wisely, he only told
me." Carroll frowned. "Naturally, I've always wondered what might have happened had I told Peter to go back to his
marriage, to forget about Lila. I suppose there's no harm in confessing to
you now that the investigation was the
one time during my life when I made a
clear choice to deceive. I didn't tell the
detectives about Lila and McConnell
because I believed it was my duty to

protect him. Perhaps it wasn't the right thing to do, technically speaking, but I've never regretted it. Of course, in the end—when that tawdry book came out—I was unable to help him.

"I don't know how much Peter told you. But he's done some amazing work in both number theory and topology over the last couple of decades, despite being sequestered away in that little cabin in the jungle. He's quite intent on living the life of a primitive, though. No computer, it boggles the mind. As I mentioned before, he sends me letters, although it's a stretch to call them letters. Generally there are a few vague lines of text—he'll mention the weather, or some improvement he's made to the house—followed by pages and pages of calculations carried out in longhand. For years I read the letters myself, but after my eyesight began to deteriorate, I started having my secretary type out the letters before I read them. Peter's handwriting is impossible."

Carroll gestured to a cardboard box on the floor stuffed with file folders.

"There they are, arranged by year. At first I just put them in a drawer, thinking he'd be home soon. Then a year passed, two years, three, and I realized he wasn't coming back. I know I should find a better place to store them—I'm the only person in the world who has a record of Peter's work—but I've become accustomed to having them close by so I can reach in and pull one out at a moment's notice. They're brilliant. This thing is filled with work that could cause quite a stir. I keep trying to persuade Peter to let me submit them for publication, but I think he's become accustomed to anonymity."

"When I met him he was very modest," I said. "He gave no indication that he'd been doing anything worthwhile."

"He's a rare breed," Carroll said. "Even before his career was derailed, it was obvious it wasn't about the glory or recognition. He simply loved the work."

"Like Lila," I said.

Carroll raised an eyebrow. After a slight hesitation, he said, "Certainly, she did enjoy the work. But one mustn't forget that your sister was quite ambitious."

I was still stuck on our earlier conversation. "You said McConnell's wife, Margaret, made threats after she found out about Lila. When was that?"

Carroll paused to think. "To my recollection it was maybe a month before—" He hesitated, as if searching for the most delicate phrasing. "Before your sister's passing."

"McConnell said he had told his wife about Lila only days before Lila went missing."

"He said that?"

"Why would he have lied to me?"

Carroll shifted in his seat and adjusted his watchband. "I can't speak for Peter. But I can tell you that he was very protective of his family. Whatever Margaret's faults were, she was a good mother. The most important thing in the world to Peter was his son, and he would do anything to make sure that little boy could stay with his mother. He would willingly take the heat for Margaret."

"I don't follow."

Carroll hesitated. "You must understand, I'm reluctant to say more, because there is no proof whatsoever to
support my theory."

"Your theory?"

"Margaret knew some unsavory characters. Lila was a thorn in Margaret's
side. I have no evidence, mind you,
only a gut feeling. And a gut feeling, I'm
afraid, is worth very little."

"I'm sorry. I have to ask you to speak
more plainly."

Carroll crossed his legs again. When
he shifted in his chair, the inner collar of
his jacket came into view. His name
had been sewn into it in red cursive letters. "It would be injudicious of me to
spell it out further. Perhaps I've already
said too much. At any rate, Peter
thought my suspicions were baseless."

"What about Strachman?" I asked.
"Why didn't he tell anyone about Lila
and McConnell?"

"Ah yes, Strachman. That was interesting, too. Strachman used his silence
as a bargaining tool."

"For what?"

"Peter and I were collaborating on a paper. Under his own aegis, Strachman would have had no access to me. To be quite honest, I disliked him. He was Peter's opposite in every way: cagey, humorless, moody. And jealous—personally as well as professionally. I guarantee you, he would have given anything to have been in Peter's shoes—to have Peter's natural talent, not to mention Lila's affection."

"He had a crush on Lila?"

"Oh, yes. But despite the fact that he would have given his right arm to date her, he was as jealous of her mathematical abilities as he was of Peter's, probably more so."

"But he won the Hilbert Prize."

"Oh, yes, that." Carroll frowned. "He never would have had a chance were it not for earlier research he'd done with Peter. That work laid the foundations for his paper on the Hodge Conjecture. Every truly original idea that grew out of that collaboration could be attributed to Peter. But it wasn't in Peter's nature to make a fuss over it. At any rate, after your sister died and the police came around, Strachman vowed his silence on the condition that he be allowed to coauthor a paper with Peter and me."

"And you agreed?"

"You must understand, Peter was very dear to me. He still is. I don't know what it is about him, but he has always brought out my paternal side."

Suddenly, Carroll smiled and stood, holding out his hand. "It's been wonderful talking with you, Ellie, but it's past my curfew. My wife will be wondering about me."

"Thank you," I said, shaking his hand.

"Would you like me to call campus security for you? They'll send someone to walk you to your car. One can't be too careful—"

"I'll be fine."

As I turned to walk out the door, he placed his hand very lightly in the small of my back. It was one of those male gestures that had always made me uncomfortable, simultaneously chivalrous and patronizing—two sides of the same coin.

"I was wondering," he said, his hand still resting in that intimate place.

I turned and faced him, so that his hand was left hovering in the air. "Yes?"

"Lila—did she ever mention me?"

"She did."

His shoulders relaxed, and there was the beginning of a smile on his face.

I left it at that. I didn't tell him that she had only mentioned him in passing, as a brilliant professor with whom she would like to work. Like McConnell, her friendship with Carroll, and her evenings at his house had been a secret she kept hidden from me.

My footsteps echoed in the long hallway. I passed by a door with a small sign that said *Stanford Journal of Mathematics.* A strip of light shone under the door. Was this the room where Strachman had come upon Lila and McConnell, all those years before?

Keys in hand, I walked quickly to my car, which I'd illegally parked in the faculty lot near the building. Someone had stuck a white envelope under the windshield wiper. I removed it—a parking ticket. Apparently, the meter maids didn't sleep.

# *Thirty-three*

∞

A few days later, when I pulled up behind Golden Gate Coffee, I spotted Henry's silver Prius. Dora whistled as I walked in. "Going somewhere special?"

"It was the only thing I had clean," I said. Maybe the black pencil skirt and knee-high boots were too much. I couldn't remember the last time I'd worn anything like it to work.

She winked. "Henry's going to love it."

In the cupping room, I began preparing the latest samples—an El Salvador yellow bourbon cultivar, a caturra from the Boquete region of Panama, and a peaberry from Costa Rica. I'd just finished pouring the water into the cups when Henry walked in from the roasting room, his face flushed from the heat.

He looked different, and it took me a moment to figure out why.

"You got your hair cut," I said.

He brought his hand self-consciously to his head. "I went to my old place in the Castro, but Dottie wasn't there anymore. The new woman got carried away with the clippers."

"It looks good."

"You always hated it short."

I smiled. "It'll grow back."

He pulled out a chair and turned it around backward before sitting down, legs straddling the back of the chair. It was a habit I'd always found oddly endearing.

"Remember that time you cut my hair?"

"Yes. I thought that would be the end of us. What a way to begin a relationship."

"Granted, it was not a good haircut," he said. "Still, the whole point was that you were the first woman I ever trusted to do it."

I felt my face heating up. It was strange. After two people had been as intimate as we had, for as long as we

had, shouldn't all possibility of embarrassment be removed?

I picked up my heavy spoon and
broke the crust on the coffee, glad to
have something to do. "It's too cool," I
said. "I'll have to start over."

He said something, and I thought I
couldn't have heard him correctly.
"What did you just say?"

"Maybe that's something we could
think about. Me and you. Starting
over."

I put the spoon down. "Are you serious?"

"Why is that such a crazy idea?"

"It's been three years, Henry."

"I never stopped thinking about you."

"After you left, I spent the longest
time waiting for you to come to your
senses, because I was certain it couldn't
just be over so abruptly. But when you
didn't come back, I realized that I must
have loved you so much more than you
ever loved me. That was the only explanation that made any sense to me.
Now you're back. I should be furious
with you."

"You never loved me more," Henry

said. "If anything, it was the other way around."

I shook my head. "If that were the case, you would have tried to make it work."

"I did try," Henry said. "How many times did I tell you I couldn't take another fight? You would agree with me, you'd promise not to get worked up over small things, and everything would be fine for a couple of weeks, a month, and then all of the sudden you'd come from out of nowhere with some grievance, attacking me for something I didn't even know I'd done."

"I was like that?"

He sighed. "Yes, you were like that."

"I'm sorry."

"I'm not asking for apologies. If anyone should be apologizing, it's me. Don't think I don't realize what a jerk I was in the end. Honestly, I'd understand if you didn't even want to talk to me. I'm just reminding you that I tried very hard to make it work. But every time we fought, it made me think you weren't really serious. The only explanation I could come up with was, for some reason, you wanted to drive me away."

"I didn't want that at all."

For a minute, neither of us said anything. I dipped the spoon into a glass of lukewarm coffee. I scooped the crust off the surface of the first glass, and went down the line until I'd removed the grounds from all nine glasses.

"It was always like this," he said softly.

"Like what?"

"We'd begin a serious conversation, and as soon as it got uncomfortable, you would start doing something else. Laundry, dishes, coffee, whatever."

I looked up at him. I knew he was right. For some reason, despite all of my effort, I couldn't break past a certain level of intimacy, even with Henry.

"You told me something once," I said. "It was early on. You said that the seed of a relationship's demise is always apparent, even from the very first moment. You said that if you look closely at the beginning, you will always be able to see the end. At the time it seemed sort of ridiculous. But then, during those last few months together, when we were fighting so much, I started to really think about your comment. And then I traced our entire relationship back to the beginning, all the way back to our first date. I wanted to find that seed, I wanted to discover the clue, the thing that foretold the end."

"Did you find it?" he asked softly.

"No. Not at all. It wasn't there. At least it wasn't there for me. And since then, over the last three years, I've wondered whether the sign was there for you. I mean, did you notice something about me on the first date, or the first time we slept together, or hell, I don't know, the first time we met, that told you how it might all end?"

He fiddled with a spoon on the table. "If I tell you something, promise you won't take it the wrong way," he said.

I was still trying to decide whether I really wanted to hear whatever it was he had to say when Mike walked into the room.

"I need you in Nicaragua again in October," Mike said to me.

"All right."

Mike looked at Henry, as if he'd just noticed him. "How long since you've been down to Central America?"

"A while."

"You should go, too. Think of it as a welcome-home gift."

The statement hung there in the room. Mike had never been one for subtlety. When we broke up, he told Henry he was making a mistake he'd regret forever. Several times during the first month after Henry left, Mike had put his arm around my shoulders and said, "He'll be back."

"Maybe I will go," Henry said. Even though I pretended to focus on the cups in front of me, I knew that Henry was looking straight at me, waiting for some kind of signal.

# *Thirty-four*

∞

The sign out front was shaped like a farmhouse—red cursive on a white background, *Boudreaux Family Dairy*. Beside that was another, temporary sign, hand-lettered on a piece of wood:

**Welcome to Farm Trails**
**Weekend**
**Pick Your Own Pumpkin**
**Dig for Potatoes**
**Meet Tabitha**
**Milk a Cow!**
**Cool Drinks**
**Fresh Cheese Here**

I turned down the lane. The driveway was flanked by pasture on both sides, bright green against the brown hills. An antique plow lay stranded in the grass.

A crow was perched on top, cleaning itself in the sun. An ancient-looking horse standing by the fence glanced up lazily as I passed. I thought of the summer afternoon right before Lila sold Dorothy, when we drove out to the stable together and Lila saddled her up for me. "Give her a good kick," Lila had said with her customary matter-of-factness. "Let her know who's boss." But when I did just that, Dorothy had taken off across the field in a wild gallop, while I held on for dear life.

Lila's horse phase seemed a lifetime ago, almost like something I'd dreamed, but driving down the dusty lane, with the fog tumbling down from the hills and Cat Stevens playing on the radio, it was impossible not to remember Lila in her riding pants, with her black sweater and black boots, ponytail flowing behind her. I couldn't help wondering how things might have turned out if she hadn't given up riding. If, instead of devoting herself wholeheartedly to math, she had done as my mother advised and kept this small hobby on the side, this pleasure that had nothing to do with her academic life. I had wondered, more than once, whether it was her ambition that was her undoing. If only she hadn't been so good at what she did, so singular of vision, surely the order of her days would have been rearranged in some significant way. After all, when it comes to the major events that shape our lives, timing is everything. Maybe Lila's schedule, altered by a fraction, would not have delivered her into the hands of her killer. And instead of spending my Saturday touring a dairy farm in search of some elusive truth, I'd be jetting across the country to visit her at Princeton or Columbia. Maybe there would be a niece, or a nephew, or both, for whom I would bring presents. Who knows, maybe I would even have a child of my own, a husband, the whole pretty picture.

I tried to imagine what Lila would look like now, at forty-two, but all I could fix in my mind was an unsettling image of one of those age-progression sketches, dark pencil-marks indicating lines around the mouth and along the forehead. I always wondered how the artists went about selecting hairstyles for those sketches, how they settled on the decision to shorten or lengthen the hair, add or subtract bangs.

I glanced up at the rearview mirror and tried to effect Lila's off-kilter smile, activating the dimple on the right cheek and squinting up the right eye by a fraction; that was the closest I would ever come to knowing how she would have turned out, but I had the feeling it wasn't close enough. As adults, would we look more alike than we had as children, or less? Probably less.

Worse than not knowing how she would have looked was not knowing the person she would have been. Although Lila had a clear idea of how she wanted her life to turn out, there would have inevitably been some surprises. How she would have reacted to these surprises, and how her reactions would have reverberated down the years, were questions I could never answer. Lila was like an unfinished novel—two hundred pages in, just when you're really getting into the story, you realize the rest never got written. You'll never know how the story ended. Instead, you're left with an abrupt and unsatisfying *non*-end, all the threads of the plot hanging loose.

About a quarter mile down the road, I passed a large shed. A few dozen cattle were lined up inside, facing the driveway, their heads thrust beneath a wooden rail, eating from a long trough. At the end of the driveway, to the right, was a small pumpkin patch, flanked by a row of red wheelbarrows and a couple of Radio Flyer wagons. Half a dozen cars were parked in the pasture. I pulled in next to a silver minivan. A young blonde woman was struggling to get two crying preschool-aged children out of their car seats. "It's a farm!" she said. "It'll be fun!"

I got out of my car and walked past the row of wheelbarrows, stepping carefully around patches of animal droppings. A small white dog materialized from behind a bale of corn husks—*Maize Maze!* a sign declared—followed by a young boy with a stick. The dog shot past me, and the boy, panting, stopped and said, "Lady, can you help me catch Rowdy?"

"Okay," I said, but I was relieved when a short, stocky man emerged from the maze and threatened not to let the boy milk the cow if he didn't stop torturing the dog. I could travel the world and feel completely at home, but put me on a farm with a few wheelbarrows and pumpkins, and I felt as out of place as if I'd landed in Oz.

The air was infused with the light, oddly pleasant odor of cow dung. A plume of smoke rose from a small shed several hundred yards away. Beyond the pumpkin patch, a table had been set up under a tent. A woman with a green bandana around her neck stood there looking bored.

"Sorry," she said. "My guys haven't shown up yet. We're not doing tractor rides until two."

"Not a problem," I said, wondering what it was about me that made her think I was in the market for a tractor ride.

"Want a sample?" she asked, cutting a cube off a wedge of white cheese.

"This is our Sonoma Jack. Melt this over a baked potato with a little fresh garlic and you'll think you've found Nirvana."

I bought some and talked with her about cheese for a couple of minutes before getting around to the question I really wanted to ask. "Is Billy Boudreaux around, by any chance?"

"There's no one here by that name. Maybe you're looking for Frank."

"Frank?"

"The owner. He's around here somewhere." She pointed across the driveway, where half a dozen hay bales surrounded a big brown cow. "He'll be doing a milking demonstration right over there in about fifteen minutes."

"Thanks," I said. I took off across the pumpkin patch, past a sign that said *Sugar Pie.* As I was crossing the road I saw that the field in front of me was made up of long rows of dry-looking dirt. I thought of the potato patch Lila had shown me that day, forever ago, when I visited Dorothy with her for the last time. I had a pit-of-my-stomach feeling, a shivery sort of reaction that caused me to turn slowly in my tracks, toward the house rising up at the end of the driveway. I'd hardly noticed it at first, obscured as it was by a row of fir trees almost as tall as the house, but by looking between the trees now I could see the wraparound porch and dormer windows, the ramshackle additions on the west-facing side of the house.

I had been here before.

It was an instinct, more so than a fully formed idea, that pulled me across the pasture to the old horse. When I was within ten feet of the animal, she lifted her head and regarded me.

I was sideways to her, something Lila had taught me. "A horse's vision is peripheral," she had said. "If you approach them straight on, they get spooked. And don't look them in the eye right away— that's what predators do."

"Hi, girl," I called out, proceeding very slowly. The horse stomped and swished her tail. As I drew closer, she took a few steps away. I stopped and stood still for a minute. Finally, I held out my arm, wishing I had an apple or carrot to offer.

The horse was old and swaybacked, graying, with protruding teeth, rheumy eyes, and a white stripe down her face. I stepped closer, and this time she didn't back away. Soon I was close enough to feel her warm, moist breath on my arm. I patted her very gently on the jaw; she snorted and blinked.

"Hey there," I said in a quiet voice.

She stomped weakly and swished her tail again. A fly landed on her left eye. She blinked, but the fly remained there. I shooed it away and began petting her flank. She inched closer. Her fur was thick and shiny, and when I touched it, to my surprise, I didn't experience the same revulsion I'd felt as a young girl whenever I touched a horse. She had that distinctive horse smell— dirt and oats and sun.

A horse is just a horse, I told myself. Don't all horses, to a layperson, look the same?

"How old are you?" I said.

I heard footsteps behind me, and turned to see a man in jeans and a plaid flannel shirt walking toward me from the direction of the barn, carrying a small bucket. "Thirty-one," he said. "She's old but tough." He came around on the other side of her and ran his hand along her back. "Just like me, huh, old girl?" he said, hugging her around the neck. He looked at me and said, "We're getting all our old-age symptoms at the same time—arthritis, failing eyesight, stiff legs, the works. My wife tells me that pretty soon she's going to have to put me out to pasture, too." He reached into the bucket and pulled out a turnip, which he cut into small pieces with a pocketknife before offering it to her on the flat of his hand. She nibbled it slowly.

"You must be here for Farm Trails weekend," he said. "We're a lot busier than usual this year. Must be a slow day in the city."

"This is your farm?" I asked.

"Mine and my wife's. As of 1983. Back when we bought it they only had a few cattle—it was an apple farm in those days—but we expanded over the years, and in 1998 we turned it into a fully organic operation. Now we have nine hundred cattle. Still small as dairy farms go, but more than big enough to keep us busy. I'm Frank Boudreaux," he said, offering me his hand.

"Ellie."

His handshake was firm but not too forceful, and I could feel the thick calluses where his fingers met his palm.

"It's a beautiful piece of land," I said.

"We think so." He patted the horse, who nuzzled her head against his shoulder. He pulled out a couple of blackberries, and she took them from his hand. "When my wife and I bought the farm, we just thought of it as a way to go off the grid, make ends meet, and have a better quality of life. We never dreamed of all this." He tended to the horse while he talked, checking her ears, dabbing her eyes with a damp cloth. Finally, he dumped the remaining turnips on the ground in front of her and said, "I'm about to milk Tabitha. That's pretty much the day's main attraction, if you want to join us."

I couldn't figure out how to tell him why I was really there. Instead I just smiled and said, "Wouldn't miss it." I patted the horse's flank and ventured a question, unsure if I was ready for the answer. "What's her name?"

"Dorothy. I'm surprised she didn't run away from you. She doesn't usually take too well to strangers." Frank glanced over at me. "Hey, are you all right?"

"We're not strangers," I managed to say.

"Come again?"

"Dorothy and I go way back. I knew her before she came out here, back when she was being stabled in Montara."

He did a double take then, studying my face. "What did you say your name is?"

"Ellie."

"Enderlin?" he asked.

I nodded.

He looked at the ground. For a few seconds neither one of us spoke. Finally he looked up. "You're not here to milk the cow, are you?"

"No."

What he said next completely took me off guard. "I think I always knew you'd show up one of these days. In a way, I suppose I've been waiting for you."

"You have?"

"Yeah. I'm glad you're here. I want to talk to you." He looked up the hill, flustered. "Unfortunately, I've got all these kids over there, waiting for me to put on a show. Why don't you stick around? This afternoon, after everyone is gone, we can sit down and talk."

"Okay," I said. I was beginning to feel a bit dizzy, like everything was happening too fast. I didn't know what to make of this man, this place. Part of me wanted all the answers. Another part of me, I realized, wasn't prepared for this.

For the next few hours, time took on a hazy, unreal quality. I sat on a hay bale in the circle of children while Frank showed us how to milk Tabitha. The children had a go, one by one, followed by their reluctant parents, and then it was my turn to sit on the little metal stool. I'd never milked a cow before, and it was nothing like I thought it would be. The teat looked like a finger, or a flaccid penis. When I squeezed and pulled, squirting the milk into a plastic cup, Tabitha lifted her tail and released a large, wet dollop of shit. This delighted the children, one of whom promptly declared it "grosser than gross." I declined to drink the milk, even though everyone else had drunk theirs.

"Drink it!" someone yelled. It was the little boy who had been chasing the dog, Rowdy. Then the other kids joined in, until they were all chanting, "Drink it! Drink it!" So I did. It was warm and weirdly sweet, and it was an effort to get it down.

"I'm not cut out for farm life," I'd said to Lila once, when we sat just a stone's throw from this very spot, on the porch of the big white farmhouse. We'd been sitting in rocking chairs, drinking lemonade. The lemonade was tart and pulpy, with little bits of sugar that hadn't melted. "I like this part," I'd said, as the ice cubes clinked in my plastic cup. "The lemonade, the porch, the rocking chairs. It's like something out of *The Waltons.* But I wouldn't care for the rest of it—digging for potatoes, slopping the pigs, mucking the horse's stall, waking up at the crack of dawn."

"You'd get used to it," Lila said.

"I don't think so."

She rocked back and forth, her face turned to the sun, and she talked to me with her eyes closed. "You have this idea of what your life is, what it should be, and you're afraid to veer too far from it. But if you had to—I mean, say, for argument's sake, the big one hit and the city went up in flames, and somehow you ended up living in the country, and the only way you could survive was to raise your own food—you could do it. You might even like it. You might decide it actually suited you *better* than the life you have now."

"Would I have MTV?" I asked, pouring myself a second helping of lemonade from the cold metal pitcher.

"No."

"Would I get to drive into the city to shop and borrow books from the library?"

"No, all the stores burned down. The library, too. There's nothing. You have to make your own clothes out of drapes, just like Scarlett O'Hara. For entertainment, you have to tell stories in the evening by firelight."

"Couldn't do it," I said. "I'd starve and go naked and ultimately die of boredom."

"But you *could*," she insisted. "You'd just have to adapt your mind to the idea of an altered reality, a new set of rules."

"What about you?" I asked. "What if you could no longer practice math?"

"That doesn't make sense," she said. "There will always be math. It's the most fundamental building block of the universe. Humankind can live without MTV and Banana Republic—even, in a pinch, without literature—but not without math."

"For argument's sake," I insisted, "let's just say that's part of the deal. No math for you. Ever."

"That's different," she said. "Everything in your life right now is just a hobby, it's expendable. But math is my calling. You don't give up your calling, no matter what."

I stood up and stepped away, tossing the last of my lemonade on the ground.

It quickly sunk into the earth, leaving a dark spot on the dirt. "I'll wait for you in the car."

"Don't be so sensitive," Lila said.

"This calling of yours. What has it gotten you? No friends, that's for sure. No boyfriends. Maybe I don't know what I'm supposed to do with my life, but at least I won't die a virgin." It was the meanest thing I could think of to say. Later, I would regret it, but at the time I wanted to hurt her, the way she'd hurt me by pointing out what I feared was my greatest shortcoming. For a genius, finding one's life's purpose was easy. For the rest of us, it was a considerably more difficult task.

After that, I sat in the car in the driveway, doors open, Billy Idol cranked up high on the tape deck. From behind my sunglasses, I watched Lila riding Dorothy through the pasture. She looked natural on the horse, like she was meant to be there. It was almost two hours before she came out to the car. At some point I dozed off. When I woke up the tape had run out, and Lila was sitting in the driver's seat, trying to get the car to start. "I think you killed the battery," she said.

"I'm sorry."

"No, I'm sorry. You're going to be great at whatever you do."

"Thanks," I mumbled. I wasn't entirely ready to forgive her yet, but I appreciated the apology. The weird thing about Lila was that she could say a thing like that—about my having no calling—without any malice; to her, it was simply a matter of stating the truth. It wouldn't have occurred to her that her honesty might be hurtful.

"I mean it," she said. "You *will*." She gave my arm a little squeeze. "I'll go find William and ask him to give us a jump-start."

A few minutes later, she came out of the house with a big guy in overalls and a Giants cap. I couldn't tell if he was wearing the overalls ironically or not. "William, meet my sister, Ellie," Lila said. "Ellie, William."

William tipped his hat and mumbled, "Nice to meet you," then went off to get his truck and jumper cables. He hooked up the cables and Lila sat in the driver's seat, turning the ignition on command. He had our car running again in a couple of minutes. When he was finished, he propped his forearms on Lila's open window, leaned into the car, and said, "Should be all right as long as you keep the engine running."

"He smells like sweat and apple pie," I said to Lila, as we pulled out onto the main road.

"You say that like it's a good thing," Lila said.

"Isn't it?"

She didn't answer.

"I think he likes you," I said.

"William?" she said, laughing. "We've got absolutely nothing in common. Actually, he's more your type than mine."

"How's that?"

"He's really into music. He was in some weird band."

It was a nothing comment, something I quickly forgot. I rarely went back to the farm, and the only other time I saw William was on the day, a year or two later, when I went out there with Lila to sell Dorothy. Now, as I sat on the stool in front of the cow, swishing the warm milk around in a plastic cup, I thought about that afternoon so long ago, the good-looking guy who seemed to have a little crush on Lila. At the time, it had seemed so insignificant. William, Billy—it was starting to make sense. *What have I done my beautiful one/ what have I done?*

After milking the cows, Frank took the kids on a hayride. "What about seat belts?" said the blonde woman who'd been struggling to get her kids out of their car seats when I arrived.

"It's a hay wagon, honey," Frank said. "Doesn't come with seat belts."

"I don't know," the mom said, but her kids screamed until she let them ride.

Afterward, Frank showed everyone to the smokehouse, where a whole pig hung by its feet, head dangling. The throat had been slit, but the face still looked alarmingly piglike. The boy who had led the "Drink it!" cheer after I milked Tabitha ran out of the smoke- house, sobbing.

After the smokehouse there was a

pumpkin-carving contest. At precisely four-thirty, Frank thanked everyone for coming and sent them all home with a free slice of sugar pie. I stood with him in front of the house and watched the last car roll slowly down the driveway.

# *Thirty-five*

∞

The foyer of the farmhouse was large and square, with wide-plank floors and fading floral wallpaper. In the center of the room was a wrought-iron sewing machine table, on which stood a vase filled with sunflowers. Upon stepping inside, I was struck by a profound sense of déjà vu. I must have been in the house with Lila on one of my handful of visits to the farm, although I had no distinct memory of it. The place smelled of floor polish, potpourri, and the musty, burnt odor that lingers after a rug has been cleaned with an old vacuum cleaner. In the room to the right, which was filled with old settees and high-backed chairs, the pale green carpet bore the marks of a recent vacuuming.

Across from the front door, a staircase led up to the second floor. There was a sudden movement upstairs, followed by the creaking of the floorboards, and I glanced up to see someone retreating into one of the upstairs rooms—a white flash of elbow, the dark shadow of a shoe. Swirls of dust circulated in bars of light at the top of the staircase.

"This way," Frank said, leading me through the carpeted room, past a large flat-screen television and a bookcase crowded with videos and DVDs, into the kitchen. The kitchen was spacious and light-filled. A gleaming, stainless-steel refrigerator towered next to an antique Wedgwood stove. A diner-style booth, complete with red vinyl seats, had been built into the bay window. The effect was charming and somewhat unsettling. I imagined the way a marriage and family would unfold inside this house, indecisively, haphazard as the décor. I suspected most houses shared more in common with this place than with my own childhood home, where each piece of furniture was chosen with an eye for its relationship to the others, and where every object had its proper place.

"Have a seat," Frank said. The vinyl squeaked as I slid into the booth. The seats smelled as though they'd been scoured with Lysol, and the gleaming windows reeked of Windex.

"Regular or decaf?" Frank asked.

"Regular, please."

He took a canister of chicory coffee down from the cupboard and measured the ground coffee into an old percolator. Just as he was setting it on the stove, a phone rang, and he excused himself. He was gone for several minutes. When the percolator began rattling, I turned off the burner and poured the coffee into cups, glad to have something to do. I wandered around the kitchen, hoping to find something that would give me clues about the elusive Billy Boudreaux. But the photos on the fridge were mainly of a little girl—elementary school shots, Girl Scout camp, high school graduation, what appeared to be a Hawaiian vacation. A collection of ceramic cookie jars shaped like various Disney characters lined a high shelf, and a set of copper pots and pans hung from a metal rack above the island.

Frank returned. "Sorry about that. It was my daughter."

"The one in the pictures?"

"Yep. She's doing a semester down in the Florida Keys, studying the effect of global warming on sponge life and coral reefs. They have this underwater laboratory down there called Aquarius, sixty feet below the surface, and they broadcast in real time over the Internet. It's addictive. First thing in the morning I'm sitting at my computer, hoping to catch a glimpse of Tally with the tanks strapped to her back."

He put a plate of brownies on the table between us. "I'd have never guessed she'd decide on a career in marine biology," he continued. "Her mother and I are completely land-bound. I'm ashamed to confess I don't even know how to swim. But that's what kids do—they surprise you. You have any?" He glanced at my left hand.

"Not yet."

For a few more minutes we made small talk, as if neither of us quite knew how to broach the obvious subject. We talked about Tally, and the farm, and his wife's previous career as the curator of a small art gallery in the city. I asked him about the large collection of DVDs and videos I'd seen in the other room, to which he replied that he was something of a movie buff. "Actually, I inherited them from my brother, Will," he said. "More than half of those are his. Over the years I've been expanding the collection."

"Inherited?"

"He has no use for them now, of course."

I waited for him to say more by way of explanation. But he didn't elaborate. For a few seconds neither of us spoke. Frank kept nibbling at the brownies, like a nervous habit. He must have eaten four of them before we finally got around to the subject we'd been dancing around all day.

"You said you've been waiting for me," I said finally. "Why?"

"One thing I've learned in this life is

that the past always resurfaces. It simply stood to reason that you'd come
around one day. You've been here before. It's all a big circle, right?"

"I'm not sure I understand."

He looked up at me. His eyes were
dark brown, the pupils so large as to
make his eyes appear almost black. My
mother had once told me that, because
the iris expands in the dark, and because juries tend to look to a person's
eyes as a sign of whether or not they're
telling the truth, a dimmer room works
in your favor when one of your witnesses is on the stand. "It's human nature to feel trust when someone has
large pupils," she said. "If you can keep
it in the vault, I'll tell you a little trick I
use. Immediately before going in front
of the jury for closing arguments, I in-
tentionally blur my vision by looking
down at my notes and crossing my
eyes until I lose focus. This dilates the
pupils, so that when I stand up in front
of the jury I look wide-eyed and honest
as Abe."

It had provided an interesting window
into my mother's nature, into the per-

son she was capable of becoming when she was at work, but I wasn't sure it was a side of her I wanted to see. After she told me that, I found myself wondering if I could really trust her emotions. When she looked into my eyes and said she was proud of me, was she telling the truth, or was she simply feeding me a line, calculated to convince me of my own worth and thereby turn me into a better person?

"Do you like stories?" Frank asked, pushing the plate of brownies aside.

"Everyone likes stories."

"I have one for you."

I took a deep breath. "Go on."

"Early one morning in December 1989, my younger brother Will showed up at our door. A month before that, we had kicked him out. He'd been living with us for quite a while, trying to get clean, and he'd been doing great, so great that I thought he might really do it this time, he might really turn his life around for good. But then he had a relapse. We'd given him so many chances, and we had a new baby at the time, and my wife, Nancy, understandably, didn't want him around. When Will was sober, he was a huge help on the farm—a hard worker, kind to the animals, got along with everyone. While Nancy was pregnant, he treated her so well, you'd have thought she was carrying *his* baby. He'd come in the house several times during the day to check on her, and when he finished with his work he'd do chores around the house so she wouldn't have to. He'd go out in the middle of the night to get milk from one of the cows—he'd gotten this idea in his head that she should have only the freshest milk, if it had sat in the refrigerator for more than an hour it wasn't good enough. 'Straight from the teat is the only way,' he'd say. 'It'll make the baby stronger.' And to this day I'm not convinced there wasn't something to that; after Nancy drank fresh milk, the baby would invariably start kicking up a storm. Anyway, for months, that baby was all Will could talk about.

"Then Tally came, and Will was amazing. She was colicky, spent the first six months of her life screaming up a storm, but her crying didn't bother him one bit. When he was out working on the farm, she could scream for hours, and nothing Nancy did seemed to work. But when Will walked into the house, he'd wash up real quick and then go take Tally out of Nancy's arms, and start blowing in her ear, making this weird, musical rumbling sound—he had such a voice, you should have heard it, I always thought he should have been the front man in his band—and her screams would turn to little cries, then peter out to a whimper, and within a minute or two she'd be completely quiet and happy. Honestly, I don't know how we'd have gotten through those first few months without him.

"At any rate, about a year after Tally was born, Will was running errands in Petaluma when he ran into some guy he used to know in the music business. He called from the guy's recording studio to tell us he wouldn't be home for dinner, and he didn't come home that night or the next, and when he finally did show up a week later he was a complete wreck—unshaven, unshowered, with that familiar paranoid look in his eyes. He went to pick Tally up from her playpen and Nancy told him she didn't want him anywhere near the baby. He denied falling off the wagon, but it was obvious. Nancy insisted that he go back to rehab, and I backed her up on it, but he refused. At one point in the argument he put his fist through the wall right there."

I looked where Frank was pointing. You could still see where the wall had been repaired and painted over.

"That was when Nancy told him to pack his bags and get out," Frank said. "I tried to persuade her to give him one more chance. I was worried that without us, he'd completely fall apart. I was afraid for his life. After all, he was my baby brother. I remembered when he was born. I remembered playing ball with him when we were kids, and helping him pick out his first guitar, bailing him out of jail the first time he got in trouble for driving under the influence. Nancy told me point-blank that it was him or her, and even though I loved my brother to death, I wasn't about to lose Nancy or my baby over him. Will pleaded with me to let him stay, he promised he wouldn't do it again, but I told him what I was really feeling at the time—that I'd given up on him. To this day I regret saying it, but at the time it was true.

"Ultimately I had to pack his bags for him, because he refused to do it. I'm not sure how I finally got him out to his car, but I did, and I drove him to the city, paid for a couple of weeks at a hotel out by the beach, gave him a few hundred dollars to get by. We spent that night in the hotel room, talking things out. He was alternately contrite and angry, crying and yelling, but he promised me he'd stay out of trouble and find work, and that I'd see him again in three months' time, clean and sober and gainfully employed. 'Maybe I'll even write some songs,' he said. There was such hope in his voice, I wanted to believe him.

"The next day, Nancy drove to the city and picked me up. I'm ashamed to admit that I felt like a burden had been lifted. I told myself that he wasn't my responsibility anymore, that he'd have to sink or swim on his own. Of course I know now it was the wrong thing to do—if I'd managed somehow to keep him out here at the farm, all the terrible stuff that came later never would have happened, and maybe he'd still be alive—but at the time I was so fed up, I just wanted him off my hands. You never know the repercussions until it's too late, do you?"

It seemed like more than a rhetorical question—as if he was actually waiting for an answer—but I was still stuck on that other part. "He's dead?"

"Six years ago," Frank said. "Tally was the one who found him, out in his car. He'd hooked a hose up to the exhaust and threaded it through the window."

"But I thought . . ."

"Hmm?"

"When we came in, I saw someone upstairs. I thought—"

"Oh, Roy," Frank said. "That's Tally's fiancé. His lease just ran out on his apartment in the city. He's staying with us for a couple of weeks until he finds a place."

"Oh."

Frank paused. "You were hoping to see him."

I nodded.

"If you don't mind my asking, how did you trace him out here? He kept a low profile for a long time."

I told Frank about Ben Fong-Torres, about the article he'd written, and his chance meeting with Billy in the Haight, and the tape.

"A tape? He never told me he was writing new songs. I'd hear him playing the guitar sometimes, up in his room, even singing on occasion, but I figured it was old stuff. I tried to get him to play for us, but he wouldn't. He said all that was part of another life. Every now and then he'd play for Tally, but not if any-one else was around." He leaned for-ward. "Do you have it with you?" he asked. "The tape?"

"Yes."

"I can't tell you how much it would mean to me to hear it."

We went into the green-carpeted

room, and Frank inserted the tape into an old cassette deck. "Wait," I said. "Before you play it, please. I'd like to hear the rest of the story."

# *Thirty-six*

∞

"Your brother's stage name was Billy, wasn't it?" I asked.

Frank was standing by the fireplace. Beside him, a pile of firewood rested in a copper bucket. "Yes, his band decided Billy Boudreaux sounded cooler than William. But to me, he was always Will. I remember once, before all the trouble started, we were in downtown Petaluma, having dinner at a little Italian restaurant, and some kid came up to him and said, 'Hey, you're Billy Boudreaux.' Will autographed the kid's schoolbook, and that was when I realized that he was living this double life. To me, he was just my kid brother, the same one who'd made miserable grades in school, the guy who could never manage to keep more than fifty bucks in the bank, but to some people he was this up-and-coming rock star. I figured you'd have to be a certain kind of person to be able to pull that off, to keep those two identities separate. One night he'd be standing in front of hundreds of screaming fans, and the next night he'd be eating Campbell's soup for dinner in his crummy studio apartment in the Tenderloin."

"You said he showed up at your door early one morning about a month after you kicked him out," I said. "What happened?"

Frank came over. There were plenty of chairs, but he sat beside me on the edge of the couch, his body facing me. He was a big, sad-looking man. Out in the field with Dorothy, he had seemed cheerful, easygoing, but now that we were so close, our knees nearly touching, I understood that he exuded the kind of sadness that takes the air out of a room. I wondered what it would be like to be married to such a man, to wake up each morning with that sadness in the bed beside you, to kiss his sad mouth and hear his sad voice saying your name.

"I guess I never really did figure out what I was going to say to you when you showed up," Frank said. "I mean, I pictured us right here in this room dozens of times, or in the kitchen, or out on the porch, and I tried to plan it out, the way I'd tell you what I know, but I never could get it right."

I still couldn't fathom how all of it fit together. I didn't understand how his abandoning his brother at a hotel near the beach had led to what, I was sure, would be the story I'd been waiting to hear, in one way or another, for twenty years.

"He looked distraught," Frank said. "He was crying. My first thought was that he'd gone off the wagon in a big way. But I'd seen him on a bender too many times to count, and I'd never seen anything like this. Nancy and Tally were in Arizona with Nancy's parents, so I didn't have to worry about them, but I was still nervous about letting him in. I guess I was actually afraid of him right then, which was something I'd never felt before, not on his worst days.

"I turned on the porch light and stepped outside. His car was idling in the driveway. I told him to go turn it off, and he did. That's when I noticed the car was all scratched up, mud on the wheels, dead insects on the windows. If there was one thing in the world he took care of, it was that car. God knows why. It was a sad excuse for a car, an old white Chevrolet, but for some reason he loved it. I think it might have had to do with the fact that he could never really keep an apartment for long, so that car was more like his home than anywhere else. Even during his worst episodes, he somehow managed to hose off the car and keep the windows clean. But not that night.

"When he came back up on the porch I asked him what was wrong, but he wouldn't tell me. He just said he was in some trouble, and he needed a shower and a place to sleep. 'I'm clean,' he said. 'Haven't done shit since you kicked me out.' I'm not sure what it was—maybe something in his eyes, maybe his tone of voice—but I believed him. What was scary was that I knew whatever he'd gotten himself into this time was a whole lot worse than drugs. But then, I guess what it all comes down to in the end is blood. He was my brother. I just couldn't turn him away.

"After he showered, I gave him clean clothes and cooked us some eggs and bacon. He ate like he hadn't eaten in days, must have drunk four or five glasses of milk. I tried to get him to tell me what was going on, but he just totally clammed up. All he would say was that he'd done something terrible, and it was an accident, and he didn't know what to do or where to go. I guess if he'd been anyone other than my brother, I would have called the police. But I couldn't bring myself to do it. For some reason, I was remembering this time when we were kids—he was seven, I was sixteen—and I'd been walking home from school along this wooded road, and I'd heard something in the bushes, some kids laughing, and I went in there to investigate. It was a couple of boys from the fourth grade class, and they had Will shoved up against a tree, and they were pissing on his shoes, these brand-new sneakers, white with red stripes, that he was so proud of. Even though Will was big for his age, they were three grades ahead of him, and he just looked so helpless there, and terrified, trying his best not to cry. I'll never forget the look in his eyes when he saw me, this look of pure and absolute trust. I just lost it, I let them have it. A few minutes later those boys stumbled away crying, with bloody lips and black eyes, and nobody ever messed with Will again. And that's what I was thinking about when Will sat in this house that night, eating his bacon and eggs. I was thinking that he was my responsibility.

"By the time Nancy got home a few days later, Will was clean-shaven and sober and as polite as could be. She let him stay. We never had any problems with him after that. He worked the farm, took care of Tally. By then the girl who'd bought Dorothy from your sister had moved on and left Dorothy with us. Will took care of her like she was his own horse he'd raised from a foal. He never rode her, but he cleaned out her stall every day, fed her, groomed her, walked with her down to the stream where she liked to drink. I'd never seen anybody so devoted to a horse. A few weeks after he moved back in with us, we were all eating dinner together when Nancy wondered out loud what ever had happened to that sweet girl who brought Dorothy out here. Nancy and I were trying to think of her name, and we both had it just on the tip of the tongue, when Will said, very quietly, 'Lila.' We hadn't even started eating yet, but Will said that he felt sick and he needed to go up to his room.

"Later that night Nancy went to check on him, but he wouldn't open the door, and he didn't come out of his room for the next couple of days. I look back on it now and think it's kind of strange we didn't know that she'd been killed. I mean, later, when I went back to look at the newspapers from that time, I saw it had been all over the place. All I can figure is that we were so wrapped up with the farm, struggling, trying to make it work, trying to figure out how to be parents, that we just weren't paying attention to the news or to anything that was happening outside our own little world.

"Anyway, your sister's name didn't come up again until six years ago. Nancy and Tally were asleep. I was sitting in this room, over there by the fireplace, just enjoying the sound of the fire, when I heard footsteps on the stairs. Will must not have seen me, because if he had, there's no way he would have done what he did next."

I took a deep breath and closed my eyes. I wanted to press pause, somehow prepare myself. I realized the story was about to change irrevocably. Moments from now, Thorpe's book, the book that had provided the only map I knew of Lila's last days, would be rendered obsolete. After eighteen years of defining the story for me, Thorpe's book would no longer hold sway. It was strange—Thorpe's story seemed so much more alive, more persuasive, every fact and supposition backed up by more facts, each sentence working so hard to convince the reader that it was all real, that it had all really happened. And yet, somehow, I knew this new story, so different, so simple and plain, was the real truth.

I leaned forward. I wanted to know, and I didn't. It was the same way I used to feel as a young girl when, after dinner, Lila and I would climb into our father's lap, and he would tell us the tale of the golden arm. "Give me back my golden arm," he would say in a deep, wavering voice, while Lila and I squealed in terrified delight, waiting for the inevitable moment when he would raise his hands into the air like claws and grab each one of us by the arm and shriek, "Gotcha!" I used to think it was our father's favorite ghost story, but when I was older he confessed to me it was the only one he knew.

"He went over to that desk right there"—Frank pointed to an antique oak secretary—"took a key ring out of his pocket, and opened a series of smaller and smaller compartments until he got to the one he was looking for.

Other than the car, that secretary was his only significant possession. Our great-aunt left it to him when he was just a kid, and after we left home and my parents sold their house, he didn't have anywhere to put it, so I kept it for him. But he'd always been the one with the key, and over the years, while Will was out living his life, I liked having this piece of him nearby, it helped me feel close to him. I didn't know exactly what he had in it, but every now and then over the years I'd see him open it up and put something in one of the compartments—a newspaper clipping about his band, a ticket stub, a photograph.

"I don't know why I sat there in silence that night when he came into the room—I was going to say something, and then I saw him pull out the key—and I don't know, I guess, in a way, I must have wanted to be let in on his secret, whatever it was. He pulled something out, then closed the drawer back, and I must have made a sound, because he turned around, startled.

"At that point I flipped on the light

switch, and I was about to make some joke about him sneaking around in the middle of the night when I saw that he was holding a necklace."

"What kind of necklace?" I asked, but I already knew.

Frank got up and went over to the mantel. He opened a little hen-shaped jadeite dish, took out a small skeleton key, and went over to the secretary. Then he did what Will must have done on that night six years before. He slid open the rolltop lid and began opening the compartments one by one, like a Chinese puzzle. Finally he came to a tiny compartment, buried so deep in the desk that I had to marvel at the ingenuity of the carpenter who made it. He slid two fingers into the drawer and pulled something out. His hand covered it so that I couldn't see, and he came over to me. I held out my palm, and when he opened his fist it slid into my hand, as cool as if it had been buried deep in the earth. It was Lila's gold chain with the topaz pendant, the necklace I'd given to her for her eighteenth birthday.

I couldn't say anything. I couldn't breathe.

"Her necklace is missing," my father had said, that day when he called me from the morgue in Guerneville to tell me that he had identified my sister's body. Sitting in Frank's living room, holding Lila's necklace up to the light, I remembered how I had felt that day, as I held the phone to my ear and listened to my father's monotone delivery. What I remembered was this: while I wasn't quite able to process, during that brief phone call, the fact of my sister's death, I had felt, quite clearly, a burning sense of injustice and disgust at the thought of someone stealing her necklace. It was just a cheap trinket, purchased with babysitting money, but she had loved it enough to wear it every day. For Lila, its value had nothing to do with the object itself, everything to do with her love for me.

Twenty years of my life had been defined by the loss of my sister, the person I had loved most in the world. But now I allowed myself to remember that she had loved me, too, absolutely and unconditionally. The secrecy of her final months, her reluctance to tell me the truth about Peter McConnell, did nothing to change that fact. It occurred to me then that she would have told me about McConnell, she would have told me about the whole affair—eventually, I knew, she would have—it was simply a part of the story that she hadn't gotten to yet.

I was stuck inside the moment, unable to speak or even cry. There was shock, but there was also an enormous sense of relief at having the necklace in my possession. It was a piece of my sister's story, a piece of my own.

# *Thirty-seven*

∞

After that, the facts I'd been waiting to hear for twenty years came out in a breathless rush.

"I didn't even have to question him," Frank said. "Will just started talking, without provocation. 'It was an accident,' he kept saying, and I had no idea what he was talking about. 'What was an accident?' I asked, and he said, 'I cared about her, I never would have hurt her.'

" 'Who?' I asked. That's when he said her full name, for the first and only time, 'Lila Enderlin.' "

This was what it came down to. The man who had helped me and Lila start our car all those years ago, the one I'd thought of as an interesting diversion on the farm, the one who didn't even merit a brief mention in Thorpe's book—it all, somehow, came back to him.

"Remember how I'd put him up in the hotel out by the beach after Nancy kicked him out?"

I nodded. I was clutching the necklace, and I could feel the pendant digging into my palm.

"Well, he never did get a job. He actually tried, but no one would hire him. He went through all the money I gave him, and then he had nowhere to stay, so he started living in his car. To make money for food and gas, he'd sing and play his guitar. He'd found that the best time was at night when people were going home from the bars. He'd go down into the Muni station, hop the turnstile to get to the westbound platform, lay his guitar case out on the ground, and start playing. Folks would be drunk, waiting around for the train, and they'd get generous when they heard him. I mean, he was good. He knew how to connect with people. He could pull in twenty, thirty bucks on a good night, enough for food, gas to get around town, a matinee every now and

then, but it wasn't enough to get a hotel room, not a decent one anyway. He
was trying to steer clear of those
dumps in the Tenderloin, because he
knew how easy it was to get sucked
back into the drugs again, and he was
really trying to stay clean. And he was
also trying to save a little money, so he
could rent a studio and record some
new songs.

"He told me he was doing it for Tally.
He wanted to stay clean for three
months. If he could do it for that long,
out there on his own, he believed he
could stay clean forever. After three
months he'd come back to the farm
and prove to me that he'd changed,
that he could be a proper uncle.

"So one night he's down there in the
Muni station, about to pack up to go,
singing his last song for the night, a Tim
Hardin tune, 'Reason to Believe,' when
he sees this good-looking woman
down the track, walking toward him.
And as she gets closer he realizes who
it is. I'd always loved that song, 'Reason to Believe.' But now every time I
hear it, it reminds me of Will's story.

"At first he keeps his head down, hoping she won't recognize him, because he's embarrassed for her to see him like that. But she comes over, and she gets close so she can see his face, you know, and she listens to him for a few seconds before she finally says, 'William, is that you?' "

Frank had the simplest way of telling a story, no big embellishments, no dramatic pauses or hand gestures, but as he spoke I could see Lila, in her green corduroy skirt, her black Converse high-tops and peacoat, walking up to her old acquaintance, tilting her head slightly, moving closer to get a better look. And I could hear her, "William, is that you?"—the kindness that would have been in her voice, and the concern, and the complete lack of judgment.

"It's your sister, of course," Frank said. "And once he gets over the embarrassment, he realizes that he's really happy to see her. She's just come from dinner and is on her way home, she seems upset, but he doesn't want to pry, so he doesn't ask what's bothering her. They make small talk for a couple of minutes, and finally she asks if he's doing all right. The way she asks, he can tell that she knows he isn't really okay, but he tries to play it off, just a short run of bad luck, he says.

"At some point she looked up at the kiosk. There'd been an accident in the Montgomery Street Station, and it was going to be another half hour at least before her train arrived. Will offered to wait down there with her until the train came, because the station can get pretty dodgy at night, but she said she didn't want to put him out. That's when he told her that his car was parked just a half-block away, and he offered to give her a ride home. She said she'd be fine, but he insisted it was no trouble."

As I listened to Frank's story, I felt the way you feel when you're watching a scary movie and the heroine goes into the dark house. The script has already been written, the movie's already been made, but that doesn't keep you from talking to the person on screen. *Don't go,* I was saying in my mind. *Don't go.* But of course I knew she'd already gotten in the car. There was no way to rewrite the script, no way to rewind the film.

"They were driving up Market when Will remembered your family's cabin at the Russian River. He and Lila had talked about it back when she was keeping Dorothy on the farm. Once, she'd even shown him a picture of the place. He was really desperate for a shower, a quiet place to stay and sort things out. And so he just asked her, point-blank, if he could stay there. And she thought about it for a minute, she seemed to be considering it, but she said she couldn't give him permission to do that. It was her parents' house, not hers, and she knew they wouldn't be okay with it.

"And this is where things got rocky. I mean, I keep telling you what a good guy Will was, and still in my heart I believe in his basic goodness, but there was this other part of him, this, I don't know how to say it, this brashness. Where he'd get an idea in his head and he just wouldn't let go of it, and if you threw an obstacle in his way, it made

him all the more determined to get
what he wanted. Sometimes it was a
great character trait—it's a big part of
what made his band successful for a
while there, without a doubt. But sometimes it could be scary. If he got hold of
any idea that was, to him, perfectly rational, and somebody shot him down,
he was capable of losing all sense
of reason. And I know that's what
happened that night. His brain just
checked out."

"Why did she accept the ride?" I said.
"She hadn't seen your brother in years.
Why didn't she call me? I would have
come to pick her up. It was a Wednesday, and Wednesday was my day to get
the car. If I'd just let her have the car
that morning—"

Frank reached over as if to touch my
shoulder, but then he pulled his hand
back. "I'm sorry," he said. "Are you
sure you want to hear this right now? I
can wait as long as you need."

"It's okay. Go ahead."

"Will wouldn't take no for an answer.
At some point your sister noticed that
they'd taken a wrong turn—but when

she told him, he just kept driving. By the time they got to the Golden Gate Bridge, she knew where they were headed. She demanded that he turn the car around, but he wouldn't. He apologized, promised he wasn't going to hurt her. He just needed to get to the cabin, he told her—by then, he'd decided it was the answer to his problems. And when they arrived, she could let him in. It was very important to him, see, that she let him in. He wanted to enter the house the proper way, like an invited guest.

"I've gone over it hundreds of times and it doesn't make any sense at all. I asked him, point-blank, what his plan was once he got to the cabin—was he going to hold this poor girl captive?— and he said he hadn't thought that far ahead. He was angry with me for even suggesting it. 'I'm not a kidnapper,' he said. When I told him that yes, that's exactly what he was, he started crying, saying none of it went the way it was supposed to, that it was all fucked up.

"He genuinely believed that while they were driving, he'd be able to appeal to her compassion, he'd be able to convince her to let him stay there, just for a week or two. He was certain he could find some sort of manual labor at Guerneville, and as soon as he got a paycheck he'd rent a place, because it was so much cheaper there than the city. He'd do work around the cabin, too, to earn his keep. He was telling her all of these things, and she just kept saying no, begging him to take her back home. But he kept driving."

I was thinking about that drive over the Golden Gate Bridge in the middle of the night, how when we were kids, Lila and I would huddle in the backseat while the car bumped over the bridge, and we'd gaze out in amazement at the fog, which looked ghostlike in the glow of the bridge lights. We usually left for the river on Friday nights, and the last half hour of the drive along dark, winding roads had always scared me. I had this feeling that something might leap out of the redwoods into our path—a deer, or the boogeyman—but Lila always tried to assuage my fear by telling me that deer avoided headlights and the boogeyman was just a stock character in scary movies.

"While he drove," Frank continued, "Lila was getting more and more nervous. She started yelling at him, demanding that he stop the car and let her out, but he wouldn't. She became frantic, and he kept telling her to calm down. Finally, on a wooded stretch of two-lane road just past Korbel, she jumped out of the car.

"Will said it happened so fast, he couldn't stop her. He immediately pulled off to the side of the road and ran down the embankment, and found her lying there, not moving. He realized how stupid his plan had been, what a huge mistake he'd made. 'She had no reason to be afraid of me,' Will told me, which just shows how full of holes his brain was by then, maybe from all the drugs, I don't know. I mean, he knew he wasn't going to hurt her, and he expected her to understand that, too."

And I was thinking about Lila, rational Lila. How she would have weighed her options as she sat in the car with her captor. How she would have calculated her chances of surviving a fall and running away, weighed them against what might happen if she didn't. A couple of hours before, she'd been having dinner with Peter McConnell, wrapped up in the drama of their affair—thinking, perhaps, that she couldn't stand what was happening to her, couldn't deal with the fact that she had fallen in love with a married man. And then, she had to recalibrate everything. Maybe, as she sat captive in the car with William, she wished that she could go back to the mundane drama of the affair. Or maybe she made a decision about what she would do if she made it back home okay—maybe she decided to break it off with McConnell, start clean. Maybe she was thinking about the Goldbach Conjecture, the problem she still had to solve, the proof she was determined to find. And then she jumped. In a way, it made perfect sense. Lila, after all, was a person of action. For her, sitting back to see what happened, granting someone else control over her fate, would not have been an option.

"Are you okay?" Frank asked.

I was bent over, shivering. There was a white patch the size of a quarter on the carpet. I concentrated on the spot and said, "Go on."

"She was resting against this big, sharp rock, and there was blood on the rock, and Will realized she'd hit her head. He couldn't hear her breathing, so he put his ear against her chest. When he didn't hear anything, he tore open her shirt to listen to her heart, and still there wasn't a sound. He tried mouth-to-mouth. He wasn't sure how to, he was just copying what he'd seen on TV. He picked up her hand and felt for a pulse. He sat there with her for ten minutes, fifteen, trying to revive her. 'But there wasn't anything I could do for her,' he told me. And while he talked, he was still crying, still holding on to that necklace. Finally he picked her up and carried her to the car."

I thought of Thorpe's description of how she had been found. Clothed, but with her blouse open, the top four buttons gone. The fact that the buttons hadn't been found at the scene had been an indication that the crime might have happened elsewhere, but no one could figure out where. Thorpe had dismissed the matter of the buttons. According to his scenario, she had died in the place she was buried.

"Before he put her in," Frank said, "he laid a blanket across the seat. That's something I've never really forgiven him for. Everything else, and the blanket is what I keep coming back to. Because it means he didn't want blood in the car. For whatever reason, while Lila lay there dead, he had the common sense to cover his tracks.

"There were no other cars on the highway. He was frantic, he didn't know what to do. His first thought was to take her to the hospital. But then he saw that there was blood on his hands, his clothes. He started thinking about what would happen when he got there, how he'd be accused of doing something terrible, when he'd never meant to hurt her at all. So instead he drove out to Armstrong Woods, carried her into the trees, and laid her down on the ground, and arranged her as best he could, as if she were sleeping. He was sitting there, staring down at her, and he saw the necklace, and he felt that he needed something to take with him, to prove that what had happened was real. Because part of him thought it was all some terrible hallucination, some bad trip. After leaving her, he drove out to Johnson's Beach, wrapped his clothes up in layers of bags, and tossed them in a Dumpster. He washed up in the river, then took her backpack out to Healdsburg and dumped it in a bin behind a restaurant. He didn't want his clothes and her body anywhere near each other. Then he drove out here, which was the only place he could think to go, and that's how I found him on the doorstep early that next morning."

I sat in silence, stunned. Everything about his story was so different from everything I had believed for so long. In this version, there was no malice, no premeditated crime. There was, instead, a random meeting in a train station with a junkie, followed by a botched kidnapping and a horrible accident. The mistake Lila had made had nothing to do, in the end, with McConnell. Her mistake had been in trusting the wrong person, in having faith in the general goodwill of people. Finally I managed to say, "How do you know he was telling the truth?"

"I know," Frank said. "My brother had a lot of problems, but he couldn't have hurt her on purpose. He just couldn't have."

"Why didn't you say anything?" I asked. "You knew what he'd done. You should have gone to the police."

Frank looked down at his hands. "I planned to, I really did. I told Will he had to turn himself in. I told him I'd go there with him. I told him if he didn't turn himself in, it would catch up to him eventually. I even said that if he didn't do it, I would. I figured that wasn't the sort of thing you could hide forever. I'd protected him from a lot of things, but I couldn't protect him from that. He refused. He said he'd lived in a lot of shitty places, but one place he knew he couldn't handle was jail. Two days after his confession, Tally found him dead in the car. And at that point I just couldn't bring myself to come forward. I researched the case—your sister had been dead for fourteen years by then. I knew no one had been arrested. It wasn't like some innocent guy was sitting in prison, paying for Will's crime. I felt responsible for Will's suicide. If I hadn't pressured him to turn himself in, he probably wouldn't have killed himself."

"You can't know that," I said.

"No, but I'll always wonder. And I figured there was nothing else I could do for him, short of keeping his name out of the papers."

Exactly what I hadn't been able to do for Lila. Part of me was angry with Frank for keeping his secret all these years. If he had come forward when Will confessed, there would have been six fewer years of uncertainty for my family, possibly six fewer years of exile for McConnell. And yet, I felt sympathy for him. I understood his reasons. He had lost a brother, I had lost a sister. I figured he could understand, better than most, what had happened in my life.

Then Frank was moving closer, and he had both arms around me, saying, "I know, I'm so sorry." It felt surreal to be in this man's arms, in this place, the mystery of Lila's death laid bare. I noticed that his shirt was wet, and then I understood why he was holding me. I was crying, and I couldn't stop.

I was thinking of Lila on that final morning, how she'd noticed the fallen limb on the deck, but we'd done nothing about it. I was thinking of the night we lay on the grass in our backyard, searching for Lyra, while she told me the story of Orpheus, who could not bring his wife back from the dead. I was thinking of who she was—my beautiful, brilliant, secretive sister—and who she might have been, if she had lived. And I was thinking of my parents, each of whom had managed to make a life with one daughter, instead of two. All these years, there was so little I'd been able to give them. Now, finally, I could at least give them this story.

I'm not sure how much time passed

before my breath came easily again. I know that the light changed in the room, and water went on upstairs, and the house's old pipes began to clang. Finally, Frank let go of me. It was a strange, awkward moment, both of us shifting out of that unexpected intimacy. I wanted to say something to him, but I couldn't imagine what. We sat there for a minute or two, neither of us meeting the other's eyes. He was the one who broke the silence.

"Ever since he died, my hope has been that, one day, his music will resurface. Some DJ will play it on a radio station somewhere, or some journalist will write about it for a magazine, and people will be reminded of him, they'll start playing his songs again. I just want him to be remembered as Billy Boudreaux, who made great music."

"You should hear it," I said. "It's a beautiful song."

He went over to the tape player and pressed play. Billy Boudreaux's voice came out raw and raspy, growing stronger as the song progressed.

*Deep in the trees I'm on my knees*
*Looking at you and not believing*
*What have I done, my beautiful one*
*What have I done*

As the song ended, I looked up and saw Frank. He hadn't even bothered to turn his face away from me. He just stood by the tape player, one arm on the mantel, staring at a spot on the wall, his tears coming soundlessly.

# *Thirty-eight*

∞

Thorpe saw my reflection in the window before he saw me. He jumped, turned to face me. The only light in the room came from the computer monitor. In its glow, he looked pale and somewhat sickly.

"How did you—"

"I knocked, but you didn't answer. The front door was unlocked, so—"

The expression on his face changed from startled to hopeful. "I'll have a key made. You can come and go as you please. Just knowing that you might show up at any moment would keep me motivated. I'd be sitting here at my desk in the middle of the night—"

"I meant to ask you, why is it that you write in the middle of the night?"

"My mind is clearer."

"I see."

"As I was saying, I'll be sitting right here in my office, struggling to squeeze out the next sentence, and then I'll hear your key in the lock. I won't get up, you won't even have to come say hello. But I'll hear you walking around downstairs, fixing yourself a bite to eat in the kitchen, taking a book down from the shelf. Maybe I'll even be able to hear you turning pages. And as I write I'll be imagining you as my ideal reader. The words I put on the page, they'll all be directed at you. Forever ago, a writing teacher told me you have to always think of the audience. I never could figure out what he meant. How does anyone know who his audience will be?"

"I'm probably not it," I said.

"Pardon?"

"Your audience."

"You could be."

"I prefer fiction, remember?"

"You're in luck. My novel is really coming along. Who knows, maybe you'll like it." Thorpe gestured toward the desk chair. "Have a seat." He was perched on some sort of ergonomic stool, clad in a beat-up pair of flannel pajamas.

"That doesn't look very comfortable," I said, eyeing the stool.

"I got it on the recommendation of my life coach. Align the body before you can align your mind, that sort of thing."

I remained standing and surveyed the desk, which was covered with papers and Post-it notes. Beside the keyboard was a white sheet of paper bearing a pencil sketch. I picked it up and looked more closely. The sketch was of my old house. There, on the second-floor window frame, was the little Victorian birdhouse.

"Look," Thorpe said. "What do I have to do to make it up to you? What do I have to say to make it so we can be friends again?"

He smelled like cigarettes. I almost felt sorry for him. I knew how hard he'd tried to break the habit. What if my doctor told me I had to give up coffee? I was pretty sure I couldn't do it.

"You were wrong about Billy Boudreaux," I said.

Thorpe raised an eyebrow. Everything about him looked bushier tonight. His hair, his beard, the eyebrows. He'd put on weight since I'd last seen him. There was something else about his hair, too. There were tiny follicle dots along the hairline where he used to be bald.

He smiled slightly. "How so?"

"He would have made a good character."

"You met him?" Thorpe looked a bit surprised.

"Yes." I didn't tell Thorpe that it had been over twenty years ago when we met. Or that he had since committed suicide. I didn't really want to tell him anything. I could see his book title now: *Music and Madness: The Unauthorized Biography of Billy Boudreaux.* When I drove to Thorpe's house, intending to confront him about the extent of his lies, I wasn't sure what I would say when I got there. But now I understood something of my own motivation that hadn't been clear to me before. I was here to prove to myself that, for once, I had the upper hand. I wasn't going to tell Thorpe anything—who killed Lila, or why. He didn't deserve to have that information handed to him. He could read about it just like everyone else. I knew just who could handle the story.

"You really should have included him," I said. "Steve Strachman, too. And the janitor, James Wheeler. Don Carroll, all of them."

"Red herrings," Thorpe said, and then he smiled again, as if he was waiting for me to say something. "Red herrings, right?"

"Maybe, but any one of them, if you looked closely enough, would have been enough to build a chapter on. Earlier today, I remembered something you told me once, when we were reading *Brighton Rock* in class."

"Hmmm?"

"We were talking about Pinkie, those gold crowns on the red-upholstered chairs in his hotel. Some guy raised his hand and asked why Graham Greene spent so much time on Pinkie, when he was just a minor character. And you said that, in order for a book to be really good, it's not enough to develop the major characters. The minor ones, too, have to be distinct. When readers close the book, they shouldn't just remember the protagonist and antagonist. They should remember everyone who walks across the page."

Thorpe reached up and fingered the dots on his forehead, as if he'd just remembered they were there. "I said that?"

"Because that's what life is, you said. It's not just about the major characters and the big events. It's about everyone, everything, in between."

"Yes," he said. "That sounds familiar."

"Do you still believe it?"

"I'm not sure I ever believed it. Maybe it was just something I said, a way to fill the time in class."

"Well, I was thinking about it when I was driving over here. And while it's probably true for books, I don't think it's true for real life. Here I am, closing in on forty, and I can count on my fingers the people who have really mattered."

"Who are they?" he asked.

"Lila, of course. My parents. Peter McConnell. Henry." I paused. "You."

"Me?"

"I was barely twenty years old when I read your book," I said. "And I believed every word of it. You wrote the story of my life before I'd had a chance to live it. You said I was directionless, but how could you have known that? I was still so young. But I thought you were so smart, I thought you knew the answers. No one had ever examined me as closely as you did, no one had ever taken as keen an interest. I figured you'd seen into my core and could make out, better than anyone else, who I was. It wasn't very smart on my part. I know I'm as much to blame as you—or more—but I became that character."

"I also wrote that you were smart," Thorpe said, "and beautiful. I wrote that you were passionate."

"I don't remember any of that."

"It's there."

"You referred to Lila as 'the good daughter.' "

"Yes, but I didn't call you the bad daughter."

"You didn't have to."

Thorpe glanced at a clock on the wall, then turned away from me and looked out the window. I followed his gaze. Moments later, someone moved in front of the window of my old bedroom. The shade went down, the light went off.

Thorpe got up and flipped the switch on the wall, flooding his office with light.

"Sorry," he said, looking back toward me.

"What?"

"She lowers the shade and turns off the light at precisely this time every night. Twelve forty-five. I could set my clock by her. Immediately thereafter I switch on my light. It's this game I play. I like to think she notices my light going on—as if we've choreographed it, a silent form of communication. At five minutes past seven every morning, she opens the shade. Except Sunday. Sunday she pulls up the shade at six-thirty, emerges from the front door at seven-fifteen, and walks down the hill to St. Paul's. Coming and going during the

week, she always looks very stylish—
sleek black dresses, black boots, elegant scarves. But on Sunday, on her
way to Mass, she wears this ill-fitting
yellow coat. Every week without excep-
tion, no matter the weather."

"Maybe the church is cold," I said.

"It is."

"You followed her there?"

"It's a church. All souls welcome,
right? I was just curious. She lives
alone, and I had this idea that she
would be alone at Mass, too. But she
isn't. She meets a fellow there, a guy
with a limp, and they sit together in the
back row."

"What else have you uncovered
about her? Date of birth? Favorite
color? Her first heartbreak?"

"That's the thing," he said. "I don't
have to. She's the subject of my novel.
I get to make all that stuff up."

"Let's say she reads the book one
day," I said.

"That's quite a leap of faith, isn't it? I
don't even know if I can publish it.
Maybe no one wants a novel from a

writer of true crime books, especially a love story."

"It's a love story?"

"Yes. I'm tired of blood. I wanted to write about something beautiful. Something I've experienced. All these books about murder—I'm an outsider, not a participant."

"What about *Second Time's a Charm*? That was a love story."

"That book was as much a farce as my marriage. No, this one is about true love. Not sexual love, something deeper. The kind of love that exists even when it isn't returned. The kind of love that can keep on going for a lifetime, with no reciprocation. Tragic love, if you will."

"Some would call that obsession, not love."

His left eye twitched. It was just the tiniest movement, but I knew I had gotten to him. For once, my words were the ones that stung. I was surprised to discover that I felt no satisfaction. I would have liked to take it back. Maybe that's what makes books so dangerous; the record is permanent, indelible.

"The woman who lives in your old house," Thorpe said. "I've seen her playing the piano, hosting dinner parties, going to church, but I've never once seen her read. If I am able to publish this novel, it may come and go without fanfare. But even if it magically jumps all the hurdles and becomes a hit, I'd say the chances of her reading it are very slim."

"For the sake of argument, what if she does? Will she recognize herself?"

Thorpe turned to me, hands in his pockets. He sat on his little stool again. "There's something I've been meaning to tell you. I've been looking for the perfect opportunity to stick it in conversation, but it hasn't really come up."

I couldn't imagine what sort of shoe he'd drop now. It occurred to me that I was ready for all of this to be over. When I walked out his door, I was certain I'd never come back. From now on, new chapters, new plot, my story.

"There's this guy out in L.A.," Thorpe said, "Wade Williams. He was just a college kid when he first read the book, but now he's this hotshot Hollywood producer. He wants to do a film adaptation of Lila's story."

I knew what was coming. In literature, characters have a habit of undergoing major transformations by the final chapter. But in reality, most people don't change. You can throw anything at them, and they will remain, in every way that really matters, the same. I turned to go.

"Wait," Thorpe said, putting a hand on my arm. "It's been a dream of mine, ever since I started writing, to see one of my books make it to the big screen."

I was already at the door to the office, my back to him. There was a weird smell in the hallway—those vanilla candles again.

"I was all set to make the deal," Thorpe said, "but then you came along. And I told him no."

I stopped, just stood there for a moment. Then I turned to him. I needed to see his face, to know if he was telling the truth.

"For what it's worth," he said, "I just want you to know the movie isn't going to happen. And I'm not going to be talking about the book anymore. It's what everyone wants to talk about when I do events—always that one, never the others. For the longest time, my ego has been living off that book. But I want you to know I'm finished with that."

I was leaning against the door frame. There was a crack on the wall across from me, stretching in a crooked diagonal from the ceiling, halfway down the wall, ending somewhere behind the desk. Every building in the city had them. The house I grew up in had them. Every time an earthquake hit, my mother would do a walk-through, looking for new telltale lines in the walls and floors. As a kid I'd been certain that one day, we'd get a crack so big the house couldn't keep standing; it would just fall apart.

"Why?" I asked Thorpe.

"When I wrote that book, I didn't mean to hurt you. I had tunnel vision. All I could see was my opportunity, my way out of teaching and into this thing that I wanted so much I could taste it. I wanted so desperately to be a writer, I forgot about everything else. So I guess this is my way of saying I'm sorry. Granted, it may be too late. But I mean it, Ellie. I'm sorry. That's what I've been trying to tell you."

"Thank you."

He was looking at me, as if there was more he wanted to say. I was grateful to him for not saying it.

He walked me downstairs. Above the mantel was the Munkácsi photograph he'd told me about before—two men on a dark street, locked in battle, their arms wrapped around one another. The photograph was violent, yet somehow beautiful, full of life.

In the entryway, something was different—the silence. In the dim streetlight that shone through the front window I could see that the fountain was empty, it had been scrubbed clean. Thorpe opened the door for me. Just as I stepped outside, he took my hand in his, pulled me toward him. I didn't resist. I let him hug me, and for a second or two I hugged him back.

As I was driving home, I thought again about what Thorpe had said all those years ago in class. Life isn't just about the major characters and the big events. It's about everyone, everything, in between.

Thirty years from now, would I remember Jesus at the farm, Maria at the café in Nicaragua, my boss Mike? At thirty-eight, I could recollect the names of only three or four of the teachers I'd had in my life, and it wasn't necessarily the best ones that stuck in my memory. I remembered Mrs. Smith from kindergarten only because she chewed with her mouth open, mean Mrs. Johnson from third grade only because her dresses always rode up too high on the backs of her puffy legs, my P.E. teacher from seventh grade only because she had once shamed me in front of my classmates for failing to catch a fly ball. I remembered the men I had slept with, but only by name; for the most part, details escaped me. I knew in the end that Thorpe would never leave my memory, nor would McConnell, or Frank Boudreaux.

I wished I could go back in time and pose this question to Lila. Her short history was made up primarily of my parents, me, and Peter McConnell. Before that night when she ran into Billy Boudreaux at the Muni station, would she have bothered to mention him in her list of relevant people? It seemed unlikely.

Heading down Clipper and across Castro, I found myself stuck on Thorpe. All through the conversation, I felt as if there was something more he had wanted to say. I put him off, thinking I already knew what it was—something about me, about us. But there, alone in the car, it occurred to me that perhaps it was something else entirely.

"Red herrings," he had said, "right?" Earlier, when I had first mentioned Billy Boudreaux's name, he had smiled ever so slightly. Was it possible that he had known, all along, much more than he let on?

I thought of that first address Thorpe gave me as we stood in his garage in the early morning—the innocent janitor, living out his final days in his modest house in Bernal Heights. Did Thorpe know it was a name that would lead nowhere? After that, though, it was Boudreaux and then Strachman. Was Thorpe thanking me for coming back each time? Was he thanking me for giving him a second chance? I was the one who had undertaken the search, but it was Thorpe who gave me the tools.

He was still Thorpe. And yet, I had a hard time admitting to myself, in some essential way, he had changed. It had been twenty years. I'd always thought that people changed only in books, not in real life. But here was Thorpe—this living, breathing person doing something I never would have thought him capable of. After all this time, he had managed to surprise me.

# *Thirty-nine*

∞

It was October, the tail end of the rainy season, and Diriomo was cool and wet, the whole town blanketed in orchids. I had arrived on a Tuesday morning, following an uneventful red-eye and a bumpy bus ride from Managua, and checked into my usual hotel. That afternoon, I would go to the co-op to taste some new samples. I had gifts for Jesus's children—a book of bird illustrations for Rosa, a paint set for Angel. But first, there was someone I wanted to see.

I changed into a sundress and sandals and set out on foot. On the makeshift baseball field, children were playing with sticks and an old tennis ball. Soon I was standing on the familiar doorstep, ringing the familiar copper bell. I heard shuffling from within, and Maria appeared, her gray hair draped over one shoulder in a long braid, tied with a yellow ribbon.

"Welcome," she said, smiling.

The place smelled the same as it had three months before, when Peter McConnell walked up to my table and said, "Do you know who I am?" Then, as now, there was the salty-rich smell of frying pork, the deep aroma of coffee, the mild scent of cornmeal. But that night the place had been dark, lit only by candles. Now sun flooded in through the windows, illuminating the surprised faces of Maria's porcelain dolls. The red curtain leading into the kitchen was pulled aside, and through it I could see Maria's stove, drenched in sunlight.

"What are you serving today?"

"*Nacatamal,*" she said. "*Está usted sola?*"

"*Sí, señora.* I am alone."

She shook her head and put a hand to her heart, as if it pained her to see me return, once again, in such a state. I sat at my usual table. Moments later, she brought coffee, then disappeared into the kitchen. I reached into my bag and took out Lila's notebook.

I had been over the notebook so many times, but each new perusal of it offered up some fresh surprise. This time, it was a tiny line of handwritten text pressed up close to the binding halfway through the notebook, so that the pages had to be forced open to read it. I brought it close to my eyes and struggled to make out the words. *An equation for me has no meaning unless it expresses a thought of God.*

Maria brought out the *nacatamal*. It was delicious, as always. When she came to clear away my plate, I asked her in my clumsy Spanish about the gentleman I'd met three months before in her restaurant.

*"Ah, sí, Señor Peter!"* she said.

*"Sí,"* I said. *"Dónde vive?"*

She went to the kitchen and came back with a pen and a piece of paper, on which she drew a map. *"Estamos aquí,"* she said, pointing to a little square box with a stick figure of a woman standing in front of it. *"Él está aquí.*" She drew a circle around another box, which was connected to the first by a series of winding roads.

"Thank you."

Laughing, she made a gesture as if to shoo me out the door. *"Señor McConnell, él es muy guapo!"*

"He is," I agreed.

On my way out, I stopped to examine a Venus flytrap on the windowsill. Its pale green leaves were open, split down the middle like fruit. A fly buzzed just inches above the plant. Finally, the insect landed on the needles. The leaf snapped shut. I wondered whether Lila had ever seen a Venus flytrap. I seemed to remember there being one in a classroom at our grade school, but I wasn't sure. It was a habit I couldn't quite break, even now—when I saw or experienced something new, I often wondered whether Lila had had a chance to experience it, too. Sometimes I felt as if I was experiencing each new thing twice—once for me, and once for her. Over the years, that sensation tapered off exponentially. There are only so many new things in the world, and the older you get, the harder it is to find them.

Though the roads of Diriomo were weblike, folding over on themselves in inexplicable ways, Maria's map was excellent. I marked it with my pen as I walked, drawing in landmarks—a mailbox, a donkey tied to a post, an old tire swing hanging from a tree—so that I'd be able to find my way back afterward.

After half an hour, I came to a white house at the end of a deserted road. From the outside it looked as though it couldn't contain more than a couple of rooms. Behind the house, and to both sides of it, was forest. The dirt yard was tidy, dotted with banana palms and prickly-looking foliage. A series of circular paving stones, each inscribed with a number—1-12-9-12-1-12-9-12—led from the dirt road to the concrete porch. I had just lifted my hand to knock when I heard a voice behind me.

"Ellie?"

I turned. It was Peter, clad in a sweat-drenched shirt, carrying two large metal buckets filled with water. He walked up the path of stones and set the buckets on the porch. "Well water," he said, breathing heavily. "When I first moved out here, I thought I wouldn't last. I couldn't imagine life without plumbing. But you get used to it. There's something satisfying about using exactly what you need, nothing more."

"Where's the well?"

"A half mile that way," he said, pointing into the woods. "It's good water. Would you like a taste?"

"That would be nice."

McConnell opened the door and motioned for me to go ahead of him. Inside, it was warm and dark. We were standing in a large, simple room. He pulled the curtains aside to let in light. To the left, running lengthwise along the wall, was a bed, and beside it a nightstand. On the nightstand was a legal pad, a wind-up clock, and a large, unlit candle. I was surprised by the size of the bed given the meager surroundings—it was a queen, with crisp green sheets and two plump pillows sheathed in bright white pillowcases. A couple of feet from the foot of the bed, a large desk was pushed against the wall. Above the desk was a window framed by yellow curtains. Beside the desk, a built-in bookcase strained under the weight of several dozen books. I recognized some of the titles from Lila's own collection: Whitehead and Russell's *Principia Mathematica,* Euclid's *Elements,* Kline's *Mathematical Thought from Ancient to Modern Times,* Gauss's *Disquisitiones Arithmeticae.* And there, lying on its side on top of a series of yellow-covered reproductions of Ramanujan's lost notebooks, was the one book with which I was very familiar—Hardy's *A Mathematician's Apology.* I'd taken Lila's copy after she died.

Although the room was spartan, there was something undeniably cheerful about the color scheme. Even the concrete floor had been painted a pale shade of blue, and beside the bed there was a woven rug in bright reds and yellows. In the far right corner stood a round table and a single wooden chair. Behind that, against the wall, was a makeshift kitchenette: antique icebox,

Bunsen burner, and a copper wash-basin on a stand.

"There wasn't any electricity when I moved in," McConnell said. "I lived here for several years without it."

I spotted a cell phone on the table. "You're modernizing."

"I gave in under duress. The company I contract for insists that they be able to reach me. Go figure. They keep trying to sell me on e-mail, but I've managed to hold my ground."

He went to the porch and brought the buckets inside, hefting them up onto the table. He took two glasses from a cupboard and dipped water into them with a ladle. The water was cool and good, with a slight metallic taste and a faint smell of grass.

"Please," McConnell said. "Sit down."

I looked around the room. There was only the one wicker chair by the table. "Sorry," he said. "I rarely have company." He picked up the chair, carried it across the room, and placed it a couple of feet from the bed. I sat down, the wicker creaking beneath me. McConnell sat on the bed, so that we were facing one another. "In fact, you're the first person who has visited me in four years."

"Who was the last?"

He hesitated. "A woman from the village."

"May I ask what happened?"

"She wanted children. I told her I was too old for that."

"You're only fifty," I said.

"I already have a son."

"One is enough?"

"There was a time I dreamt of having three or four. But I rather failed on the fatherhood front, didn't I? Some errors don't bear repeating." He smiled sadly. "Technically speaking, one is a beautiful number. One is its own factorial, its own square, its own cube. It is neither a prime number nor a composite number. It is the first two numbers of the Fibonacci Sequence. It is the empty product: any number raised to the zero power is one. It might be argued that one is the most independent number known to man. It can do things that no other number is capable of."

"A sequence of natural numbers always ends with one," I said.

"You've been doing your homework."

"It was in Lila's notebook. The Collatz Conjecture. According to Erdos, 'Mathematics is not yet ready for such a problem.' "

He took a sip of water, wiped his mouth with the back of his hand. "You went to see an old friend of mine."

"Yes, Don Carroll. He spoke very highly of your work."

McConnell glanced at the floor, embarrassed. "He always was in my corner."

"In his office I saw a book with a double torus on the cover. I wanted to ask you about Lila's tattoo. Why did she choose the double torus?"

"She had a thing for topology. In topology, you can bend and stretch shapes and they remain essentially the same—a sphere is identical to any sphere or cube, or in fact any solid shape, such as the bed you're sitting on, or the rug beneath our feet. But the moment you put a hole in a shape, it is no longer equivalent. So a double torus, which looks like two doughnuts stuck together, is equivalent to anything else with two holes, say a trophy with two handles. Lila liked the idea that a thing could be dramatically transformed while remaining, in every way that really mattered, the same. The double torus is a particularly rich form in that respect."

"In the notebook," I said, "Lila had a quote: 'An equation for me has no meaning unless it expresses a thought of God.' "

Peter smiled. "Ramanujan. He believed his inspiration came from Namagiri, his *kuldevta,* family deity."

"Do you see God in the numbers?" I asked.

"An equation isn't necessarily about numbers. It's about patterns. The universe is governed by mathematical patterns. Gravity, string theory, chaos theory, quantum mechanics—all of it can be expressed in terms of equations. $F = GMm/R^2$, for example, one of the most basic equations of our universe. There's an argument that if you can create an equation for anything, that thing exists. Because one can write an equation that represents a vast, empty, three-dimensional space, such a space exists. If the essence of God is creation, then yes, a beautiful equation can be said to express a thought of God."

He looked away, and smiled to himself. "I was always a bit lowbrow compared to Lila. My favorite Ramanujan story is about when Hardy was visiting him in the hospital, and Hardy said: 'I rode here today in a taxicab whose number was 1729. This is a dull number,' to which Ramanujan replied, 'No, it is a very interesting number; it is the smallest number expressible as a sum of two cubes in two different ways.'" He paused. "But you didn't come here for a math lesson."

"Lila's notebook," I said, hesitating. "Why did you have it?"

"She gave it to me that night at dinner. She had come up with a new idea—a 'brain flash,' she called it—regarding an approach to the Goldbach Conjecture, and she wanted my opinion. But, unfortunately, I told her I didn't want to talk about math. For one night, I wanted to put work aside and talk about other things, personal things. We needed to address the issue of my marriage, what we would do in the long term. I also felt there was still so much I didn't know about her, so many questions I wanted to ask. Ultimately, she consented, on the condition that I take her notebook home and examine her new work, so that we could discuss it the next day."

"And what did she tell you?" I asked. "That night, what did you learn about Lila that you didn't know before?"

"I asked her to tell me what the best moment of her life had been."

"Did she?"

"Yes. She told me about a trip the two of you had taken to Europe together right after you graduated from high school."

"Pascal in Paris," I said, smiling.

He gave me a questioning look.

"It had been a dream of hers," I said, "to visit Pascal's grave. On that trip, she finally did. I'd never seen her so excited."

"That wasn't it," Peter said.

"It wasn't?"

"No, it was in a hostel in Venice. The two of you had been traveling for a couple of weeks, and all of your clothes were filthy. You didn't mind the dirty clothes very much, Lila said; you were able to roll with the punches, and for you everything about the trip, even the dirty laundry, was a great adventure. But Lila liked things a certain way, and she hated being dirty. That day, she had gone off in search of a Laundromat, but hadn't been able to find one. You were sleeping in a room with a dozen bunks, women and men together. In the middle of the night Lila woke up, and realized you weren't in your bed. She thought you must have gone to the bathroom, but after a couple of minutes, when you hadn't returned, she became worried. She climbed down from her bunk and went to the bathroom to find you. You weren't there. She wandered up and down the hallways, softly calling your name. A few of the rooms were private, and had the doors closed. As she became increasingly worried, she began putting her ear to those doors, listening for you. Then she heard banging down below. Alarmed, she went down the dark stairwell to the basement. She saw you before you saw her. You were working in the dim light of a single bulb, standing over an old hand-operated washing machine. She asked what you were doing. 'What does it look like?' you said, smiling. What Lila remembered from that night was that you actually looked happy to be standing there in the cold basement in the middle of the night, washing clothes by hand. And she knew that you wouldn't have minded wearing dirty clothes for another week or two. You were doing it for her."

"She said that?" I asked. I had a vague memory of a hostel in Venice. But I didn't remember anything about the midnight trip to the basement to wash our clothes. It amazed me that Lila had remembered, and that it had meant so much to her.

"Yes. When I asked her what the best moment of her life had been, she told me that story."

"But it was nothing," I said.

"To her, it was."

"Thank you for telling me that."

I heard steps on the porch. I glanced out the window. A young boy dropped a small bundle beside the door before pedaling away on an old bike, wheels squeaking.

"It's Pedro," McConnell said. "He brings me pencils each month."

"Another question," I said, as the squeaking of Pedro's bicycle faded.

"Hmm?" He reached over and smoothed the pillowcase at the head of the bed. My gaze followed his hand, the gentle movement of his long fingers over the white fabric. For a moment it was as if I had been transported to another place and time, and had been given the gift of seeing into his most private moments—McConnell in the hotel room in Half Moon Bay, running his hand over Lila's pillowcase after she had left, memorizing the impression of her head against the pillow.

His voice brought me back. "Ellie? Where are you?"

I met his eyes again. "Sorry, I was just thinking about something—"

"Your sister used to do that. Just wander away in the middle of a conversation. At first I was offended, until she explained it to me—"

"As if she'd stepped into another room," I said, "and she became so focused on the things in that room that the door shut behind her. You'd have to make physical contact to shake her out of it."

"Exactly. The moment I touched her shoulder or held her hand, she'd come right back to me, and explain in the most lucid terms what it was she'd been concentrating on. Every time, it gave me the impression of having performed some strange magic trick, as if my touch was enough to lead her back from another world. Funny, I always assumed I was the only one who could do that." He paused. "You wanted to ask me something?"

"Why did you return the notebook to me?"

"I've memorized every page of it, I don't need the physical object when every figure, every scribble, is stored in my mind. Beyond that, I thought you should have it."

"I thought it would provide some clue," I said. "I thought there would be some key in those pages that would unlock the mystery of what happened to Lila. I was disappointed when I didn't find it."

"You came back because you still aren't sure, didn't you? You went home, you looked for answers, and you didn't find them. But I've told you everything I know. I'm sorry, I wish I could help you, but I have nothing more to offer."

His gaze came to rest on my throat. He leaned forward, reaching toward me. For a split second, when I felt his warm fingers brushing my neck, I had the strange feeling that he might kiss me. I decided, in that moment, that I would not back away. "It's hers," he said, astonished.

I had misread him. I could feel the slight pressure of the gold chain against my neck as he held the topaz pendant between his fingers. He let go, and the tiny stone fell back against my skin. He touched it again. I looked into

his eyes, and he was a million miles
away.

I reached into my bag and pulled out
the magazine. I handed it to him.

He looked at the cover, uncomprehending. *"Rolling Stone?"*

"Turn to page sixty-three."

He looked at me for a moment more,
and he seemed like he was about to
say something, but then he started flipping through the pages. The top half of
the spread was covered with a photograph of the Potrero Sound Station.
The title of the article was "Billy
Boudreaux's Last Act." In a slightly
smaller font was the byline, Ben Fong-
Torres. Ben had pulled some strings
and managed to get the piece in at the
last minute.

"What's this?" Peter said.

"Look at the bass player," I said. I'd
studied the photograph for so long, it
was burned into my memory. In the
foreground was Kevin Walsh, holding
the microphone so close to his mouth it
looked as though he might swallow it.
Billy was in the shadows, his face
barely visible. But the way the stage

was lit, you could see his powerful arms, fingers poised on the strings. "That's Billy Boudreaux."

Peter looked up at me. "I don't understand."

"Take your time," I said. "I'll go outside."

I stood on the porch, waiting. I picked up the bundle of pencils and breathed in the woody, clean smell. I was out there for twenty minutes, watching dogs pass on the dirt road, looking for birds in the branches, before I heard the bedsprings creak. Peter came onto the porch and stood beside me. "Where did this come from?" he asked quietly.

"It's a long story."

We stood there for a few minutes, looking out at the road. It began to rain. The raindrops were huge, leaving pockmarks in the red dirt yard. I didn't know what to say. I hoped he knew that I felt responsible, in some way, for what had happened to him. I hoped he understood that this was the best I could do.

"You could go home now," I said. "It's been in the news, you know. I think there are some people who want to apologize to you."

"Someday, maybe. For now, this is home."

"The numbers," I said, "on the paving stones. What do they mean?"

"12-9-12-1," he said. "L-i-l-a. I used eight stones, spelled it out twice, because eight represents infinity."

"She'd like that," I said.

He laughed slightly. "Actually, I think she would find it alarmingly sentimental. But then, I've had a lot of time on my hands. A guy can become sentimental when he lives at the end of a dirt road for too long."

He moved closer and put an arm around my shoulders, just for a moment, and then dropped it. "The first time I saw you in town," he said, "you were standing beside a fruit stand, your back to me. It was about to start raining. I could tell you were a foreigner, and I wanted to go over and tell you to find somewhere to sit out the storm. Foreigners are always surprised by the rain. It comes down so hard, so fast, you hardly have time to get out of it.

Then there was a clap of thunder. It startled you. You turned around and looked up at the sky. And for a second, maybe two, I thought everything they say about Diriomo was true. I believed that it really was a *pueblo brujo,* bewitched village. Because at that moment, when you looked up at the sky, I thought you were her. And for a fraction of a second, I had this picture in my mind of everything coming together, my whole life reorienting itself, as if the last decade had been a dream."

We stood there in silence for another minute or two before I said, "I should go. I'm visiting a farm this afternoon."

"Wait. You can't go out into this rain like that."

He went into the house and came out seconds later with a white poncho, just like the one he'd been wearing in the photograph in Carroll's office. "Lift your arms," he said. I did, and he pulled the poncho over my head. It reached all the way to my ankles. "You look like a ghost," he said, smiling.

We hugged, a complete hug this time, and I breathed in the pencils-and-rain smell of his skin. I thanked him and stepped out into the downpour. I took my time following the path of stones— 12-9-12-1-12-9-12-1—from his porch through the rain-soaked yard. When I got to the end, he called out to me— "Wait!"

He ducked into the house. A couple of minutes later he came out again, plodding across the wet paving stones. His shirt and pants immediately became drenched, clinging to his body. His hair stuck to his head. He handed me a package, something hefty and book-like, wrapped in layers of plastic bags.

"What's this?"

The rain stopped, just as suddenly as it had begun. I reached into the bags and pulled out a large manila envelope. Inside the envelope, a sheaf of paper, two inches thick, covered in numbers and symbols.

# *Forty*

∞

The new café was on Twenty-first Street between Mission and Valencia, tucked between a used bookstore and a clothing boutique. When I arrived at three in the afternoon, the neighborhood was gearing up for the *Día de los Muertos* procession. As I rounded the corner, I could see Henry down the block, standing on a ladder in front of the café. When I got closer I saw that he had a paintbrush in hand, and was touching up a smudge on the signage above the storefront. The letters were pale green, lowercase.

"Great name," I said.

"You like it?"

"Shade," I read. "It's perfect."

"I'd hug you, but I'm covered in paint and sawdust."

"All set for opening day?"

"Getting there. Have time for a cup of coffee?"

"Always."

Inside, he showed me the beautiful chrome espresso maker, the antique roasting machine. A series of framed photographs depicted the coffee farmers whose co-ops would supply the beans for the café.

"Everything is reclaimed or recycled," Henry said proudly. "These are the original light fixtures from the Coronet movie theater. The bar and tables are made out of redwood from an old Doelger house they tore down last year in the Sunset. The chairs are from the old U.S. Mint."

"It's beautiful." I pulled a small paper bag out of my purse. "Here, I brought you something. A new blend from Jesus."

He opened the bag and sniffed. "Mmmm, chocolate and toasted hazelnut."

"Wait until you taste it," I said. "Cayenne and citrus. A lovely vanilla bourbon

note in the end. I think it should be your
signature coffee."

He went behind the counter and fed
the beans into the grinder. The noise of
the machine was a welcome distraction. I'd seen Henry half a dozen times
since our aborted conversation in the
cupping room at Golden Gate Coffee,
but each time, there were other people
around. "I don't know if Mike told you,"
he said, "but I requested that you handle my account. Nobody else."

I nodded.

"How was the Nicaragua trip?"

"Really good. I would have asked you
to come along, but—"

He stood with his hands in his pockets. He looked tired. When he smiled, I
noticed that crow's-feet had begun to
form around his eyes. When I'd met
him, he looked so young. He *had* been
young, I reminded myself; so had I.

"Funny," he said, "when Mike suggested that I go with you, I had this
whole picture in my mind of how it
would play out—me and you down
there, eating at little hole-in-the-wall
restaurants, running back to our hotel

in the rain—the way we used to. I kept waiting for you to give me the go-ahead. Every time I saw you at the office, I hoped that would be the day you'd change your mind. At the very least, I thought you'd let me take you to dinner, catch up."

I hesitated. "There was someone I needed to see down there."

"I know. I heard. It's all pretty amazing."

A burst of music drifted through the door as a group of old men with trumpets passed by.

"We never really talked about what happened in Guatemala," he said.

"It's okay, Henry. It was a long time ago."

"Not that long." He spooned the grounds into a coffee press and poured in the steaming water.

"I'd forgotten that about you. You're still devoted to the French press."

"It's the only civilized way."

I watched the street while he waited for the coffee to steep. He brought two porcelain cups—one blue, one yellow—over to the table.

"Pretty."

"An estate sale. I thought it would be nice if all of the dishes were sort of random." The 21 Valencia bus went by, and the chandelier above our table rattled. He poured the coffee and sat down.

"That night in Guatemala," he said. "I guess I just got scared off. I didn't want to fight anymore. We were always fighting."

"I know," I said. "I'm sorry."

A series of loud pops erupted outside, followed by shouts and laughter. I turned to see a group of teenage girls heading toward Mission, setting off firecrackers in the street. They wore identical black dresses and dark red lipstick, their hair slicked back in ponytails. At that moment, as if she could sense my gaze, one of the girls turned, met my eyes, and slowed down. I waved at her, and she waved back.

Henry sipped his coffee. "You seem different."

"Different how?"

"You were always so nervous, fidgety, always looking over your shoulder."

"And now?"

"I don't know. You've relaxed."

"That's another thing I'd forgotten about you."

"Hmm?"

"You could always see right into me. It made me uncomfortable. You knew me too well."

"That's a bad thing?" Henry asked.

"At the time, I thought it was."

We sat for a minute or two in silence, watching the police set up barricades for the parade.

"Remember that time?"

"Yes." I knew that he was talking about the night, several years ago, when we took part in the Day of the Dead procession—his idea.

"You looked good in your skeleton suit," he said.

"Did I?" I laughed.

I remembered that the white makeup made my face feel tight. And I had carried a picture of Lila in my pocket. I'd taken the photo with a little point-and-shoot camera at the stable in Montara, not long after she got Dorothy. I'd forgotten to turn off the flash, and in the photograph, Dorothy is startled by the light, rearing up. Lila is leaning forward, hanging on, but she doesn't seem the least bit scared. She looks as if she's having the time of her life.

"Do you remember that picture?" I asked.

"Of course. You put it on the altar. And then, as we were walking away, you took it back."

"You saw that?"

Henry nodded.

"Why didn't you say anything?"

"I figured you had your reasons."

"After I put the photograph there, I changed my mind. I didn't want to give her up, even if it was just a picture."

Through the open door, I could feel the evening growing cooler. The light was fading. "You were right," he said finally. "This should be my trademark coffee. It's amazing."

I reached across the table and took his hand. He seemed startled, but he didn't pull away. His blue eyes were so unusual, so beautiful. It was the first thing I'd noticed when I met him; I imagined it was the first thing everyone noticed. How could they not? In certain kinds of light, his eyes were so pale they appeared almost clear. Sitting there, I considered the unlikely genetics, the strange combination of his parents' chromosomes that conspired to give him his most striking feature. For my entire adult life, I had believed what Miss Wood, my high school biology teacher, had told me: that one day such eyes would be gone, a distant memory of a faded civilization. Blue eyes resulted from recessive genes, Miss Wood had said; because of this, one day they would no longer exist. One day, the world would be filled with nothing but brown-eyed people, the dominant gene running its course, taking over the planet. It was the doom of mediocrity, she said, dominant genes battling the recessive genes until one day every human would be the same.

I had never really questioned Ms. Wood's reasoning, accepting it like so many other wrong things I learned in high school. And so, for years, with Henry, I always looked into his eyes with a bit of melancholy, assuming that our children would have no chance of inheriting his eyes. They were like a beautiful, pale light coming from a star that had died many years earlier.

Only recently had I discovered that Miss Wood had misunderstood one of the most basic and most important tenets of biology. It was McConnell who explained this to me, during that conversation in his room in Diriomo a couple of weeks before. "You look so much like her," he had said. "Except for your red hair, of course." And in response, I had said something about how, one hundred years from now, red hair would be obsolete.

"Not true," McConnell had said. And he'd gone on to tell me the story of the biologist Reginald Punnett, who believed that recessive genes would continue to recur in the population at a steady rate, indefinitely. Unable to come up with any science by which to prove his theory, Punnett turned to his friend, G. H. Hardy. According to Punnett, Hardy thought about it for a few minutes, and then quickly scribbled a simple, elegant equation which proved

Punnett's theory beyond doubt. Punnett was amazed. He immediately suggested that Hardy submit his work for publication. Hardy was hesitant at first, believing that such a problem must have already been solved and that it was not his place, as a mathematician, to propose work in a field so completely foreign to him.

"Ultimately," McConnell had said, "Hardy relented and submitted the work that is now known as the Hardy-Weinberg Principle and is taught in all of the more reputable high schools and colleges around the world. Blue eyes, red hair—they'll be around as long as humans are. It's a huge deal in biology, but when he wrote his famous *A Mathematician's Apology,* he didn't even bother to mention it."

Now, for the first time, I looked into Henry's eyes and felt none of that old melancholy. A hundred years from now, Henry's great-grandchildren might look at photographs of him and understand exactly where they got their beautiful blue eyes.

"Why are you smiling?" Henry said.

"No reason."

For a couple of minutes we just sat there. I remembered what Don Carroll had told me—"a perfect match is almost as rare as a perfect number."

"That day at the office," I said. "You were about to tell me something, and then Mike walked in. Remember? I'd just asked if you could tell, the first time you met me, what exactly would do us in."

He leaned closer, wrapped my hand in both of his. There was no hesitation in his voice, and I wondered if he'd been waiting, all this time, to give me an answer. "When I was a kid I always had this dream where my father finally bought me this bike I'd been desperate for—it was one of those Schwinn five-speeds with the choppers in the front. It was dark green, and it was called the 'Pea Picker.' Anyway, in the dream, whenever I reached out for it, it would start rolling away. I never did catch it. In Guatemala, it occurred to me that you were like that bike. You were there with me, but then you were also just slightly out of reach."

"So, I'm the Pea Picker?"

"Well . . ."

More noise in the street, more fire-crackers, but this time, neither of us turned to look.

"Do you know the story of the constellation Lyra?"

He shook his head.

I told Henry the tale as Lila had told it to me that night thirty years before. I told him about how Orpheus had gone to the Underworld to bring his wife, Eurydice, back from the dead, and how, in the last moments, he had broken his promise to the gods and turned back to look at her. "When he looked at her, she slipped away," I said. "After Orpheus died, Zeus tossed his lyre into the sky, forming the constellation Lyra."

"Sad story."

"Yes," I said, "but the actual facts are rather unsentimental: Lyra has a right ascension of 19 hours and a declination of 40 degrees. It contains the stars Vega, Sheliak, Sulafat, Aladfar, Alathfar, and the double-double star Epsilon. Four of Lyra's stars are known to have planets. The best time to view the constellation is in August."

Henry smiled. "I'm not sure I follow."

"The whole thing about Orpheus and Eurydice, how he made this crucial error and lost her forever—it's just a story. You can take it or leave it. Stories aren't set in stone. It took me the longest time to realize that."

Later, I helped Henry with some last-minute details—hanging a mirror in the restroom, putting candles and bud vases on the tables, sweeping the floors. By the time I left, it was dark out, and the streets were crowded with costumed revelers. I walked down Valencia, pressing against the throng. A troupe of scantily clad dancers swirled around me, moving in unison to the spooky beat of the drums. The air reeked of incense. A pair of police officers drove slowly down the street, motorcycles rumbling. I stepped aside to avoid a group of men dressed in tattered suits, carrying an enormous funeral pyre. On top of the pyre was a naked woman, painted head-to-toe in white.

I tried to push my way through the crowd, but I was going the wrong direction. Soon I was swept up in the raucous, swirling mass moving south down Eighteenth Street. The music, the voices, the bodies, the smell of sweat and alcohol and incense, made me feel as if I had been caught up in some impossible dream. The costumes were dark and ghoulish, but the atmosphere was festive. For several seconds I walked side by side with a tall, gaunt man in a tuxedo and bowler hat, his lips starkly red against the white face paint. He held hands with a small woman in a long white dress, wearing a cloak of purple feathers so heavy she stooped under its weight. A man in skeleton gloves brushed past us, playing a trombone. The tuxedo man broke away, down another street, and I was surrounded by Mexican schoolchildren clad in red, singing a familiar melody to the shush-shush of their maracas. Their teacher, a beautiful twentysomething girl, was also dressed in red; her face was painted white—a skeleton, though a happy, smiling one. As the teacher led them in song, a mariachi band appeared from across the street to accompany them on guitars and bass.

I don't know how many minutes I was jostled along by the crowd before I arrived at Garfield Park. The place was crowded with altars that had been erected in honor of the dead. There were dozens of them, ranging from the very simple to the stunningly elaborate. On the altars people had left flowers, toy skeletons and bones, books, shot glasses filled with tequila, little white skulls made of sugar. And on every altar, stretching through the park and into the dark alleyways beyond, were photographs. Thousands of pairs of eyes staring out from the candlelit altars. Here the crowd had grown less rowdy. People were politely pressing past one another in order to place their photos on the communal altars. As I moved closer, I realized that I had fallen into a long line, marching slowly toward the largest of the altars. In front of me, a young girl dressed in white was clutching a photo with both hands, tears in her eyes. She kept glancing over toward the McDonald's, where her father was waiting for her. Behind me, two older women were holding hands, speaking in Spanish.

For so long I had lived a solitary life, hoarding my memories of Lila like some secret treasure I couldn't afford to lose, sifting through them, day by day, on my own—as if my sister's death was a thing no one else could understand. Now, everywhere I looked, I met the faces of the dead.

Inside my coat pocket was a photograph of Lila I had taken about a month before she died. In it, she's sitting at the dining room table, head bent slightly over the familiar notebook, pencil poised against the page. From the angle of the photograph, it's clear I must have taken it from the opposite end of the table, just a few feet from her. She's not looking at the camera, but at the notebook, as if completely unaware that there is anyone else with her in the room. Her dark hair is piled on top of her head, fastened with a tortoiseshell clip, and on her face is a look of pure concentration. But if you study the set of her mouth, her eyes, something else is clear in her expression. It is a look of delight, as if something has just dawned on her.

For years, I'd kept the photograph in a box, worried that I might bend it, or worse, lose it. Now, standing before the communal altar, I slid it out of my coat pocket and held it up to the candlelight. I thought of Peter McConnell, how he'd never needed photographs of Lila to keep his devotion alive. He'd had the notebook, and his memories of her, and for him that was enough.

What's this?" I had asked several days before, standing on a stone step in McConnell's soaked yard, holding a thick envelope.

"It's the proof."

"The proof?"

He nodded. I just looked at him for a few moments, uncomprehending. Then I understood. "*The* proof?" I said, incredulous.

"*The* proof."

"For the Goldbach Conjecture?"

"Yes." From the expression on his face, I could tell he was almost as astonished as I was.

"I don't understand. I thought you'd given up."

"I had," he said. "And then I met you, talked to you, and everything turned upside down. My memories of the final conversation I had with Lila that night in the restaurant came rushing back. I remembered something she said before I turned the conversation in a more personal direction, something about a combination of Brun's Sieve Method, the Vinogradov Theorem, and what she referred to as an 'unusual but perfectly elegant third piece.' At the time, I thought little of it. We'd been down so many roads in our pursuit of the Goldbach proof, and I assumed we would go down many, many more. I took it for granted that the sheer complexity of the problem meant that the key we were looking for was years, possibly decades, in the future. A few months after I'd moved here in the early nineties, I finally persuaded myself to open her notebook and search for the 'unusual but perfectly elegant third piece' she had referred to. I went through the notebook with a fine-tooth comb, and over time I considered thousands of different variations, but nothing worked. Still, I continued working, and, as you learned from Carroll, I managed to conceive of a number of interesting results in the process. But I never felt that I was coming anywhere close to a final proof of the Goldbach Conjecture.

"Then I met you. That night with you in your hotel room was almost unreal. The combination of the rum, and the darkness, and the sheer strangeness of it all, had an almost hallucinatory effect on me. I found that if I narrowed my eyes just so, slightly blurring my vision, and tuned down my ears a notch, kind of halfway listening, it was very much like being in a room with *her.* On my long walk home through the rain that night, I re-created her voice in my head, her face, the way she moved her hands when she spoke. It was more than strange; it was, without doubt, the closest I have ever come to a spiritual revelation, and for the first time I understood Ramanujan's claims of divine inspiration. Because as I made my way through the wet streets that night, I saw, in a sort of grainy, movie-reel vision, Lila forming the phrase with her lips. I actually *heard* her speaking. And I realized I'd been remembering it incorrectly all along. She'd actually been smiling when she said it, this quiet, mischievous smile. Her exact words were not 'an unusual but perfectly elegant third piece.' They were more lyrical than that. She had said, I became certain, 'an unusual but perfectly elegant third *element*.' "

"I don't understand."

"Don't you see? It was a riddle. I'm sure she planned to explain the riddle to me before long if I didn't figure it out, but she never got the chance. That night, after I met you, arriving home drenched and halfway drunk, I sat down at my desk and placed a diagram of Brun's sieve to my left, a statement of the Vinogradov Theorem to my right, and between them I placed my worn-out, hand-me-down copy of Euclid's *Elements*—'an unusual but perfectly elegant third element,' she had said. A clue. It had been there all along, if I'd only paid closer attention. *Elements* comprises thirteen books, and, rather than risk missing something, I began with book one, page one. I parsed it page by page, stopping only to grab something to eat or to crash on my bed for a few hours, or to fetch water from the well. I did this for forty-three days straight. I went through dozens of pencils, reams of paper. And in the end, in a place where it never would have occurred to me to look, I found the key that Lila had been pointing to, the key that unlocked the whole thing."

The sun shone down through the wet branches of the trees, making everything shine with a crazy kind of light. Large drops of water collected at the tips of McConnell's hair and plopped down on his face, his shirt collar. He looked manic and inspired, and I knew exactly, without any doubt or reservation, why Lila, who swore she would never waste her time on love, had fallen in love with him.

"What will you do with it?" I asked.

"I'm giving it to you. It's yours to decide. It's not important to me anymore. I only did it for Lila."

"You can't mean that."

He looked at me as though I'd missed the whole point, as if I hadn't understood a thing he'd said to me. "But I do. An enormous burden has been lifted. I've done the biggest thing I could ever have imagined doing in my lifetime, and I did it just the way I planned to twenty years ago—in collaboration with Lila."

Back in my hotel room, I had stared at the pages for hours, trying to understand even a few lines of the dense, impenetrable mass of numbers and symbols. But it was no use. It was Lila's language, not mine.

I had made a copy for myself—a misplaced archival instinct, I suppose, a desire to have a record, even of something I would never begin to understand—and taken the original to Don Carroll, who received it with astonishment. He would get it published, he said, jointly, under McConnell's name, and my sister's. It would take some finagling, some calling in of a favor or two—after all, McConnell had been absent from the math world for twenty years, and his claim of having proved one of the most difficult problems in the history of mathematics would be met with intense skepticism— but it could be done. There would be a peer review. And if the proof was found to be accurate—Carroll had faith that it would—the world would take notice. Once again, I realized, my sister would be famous. But this time, she would become known for her talent, her mind. Not for what had been done to her, but rather for what she had done.

Now I took one last look at the photograph of Lila at the dining-room table with her notebook. Then I placed it on the altar. Lila at her best, in a moment of discovery.

I made my way through the writhing park, out into the darkened street. Once again, there was the crush of bodies. Dozens, hundreds, a river of the dead flowing through the city, dis-

persing slowly through the side streets
into the neighborhoods. I kept trying to
find my way out, but there appeared to
be no exit. Every painted face led to another, and another, so that it felt as if I
was going deeper into the crowd. After
a while I came upon four men in black
capes, carrying a wooden gazebo
draped with skeletons. The gazebo
was fitted with handles, and they carried it low to the ground, walking
slowly. I was stuck behind them, unable
to go around. Then the gazebo began
to rise into the air, and one of the men
caught my eye. He signaled me with his
eyes, and I realized they were lifting it
so that I could pass underneath. But as
I moved ahead, they lowered it again,
and I was trapped inside the moving
structure. It was lit from within by three
small battery-powered lights. The walls
were painted white, and plastered with
photographs. All I could see was the interior of the box, and the feet of the
men who carried it, marching along. After a few seconds, it was impossible to
tell the feet of the four men from the
others swirling around us. I knocked on

the walls, but no one heard me; if they did, it made no difference. I could hear the crowd pressing against the side of the gazebo, and the dull throb of drums in the distance. The smell of fresh paint made me dizzy. But to my surprise, I felt no sense of panic. After perhaps a minute I gave in to the moment. As long as I kept pace with the men, it was not uncomfortable. As I walked, I studied the photographs. Men, women, children, different ages, different settings. In one I thought I recognized the cloud forests of Guatemala; in another, the garlic fields of Gilroy; in yet another, the windswept beach at the western edge of the city. The smell of the paint grew thicker, and my head began to feel heavy. It was like a dream, one over which my rational mind held no jurisdiction. I would simply wait for it to end.

I don't know how many minutes had passed—five, ten, fifteen?—when the structure began, slowly, to rise. When the bottom of the gazebo was level with my shoulders, I ducked my head and emerged. I breathed deeply, filling my lungs with the cool night air. The men stumbled drunkenly to the left, seemingly oblivious to me, and I realized they probably had not even known I was there.

I looked around to get my bearings. The sound of drums was distant now. The crowd had all but disappeared. I found myself alone, on an unfamiliar block. There were no signs, no landmarks, no points of reference. The street was really no more than a sliver of an alley, lined with trees and home to a row of old Victorians, each one of them marked in its own way by a kind of graceful disrepair. A cat wailed in the distance. In a second-floor apartment, a girl in a yellow nightgown walked slowly past the window. A tall figure moved toward her. A slender arm reached out to turn off a lamp, and the room went dark. Everything about the moment was stunningly familiar. Had I been here before? Had someone described this very scene to me? Or, maybe, I had simply read it all in a book. Sometimes it felt as if books and life formed a strange origami, the intricate folds and secret shadows so inex-

tricably connected, it was impossible
to tell one from the other.

At the end of the street, by instinct, I
went right. The Victorians gave way to
apartment houses and taquerias, bars
and burger joints. I don't know how
many minutes passed before I came to
Dolores. Left, and up the hill, past a
small park littered with the evening's
debris—empty bottles, a discarded red
cape, a string of paper skeletons hanging from a lamppost, lifting and lower-
ing in the breeze. My legs were sore,
but I kept walking. It wasn't until I
reached Twenty-eighth Street that I realized where I had been headed all
along. By the time I began the steep
uphill climb, I felt as if I'd been walking
for hours. It was quiet on my old block.
Even though it was less than a mile
from the heart of the Mission, it seemed
like a different city. Halfway up, I
stopped beside the familiar bottlebrush
tree, turned, and looked up. The light in
my old bedroom was on. The birdhouse on the windowsill cast a strange
shadow on the sidewalk. I checked my
watch—half past midnight. I sat on the

bottom step of the house and waited. The breeze picked up, carrying with it the scents of my mother's old garden— peppermint, lavender, sage.

At 12:43 I stood and faced the house, looking up at my bedroom window. At 12:45, just as Thorpe had said, the shade came down, and the light went off. I glanced up the hill toward Diamond Heights. There was Thorpe's big house, jutting over the cliff like a spaceship, its modern angles oddly in tune with the hill and the trees. *Now.* I don't know if I said the word aloud, or if I merely thought it, but just then, the light in Thorpe's office went on.

I thought of Diriomo, where objects and moments seemed to obey the laws of some hidden symmetry, where the most mundane moments seemed ordered, orchestrated, nothing truly left up to chance. I had long believed that Diriomo was an exceptional place, where the ordinary laws of randomness did not apply. But maybe I had been wrong. Maybe there was symmetry everywhere, and the patterns of our days held no less certainty than the mathematical patterns of the universe. Maybe, in order to see the patterns, one simply needed to take a few steps back, turn the page upside down, approach everything from a different angle.

I imagined the woman in my old bedroom climbing into bed. Did she fall asleep as soon as she rested her head on the pillow, or did she lie awake making plans, brooding over the events of the day? How much did she know about the family who lived here before? At this very moment, unbeknownst to her, she was becoming a character in Thorpe's new novel. What would she do in that novel, I wondered, that she would not do in real life? What decisions would be made for her that she would never make for herself? What name would Thorpe give her, and what words would he put in her mouth? Would she read the book one day, and recognize herself?

This was a city of windows. Behind every window were enough stories to fill a book. I thought of the photographs inside the white gazebo, how each face was the starting point of a thousand different stories. Some of them were true, and some were not. I thought of my family's story—how, for so long, we let it be told by someone else.

I closed my eyes. If I concentrated hard enough, I could almost hear my parents' voices coming from within. Of course they were not there, but there was something to be said for reinvention. In the world as I reordered it, at that moment, standing on the steps of my childhood home, my parents had never divorced, never moved away. They sat at the kitchen table, talking. My father was telling my mother a story about a business trip he'd recently taken to Sweden, some chance encounter with an old college friend in the airport in Stockholm. My mother met his story with her own, about a decade-old guilty verdict against one of her clients that had recently been overturned. Each one of these stories had indeed been told to me by my parents in recent weeks, but separately. My mother told me hers as we sat in her new garden in Santa Cruz, among the bright bougainvillea and soft, silvery lamb's ear. My father told me his over the phone from London—another business trip. In reality, they were thousands of miles apart. Only in my imagination did my parents come together, talking with their old ease, as if nothing had ever happened to split their world apart. I realized I could have stood there for hours, listening, inventing.

"There was only one perfect ending," Thorpe had said of his first book. "Once I understood what it was, writing the story was like following a map." At the time, he was sitting at the table in his house at the top of the hill, and he was staring at me, as though he was trying to decide if I was really there, or if he had only imagined me.

Even then, I knew he had been wrong. There is no such thing as a perfect ending, no such thing as an infallible narrative map. "Arbitrarily one chooses that moment of experience from which to look back or from which to look ahead." Every story is flawed, every story is subject to change. Even after it is set down in print, between the covers of a book, a story is not immune to alteration. People can go on telling it in their own way, remembering it the way they want. And in each telling the ending may change, or even the beginning. Inevitably, in some cases it will be worse, and in others it just might be better. A story, after all, does not only belong to the one who is telling it. It belongs, in equal measure, to the one who is listening.

# *Acknowledgments*

I wish to thank my wonderful agent, Valerie Borchardt, and my excellent, insightful, and very patient editor, Caitlin Alexander.

Many thanks to Lauren Mountanos at Mountanos Bros. Coffee for the eye-opening tour and for her wealth of coffee knowledge. Thanks to Dora for demystifying the art of cupping.

My gratitude to Susan MacTavish-Best and Jim Buckmaster for giving me the keys to the house on the hill when I needed a warm, quiet place to write. Thanks to Ben Fong-Torres for being Ben Fong-Torres.

Thanks also to Katie Rudkin, Madeline Hopkins, Chris Jones, Brenda

Orozco, Jay Phelan, Erin, and, as always, Bill U'Ren.

Above all, thanks to Kevin, where all of my stories begin and end.

# About the Author

MICHELLE RICHMOND is the author of *The Year of Fog, Dream of the Blue Room,* and *The Girl in the Fall-Away Dress.* Her stories and essays have appeared in *Glimmer Train, Playboy, The Oxford American,* and elsewhere. She has been a James Michener Fellow, and her fiction has received the Associated Writing Programs Award and the *Mississippi Review* Prize. A native of Mobile, Alabama, Michelle lives with her husband and son in San Francisco, where she is at work on her next novel.